"Nadine, one of my coworkers, says there are plenty of attractive men working in this building. Your guy must be one of them," Mason said.

"He's definitely suave. But he has an edge about him, too. Just enough to keep a woman guessing. Without making him too complex, that is."

Thom Nichols. Damn it! Sophie was talking about that phony two-timing womanizer. "Do you really think any man could be as perfect as you're making this one out to be?"

The long sigh she released troubled Mason. Even if he didn't have a chance in a million with Sophie, he'd hate to see her hurt by Thom.

"Well, I think he's perfect for me," she reasoned. "And Valentine's Day will be here in a couple of weeks. By then I plan to have Mr. Right exactly where I want him."

She patted the side of her hip, but rather than envisioning Thom standing next to Sophie, Mason was visualizing himself at her side. And suddenly he was determined to make the image come true.

AN UNEXPECTED HERO

USA TODAY Bestselling Author

STELLA BAGWELL

&

NANCY ROBARDS THOMPSON

2 Heartfelt Stories

Her Sweetest Fortune
and *Fortune's Surprise Engagement*

Special thanks and acknowledgment are given to Stella Bagwell and Nancy Robards Thompson for their contributions to the Fortunes of Texas: The Secret Fortunes continuity.

ISBN-13: 978-1-335-42737-3

Recycling programs for this product may not exist in your area.

An Unexpected Hero

Her Sweetest Fortune
First published in 2017. This edition published in 2022.

Fortune's Surprise Engagement
First published in 2017. This edition published in 2022.

For questions and comments about the quality of this book, please contact us at CustomerService@Harlequin.com.

Harlequin Enterprises ULC
22 Adelaide St. West, 41st Floor
Toronto, Ontario M5H 4E3, Canada
www.Harlequin.com

Printed in U.S.A.

CONTENTS

After writing more than one hundred books for Harlequin, **Stella Bagwell** still finds it exciting to create new stories and bring her characters to life. She loves all things Western and has been married to her own real cowboy for forty-four years. Living on the south Texas coast, she also enjoys being outdoors and helping her husband care for the horses, cats and dog that call their small ranch home. The couple has one son, who teaches high school mathematics and is also an athletic director. Stella loves hearing from readers. They can contact her at stellabagwell@gmail.com.

Books by Stella Bagwell

Harlequin Special Edition

Men of the West

Her Kind of Doctor
The Arizona Lawman
Her Man on Three Rivers Ranch
A Ranger for Christmas
His Texas Runaway
Home to Blue Stallion Ranch
The Rancher's Best Gift
Her Man Behind the Badge
His Forever Texas Rose
The Baby That Binds Them
Sleigh Ride with the Rancher

Visit the Author Profile page
at Harlequin.com for more titles.

HER SWEETEST FORTUNE

Stella Bagwell

To Susan Litman for all her hard work
on the fabulous Fortune saga. Thank you!

Chapter 1

She had to do something and fast!

For the past several hours, the words of warning had made a monotonous loop through Sophie Fortune Robinson's mind, making it virtually impossible to concentrate on the work scattered across her desk.

As assistant director of human resources at Robinson Tech, it was Sophie's responsibility to make sure two new training programs were ready to be implemented in a few short days. At the rate she was going, the task would never get finished.

Darn it! If Sophie hadn't turned a corner at just the right moment, she would've been spared the sickening sight of her dream man with another woman. Now the image of Thom Nichols stepping off the elevator with his arm wrapped around Tanya Whitmore's slender waist was stuck in Sophie's head.

The sexy grin he'd been giving the willowy blonde

had made it quite apparent he was enjoying every minute of her company. The realization had left Sophie nauseous and even more desperate. She couldn't sit back and wait for Thom Nichols to take notice of her. She had to come up with some sort of strategy to snare the man's attention.

But how did a woman go about making herself appealing to the sexiest man alive? There was hardly a female working at Robinson Tech who didn't sigh at the mere mention of Thom's name. Sophie didn't want to think of her opposition in terms of numbers: it would be too staggering. Besides, she already knew the task of snaring her man wasn't going to be easy.

But Sophie's father, the giant tech mogul Gerald Robinson, had lectured her plenty of times about setting goals and achieving them through hard work and confidence. The same could be applied in this situation. Her goal was to have Thom Nichols as her Valentine dream date.

Now, if she could just figure out how to make that happen.

"Sophie? What are you doing here at this hour?"

Since everyone in her department had left hours ago, the unexpected voice caught her by surprise, especially when she'd been sitting there with her head in the clouds.

Glancing over her shoulder, she saw Mason Montgomery shoving back the cuff of a pale blue dress shirt to study his watch. The tall, dark-haired computer programmer had probably seen her staring off into space like some lovesick teenager. The notion sent a flood of pink embarrassment to her cheeks.

Mason was far too intellectual and mature to understand a woman's crush on an attractive man. Or was he? With him working just across the hall from her, they'd often exchanged greetings and talked about work or current events, but they'd never been more than casual friends. He was a crackerjack programmer who'd created several highly successful apps for the company. He was also mannerly and nice-looking in a boy-next-door kind of way. He just wasn't Thom Nichols.

"Oh, hi, Mason. I guess I've been so engrossed in my work I didn't notice the time." Which wasn't a complete lie, she thought. It had been hours since she'd glanced at the clock on her desk, but only because she'd been too busy fantasizing about her Valentine date. At least, the man she was hoping would become her Valentine.

A frown furrowed his forehead. "Surely your father doesn't expect you to wear yourself out. I realize he's a stickler about deadlines, but I don't think he'd want his daughter to collapse with fatigue."

Laughing, Sophie swiveled her chair so that she was facing her late night visitor. "Most everyone in the building thinks Gerald Robinson is a taskmaster, but he's really just a big teddy bear with a loud growl."

His smile exposed a row of straight white teeth and Sophie could see the expression was sincere. She liked that about Mason Montgomery. He always seemed genuine. But Thom's dazzling smile could charm the fleas right off a cat. How could any other man compare to that?

"Drop the *teddy* and I'll believe you."

She tossed strands of long brown hair over her shoulder before gesturing to a thick folder lying open on her desk. "I've been going over a presentation for a new job-training program the company will soon put in place.

Actually, there's a new program for your department and marketing."

His brows lifting with interest, he moved inside the cubicle and rested a hip against the side of her desk. "Oh? Robinson Tech is going to put its programmers through more training?"

She laughed at his wary expression. "Only the newly hired employees. Not the old veterans like you."

"Ouch!" he said with a chuckle. "I'm not so sure I like that *old* part."

Shaking her head, she gave him another smile. "I just meant you've worked here for a long time. As for your age, you couldn't be much older than me. I'm twenty-four."

"Try five years," he admitted. "I'm twenty-nine."

"Ooooh, that's terribly old," she joked, then added in a more serious tone, "Speaking of working late, I've noticed you've been burning the midnight oil here lately. You know, my father wouldn't want you collapsing from fatigue, either."

His brown eyes twinkling, he picked up a hunk of raw amethyst Sophie used for a paper weight. "We're getting a new app ready to roll in a few days. I want to make sure there are no glitches before Wes sends it on to your father for final approval. Sometimes that means losing sleep and a meal or two. But there's no need for you to worry you might have to scrape me off the floor. I've been eating my spinach."

Mason was hardly a muscle man, Sophie decided, as she studied him from beneath her lashes. But he had a trim, athletic build that implied he hit the gym on a regular basis. Although from the long hours he put in at Robinson Tech, she couldn't imagine where he found the extra time for himself.

"Mmm. I like my spinach in enchiladas," she said. "But I'd eat it raw or standing on my head if it would make me as tech savvy as you."

He shook his head. "And I wish I had your gift for communicating with people. I've seen you in action—how easy it is for you to soothe irate employees. I wouldn't have the patience to listen to their complaints, much less calm their tempers. And you can do something around here that no one else can do."

Intrigued, she leaned back in her chair and arched a brow at him. "Oh? I can't imagine what that might be."

"You can put a smile on our boss's face. I've never seen anyone but you make Gerald Robinson happy."

Her short laugh dismissed the compliment. "That's only because I'm the baby of his eight children. My siblings all complain that our father lets me get away with murder. But that's not really true. I just happen to be a positive thinker."

A doubtful grin lifted one corner of his mouth. "Positive thinker, huh? So that puts you in your father's good graces?"

She shot him a clever smile. "In a roundabout way. I happen to think if you can dream it, you can do it. And Dad likes it when people get things done."

Mason tossed the piece of lilac-colored quartz from one hand to the other and forced his gaze to remain on the rock rather than Sophie's lovely face. Not for anything did he want her to think he was staring. Even though he wanted to.

Of all the women who worked at Robinson Tech, Sophie had to be the most beautiful, he decided. Her long brown hair hung straight against her back, while her creamy skin glowed as though she was lit from within. And those brown eyes fringed with long, black lashes were like looking into a cup of hot, sweet chocolate.

She was the youngest child of the famous Fortune Robinson family. Their wealth was the sort that a simple man like Mason could only dream about. And yet none of those obstacles had stopped him from watching her from afar and wondering how it might be to actually take her on a date. If that made him a fool, then he was a big one, even by Texas standards.

"So you're a dreamer." His gaze settled on her face and suddenly he felt a hard tug deep inside him. Unfortunately, the sensation had nothing to do with him missing dinner and everything about the effervescent glow in her eyes. "Tell me, Sophie, what does a woman like you dream about?"

Her cheeks turned a darker pink. A telltale sign that when he'd walked up on her a few moments ago, she'd been thinking about a man. What else could put that sort of spaced out look on a woman's face?

She shrugged one slender shoulder and the slight movement caused Mason's gaze to dip from her face to the curve of her breasts pushing against the magenta colored top, then farther downward to where a close fitting black skirt stopped just above her knees and a pair of strappy high heels covered her small feet.

"Oh, I dream about lots of things," she said. "Like work and travel and family. But mostly I dream about—"

His eyes lifted to see a smile tilting the corners of her soft, pink lips. As Mason studied the moist curves, he felt the sudden urge to clear his throat.

"About what?" he prodded.

Her gaze dropped shyly from his. "Finding true love

like some of my brother and sisters. They're married and happy and planning families of their own." She sighed. "But I need the right man for that. And I think I've found him."

The right man. Austin, Texas was full of eligible bachelors, but he couldn't imagine any of them being good enough for Sophie. So who could possibly be the right man for this pampered princess, he wondered, while attempting to swat away a stab of foolish jealousy.

Folding his arms against his chest, he hoped he appeared cool instead of moonstruck. "Does the lucky guy know he's targeted yet?"

With a nervous little laugh, she said, "Uh, not exactly. But I'm planning on letting him know soon. Very soon."

It was stupid of Mason to feel deflated, but he did. Sophie could fly to any place in the world anytime she wanted. The man who'd caught her eye could be in Paris or London, anywhere besides Austin. "Do I know this guy?"

She picked up a pencil and tapped it against a notepad. As Mason looked at her dainty hands with their perfectly manicured fingernails, he doubted she'd ever had to lift more than a pencil. But to her credit, she and her siblings contributed long hours to their father's company, even though their financial security had been set the day they'd been born.

She said, "I'm not ready to name names, but yes, you certainly know him. He's handsome and very smart. And has a great job here at Robinson Tech."

Hey, she could be describing him, Mason thought hopefully. He was smart and certain people had told him he was handsome. He also had a great job with the company.

"Sounds like a nice guy," Mason admitted.

A wistful smile put a foggy look in her brown eyes. "Oh, he's very nice. And practically oozes charisma. When my guy walks into a room all the women catch their breath and stare. And wish *he* belonged to *them*."

Dang. That definitely crossed him off the list of possibilities. Though finding a date for himself wasn't exactly as difficult as moving a mountain, Mason hardly had women swooning at his feet. He was the one with the shoulder they wanted to cry on. The one they came running to whenever some reckless rebel threw them over for a biker chick or rich cougar. Always the friend, but rarely the lover. That was good ole Mason.

"Nadine, one of my coworkers, says there are plenty of hunky men working in this building. Your guy must be one of them," he said.

A sly look crossed her face. "He's definitely suave. But he has an edge about him, too. Just enough to keep a woman guessing. Without making him too complex, that is."

Thom Nichols. Damn it! She was talking about that phony, two-timing womanizer who ate women for breakfast and spit their bones to his Doberman pinscher. But Mason could hardly express his opinion about the man to Sophie. He'd learned long ago that putting down a boyfriend was not the way to score points with a woman.

Clearing his throat, he asked, "Do you really think any man could be as perfect as you're making this one out to be?"

The long sigh she released troubled Mason greatly. Even if he didn't have a chance in a million with this woman, he'd hate to see her hurt by lothario Thom.

"Well, I think he's perfect for me," she reasoned. "And Valentine's Day will be here in a couple of weeks. By then I plan to have Mr. Right exactly where I want him."

She patted the side of her hip, but rather than envisioning Thom standing next to Sophie, Mason was visualizing himself at her side. And suddenly he was determined to make the image come true. She might be thinking of Thom as her Mr. Right, but Mason was going to do everything possible to make her see she was all wrong about the plastic marketing strategist. And that Mason was her *real* Mr. Right.

Placing the amethyst back on a neat stack of legal papers, Mason straightened away from the desk. "Well, it's getting really late and I still have a few things to do at home before the morning gets here and everything starts over."

"You should get yourself a maid," Sophie suggested. "You'd be surprised by how much she'd ease your workload."

Mason was thinking he'd much rather have a woman to warm his bed than a maid to clean his house. Preferably one with long brown hair, killer legs and a waist that would fit right between his two hands.

Grinning, he winked at her and started out of the cubicle. "No thanks," he tossed over his shoulder. "I'll just eat more spinach."

"Have you lost your mind, Sophie? You, of all people, chasing after a man! I just don't get it."

She glared at her sister Olivia, who'd made herself comfortable in one of the matching wingchairs in the sitting area of Sophie's enormous bedroom suite. Even though Olivia had recently moved into a place of her own, she often stopped by the Robinson estate to visit. Sophie had always admired her older sister and often sought her advice on personal matters. Only moments earlier, Sophie had confided her plans to snare Thom Nichols and much to her chagrin, Olivia had immediately exploded with protests.

"No. You wouldn't understand," Sophie said, trying to keep the bite of sarcasm from her voice. "You don't have the same dreams that I do. You don't care if you ever have a man in your life."

Sighing, Olivia crossed her legs, as though talking sense to her younger sister was going to be a long, arduous endeavor. "We're not talking about me, Sophie. This is about you. You making a fool of yourself by chasing after a man."

Hadn't their own mother made a fool of herself by living with a man who'd cheated on her for years? Sophie felt like flinging the nasty question at Olivia, but bit it back instead. It wasn't her place to judge either of her parents for the artificial state of their marriage. For some reason Sophie couldn't fathom, the two remained steadfastly together. Even so, the connection between her mother and father was about as warm as a trip to Antarctica. And Sophie was determined that she would never settle for such a cold relationship with a man.

"I'm not actually going to chase him," Sophie corrected as she walked over to the double doors that opened to an enormous walk-in closet. "I'm just going to give him a little nudge—a reminder that I'm in the building and available."

Olivia snorted. "Thom Nichols believes every

woman in the building is available to him. I just don't see the attraction you have for the man."

Gasping, Sophie shot a look of disbelief at her sister. "Are you joking? He has to be the sexiest man alive! Well, at least in the state of Texas!"

"We live in a mighty big state, Sophie. Just how would you describe a sexy man? Would you know one if you saw one?"

Momentarily ignoring Olivia's barbed questions, Sophie snatched several pieces of clothing from the closet and carried them over to a king-sized bed.

"Apparently you need a lesson in identifying a sexy hunk from the regular crowd," Sophie told her. "He's tall, dark haired, has a killer smile and walks with just enough swag to let a woman know he's full of confidence."

"Hmmp. You mean with just enough conceit to let us know he's struck on himself."

Sophie glanced over to see Olivia shaking her head with disgust. Her sister's cynical attitude irked her and saddened her at the same time. With gently waving hair that was a much darker brown than Sophie's and beautiful features to match, her older sister could attract any man she wanted, but so far she viewed men and marriage as something worse than a chronic disease.

"Why do you have to be so jaded?" Sophie asked. "I wish now I'd never told you about my plans to go after Thom. It's obvious you don't understand how I feel."

With a rueful sigh, Olivia pushed herself out of the chair and walked over to Sophie. "You're right, I don't understand. So why don't you tell me how you feel about Thom?"

In an effort to gauge her sister's sincerity, Sophie

looked into Olivia's brown eyes that were incredibly similar to her own.

"Do you honestly want to know?" Sophie asked. "Or are you just patronizing me?"

"I honestly want to know." She reached over and plucked a black knit dress from the pile of clothing on the bed. "I need to understand why a young, beautiful woman like you feels the need to change yourself just to snag a man. If you have to be someone you're not in order to make him like you, then you're deluding yourself that it will ever work."

Deflated by Olivia's negative viewpoint, Sophie sank onto the bed. "I've had my eye on him for a long time," Sophie told her. "And the more I've watched him, the more I'm sure he was put on this earth to be my one true love."

Olivia let out a loud, mocking groan, then immediately plopped a hand over her mouth. "Sorry. I couldn't help it."

Sophie turned her misty gaze on a far corner of the room and swallowed hard. Not one of her seven legitimate siblings believed she was mature enough to take on a serious relationship with a man, much less think about marriage or a family. They all viewed her as the baby, the one offspring of Charlotte and Gerald Robinson who had been so sheltered, it would take years for her to grow up and acquire a head full of wisdom. Sometimes she even wondered how she'd gotten her job at Robinson Tech. Was it because she was well trained for the job, or because her father was the boss?

"Sure. I know. It all sounds silly to you," Sophie mumbled.

"Oh, Sophie, don't be so defensive." Easing down

next to her, Olivia wrapped an arm around Sophie's shoulders. "I'm sorry. It's just that I don't think you grasp yet what love is. And I don't want you to get hurt while you're learning."

Blinking at the tears stinging her eyes, Sophie looked directly at her sister. "I'll tell you one thing. I know what love *isn't*," she said in a brittle tone. "It isn't like this sham between our parents! Furthermore, I'd stay a spinster for the rest of my life if it meant avoiding the sort of marriage our mother has endured over the years."

"Sophie!" Olivia scolded. "How can you say that? Dad has given Mother and all of us kids anything and everything we could possibly want."

"So in other words, you're saying Mother stays with Dad because of his money and this." Sophie waved her arm, indicating the spacious room with its extravagant furnishings. "This high-class lifestyle he can provide her."

Frowning, Olivia tossed the black dress back onto the bed, then looked toward the door as though she feared their mother might walk in at any moment. "That's an awful thing to say, Sophie!" she said in a hushed tone. "Mother stays with Dad because she loves him!"

"Really? How could that be when she and the whole world know that Dad has had numerous affairs? You're telling me that love can actually exist under those conditions?"

"Of course I am," Olivia insisted. "Why else would she stay if she didn't love him?"

Sophie had been asking herself that very question for some time now, and the more she did, the more she considered the idea that their mother might be hiding something from the whole family. But since that was only speculation, she was hardly going to mention her suspicions to Olivia. And she definitely wasn't going to comment about their father anymore tonight. In Olivia's eyes, Gerald Robinson could do little wrong. She'd chosen to forgive and forget about his philandering. Probably because Olivia happened to be one of their father's favorites and he doted on her even more than he did Sophie.

Instead she switched the conversation back to her dream man.

"Thom is handsome and dynamic," Sophie told her. "And I plan to make him mine by Valentine's Day."

"Exactly what does your plan entail?"

Sophie walked over to the cheval mirror and twisted her hair into a loose knot atop her head. "Don't worry, I'm not going to change who I am. I'm only going to tweak the outside a bit. Maybe some highlights in my hair or some new clothes. Some sexy knee-high boots might do the trick."

"And when you do catch his attention? Then what?"

Sophie smiled confidently at Olivia's image in the mirror. "Then he'll begin to look at all of me. Not just the outside."

With a rueful shake of her head, Olivia warned, "You are headed for disaster, my dear sister. Thom Nichols wants two things from a woman. Sex and money. He's hardly interested in finding the love of a lifetime."

Sophie's lips pressed into an angry line as she turned to face her sister. "Go ahead and be cynical and negative. Do your best to make me look foolish just because I want a man to love and for him to love me!"

Olivia threw up her hands in a gesture of surrender. "I give up. I can see this is something you're going to have to figure out for yourself. And far be it from me to ruin your quest for love."

"You'll see," Sophie countered with conviction. "By Valentine's Day I'm going to have my man."

"I hope you do get the right man—for you, that is. And I hope by Valentine's Day you'll begin to see the whole picture. Presently, this crush you have on Thom is giving you tunnel vision."

Sophie frowned with confusion. "What is that supposed to mean?"

"The only man you see in front of you is Thom. You might allow yourself to look around a bit. You might find out that Mr. Right is someone else."

Sophie scoffed. "I'm not shopping for high heels. I know what I want when I see it. I don't have to keep looking for another man. Thom is perfect for me."

A wan smile on her face, Olivia leaned forward and kissed Sophie's cheek. "It's getting late. I'll see you tomorrow."

As Sophie watched her sister leave the bedroom, a tinge of sadness began to push her frustration aside. A few kind words of encouragement from Olivia would have been far nicer than a prediction of failure. She'd made it sound like Sophie didn't have enough sense to differentiate between a skirt chaser and a gentleman.

Sighing, Sophie sank onto the edge of the bed and plucked a family photo from the nightstand. The framed image was one of the few pictures that included all her brothers and sisters. With their busy lives taking them in all directions her whole family wasn't often together. But this particular photo had been taken at their parents' twenty-fifth wedding anniversary and everyone, including Charlotte and Gerald, looked happy. Yet that had been eleven years ago, long before anyone knew about Gerald's hidden identity or his affairs.

A year ago, her older brother, Ben, had been instrumental in uncovering the truth. Their forceful father, one of the most famous tech moguls in the world, wasn't really Gerald Robinson. He was Jerome Fortune, a member of the famous Fortune family. As if that wasn't enough of a stunner, during the investigation, Ben had found a thirty-three-year-old illegitimate son of Gerald's named Keaton Whitfield living in London.

Since that time, their newly discovered half brother had moved to Austin and started building a rapport with all his siblings. Sophie had to admit she liked Keaton and didn't begrudge his place in the family. Yet the whole revelation of her father's other life had shaken her to the core.

All at once she'd had to accept the fact that her father had never been the man she'd believed him to be. And as for her mother, who could possibly know why Charlotte had hung around for all these years? It sure as heck wasn't for love as Olivia had suggested.

Face it, Sophie, your parents are phonies and so are you! The only reason you have an important position at Robinson Tech, or anything else for that matter, is because of your name. It certainly hasn't come from your brains, or beauty, or hard work. The sooner you realize the truth, the better off you'll be.

Disgusted with the degrading voice in her head, she put the photo back and squeezed her eyes shut.

If her parents were shams, then their marriage was even more of a joke, Sophie miserably concluded. So what did that make their children? Mere symbols of a fake love? Moreover, what did it make Sophie?

Her lips pressed into a determined line, Sophie looked over at the clothes she'd tossed onto the bed. In one aspect, Olivia had been correct. The outside of her wasn't nearly as important as the inside. Yes, she wanted to look just as attractive as her sisters and all the other beautiful women of Austin. But she also wanted everyone to see she was more than just the youngest child of a famous and wealthy family. And she was hardly a fool for wanting the same genuine sort of love that her siblings Ben, Wes, Graham, Rachel and Zoe had found, she thought.

By Valentine's Day, Thom was going to see she was worthy of him. And then everything she'd ever wanted in her life was going to fall into place.

Chapter 2

"They make a nice-looking couple. The office heart-throb and the boss's daughter. Can you think of a more perfect pairing than that?"

"Yeah, about a million of them," Mason muttered under his breath.

"What did you say?"

Mason forced his gaze away from Sophie and Thom, who were sitting together at the far end of a long utility table. In the past year he could count on one hand the times he'd seen Thom taking midafternoon coffee in the second floor breakroom. Which could only mean that Sophie had gone to work on her plan and persuaded him to join her.

Mason looked over at the platinum-haired woman sitting next to him. Nadine had been working in the programming department for many years, long before Mason had ever taken a job at Robinson Tech. Divorced and somewhere in her forties, she pushed the envelope of the company's dress code, but her flamboyant appearance belied her shrewd mind. Even though Mason had graduated in the top half of his college class, he didn't possess half the knowledge about programming that Nadine held in that sassy head of hers.

"I said they're all wrong for each other. Totally wrong."

Nadine turned a frown on Mason. "You don't say? How did you come to that conclusion?"

Mason squeezed the foam cup of cold coffee so hard it nearly collapsed in his hand. "It should be obvious," he said. "Everyone in this building knows he's a player."

Nadine shrugged. "So? Maybe that doesn't bother Sophie. Besides, when I called them a couple I didn't mean it literally. Geez, Mason, lighten up. The two of them are merely having coffee together. Not discussing their marriage vows."

If Nadine had heard Sophie talking last night about snaring Mr. Right, she wouldn't be making light of the situation. Couldn't Nadine see how Sophie was leaning her head toward Thom's and smiling at him like he was the last male on earth? It was more than obvious that she was on a serious mission to catch Thom Nichols. And what was even clearer was that Mason couldn't just sit around and watch himself lose the lady of his dreams to a no-good womanizer.

"I wouldn't be so sure," Mason muttered as he studied Sophie from the corner of his eye. Today she was wearing a short black dress that resembled a sweater. The fabric outlined her petite curves while black suede boots with chunky heels fit snugly around her shapely calves. A pink-and-black printed scarf hung around her neck, as did dangling jet bead earrings. She looked more than lovely, he decided. She looked downright sexy. And the fact that it was Thom who, at the moment, was receiving her undivided attention clawed jealously at Mason.

"Why, Mason Montgomery, I do believe I hear a green streak in your voice," Nadine declared. "Are you interested in Sophie Robinson?"

"Fortune Robinson," he corrected. "Remember? The family discovered they're actually a part of Kate Fortune's bunch. You know—the famous cosmetic heiress."

Nadine nodded. "I remember about a year ago when the news came out about Gerald. But I keep forgetting about the kids tacking on the Fortune name." Pausing, she clicked her tongue. "Poor little Sophie. She's such a sweet girl. It must've been hard on her—learning all that scandalous stuff about her father."

Mason could hardly imagine how it would feel to learn your father was actually someone you never knew. His own dad was a hard working pipeline technician for a gas and oil company in San Antonio. Hadley Montgomery had always been a strong anchor for Mason and his two older brothers. Finding out he'd had a secret life would shake the very ground Mason walked on.

"I imagine Sophie and her siblings have tried to keep a stiff upper lip through all of it," Mason replied. "After all, they can't help what their father has done."

Mason suddenly heard Sophie's light laugh at the far end of the table. The happy sound cut straight through him and he wondered if he was destined to become a fool over women. It hadn't been that long ago that Melody had broken his heart by deserting him for another man. He was an idiot for thinking things could be different with Sophie. She was already so besotted with Thom Nichols it was like she was wearing blinders.

Nadine's shrewd chuckle momentarily distracted him. "Well, the revelation about Gerald most likely made all the siblings richer than they were already. Can you imagine how it must feel to have that sort of wealth? They'll never have to worry about paying a utility bill or wondering if they can afford to eat more than macaroni and cheese for supper."

Along with her crush on Thom Nichols, Sophie's wealth was one more wall standing between them. But Mason was determined to knock down those obstacles and clear the path for a chance with her.

"Sophie might be filthy rich, but she's not a snob. She works very hard."

Nadine shot him an impish smile. "How would you know? I never see you cross the hall to HR. You always have your head buried in your own work."

If Mason explained to Nadine that he often spotted Sophie working late at night, then he'd also be admitting he had a habit of staying long after quitting time, too. And Nadine might misconstrue things and get the idea that Mason put in overtime just for a chance to see Sophie alone. Which was completely untrue. Until last night, he thought sheepishly.

"For your information," Mason said matter-of-factly, "the state bird of Texas is the mockingbird and we have plenty of them flying around the building. They tell me lots of things."

"Pertaining to Sophie, I presume." Nadine picked up her smartphone and pretended to swipe. "I'm going to find the best psychiatrist in the city of Austin. Hopefully a doctor can help you with this bird disorder you've developed."

Shaking his head, Mason shoved back his chair. "My coffee is cold. I'm going back to work. Are you ready?"

Groaning, Nadine ran a hand through her wispy blonde hair and glanced around the room. "Sure, I'm ready. There's no men around here giving me the goo-goo eye anyway."

Mason smirked. "If a man was, you'd promptly tell him to go stick his head in a garbage can."

Nadine laughed. "Not if he was the *right* man."

Mr. Right. Mason was sick of hearing that term and even sicker of picturing Thom Nichols as the definition.

He rose to his feet and started to follow Nadine out of the breakroom, when behind them, Sophie suddenly called out to him.

"Here's your chance," Nadine whispered. "Better go say hello. I'll see you later."

Feeling like a nervous teenager, but trying to be cool, Mason walked to the end of the table where his dream lady and Mr. Heartthrob were chatting as though they'd been friends forever. To say this was a fast turn of events would be putting it mildly.

"Hi, Mason!" she said cheerfully. "I saw you leaving and wanted to say hello before you got away."

"Hello, Sophie. Thom." He smiled at Sophie then forced a polite glance at Thom. The other man reminded Mason of one of those handsome movie stars who always played the hero on screen, but in reality couldn't do so much as change a flat tire if a dozen lives were depending on him. "How's the coffee?"

"Great," Thom quickly answered and gestured to the small thermos sitting in front of him. "Sophie brought her own special brew from home and talked me into trying some."

Mason wanted to knock the leering smile he was giving Sophie right off the other man's face. Instead, he focused his gaze on Sophie.

"Good planning," he said sagely. "About the coffee, I mean."

Color swept across Sophie's cheeks and Mason knew she'd picked up on his subtle comment.

"I try to think of the little things. They make the work day go brighter," she said with a wide smile, then looked adoringly at Thom. "Did you know Thom is heading the marketing for your new sports app? The media blitz he's planning is bound to make it a huge seller."

Mason had rather believe the app would be a huge seller because he'd developed a good product. Not because of a slick talking salesman who could convince folks on Galveston Island to buy a set of snow chains.

Mason said, "I like to think Sports & More is a worthwhile project that deserves plenty of marketing."

"You're lucky, Mason," Thom spoke up. "Mr. Robinson made the decision to spend a bankroll on the marketing for Sports & More. You must have done something right this time. I love sports, but to be honest, I perform better on the dance floor than I do the gym floor."

In Mason's opinion, the grin Thom was giving Sophie could only be described as lecherous. Which made it even more puzzling to Mason as to why she'd want a guy like Thom in her life. But women viewed things differently than men, and clearly she was seeing something in Thom that Mason was missing. Whatever the reason for her infatuation with the man, Mason couldn't just stand passively around and watch this beautiful woman get her heart crushed.

"I'm sure you've had lots of practice doing the... hustle," Mason replied.

Sophie's brows arched upward, but she didn't make any sort of reply. Thom merely let out a cocky laugh. Mason decided he should make a quick exit before he really insulted Thom and made both of them angry.

Glancing at his watch, Mason said, "Well, my break is over. Nice to see you two."

Once he'd returned to his desk, it was only a matter of seconds before Nadine sauntered into his cubicle and propped a hip on his desk. "Okay, what happened? Did you score points with the girl?"

Frowning, he tried to focus on the computer screen in front of him, but the only thing in front of his eyes was Sophie. "I wasn't trying to score points. Which is just as well. I came close to calling Thom a creep right to his face."

Nadine groaned. "Let me give you some advice, Mason. The more you toss insults in Thom's direction, the more she's going to defend him."

He turned and glowered at her. "I know that much. It's just that whenever I'm around the guy I get the urge to vomit. And then things start coming out of my mouth before I can stop them."

"Look, my friend, if you're really interested in snagging Sophie's attention, you need to forget about Thom Nichols and start concentrating on how to make yourself more appealing to her. If you do things right, she'll start looking at you instead of him."

"You think so?"

"Trust me. You have loads to offer a woman." She patted his shoulder. "I better get to work. Wes has assigned me the job of coming up with a mother/baby app store. I can't imagine what our boss was thinking. My daughter is twenty years old now. What do I remember about having a baby?"

"Hmm. I expect it's like riding a bike. Once you learn, you never forget."

Nadine laughed, causing Mason to chuckle along with her.

"Well, a person can get rusty if he doesn't practice," he agreed. "But you can always knock off a little rust."

"And how am I supposed to do that? Have another baby?"

"Why not? Women your age are having babies all the time."

Her expression softened in a way Mason had never seen before and then she reached out and gently patted his cheek. "You are the sweetest man ever. Sophie's an idiot if she doesn't latch on to you."

Sweet. Mason didn't want to be a piece of candy. He wanted to be viewed as authoritative, masculine and tough. He wanted women, particularly Sophie, to see him as a take-charge kind of guy who could melt a heart with just one smoldering look. He wanted to be more like his brothers, Doug and Shawn. Neither one of them ever had to worry over catching a woman's attention. Their problem was trying to decide which one they wanted and on what night of the week.

But Doug was an assistant prosecutor in Bexar County, a fierce lion in the courtroom. And Shawn was a lieutenant on the San Antonio police force. They were both handsome and forceful, with jobs that women admired. Even as children, Mason had never felt as though he could compete with his stronger, older brothers. And time hadn't changed Mason's feelings. Sure, he had a great job and his physical appearance wasn't exactly homely. But compared to his brothers, he was a geek.

If he ever expected to get Sophie to notice him, then he was going to have to be more like Doug and Shawn and a whole lot less like himself, he thought grimly.

More than an hour later, Mason was working when Sophie suddenly walked into his cubicle, nearly sending him into shock. The only time she'd ever stopped by his desk was when she'd personally helped him with a health insurance issue.

But it was clear this visit of hers had nothing to do with insurance. She was grinning from ear to ear and practically dancing on her toes.

She pulled up a chair and leaned her head close to his. The soft scent of her perfume swirled around him and tugged on his already dazed senses.

"Mason, I'm sorry if I'm interrupting your work," she said in a hushed tone. "But I'm so excited I had to tell someone! And since I shared my plans with you last night— Well, it's happened!"

Totally bemused, he stared at her beaming face. "It has?"

"Yes! Already! Can you believe it? Here I was thinking I was going to have to do handsprings out in the hall to get Thom to take a second look at me and all it took was a cup of exotic coffee."

Mason had never felt so deflated in his life. "You two looked pretty chummy in the break room."

"Chummy? Mason, you're so funny." Laughing

lightly, she gave his knee a gentle squeeze. "He's asked me out on a date! A real date! Tonight! Isn't it incredible?"

Mason felt like handing her the letter opener on his desk and telling her to stab him right in the gut. The act would have been more merciful than the news she was giving him.

He looked into her brown eyes and wondered if they would ever shine for him the way they were shining at this moment.

"A date, huh? That was fast work."

"You're telling me! I only started my plan today. I never expected to have results this quick." Her expression suddenly sobering, she glanced around the large room to make sure no one was listening. "Mason, you're a really honest guy. Tell me, do you think Thom might've asked me out just because—well, because I'm Gerald Robinson's daughter?"

Hell yes! Mason wanted to shout the words at her. But he held them back. One thing he was certain of, Sophie was a soft, gentle person. It would hurt her deeply if she thought her dream man might be using her for his own gain. Mason couldn't do that to her. Not right now. He couldn't bring himself to shatter the deliriously happy look on her face.

The more you insult Thom Nichols, the more Sophie will defend him. At this moment, Nadine's words couldn't have been more right.

Unable to keep looking her in the eye, Mason's gaze drifted to the computer screen. But for all he could see, the words might as well have been written in a foreign language. "Oh, Sophie, I wouldn't worry about that. Thom already has a good position in the company. He hardly needs you to help him get in your father's good graces."

"I guess that's true enough," she said quietly. "I shouldn't have ever let the idea cross my mind. It's just a date. Not a marriage proposal."

Thank God, Mason thought. If that ever happened, he'd have to speak up.

"That's true. And anyway, you're an intelligent woman. You'd know right off if a man was trying to use you."

Her eyes grew soft. And then suddenly without any warning at all, she leaned forward and pressed a kiss to his cheek.

"Thank you, Mason. You're wonderful!"

To his utter amazement, she pressed another kiss to same spot she'd already branded with her lips, then jumped to her feet.

"Stop by my desk tomorrow and I'll let you know how things go," she told him, then with a wiggle of her fingers she hurried away.

Mason lifted fingertips to the spot she'd kissed not once, but twice. The skin was still tingling as though she'd stuck a naked electric wire to his cheek. If a simple kiss to the side of his face had caused this much re-action, the feel of her lips against his would probably have him dancing like a drunk idiot atop his desk.

Darting a glance toward Nadine's desk, he realized the woman must have seen the whole interchange between him and Sophie. She was smiling broadly and giving him a thumbs up. The encouraging signal had Mason stifling a loud groan. Nadine didn't know Sophie had merely stopped by to announce her date with Thom. And at the moment, Mason felt too sick to set his coworker straight.

* * *

Later that evening at the Robinson estate, Sophie was hurrying to her bedroom when her mother called out to her.

"Sophie? Why are you running through the house like a child?"

Laughing, Sophie stopped in her tracks and waited until her mother caught up to her.

"Probably because I feel like a happy kid tonight. Don't you ever feel that way, Mother? Like kicking up your heels and doing pirouettes?"

"I like to think I'm in good physical condition for my age," Charlotte told her daughter, "but I'm not exactly ready for ballet leaps and spins."

For a woman in her midseventies, Sophie's mother still looked youthful. Of course, it helped that she could afford to get routine facials and have her own personal trainer, along with a chef who designed meals to keep her weight down and her skin and hair glowing.

Smiling brightly, Sophie said, "I refuse to believe that, Mother. I happen to think you could dance all night."

Charlotte pursed her lips with disapproval. "Those occasions are long over for me, Sophie."

Sophie frowned. "That's nonsense. Dad doesn't think in those terms. He still does plenty of fun things."

"Fun," Charlotte repeated in a mocking tone. "Your father views the whole world as his playground. That will never change."

It was a rare occasion that Charlotte made any sort of comment about her husband. More often than not, she went about her business as though Gerald didn't exist.

Looping her arm through her mother's, Sophie urged her down the hallway to her bedroom. "Come sit and help me pick out something nice to wear," she told Charlotte. "I have a date tonight and I want to look extra special."

"Who is this special date?" her mother asked, taking a seat in one of the wingback chairs. "Do I know the young man?"

"I doubt it," Sophie called from inside the closet. "He works for the company—in marketing. His name is Thom Nichols."

"Nichols," Charlotte repeated thoughtfully. "Is he related to Drew Nichols, who owns Austin Capital Bank and Trust?"

"I have no idea," Sophie answered as she stepped out with clothes tossed over her arm.

Charlotte gasped with dismay. "You have no idea? You're going out with the man and you don't know any more than that about him?"

The branches of a family tree were very important to Charlotte. So was public perception. Which made Sophie wonder how her mother had stood so stanchly by her husband when the news of his London love child had hit the rumor mill in Austin.

"Oh, Mother, I hardly need to know the size of Thom's wallet before I go on a date with him."

Her spine ramrod straight, Charlotte scooted to the edge of the chair. "I am not talking about money. As a Robinson you have a social standing to uphold and—"

"A Fortune Robinson," Sophie interrupted dourly. "Surely you haven't forgotten I have an extra name now. But then, I suppose as a Fortune, I have an equally important reputation to uphold."

Her hands clasped tightly together in her lap, Charlotte said stiffly, "The added name is a fact I don't care to ponder on."

"That's perfectly understandable," Sophie said gently. She walked over and sank onto the dressing bench facing her mother. "Ever since Keaton has come into the family I've been wondering about you, Mother."

A shutter fell across Charlotte's face, making her features unreadable. "There's no reason for you to be wondering about me. I'm fine. And I'll remain fine."

Not wanting to add to her mother's suffering, Sophie chose her next words carefully.

"Actually, I've watched the way you've conducted yourself through this whole scandal, Mother, and I've been amazed. I couldn't have been nearly as strong and steadfast as you've been."

The rigidness of Charlotte's face eased a fraction as her glance returned to Sophie. "It's not been a picnic for me by any means. But I understand your father completely. Actually, I understand him better than anyone," she said. "And sometimes a wife just has to put on a brave face and look the other way."

The other way? Sophie was incredulous, but she carefully hid the reaction from her mother. Charlotte had grown up in a past era, where women had different roles in life. Especially when it came to men and marriage.

"Maybe so, Mother. And I know a person is supposed to be forgiving. But I happen to think you deserve better from Dad. For the life of me, I can't imagine why you stay married to him."

Her mother shot her a stern look of warning. "Your father and I have a complicated relationship. It's also unbreakable. I can assure you of that."

Unbreakable because her mother refused to let go of a cold marriage? Or maybe it was her father who kept his wife bound to his side for purposes other than love?

"Anything can break, Mother, with enough pressure."

"Gerald has provided me, you and everyone in his family with a wonderful life. Not one of you children has a thing to complain about. So don't."

The firm tone of Charlotte's voice told Sophie not to push the issue, so she would honor her mother's wishes and let the subject drop. But that didn't mean Sophie would stop speculating and wondering if there could be more to her mother's loyal devotion to her cheating husband.

Smiling, she focused on her upcoming date instead, standing and holding up a pale pink mini dress with black accents. "What do you think about this for dinner and a movie?"

"Dinner and a movie? You're calling that a special date?"

Sophie's laugh tinkled through the bedroom. "It's the man that's making it special. Not where we're going."

Clasping the dress to her, Sophie waltzed over the plush carpet, while her mother eyed her with speculation.

"Sophie, you always were an impulsive, dreamy child. I'd hoped that by the time you graduated college you'd be more realistic and settled. But it's clear you're still flittering around like a butterfly, believing life is nothing more than a rose garden. One of these days you're going to have to face the real world."

Pausing in front of Charlotte's chair, Sophie fought hard not to roll her eyes. If it wasn't so sad, her mother's comment would be laughable. Did she think pretending to have a loving, caring husband wasn't delusional?

"I crammed four years of college into three and I've held down a demanding job ever since," she said stiffly. "I'd call that very real, Mother."

Charlotte's features softened somewhat. "Oh, Sophie darling, there's no sense in you getting all defensive. I only meant—well, you're a romantic soul. You believe life is full of hearts and flowers and kisses. And I suppose there's nothing wrong with that—in small doses. But you also need to be firmly grounded."

When Sophie came home sporting an engagement ring, then her mother would see her butterfly daughter was perfectly capable of landing safely on her feet.

Determined not to let anything spoil her evening ahead, Sophie dropped a kiss on her mother's smooth cheek. "Don't worry, Mother. I promise not to let Thom sweep me off my feet tonight."

But I'm sure as heck going to try to sweep him off his.

Chapter 3

Several hours later, a bored Sophie stared at the theater screen while fighting back a yawn. She'd never been into action movies and this one, with its ridiculous, computerized explosions and car chases, was hardly enough to hold her attention.

When Thom had asked her what movie she'd like to see tonight, Sophie had generously insisted he choose, with hopes he'd view her as easy to please. She'd hardly expected him to take her to see *Road Devils: The Final Battle.* So far there hadn't been one meaningful exchange of dialogue. But that hadn't seemed to bother Thom; he appeared to be enthralled with the story. For the past hour and a half, he'd rarely glanced in her direction.

So much for taking pains with her hair and makeup, she thought wryly, as she sipped her diet soda and darted a glance over at Thom. At the moment, he was munching on butter-drenched popcorn, his gaze fixated on the gun battle on the screen. Even though he'd not been all that attentive, she had to admit he looked devilishly handsome tonight in close-fitting brown trousers and a black shirt. But was gazing at a good-looking face all she wanted?

The question had barely had time to roll through her mind when suddenly, for no unexplainable reason, Mason popped into her thoughts. Would he have brought her to this sort of juvenile flick?

Are you going crazy, Sophie? You've been bragging to everyone how you're going to snag Thom. Now you're finally out with him and you start thinking about Mason Montgomery! He's just a friend at work. He's not the man of your dreams!

The scolding voice in her head was correct. This was hardly the time for her thoughts to be straying to Mason. Yet this was the second time in the past few hours that a vision of the other man had appeared to her.

Earlier, when she and Thom had been sitting in a restaurant eating a simple meal of fish and French fries, a dish she'd learned was Thom's favorite, the image of Mason cutting into a rare steak and sipping red wine had popped into her mind. It was ridiculous! She had no idea whether Mason liked to eat such a masculine meal. Besides, Thom was the he-man of the two. Wasn't he?

"Wow, that was a great ending, don't you think?"

Ending? Sophie glanced around to see the credits were rolling on the screen and people were already filing toward the exits.

"Oh. Yes, for sure. It was very exciting," she said, hoping he wouldn't guess she'd mentally blanked out the last hour of the movie.

He tossed his empty soda cup into the popcorn tub and dropped the whole thing to the floor for the janitors to clean up.

"Ready?" he asked.

She nodded, while telling herself his untidiness was hardly anything to be concerned about. He was probably very orderly at his own place. Besides, it wasn't like she had to clean up after him.

Are you even ready to see this guy's apartment, Sophie? And what would you do if he tried to seduce you into his bed?

Frowning at the silly questions that continued to pop into her head, she nodded at him and reached for her coat. After he'd helped her into the garment, the two of them left the theater. Once they were outside, Sophie dropped her soda cup into a nearby trashcan.

As they walked across the parking lot to his car, Thom glanced at his watch. "It's getting rather late. I think we should call it a night. We both have to be at work early in the morning."

So much for worrying about going to his apartment, she thought. He couldn't even manage a stop off at a coffee house.

Sophie tried not to show her disappointment. After all, this was their first date. Just one of many, she hoped. She shouldn't be expecting him to behave as though he was reluctant to tear himself away from her company.

"Fine. I can always use the extra time to shampoo my hair and shave my legs—again."

He tossed her a puzzled look. "What?"

She chuckled and then realizing he was clueless, she shrugged. "Oh, nothing. Just a girl thing."

"You're a good sport, Sophie. I like that about you."

At least there was something about her he liked, Sophie decided. Although she would've preferred to hear him say how competent she was at her job. The way that Mason had complimented her.

Mason. Mason. Why did the man keep lurking at the edge of her mind?

Thankfully, Thom put his arm around her waist and as they walked the remaining distance to the car, she was able to push the ridiculous question from her mind.

When they reached the sleek, little sports car, he politely helped her into the bucket seat. No sensible economy car for this guy, Sophie decided. Apparently he wanted his mode of transportation to match his image. Cool and sexy.

She'd been sitting only inches away from the man for the past few hours. By now she should be feeling the itch to get closer. Instead, she was wondering about the other women he'd dated. No doubt most of them had been eager to get their hands on him. Shouldn't she be wanting to scoot closer and snuggle her cheek against his shoulder? Was she just not getting herself in the right frame of mind?

Minutes later, Sophie was still mulling over the troublesome ideas when they approached the iron security gates connecting the high stone walls surrounding the Robinson Estate.

After Sophie keyed in a code to allow them entry, Thom drove down a long drive lined with live oak trees. In the summer months, the multi-winged mansion was shaded by more live oaks, along with several massive pecan trees. Presently, winter had bared the branches of the pecan trees.

Normally, when Sophie went on a date, she met the

guy at a chosen spot downtown. It saved him the inconvenience of driving to the estate and dealing with security. It also took away the intimidation factor. A few of her past dates had taken one look at her home and never asked her out again. But Thom was far more self-assured than that and she'd wanted this whole evening to feel like a special beginning.

After parking in the wide circular drive illuminated by solar footlights, Thom helped her from the car and walked her to the door. The arm at the back of her waist felt strong and sturdy, but she wasn't getting any warm or cuddly vibes from the contact. Maybe that was because she was still a little miffed at being brought home early as though she had a curfew.

"This is some serious digs, Sophie," he said as he eyed the elaborate entrance to the only home she'd ever known. "Bet the inside is even fancier than the outside."

The subtle hint brought Sophie up short. Did he want her to invite him in for a drink—with her father?

Hating herself for thinking such unseemly things about this man, she forced a smile on her face. "It's nice and comfortable," she said simply. "I'd invite you in, but like you said, it's getting late and I wouldn't want to disturb my parents. You understand, of course."

He smiled back and Sophie was relieved that he didn't appear to be offended. This was Thom. Her Thom. She wanted things between them to start off well. Even so, she had no intentions of being a pushover.

"Sure. Maybe next time," he suggested.

Tilting her head back, she studied his perfectly carved features. "Would you like there to be a next time?" she asked.

He shrugged. "Why not? I'm willing if you are."

His response wasn't exactly what she'd been hoping for, but this was just the beginning of things, she assured herself.

Lowering her lashes, she said demurely, "Yes. I'm willing."

"Great."

The simple word was said offhandedly as he shoved back the sleeve of his jacket to check his watch. Again. If time was more important to him than she was, she thought bleakly, she was doing something very wrong.

"Well, it's rather cold out here," she said. "Maybe we'd better say good-night."

Sophie turned toward the door, but before she could key in the entry code, his arm snaked around her waist and drew her toward him.

"I can't let you go in without a proper good-night," he said with practiced ease.

Finally! The word was zipping through Sophie's mind as she planted her hands on his chest and tilted her head slightly back. At last! Her dream man was going to kiss her!

Her heart tripping with anticipation, she waited for his kiss. But shockingly, when his lips met hers, her initial instinct was to push him away and step back. Somehow, she managed to catch herself before the crazy reaction ruined everything. Then, forcing herself to lean into him, she attempted to put real feeling into the kiss.

His lips moved expertly over hers with just enough pressure to convey that he was interested. The feeling was pleasant enough for Sophie, but there was no passion igniting inside her. No sweet singing birds sounding in her ears. No trembling in her knees. Even after he lifted his head, she was still anxiously waiting, expecting some last-minute explosion.

Smiling smugly, certain the dazed look on her face was a result of dreamy desire, he patted the top of her head. "Good night, Sophie. See you tomorrow."

"Yes. Good night."

As Sophie watched him walk back to his car, she was struck by the stunning realization that something was very wrong with her.

Thom Nichols, the man of her dreams, had just kissed her and she hadn't felt a thing.

The next evening Mason was still at his desk, deep in work, when Nadine stopped by his cubicle.

"Hey, guy, haven't you looked at the clock? It's quitting time."

He glanced around to see Nadine was already buttoned up in a fake fur coat that resembled a cheetah. In spite of her smile, she looked drained.

"I'll be going soon," he told her. "I have a few more things I want to finish. How's the mother/baby app going?"

Groaning, she rolled her head one way and then the other. "I'm losing my mind. That's how it's going. Wanna help?"

Mason chuckled. "I have plenty of work waiting on me. Besides, I know nothing about mothers and babies."

Nadine grinned suggestively. "This would be a good opportunity for you to learn."

"Hah! It'll be years before I have a child. If ever," he said flatly.

"Aw, come on, Mason. I can see deep down you were made to be a family man. Don't disappointment me."

Mason shot her a glum look and Nadine promptly stepped into the cubicle as though she'd forgotten she was on her way out of the building.

"It's been months since Christa threw you over for that high-rolling real estate agent. If you're still pining over her, let me assure you, she's not worthy to wipe the sweat off your brow, much less be your wife."

Mason gave her a weary smile. "Thanks for the compliment. But forget about Christa. Believe me, I have."

"Really? Then tell me why you've been going around all day like you've lost your dog?"

"I don't have a dog."

"Don't evade the question. Something…" Her red lips formed an O as she shot him a shrewd glance. "It's about Sophie, isn't it? You were very unhappy at seeing her with Thom in the breakroom yesterday. What's happened? You think you've lost your chance with her or something?"

Mason tossed his pen onto the desk, where it promptly rolled to the back and fell between the wall and the kickboard. A sign of just how his luck was going, he thought dismally. "She went out on a date with him last night."

Nadine's brows arched upward. "Really? How would you know that?"

"Yesterday, when you saw her here at my desk, she was telling me that Thom had asked her out. She was jumping up and down with excitement." He shook his head while trying to ignore the heavy feeling of dejection settling in the pit of his stomach. "She has her heart set on having a big Valentine's date with Thom. And knowing Sophie's determination, she'll probably get it."

"Poor girl. She's letting that pretty face of Thom's

blind her. I expect it won't take long for the blinders to fall off and then she'll start looking for a man with real substance. And we know where she can find one of those," Nadine added with a sage grin.

"Do we?"

Before Nadine could answer, Dexter Johnson, another programmer, stopped by Mason's cubicle.

"Oh. You two are still here. Are we supposed to be staying over for a meeting or something? I didn't get a memo about it."

In his midthirties, Dexter had black hair that waved in a giant bush about his pale face. A wide smile exposed a set of longer than normal eyeteeth, prompting the nickname Vamp. And though it was done with affectionate teasing, Mason didn't approve of his colleagues' humor. When it came to computers, though, Dexter was practically a genius. Along with that, he was a nice, unpretentious guy.

"Don't worry, Dexter. There's no meeting. Nadine and I are just having a little visit."

"Oh, well, I'll let you two get on with it."

Before he could move on, Mason said, "You don't have to go. Pull up a chair and join us."

Even though Dexter was clearly warmed by the invitation, he quickly shook his head. "No thanks. I need to get home. They're predicting sleet tonight. Not good walking weather. And I'm too chintzy to catch a cab."

Nadine wrapped her arm around Dexter's slender shoulders. "Forget about walking, or the cab. You can ride with me. Your apartment is right on my way."

Dexter's thin face brightened. "Are you sure? I don't want to be a bother."

"No bother at all. I'm happy to have the company. So

if you're ready, let's go." She urged Dexter away from the cubicle, while tossing a smile over her shoulder at Mason. "Get your swagger on, Mason. Your time is coming. Good night."

Mason waved, then turned back to his computer.

Swagger? Him? He was hardly the guy who roared in on a motorcycle wearing black leather chaps and a slick pompadour. How was Mason supposed to get swagger when everybody saw him as the boy next door with the kind face and comfortable shoulder?

For the next two hours, Mason tried to dive into his work and forget about Sophie's date with Thom. But each time he thought he'd cleared his mind, her pestering image came right back to him.

Sophie had told him to stop by her desk today and she'd give him a report on her date. But regardless of how much he wanted a chance to talk with her, he was hardly keen on hearing about Thom Nichols sweeping her off to some magical spot and kissing her until she fainted with delight.

No. Mason didn't need to hear any of that. But when he finally shut down his computer and walked out into the corridor to leave, he spotted a light still burning in human resources and knew it had to be Sophie. No one else put in the long hours that she did.

With his jacket slung over his shoulder, he stood near the elevator doors, trying to decide whether to go speak to her, when the light suddenly went dark and Sophie stepped into the corridor.

Spotting him immediately, she waved. "Mason! I didn't know you were still here."

His heart tripping at a ridiculous rate, he watched her stride quickly toward him, while thinking she looked as fresh as if it was eight thirty in the morning and she'd just arrived, instead of nearly three hours past quitting time.

"Hi, Sophie. I just now saw the light and wondered if it was you," he confessed.

Her lower lip thrust forward in a playful pout. "And you weren't going to stop by and see me? Shame on you. I expected to see you today."

So she could brag about her date with Thom, he thought sickly. "Well, I've been very busy today. I'm still doing last-minute tests on the sports app. And then there's a new project."

"You're so incredibly smart, Mason. I doubt you ever worry about the work you produce. In fact, I've heard Wes bragging on you before. You're one of his favorites," she added, then gave him a coy wink. "But don't let him know I told you so."

At least there was one Fortune Robinson who appreciated him, Mason thought dryly.

"I wouldn't think of repeating that little tidbit," he assured her.

For some reason he felt compelled at the moment to grab the bull by the horn, as the saying went. Raking a hand through his hair, he asked her, "Uh, seeing as how you're leaving, too, would you like to grab a cup of coffee?"

For one split second she appeared surprised by his invitation and then a bright smile lifted the corners of her lips. "Sure. I'd love a cup."

Feeling as though the floor beneath his feet had just turned to air, he reached for the coat she was carrying. "Better let me help you with this," he said. "I hear there's bad weather coming tonight."

Standing behind her, he held the coat so that she could slip her arms into it and Mason was immediately struck by her petite stature and the grace with which she moved. As always, she smelled like a cloud of sunny flowers and he longed to drop his face to the crown of her hair and draw in the subtle scent.

"Thanks," she told him as she buttoned the coat and wrapped a dark purple scarf around her neck. "I hate being cold. I'll be happy when three-digit temperatures get here."

He chuckled. "Don't worry. Summer will be here before you can say the rat ran over the cheese barrel."

She shot him a quizzical look. "'The rat ran over the cheese barrel.' Where did you get that phrase?"

He grinned. "I made it up."

She laughed then, and looped her arm through his. "You're so funny, Mason. Thank you for making me laugh."

Funny. How was he supposed to get any kind of serious swagger going when Sophie viewed him as some sort of standup comedian?

He didn't know, but he had to get his new and improved Mason going soon or Thom Nichols was going to snare this sweet Fortune on his arm.

Chapter 4

Bernie's was five doors down from the Robinson Tech offices in an old building that had once been a pharmacy with a soda fountain. Down through the years, the medicinal side of the business had fallen by the wayside and the remaining space turned into a casual diner that catered to nearby office workers.

Sophie had always adored the place because of its homey, nostalgic feel and simple food that could be eaten with your fingers. Something their mother had never allowed her and her siblings to do while growing up on the Robinson estate.

"Where would you like to sit? The counter or a table?" Mason asked as they entered the eating establishment.

Sophie glanced from the Formica and chrome tables to the long wooden counter with red stools.

"Hmm. Let's sit at the counter. I'm still a kid at heart. I like to swivel around. Don't you?"

"Merry-go-rounds make me nauseous and bar stools make me even more drunk," he joked.

She laughed. "I think that's a result of the drink sitting in front of you rather than the swiveling bar stool."

He grinned. "You might be right."

He reached for her hand and as he led her around a group of tables to reach the counter, Sophie couldn't help thinking how nice his hand felt against hers and how completely natural it was to be in his company. With Mason she didn't have to worry about how she looked or the things she said. She didn't have to work at impressing him. He liked her as she was and that was the reason she'd been so happy to see him a few minutes ago in the corridor outside her office. Talking with Mason always made her feel better.

After taking seats at one end of the counter, they removed their coats and draped them across their laps. Then a barrel-chested man wearing a white apron came over to take their orders.

"Good evening, Miss Sophie," he greeted her with a toothy grin. "How are you tonight?"

"I'm fine, Leo. Thank you for asking. And you?"

"I'm cold," he complained as he rubbed a hand over his bald head. "I want the sun to come out. The birds to sing. The bluebonnets to bloom."

"From your lips to God's ears, Leo," she said. "I'm cold, too. So give me a cup of the strongest, hottest coffee you have. And do you have something good for dessert this evening?"

"Bread pudding with raisins and rum sauce."

"I'll take a dish." She looked over at Mason to see he was arching a brow at her. "What? Is something wrong?"

"I didn't know women ate rich desserts. I mean, women that look like you."

Leo chortled and Sophie found herself blushing. She'd not ever thought about Mason looking at her figure in any form or fashion. But she needed to remember he was a man and a very nice looking one to boot. Something she'd not really noticed until recently.

"Well, I make sure I work off the calories. Every little bite of something sweet is worth the pain to me."

Clearing his throat, he looked at Leo. "Give me what she's getting."

Leo glanced curiously from Mason to Sophie before he ambled off. "Coming right up."

Sophie cleared her throat. "I suppose you want to hear about my date with Thom."

Behind the bar, a small radio was tuned to a blues station, while above their heads a flat screen TV was silently broadcasting an NBA game. Mason appeared to have his attention focused on the basketball game, but Sophie got the feeling that he was waiting intently for her to continue.

"That's right," he said off-handedly, "you and Thom did have a date last night. I'd almost forgotten."

Had he really forgotten or was he just teasing, Sophie wondered. With Mason it was hard to tell. Frankly, Sophie was relieved he wasn't making a big issue of asking her about the date. Not after the way it had bombed so miserably.

"Well, you do have more to think about than me," she said, while wishing Leo would hurry up with their order. She needed to do something with her hands. For some strange reason she kept wanting to reach over and rest one on Mason's arm or knee. What was the matter with her anyway? It wasn't like her to touch any man. Even Thom. A point that had been all too evident last night.

He turned his head and Sophie found herself looking into his brown eyes. They were very dark with a few lighter flecks radiating out from the pupils and at the moment they appeared to be zeroing in on her lips. Which gave her the ridiculous urge to flick her tongue out and lick away the tingling sensation.

"So how was your date? Have a good time?" he asked.

The need to clear her throat hit her once again, but Sophie resisted. Not for anything did she want Mason to think she was hemming and hawing about her date with Thom. Especially one that she'd announced to him with such fanfare.

"It was nice," she said simply.

"Nice? I figured you were going to tell me it was spectacular, stupendous, and a bunch of other S words."

How about *silly* or *slow*, Sophie thought, then quickly scolded herself for such negative notions. Maybe her date hadn't been half of what she'd wanted or expected from Thom. That didn't mean he was wrong for her. She truly believed he was her Mr. Right. After they spent more time together, she was certain their relationship would start to gel perfectly.

The bright smile she forced on her lips was hardly genuine, but she couldn't let Mason guess that her date with Thom had been about as exciting as watching an inchworm cross a sidewalk.

"It was a start," she said. "By the time Valentine's Day rolls around, I'm sure things will be getting—uh, heated."

A wan smile slanted his lips before he turned his attention back to the game. Sophie was glad she could use the diversion to change the subject completely.

"Are you a big sports fan?"

"I'm not a fanatic by any means. But I enjoy basketball and baseball." He inclined his head toward the small screen. "The San Antonio Spurs are playing at home tonight and I'm wondering if either of my brothers are at the game. Both of them have season tickets. Sometimes I drive down and go with them."

She looked at him with interest. "Oh. You have brothers?"

He nodded. "They both live in San Antonio. One is a lieutenant on the city police force. The other is an assistant district attorney for Bexar County."

"Mmm. That's impressive. You must be very proud of them."

He shrugged. "Yeah. They're both a bit older than me. So I've pretty much spent my whole life trying to be as successful as they are. But I doubt I'll ever make it."

Leo arrived then with their coffee and dessert. As she stirred half and half into her cup, she studied his strong profile.

"Now why would you say something like that about yourself?" she asked him. "Don't you consider working for Robinson Tech as being successful?"

"Since I'm working for your father, I plead the fifth," he said, his voice full of wry humor.

"No. Seriously, Mason. You're a brain. Everyone says so. And the new sports app you've created has great potential. Otherwise, Dad would never be investing money in a media blitz."

He sampled the pudding before he replied, "Yes, I can create things to use on our computers and smartphones. But that isn't like my brother Shawn facing bullets on the streets. Or Doug arguing in court to make sure a dangerous criminal is put behind bars. They both work to make our lives safer. What I do is—well, it's for entertainment. What my brothers do is meaningful."

Strange how very much she could relate to this man. For as long as she could remember, she'd always considered herself the inferior one of the family. The youngest sibling that didn't quite stack up to the others. It was an awful feeling and she hated to think that Mason ever suffered in such a way.

"So what? Everyone needs a little entertainment and fun in our lives," she told him. "If we were all rocket scientists or doctors it would be a pretty boring world, wouldn't it?"

"You don't have to placate me, Sophie. I can live with my lot in life."

She laughed softly as she dug into the bowl of bread pudding. "Coming from you, that's ridiculous. Now, me, I have a reason to feel lacking. All of my siblings are attractive and highly successful. Take Wes, for instance. He's the vice president of research and development. He's a creative whiz and now has a beautiful wife who adores him. I'm in human resources because I'm good at resolving arguments. And my love life is—well, not exactly there yet."

"Wes and Vivian seem like the perfect match. Just like the app they promoted during Valentine's Day last year. My Perfect Match is still making the company tons of money." His cup paused halfway to his lips as he glanced at her thoughtfully. "What do you think about that concept of dating, anyway? That a couple should get together because their views and likes are the same?"

"I'm not sure I believe in it. I mean, where's the passion? Take you, for instance. How you kiss would be a heck of a lot more important to me than how you vote at the ballot box."

He sputtered, then coughed. "I'm afraid I'm not that experienced in either of those departments. I—well, I do both things. I'm just not sure if I'm doing them right."

"Oh, Mason. You're so—"

"I know," he interrupted, "I'm so funny."

This time she couldn't stop the urge to reach over and give his knee a gentle squeeze. "I mean that in the nicest possible way, Mason."

He smiled at her and for a split second, Sophie thought she spotted a warm gleam in his eyes. But just as quickly she dismissed the idea. Mason wouldn't be thinking of her in that way. They were friends. Nothing more.

"Yes, I know you do."

She pulled her hand away from his knee and gave herself a mental shake. "So tell me what you think about My Perfect Match. You have to agree it brought my brother and Vivian together."

He chuckled. "It brought them together in a roundabout way. Not because the computer matched them up. As for me, I believe a person needs to let nature take its course. My dad says it was love at first sight for him when he first saw Mom. That was at a junior high prom. He asked her to dance, even though he didn't know how. Fortunately she overlooked that minor problem and they've been together ever since."

"Since junior high? What about the love at first sight—is it still going?"

"Strong as ever," he answered. "Which only proves that opposites do attract. Mom likes pop music and Dad prefers country. Mom loves Italian food, while Dad wants meat and potatoes. They both agree to go to the coast to relax, which means Mom wants to lie on the beach, while Dad fishes. But they complement each other in lots of ways and respect each other's opinion. Something that has kept them in love all these years."

Sophie couldn't imagine how it would be to have parents that were actually in love and wanted to spend time together. "I guess it must be obvious to you and your brothers that your parents love each other," she said, unaware of the wistful note in her voice.

"If you're asking whether we ever catch them kissing in the kitchen, then yes. That happens quite often. Why? Doesn't that ever happen in your house?"

The only time Sophie saw her mother in the kitchen was to give the cook instructions. As for her father, he never entered that part of the house and usually took his meals in his bedroom or study with a stack of work at his elbow. As for kissing his wife, she couldn't remember ever seeing it happen. Which made Sophie wonder how the two of them ever got close enough to create eight children. There must have been a spark at some point, she reasoned. But somewhere along the way, the sparks had been doused with ice.

She said, "Not exactly. My parents have been married for thirty-six years. A record these days, I suppose. But they mostly go their separate ways. And follow different interests."

"Hmm. Well, I'm sure your father is a very busy man," he replied tactfully.

Busy could hardly describe her father's life. He was always on the go, jetting around the world for one reason or another. Whenever he was home, he usually had a phone to his ear or was dashing off to a meeting or work.

Sophie couldn't count the times she'd wished she'd been born into a regular family. With a father who held a common job and considered time spent with his children far more important than earning money. And more importantly, a father who would never dream of cheating on the wife he loved.

But she couldn't express any of this to Mason. It would reflect badly to start pouring out her family problems to a Robinson Tech employee. Besides that, it would be downright embarrassing. Mason was a nice guy from a loving, close-knit family. He wouldn't understand what it was like to have a father who'd faked his own death and kept a woman in every port.

Sipping her coffee, she tried to push away the sadness that had suddenly crept over her. "Do your parents still work or are they retired?"

He chuckled. "Retired? They're both in their late fifties, but I doubt either of them will ever retire unless health issues force them to. Dad is a pipeline technician for a gas and oil company based in San Antonio and Mom is a high school English teacher. And before you ask, yes, she still corrects our grammar."

Sophie laughed softly. "I'm sure she never had to correct you."

He chuckled. "Oh, no. I ain't never used bad grammar."

She dipped into the pudding and realized with a start that she was very near the bottom of the bowl. She'd been so engrossed in Mason's conversation she hadn't even noticed.

"Are your brothers married?"

"No. Doug came close once, but things didn't pan out for him." He shrugged a shoulder. "Both my brothers are too busy playing the field to settle down. But I expect they will someday."

And what about you, Mason? Are you longing to find someone to love as much as I am?

Strange that those questions would be going through her mind, Sophie thought. And stranger still that she was thinking what a great husband Mason would make for some lucky woman. He was a good-looking guy with a manner that was a nice mixture of gentle and strong. He was a hard worker, polite and trustworthy.

He just wasn't Thom.

Okay. Nice. A start. As Mason and Sophie walked back to the parking garage of Robinson Tech, he happily repeated Sophie's lukewarm date description to himself. All day he'd been expecting to hear Sophie gush about her date with Thom. He'd been dreading seeing the dreamy look in her eye and knowing that Thom had put it there. Instead, she'd barely mentioned the date and the look in her eyes had been cold sober instead of a lovey-dovey haze. Which could only mean that Sophie's evening with Thom had been lackluster.

Maybe Mason had a chance with Sophie after all.

The celebration going on in his mind must have caused him to miss her next words, because suddenly he became aware of her calling his name.

"Mason? Hello? Have you gone into a trance?"

Giving himself a hard, mental shake, he looked at her.

"I'm sorry, Sophie. I was thinking about—uh—work. Were you saying something?"

Laughing lightly, she looped her arm through his and the affectionate gesture made Mason want to forget that they were walking down a city sidewalk. At the moment, the street was mostly quiet, the concrete walkway covered with shadows. He could pull her into his arms and kiss her soundly on the lips before anyone noticed. Except her. And for all he knew, she might just slap his face.

She said, "I was asking if you had anything special planned for Valentine's Day. I'll bet you have some lovely woman hidden somewhere that none of us knows about."

The woman was hidden, all right, Mason thought drolly. She was so hidden he couldn't find her. Unless he looked at the one who was momentarily hanging on to his arm. But she had her heart set on another man.

He called himself ten kinds of fool for wanting this woman. She was so out of his league they might as well be living on separate ends of the galaxy. And yet he couldn't stop this yearning inside him.

"Uh—no. No special plans. I'm not sure the woman I have in mind would agree to go out with me anyway."

"Oh, Mason, I can't believe that. I'll bet she's just dying for you to ask her out. Why don't you try it? No one should spend Valentine's Day alone."

He choked, then sputtered as he attempted to clear his throat. "It would certainly surprise her."

As Dexter had predicted, the temperature was growing much colder and a fine mist of ice particles was beginning to gather on his jacket. That must be the reason

Sophie had hugged herself closer to his side, he decided. She was cold.

"Then I say go for it. That's what I plan to do with Thom. Just give it my best shot and pray that all turns out like it should." She glanced thoughtfully over at him. "If I remember right, I used to see you with a cute blond. I think she worked in marketing."

Yeah, all the promiscuous people work in the marketing department, he wanted to tell her. Instead he said, "Yes. That was Christa Dobbins. She's gone now. She left Robinson Tech and moved in with a high roller."

"A gambler?" Sophie asked incredulously.

"No. I meant high roller as in money. The man is some sort of hot shot real estate agent."

"Oh, so she got dollar signs in her eyes. I'm sorry things didn't work out for you."

At the time, Mason had been sorry, too. He'd believed Christa was the woman he wanted to spend the rest of his life with. But now in hindsight, he was relieved he'd not gone so far as to give her an engagement ring. Given Christa's roaming eye, she would've made a horrible wife.

"No need to be sorry. We weren't *that* serious." At least, Christa hadn't been, Mason thought dourly. As for him, he'd been a sap for a while, but hopefully he'd learned from the broken heart.

By now they had reached the parking garage and as they stepped inside, Sophie pointed to the elevator. "I'm parked on the second floor. What about you?"

"Second floor, too."

"Great," she said, still clinging to his arm. "You can walk with me the rest of the way. I hate being here alone at night."

Concerned, he looked down at her. She always seemed like such a tigress that he couldn't imagine her being afraid of anything. "Are you afraid someone might jump you?"

"Well, I'm not overly concerned. It's just that…well, I'm a Fortune Robinson. And sometimes bad people have bad things on their minds—especially when it comes to money. Dad has always advised us kids to be alert and smart when we're out alone."

"Hmm. I see. I guess money can cause problems."

Feeling more protective than he could ever remember, Mason curled his arm around her shoulders. "You don't have to worry about that tonight. Not with me."

The grateful smile she gave him made Mason feel like he could jump over the moon.

"Thanks, Mason," she said, then gestured toward a small red sports car parked near a stairwell. "That's mine."

Mason walked her to her vehicle then waited patiently for her to dig out her keys. Once she had them in hand, she pressed a button and the engine sprang to life, along with the headlights.

So much for the problems of being rich, he thought. He doubted the heater in his well-used car would warm up before he reached his apartment.

And you think you have a chance with this woman? You have definitely slipped a cog, Mason. She's accustomed to luxury. You deal in the essentials. Get real. Or get ready for a giant disappointment.

"Well, I should be getting home," she said. "Thanks for the coffee and dessert, Mason. And I really enjoyed our chat."

"I enjoyed it, too." Far, far too much, he thought. "Uh, maybe we can do it again sometime."

"Oh, for sure," she happily agreed.

His brows lifted skeptically. "You don't think Thom might be jealous if he heard about it—us having coffee, I mean?"

Her laugh echoed through the parking garage and Mason inwardly cringed. He supposed it was ludicrous to think a sex symbol like Thom Nichols would ever be jealous of him.

"Of course not. You and I are friends. And anyway," she added coyly, "as much as I want Thom to be my Valentine, I'd never let him pick and choose my friends."

Friends. Mason supposed that was better than nothing. At least, it had gotten him a little coffee date with her. Now if he could just figure out how to get her to make the leap from friends to lovers.

"That's good—that you don't intend to let him take away your independence," he told her. "A woman needs to hang on to a certain amount of self-reliance."

A wan smile lifted one corner of her pretty pink lips. "I wish my mother could hear you say that."

Her unexpected comment had him casting her a puzzled look. "Really? Why is that?"

She shrugged, then shook her head. "Nothing important. She's just a bit old-fashioned about things. That's all. Good night, Mason."

Before he could stop himself, he bent his head and pressed a soft kiss to her cheek. "Just a little goodbye between friends," he murmured.

Something flashed in her eyes and then with her hands anchored on his forearms, she rose on her toes and planted a kiss to the middle of his chin.

"Yes. Just between friends," she said gently, then quickly opened the car door and slid inside.

Mason stepped out of the way and the next thing he knew the taillights of Sophie's car were disappearing out the exit and he was staring after them like a little lost puppy.

Get a grip, Mason. She's only a woman. The world is full of them.

Yes, but none of them looked or sounded or smelled like Sophie Fortune Robinson, he argued with the sarcastic voice going off in his head.

But right now Sophie wanted Thom. Or at least, she believed she did. A detail that Mason had to change before Thom turned on that phony charm of his and managed to get his foot in the door of the Fortune Robinson mansion and stepped right into Sophie's heart.

Chapter 5

The next afternoon, Dennis Noland, the director of human resources, made a rare stop by Sophie's cubicle. The tall, thin man with graying black hair looked unusually harried as he pulled up a chair.

"This is a nice surprise," Sophie told him. "Although from the looks of you, I'm not so sure you have good news."

The man batted a dismissive hand through the air. "It's nothing about work. My wife has been sick and our daughter is having marital problems. Lanna is six months pregnant and wants to move in with us. Sophie, we still have a twelve-year-old son at home. I don't want her problems spilling onto him." He raked a hand through his rumpled hair, then shook his head. "Sorry. I didn't mean to walk in here and start pouring out my personal problems. Hell, I'm supposed to be an expert at dealing with this sort of stuff."

From the moment Sophie had been promoted to Dennis's assistant director, he'd been like a papa bear watching over his cub. He'd always given her enough rein to build her confidence, yet was never far away if she had any doubts. If Dennis had ever believed she'd gotten the position because of her father, he'd never implied or even hinted that was the case, and she was grateful to him for that.

Reaching over, she gave his arm a reassuring pat. "Forget it, Dennis. You can pour it out to me anytime you feel the need. And as for dealing with people, employees are far different than family members. You'll figure out how to handle your daughter's problem in the best possible way."

He blew out a long breath. "Thanks, Sophie. I hope I can live up to your faith in me. But that's enough about family matters. I stopped by to see if you've finished with the details on the training program for the marketing department. Since it's supposed to go into effect next week, I'd like to give the employees time to look over everything."

Thank goodness she'd been working overtime every night, Sophie thought. Otherwise, she wouldn't have been close to finishing this bloated project.

"It'll be ready in the next hour," she told him. "I'll have Reece print and bind enough copies for the entire department. In the meantime, you go get some coffee. Better yet, call your wife. That should make you feel better."

Nodding, he rose to his feet. "Talking with Aileen always makes things look brighter." He gave her a wan smile. "How did you know that? You're not married."

Not yet, Sophie thought, but if she could steer fate in

the right direction, she might be married in the near future. Then everyone would see her as Mrs. Thom Nichols, a smart, mature woman, who was desirable enough to win the most eligible bachelor in Robinson Tech.

"Just a guess," she said sagely.

"Well, I'm sure you've watched your parents and learned that a man and wife need each other to lean on." He mustered a grin. "So I'm going to go do a little leaning for a few minutes. If you need me, you know where to find me."

As Sophie watched him walk off, she realized neither Dennis nor anyone would ever guess the truth about her parents. In public they put up enough of a front to make it appear as though they were a normal, loving couple. But she knew if Gerald needed to talk to someone to help brighten his mood, calling Charlotte would never cross his mind.

Just one more reason Sophie was going to make sure that she married a man who loved her utterly and completely and that she loved him just as much. She wouldn't settle for anything less.

Unbidden, a picture formed in her mind. A memory, really. She suddenly saw Mason and the way he'd looked at her just before he'd pressed a kiss to her cheek. At that very moment, she'd felt a reckless impulse to throw herself against him and lift her mouth to his. If she hadn't jumped in her car and abruptly driven away, she might have succumbed to the crazy urge.

Dear Lord, something strange was going on with her mind! Mason wasn't the man in her future plans. He wasn't the guy she'd been gazing at for weeks and imagining herself walking down a petal-strewn aisle to meet at the marriage altar.

Why was Mason's image pestering her now with his half-cocked smiles and warm brown eyes? Why did she keep remembering the fondness in his voice as he talked of his family? And why did touching him feel so comfortable and right?

Because Mason is a friend, Sophie. And friends make us feel cozy and happy and relaxed. And most of all, a friend makes us feel loved.

Loved. Yes, strange or not, Mason did make her feel loved.

But she didn't want a friend. She wanted a companion, a lover, a husband.

She wanted Thom. Didn't she?

Later that afternoon, Sophie stood in the marketing department, when Olivia suddenly walked up behind her and said in a hushed tone, "Mr. Sexy is giving you the eye. I think he's getting impatient because you've not spoken to him yet. Just look at him leaning against the wall. He thinks he's cooler than a grape Popsicle on a hundred degree day with a line of women just waiting to take a bite of him. Really, Sophie, what do you see in the guy?"

"Every female in this room—other than you, that is—would give their eyeteeth to get their hands on him."

"He's nothing more than eye candy," Olivia argued.

"He's a brilliant marketing strategist. I've even heard Dad say that much."

"Oh, he's definitely smart," Olivia agreed. "In the slyest possible way. All I can say is be careful."

Sophie gave her sister a confident smile. "Don't worry. When it comes to Thom, I know exactly what I'm doing. What are you doing here in marketing anyway?"

"Checking on some media matters. What about you?"

"Spreading word about a training program soon to go into effect."

With a little wave, Olivia said, "Better go do your spreading. But if I were you I'd make Thom wait until last. Let him know you're not easy."

Darting her sister an annoyed glance, Sophie made her way to Thom's cubicle. She could feel every female eye watching the two of them. The idea that they might be jealous of her was a heady thought. And yet in other ways it made her uncomfortable. If Thom was that much of a prized possession, how did she expect to hang on to him?

She couldn't let herself worry about such things now. She had to concentrate on snagging him first.

"Hello, Sophie. I was about to think you were going to ignore me."

Smiling coyly, she shook back her hair, making her long silver earrings jingle against her neck. "Not at all. I was working my way to you."

He held up the folder she'd instructed Reece to pass out a little more than an hour ago. "I see the old man thinks we need more training."

A frown pulled her brows together. "Excuse me? Old man?"

"Yeah. Your father. He's the boss of this place, isn't he?"

Not liking the sarcastic tone in his voice, she started to walk away, then decided that would hardly be conducive in creating a meaningful relationship with this man.

"If you're referring to the new training program,

then no. It wasn't Dad's idea. It was Ben's. Why? Do you have a problem with it?"

He must have sensed her displeasure because he suddenly cleared his throat and straightened to his full height. "No. No trouble. I can't see how anyone expects us to get our work done if we have to stop and attend training classes. Is there really that much new stuff going on in marketing that we don't already know?"

She got the feeling Thom had to check himself to keep from saying "I" instead of "we." Well, she did like for a man to feel confident about himself; however, she couldn't stand a know-it-all. She hoped she didn't learn Thom was the latter.

"Digital technology has opened up a whole new world of connecting with the consumer. Robinson Tech needs to remain on the leading edge of that connection."

He reached out and touched a finger to her cheek and Sophie had to fight to stop herself from stepping back from the contact.

"Sorry, Sophie. I suppose if my family owned the company like yours does, I'd be defending its strategies, too. But let's forget about work," he said suddenly. "What are you doing Sunday night?"

Eating bread pudding with Mason. Now that would be a nice thing to be doing.

Mentally shoving aside that image, she gave Thom her best smile and tried to feel excited. "What did you have in mind?"

He stepped closer and bent his face next to her ear. "Some special time together," he said with a purr. "I'll pick you up at seven."

Even though he seemed to be taking her for granted, she decided not to make an issue of his approach. What did it matter how he asked her out? Another date with Thom was exactly what she'd been hoping for.

"Sounds good," she said, deliberately stepping back to put a respectable distance between them. "Should I dress up? Or will it be casual?"

"Casual. Definitely. I have tickets to a wrestling match at the U of A. It's going to be a blast."

She pressed her lips together to keep them from gaping open. Was he serious? "Collegiate wrestling?"

His eyes gleaming, he shook his head. "No. That's too tame. This is the pro stuff that gets wild and entertaining. Believe me, I had to fork over a small fortune to a scalper for the tickets. The event has been sold out for weeks."

She couldn't say no now. Not after she'd already agreed to the date. Yet she was already imagining herself sitting for hours, watching hulking, sweaty men straining to throw each other to the floor. She wasn't sure she could endure it.

"Sounds interesting," she said with fake enthusiasm.

His cocky smile grew deeper. "I felt sure you'd like the idea. We'll drink beer and yell our guts out. I can't wait."

Neither could Sophie. She was already wishing the whole evening was over.

"I'll bring some throat lozenges so I won't lose my voice."

"That's my girl," he said with a patronizing wink. "You know, this thing with you and me is working out fine. We're compatible. Just like My Perfect Match."

That's because they were destined for each other, Sophie thought, and if she had to sacrifice a little to get the man she wanted, then she could endure most anything. Even overgrown men dressed in tights.

* * *

Later that day, Mason had just stepped out of the men's room on the top floor of the building when he spotted Sophie emerging from the elevator. Pleasure shot through him as she gave him a little wave and started walking in his direction.

"Mason, how nice to run into you," she said. "What are you doing all the way up here?"

She was wearing a close-fitting skirt today that stopped just short of her knees. The fabric was a geometric print of greens and blues. A crisp blue shirt was tucked inside while a wide leather belt cinched in her tiny waist. She looked professional yet very sexy and he wondered just how much Thom had taken notice of her since their date together. The man had his pick of women, but even he was probably surprised at having the boss's daughter interested in him. And no doubt pleased to be given the chance to step into such a famous and wealthy family.

"Believe it or not, I've just had a brief meeting with your father. He actually wanted to commend me on creating the Sports & More app."

Her face brightened. "That's wonderful, Mason. Dad doesn't often do that sort of thing. You should feel honored."

"Actually, I'm feeling relieved. I was quaking when I walked into his office. He's not the sort of man you have a simple chat with."

She chuckled. "No. Dad can be formidable at times. But he recognizes good work when he sees it."

"So what are you doing up here on the top tier?" he asked.

"I'm on my way to speak with Ben. I'm getting loads

of grumbling from the marketing department about the new training program. I thought my brother should be forewarned."

"Oh. Then I should let you be on your way."

She glanced at her watch, which had a fashionably large face circled by rhinestones. What was he thinking? Sophie had probably never worn a rhinestone in her life. No, those sparklers were most likely diamonds.

"Ben isn't expecting me for another five minutes," she said, then asked, "So did you take my advice and ask that special woman of yours on a Valentine's date?"

The question whacked him between the eyes and for a moment he was too dazed to answer.

Put on your swagger, Mason. She needs to believe women are throwing themselves at you whether they are or not.

As he fumbled for the right words, he straightened the knot of his red and blue tie. This morning when he'd dressed for work, he'd thought the neckwear had given him that sharp businessman look. But the way Sophie was studying him now, he was beginning to wonder if he appeared to be coming down with smallpox.

"Oh, yes, the date. Well, I'm trying to decide which one I want to give hearts and flowers. Most women place a serious romantic significance on Valentine's Day and I want to make sure I'm sending the right signals to the right woman."

"I understand. You don't want to hurt her by giving her false hope and perhaps cause her to believe you're about to present her with a ring. That's so thoughtful of you."

Mason felt like the biggest liar that had ever walked the earth, even though he wasn't actually fibbing about anything. He did want to send the right signals to the right woman. Sophie just didn't realize that *she* was the woman. Yet giving her, or any woman, a ring was something he'd not considered.

When Christa had thrown him over for the rich real estate guy, his self-esteem had fallen flatter than a punctured tire. Even now, after months had passed, he still had to remind himself that everyone made mistakes and he'd made a big one in trusting the flirty blonde with his heart.

"Is that what you're thinking?" he asked. "That Thom might give you an engagement ring for Valentine's Day?"

A blush instantly transformed her cheeks to a deep pink, while a sly smile tilted the corners of her lips. "Well, it's a little early for those kinds of thoughts. But things are definitely moving in the right direction. He's asked me on another date for tomorrow night. So he must like something about me," she added with a bat of her eyelashes.

Yeah. He likes your money and everything your daddy can do for him. Aloud, Mason said, "I'm sure he finds you enchanting, Sophie."

Her brown eyes turned soft and warm as she suddenly stepped forward and rested a hand on his forearm. The simple touch caused Mason's heart to leap into high gear and even though they were standing in the middle of the corridor and a few steps away from her brother's office, he wanted to take her into his arms and taste her lips.

"You're so sweet, Mason. The woman you choose for your Valentine's date is going to be very lucky."

He breathed in deeply, then wished he hadn't as her

sweet scent filled his head. He'd be smelling her for the rest of the day and into the night. "Thank you, Sophie. And I hope you enjoy your date tomorrow night."

"I do, too." Smiling cheerfully, she turned and entered her brother's office. "Wish me luck!" she called over her shoulder.

The only thing Mason wished was for the blinders to fall off Sophie's eyes, so that she'd look right past Thom…and straight at him.

"How about wishing you happiness?" he suggested.

"That's even better!"

With a little wave she disappeared behind the glass door, leaving Mason standing there trying to gather his thoughts.

It was already the fourth day of the month. That meant Mason only had ten days left to turn Sophie's head. So far Thom appeared to have missed the mark in the romance department; otherwise, she would've been waltzing around Robinson Tech on a dreamy cloud these past couple of days. Mason could only pray her date with Thom tomorrow night was a complete flop.

This was supposed to be a blast?

For the past hour and a half Sophie had been asking herself that very question while hundreds of spectators around her screamed and clapped and yelled things like: Break his arms! Kick him! Finish him off! And to make matters worse, Thom was one of the loudest.

As though the deafening roar of the rowdy crowd and the sight of men and women wrestlers trying to break their opponent's bones wasn't enough to deal with, a fanatical female fan seated behind Sophie had lurched forward and spilled a glass of cold beer down her back.

The woman had been very apologetic and had tried to help Sophie sop up the mess with a handful of tissues, but the effort had done little.

Sophie had never been so relieved in her life when the wild event finally ended and she and Thom headed across the jammed parking lot to his car.

"Oh, man, that was the greatest! When Rocco tore off Meteor's mask I thought the arena was going to erupt!"

"It did," Sophie said flatly. "I'm still wet."

Grinning, Thom reached over and curled his arm around her shoulders. "Sophie, honey, I'm so proud of you for the way you handled that little accident. No cursing or catfight. Just first-class all the way."

Had he honestly dated women who'd resorted to that, she wondered. Oh, God, this just wasn't working. Thom was turning out to be nothing like she'd expected.

"You know, you're the first girl I've found that actually likes the things I do. That's why I asked you out again. We seem to click. Don't you think?"

Sophie had felt a click, all right. Like a light switch being flipped to the off position.

"So what do you do when your dates have different interests than you?"

"Oh, that's it for me. I drop them. I mean, why waste precious time and effort on something that isn't going to work?"

Why indeed, Sophie thought, but kept the retort to herself. The guy was clueless, not to mention self-absorbed. "So you never think about doing something the woman enjoys?"

"Not really. If I have to make myself miserable just to make her happy, then things aren't going to work anyway. It's just like the My Perfect Match app that Wes and Vivian promoted last Valentine's Day. A man and woman have to like the same things to make a relationship last."

She wanted to remind Thom that her brother and Vivian had learned a crucial lesson while they promoted the dating app. They both discovered that it took passion, respect, sacrifice and genuine love to hold a couple together. Did Thom ever think in those serious terms, or was he all about making himself happy? At this very moment she had the sinking feeling that Thom was all about Thom.

"But we don't have to worry about that," Thom followed up on Sophie's silence. "Looks like we enjoy the very same things. Lucky, huh?"

Luck had nothing to do with it. Sophie had put her flirt on and made it obvious to Thom that she was interested in him. Luck hadn't made her join the endless numbers of women at Robinson Tech who gazed at this man from afar and fell under the spell of his good looks and flashy smile.

She'd heard through the office grapevine that he'd gone through several girlfriends. Yet Sophie hadn't allowed the talk to scare her off her mission. After all, gossip was rarely accurate, she'd reasoned. But now, she was beginning to think the talk about Thom sifting through a stack of women might be true.

"Yes," she finally forced herself to say. "It's fortunate when two people click."

His arm squeezed her shoulders and drew her closer to his side. Two weeks ago when Thom was only her dream man, the gesture would have sent her flying to the moon. Now, she actually wanted to put some distance between them. Like ten or fifteen miles for starters.

Oh, God, how had her thinking gotten so messed up? What was she doing with this narcissistic man?

"After all the food I consumed during the match, I couldn't eat another bite. But I'll take you by a burger place or something if you're hungry."

How thoughtful that he'd go to so much trouble for her, Sophie thought wryly. During the wild event, Thom had eaten two hotdogs and a giant serving of nachos. She'd sipped on a diet soda. Along the way, she'd lost her appetite for him and any kind of food.

"Oh, no. I couldn't eat a bite," she swiftly declined, then added, "Actually, after all that excitement, I think I'm ready to go home. Monday mornings are always rough in my department. I'd like to get plenty of rest tonight."

For a moment, her suggestion to end the evening appeared to have taken him aback, but then he smiled and gestured toward his car which now was only a short distance away.

"Sure. I need to run an errand before I go home anyway."

To buy another mirror so you can sit around and admire yourself, Sophie wanted to ask. Then quickly shamed herself. What was the matter with her anyway? This was only her second date with Thom. She was simply annoyed because she'd had to sit through more than two hours of a raucous sporting event, instead of being treated to a quiet romantic evening with just the two of them.

The drive to the Robinson estate took nearly twenty minutes and most of that had passed without much conversation. Not that talking would have meant that much to him anyway. As soon as Thom had helped her into the car and started the engine, he'd tuned the radio to a satellite sports station and cranked up the volume. By the time he pulled up in front of the house, Sophie had heard all she'd wanted to hear about multimillion-dollar athletes and their legal troubles.

As soon as he cut the engine, Sophie grabbed her shoulder bag and reached for the door handle. "Thanks for the evening, Thom. It was…nice."

Shifting toward her, he said, "It's still rather early, Sophie. Are you sure you wouldn't like to invite me in for a cup of coffee or something?"

She noticed his deep voice had taken on a purring sound that should have caused goosebumps to rush over her skin. Any normal red-blooded woman would be leaning toward him, inviting him to kiss her. Instead, she wanted to stick her head out the window and gulp in several breaths of clean air.

Moments of silence passed as she floundered for some sort of excuse, then finally she said, "Tonight really isn't a good night. My mother—"

"I'd love to meet your mother," he quickly countered before she had a chance to finish. "With a daughter like you, she'd have to be a very lovely woman."

"That's nice of you, Thom."

Grinning, he leaned closer until his face was only inches from hers. "I know when I'm looking at a good thing."

If that was supposed to be a compliment, she wasn't impressed. "Well, my mother goes to bed early. She wouldn't appreciate us waking her at this late hour."

"Hmm. I'm sure with a house this size, we could

find a spot far away from her room. She'd never even know we were around."

"I don't—"

Before she could finish, he'd planted his lips over hers and Sophie had little choice but to respond with as much fervor as she could muster. But the intimate contact left her as cold as the temperature outside the car and she had to force herself to go through the motions.

She must be frigid! The frantic thought raced through her mind as Thom finally eased away from her and rested his hands on the steering wheel. How could she kiss this man and feel nothing? Except the need to escape. Oh, Lord, if Olivia ever learned of this, she'd be gloating. She'd never quit saying I told you so.

The desperate thought had Sophie impulsively reaching for his hand as she tried to salvage what little was left of their evening. This had to be her fault. She wasn't trying enough. There had to be a sexy part of her just waiting to burst into flames. She had to find it and fast or Thom was going to lose all interest.

"Thank you for tonight, Thom."

"Are you sure you really want me to leave?" He squeezed her hand and urged her ever so slightly toward him. "I could still use a drink."

"Next time, I promise. I'll see you tomorrow at work," she said in a rushed voice. "Good night."

Before he had the chance to make any more moves, she practically leaped from the car and without a backward glance, hurried straight to the house.

By the time she was standing inside the foyer, she heard Thom's sports car drive away. The sound left her with a feeling of immense relief, coupled with a sense of utter disappointment. A few days ago, she'd been dreaming all sorts of beautiful images of Thom taking her into his arms and kissing her until she was drunk with desire. She'd pictured him sliding an engagement ring on her finger. A ring she could flash to her family and friends to give them proof that she was wanted by one of the most eligible bachelors in Austin. Winning Thom would be proof she was worthy of a man's love.

Had she been totally wrong about him? Even about herself?

Tears suddenly burned the backs of her eyes and as she closed the lids and waited for the sting to subside, Mason's face suddenly appeared in her mind.

Mason seemed to understand all the things Sophie was thinking, feeling, even hoping. She had no doubt that if he was standing in front of her now, she could rest her cheek against his chest and he would do everything in his power to comfort her.

Mason. Was he the reason she couldn't feel anything when Thom touched her? Had Mason gotten into her subconscious and started controlling her thoughts? Or had she unwittingly invited him to walk straight into her heart?

Either way, she had to get a grip on herself and her mixed emotions. Otherwise, her plans for her future with Thom were going to evaporate long before Valentine's Day ever arrived.

With a heavy sigh, she walked through the quiet house. Apparently her father was out of town again or buried in his study, strategizing on making his next million. The thought had her glancing in the direction of her mother's bedroom.

A lonely strip of light told Sophie her mother had already retired to her private sanctuary to read or watch

TV. She wouldn't be pillowing her cheek on her husband's shoulder or cuddling close to the warmth of his body. There would be no good-night kiss or talk of a tomorrow together.

The sad realization was not a new one for Sophie, but tonight it struck her even more deeply. She'd never thought she'd inherited her mother's traits. Everyone said she had the fighting spirit of her father. But after tonight and that tepid kiss with Thom, she could only wonder if she was going to end up like her mother. Too cold to let herself really love anyone.

Chapter 6

The next morning, as soon as Sophie walked into the HR department, Dennis met her with a new project, one that would keep her busy for the next few weeks. Which was just fine with her. She needed something to take her mind off the disappointment she was feeling over her lack of chemistry with Thom.

A few minutes ago, Olivia had stopped by her desk on the pretense of asking questions about the new training program, but Sophie knew her sister really wanted to know about her date last night. It had taken all of Sophie's willpower not to break down and admit to Olivia that she feared she'd made a mistake in going after Thom. But the memory of her sister's know-it-all prediction of failure had given Sophie the strength to keep her real feelings to herself. No doubt Olivia would gloat in the future. But for now, Sophie wasn't ready to throw in the towel. Who knew? Thom's behavior might get better. Or Sophie might find some way to melt the frigid ice inside her.

"Break time, Sophie. Better make the most of it before Dennis throws another stack of work on your desk."

Sophie looked up to see Faye, a middle-aged woman who worked in a nearby cubicle. Married with four children, Faye always had a cheerful smile, no matter what was going on at work or home, and Sophie admired her for being such a positive person.

"Oh, I hadn't noticed the time. A cup of coffee would be nice. If I can unglue myself from this chair."

Chuckling, Faye walked on toward the exit. "I'll try not to drain the pot dry before you get there."

After putting her computer into safe mode, Sophie made her way to the nearest ladies' room. As she walked, she noticed the bright winter sun streaming through the windows at the far end of the corridor and the sight lifted her otherwise dreary spirits. The day was beautiful. She was determined to forget about her problems and enjoy every second of it.

Inside the ladies' room, she smiled a greeting to some coworkers before making her way to a vacant stall.

Moments later, she was adjusting her clothing and hoping the last of the pastries hadn't been taken from the break room, when she suddenly caught the sound of women's voices beyond the stall door. Although they were speaking in hushed tones, she could hear them clearly.

"Who does she think she is, anyway? Princess Sophie Fortune Robinson?" one woman said in a sarcastic tone.

Another female voice replied, "I don't know, but I

can tell you one thing for sure. The only reason Thom Nichols would ever give her a second look is because of her daddy. Everyone knows Thom wants to move into an executive office. What easier way to do it than date the boss's daughter?"

They were talking about her! But why? She'd never used her family position to climb over any Robinson Tech employee. She always tried to be kind and helpful to everyone. And what they were saying about Thom...

"Exactly," the first woman added. "I mean, she's really not very pretty. And those clothes she wears—"

The woman followed up with a groan and Sophie glanced down at the skirt and blouse she'd dressed in this morning. She'd thought the shirred purple skirt was chic, along with the pale pink blouse tucked in at the waist.

"Well, her clothes obviously cost a fortune, but someone ought to tell her how to wear them," the second woman replied.

"She's a spoiled daddy's girl. That's the only reason Sophie got her job and everyone in this company knows it. You'd think Thom would have better taste."

"Hah. Money always makes up for beauty and class."

And both of you have neither, Sophie wanted to shout at the women.

Blinking back tears, she waited in the stall until she was certain the two women had left before she finally found the courage to emerge. As she washed her hands and dried her eyes, she told herself there would always be women who hated her simply for who she was. And yet their words had cut deep.

Was Thom dating her just because of her father? Just because he had his eye on an executive position?

Fighting back tears, but quickly losing the battle, she rushed from the ladies' room and headed back to her desk. No way could she go to the break room now. Everyone, including those two nasty mouthed women, would see her tears and the gossip would start all over again. Only this time they'd be laughing behind her back.

Quickly striding down the corridor, she kept her head down and tried to wipe away the tears that continued to stream down her cheeks.

"Sophie!"

Suddenly two male hands caught her shoulders and she looked up through a watery wall to see she'd very nearly run smack into Mason.

"Oh, Mason!" His name came out with a mixture of anguish and relief, and before she realized what she was doing, she grabbed the front of his shirt with both hands. "I'm so glad it's you."

"Sophie, what's wrong? Something has upset you."

She blinked and did her best to smile. Not for anything could she repeat what she'd heard in the ladies' room to this man.

"I—I'm just having a bit of a rough morning. I'll be okay."

Sophie was crying! The sight of her tears shook Mason far more than he would've ever expected and before he could think about what he was doing, he slipped his arm around her shoulders and urged her toward a nearby alcove where a pair of dark green couches was flanked by tall fig trees and surrounded by a row of arched windows.

"Come with me and let's sit for a minute," he told her. "You can't return to your desk in this shape."

He helped her onto one of the couches, then took a seat next to her. She promptly produced a tissue from a tiny pocket on her skirt and dabbed her cheeks. Even though her brown eyes were red and watery they were still the most beautiful eyes he'd ever gazed into, Mason decided.

"I'm so sorry that you're seeing me like this, Mason. This isn't me. I can't even remember the last time I got weepy."

Now that Mason thought about it, he couldn't remember a time he'd seen Sophie without a dazzling smile on her face. She was always happy and upbeat. So what had caused all the tears, he wondered. Thom?

"Did you have a run-in with an employee?"

She shook her head and Mason felt a small measure of relief.

"No. I'm just doubting myself a little. Sometimes a woman has days when she feels…less than beautiful. I guess this is one of mine."

Reaching for her hand, he pressed it between his. "Sophie, listen to me. You don't have any reason to doubt yourself as a woman or as the assistant HR director. You're beautiful and capable. Don't let anyone tell you differently. Okay?"

Her somber gaze slowly surveyed his face and Mason suddenly felt a connection between them that he'd never felt before. It was warm and strong and deep enough to make his heart beat with hope.

"You're right. I shouldn't allow anyone or anything to stop me from feeling positive about myself."

"That's the spirit." He tucked his forefinger beneath her chin. "Now let's see that gorgeous smile of yours."

Her cherry colored lips automatically curved into a smile, but the expression didn't light her eyes and that worried him.

"That's better," he said, "but you still don't look completely happy to me."

Shaking her head, she glanced away, then bit down on her bottom lip. "Mason, do you think—well—that Thom is really interested in me?"

Thom! The wolf in designer clothing! Mason would like to punch him in the jaw and warn him to stay as far away from Sophie as he could possibly get. But Thom appeared to be what Sophie wanted and it certainly wouldn't score any points with her to beat the jerk to a pulp.

"What makes you think Thom might not be interested? He's dated you twice now. By the way, how did last night go?"

With her stare glued to the window, it was impossible to see what was going on behind her eyes. But Mason got the impression she wasn't ready to talk about any of it. Whether that was because the date had been good or bad, he could only guess.

"Oh, it was…enlightening. Thom seems to think we're perfect for each other. He believes if we registered with My Perfect Match, the computer would put us together instantly."

Sure. Perfect for Thom, Mason thought. He ventured to ask, "Is that what you think? That you're perfectly matched?"

She shrugged and the indifferent response surprised Mason. It also sent his spirits on another soaring leap.

She wasn't singing Thom's praises. She wasn't prattling on about having a fabulous time in his company. According to her less than enthusiastic reaction, something wasn't working out quite right with the two of them, Mason decided. Which meant he still had a chance to win her over.

"I've always thought he would be perfect for me. But I'm realizing now that I need to get to know him better. People are always different outside of work. But then, you probably see that same thing with the women you date."

Oh, yes, his women. He scoffed inwardly. He hadn't dated since his fiasco with Christa, but that was a fact he was going to keep to himself. For now, at least.

"Yes, sometimes people can turn into real monsters when they're not under the scrutiny of a boss. Actually, once I leave Robinson Tech in the evenings I grow fangs and wolf hair."

She looked at him and giggled and the sound made him smile. More than anything he wanted Sophie to be happy.

"Mason, you're so funny."

"It's good to hear you laugh," he told her.

She squeezed his fingers and Mason wished they were in a private place where the rest of the world couldn't intervene. He wanted so very much to pull her into his arms and tuck her head beneath his chin, to show her how much he wanted her. But would he ever have that chance? And even if he did, how would she react? She seemed to like him. But liking was nothing like wanting. Or loving.

"You always make me feel better," she said softly.

His thumb stroked the back of her soft hand. "Sophie,

if anyone ever hurts you—if you ever need me—I'm right across the hall. All you have to do is come to me for help. You know that, don't you?"

Smiling now, she leaned close and pressed a kiss to his cheek. The touch of her lips, the scent of her skin and hair whirled his senses to a drunken daze.

"Yes, I know," she whispered. "Thank you, Mason."

She rose to her feet and Mason was forced to release her hand.

"I'd better get back to my desk," she said. "Dennis just handed me a new project this morning."

Rising from the couch, he took hold of her arm. "Come on, I'll walk you back."

At the door of the HR department, Mason stood with his hand still wrapped around Sophie's arm and even though it was time for him to let go, he was reluctant to end the sweet contact.

"So will you be working late tonight? Or do you have another hot date with Thom?"

She glanced up and down the busy corridor as though she expected the suave snake charmer to appear at any moment. Did she think Thom might actually be jealous of him? The notion made him want to puff out his chest.

"What makes you think it was hot?" she asked guardedly.

"Hmm. Well, isn't Thom in the running for sexiest man alive?"

"I don't know about that," she replied and then her gaze landed back on his face and she smiled brightly. "Uh, I'm pretty sure I'll be working late tonight. What about you?"

He nodded as he anticipated spending a few private minutes with her. "Definitely. Mr. Robinson—your father—and Wes have given me the task of producing a health app to go along with the Sports & More app. And they both want the finished product on their desks as quickly as possible."

She smiled again and this time her eyes sparkled. Mason wanted to shout hallelujah at the sight of her lifting mood.

"Congratulations," she said. "Obviously you're doing all the right things. Maybe you'll have a chance to tell me more about the new project tonight."

This had to be his lucky day, Mason decided, as a ridiculous thrill rushed through him. He'd climbed out of bed this morning feeling as though winter was never going to end. Now, just hearing Sophie suggest she'd see him tonight made it feel like daffodils and green grass were just around the corner.

"Sure. We'll have another coffee or something."

Nodding, she started through the door. "That would be great. See you later."

Mason was walking down the hall, whistling happily under his breath, when he noticed Thom approaching him from the break room. Judging by the smirk on his face, the other man wasn't exactly in a friendly mood.

"Hey, Montgomery, having trouble with your job?"

Mason arched a brow at him. "No. Are you?"

Thom inclined his head toward the human resources department. "That's where an employee goes when he feels…slighted."

Mason had never liked Thom Nichols and the feeling had only intensified since Sophie had told him her plan of trying to snare the man for her Valentine's date.

"I couldn't be happier about where my career is headed. And my private life," Mason said coolly.

"Same here," Thom quipped. "Dating the boss's daughter certainly has its merits. Before long I might be moving to an office on the top floor. Maybe right next to old man Robinson himself."

Only in your dreams, Mason thought. "She has a name. Why don't you use it?"

Thom rolled his eyes. "Montgomery, you always were a polite sap. If you'd loosen up and quit the stuffed-shirt act, you might get somewhere with the women. In fact, Christa might still be around."

It was all Mason could do to keep from ramming his fist into Thom's gut. But Mason wouldn't give him the satisfaction of knowing he'd gotten under his skin.

"Christa is none of your business."

A phony smile exposed Thom's white teeth. Mason figured he'd spent thousands to make them perfect.

"Just like Sophie is none of yours."

So that's what this little chat was all about, Mason concluded. Thom had spotted him and Sophie talking. Well, well. Who would've thought Mr. Sexy could ever doubt his ability to keep a woman interested?

"Sophie is a friend," Mason said flatly. "And I don't want to see her hurt."

Thom's nostrils flared as he unnecessarily straightened the knot of his tie. "I have no intentions of hurting Sophie. So don't give her a second thought."

Like hell, Mason muttered to himself. To Thom, he said, "I hope you don't try to tell Sophie who she should be thinking about. Women aren't too keen on that sort of domination."

Thom shot him an incredulous look, then after a moment, burst out in sarcastic laughter. "You? Giving me advice on handling a woman? That's hilarious, Montgomery." Then he abruptly walked away.

Mason stared after him, thinking he'd rather be struck by lightning than to let Thom get his greedy hooks into Sophie's soft heart.

Later that evening, well after most everyone had left, Sophie continued to work at her desk. She told herself she wasn't going to cross the hall and seek out Mason. No, if he wanted to have coffee with her, then she'd wait until he showed up to ask her. And if he didn't, she'd go home and forget about him.

Which was exactly what she should do. After all, Thom was the man she was after. He was the man who should be inviting her to the coffee shop. Not Mason. But the only time Thom had mentioned coffee was when they'd been sitting in front of the Robinson doorstep.

Olivia would warn her that Thom was using her to wiggle his way into the bosom of the family. Although Olivia was so jaded she would naturally think in those terms, Sophie was beginning to realize her sister might be right. The more Sophie thought about Thom's behavior, the more she was realizing his feelings for her were far from sincere. She didn't want to believe she was dumb enough to have developed a crush on that sort of man, but it appeared as though she had.

Eventually, her rambling thoughts got the better of her and she grabbed her handbag and headed to Mason's cubicle.

Mason was the only person left in his department and as she neared his desk, she paused to take a longer look at the man who'd always been so kind to her. At the moment, his head was bent over a stack of papers, causing a lock of his dark hair to flop away from his forehead. His brows were pulled together in deep concentration as he shrugged one shoulder and then the other in an effort to ease the stiffness.

She must have unconsciously made a move or taken a step, because he suddenly turned toward her. As soon as he spotted her, he stood and smiled.

"How long have you been there? You should've yelled at me."

She entered his cubicle. "You were in deep thought. I didn't want to disturb you."

"You could never disturb me."

He pulled up an extra chair and gestured for her to sit. "Make yourself comfortable, Sophie, while I clean up. Have you finished work for the evening?"

"Yes. My mind refused to focus any longer so I gave up and decided to see if you were faring any better."

Sophie sank into the chair and all of a sudden a strange awareness came over her. For no reason at all, she noticed the room was quiet and practically dark. And Mason was sitting only inches away from her. He smelled like piney woods and fresh rain, and she noticed the dark hair inching over the back of his collar had a rich, shiny texture. Beneath his mustard-colored shirt, the muscles of his back and shoulders rippled ever so slightly as he moved. What would it be like to touch all that masculine strength? How would his lips taste? How would his hands feel against her skin?

The thoughts stirred the feminine parts of her and stung her cheeks with unexpected warmth. What was she doing thinking such erotic things about this man? He was her friend, not her lover!

"I've accomplished enough for one day." He stuffed

the stack of papers in his desk, then swiveled his chair toward hers. "There. That's out of the way. Are you ready to head to Bernie's?"

As she crossed her legs and smoothed the hem of her skirt, she noticed his eyes traveling down the length of her calf which was covered with the soft brown leather of her dress boot. It was the first time she'd ever seen him looking at her in such a physical way and it only added more fire to her heated thoughts.

"I—uh—well, I thought we might talk a minute before we leave." She nervously licked her lips as her gaze dropped to her lap. "Unless you're in a hurry."

"No hurry. I don't have anything waiting for me at home. Do you?"

Home. Not since she and her brothers and sisters had been children and the house had held the sound of voices and laughter had she thought of the Robinson estate as home. The place she lived in now was little more than rooms that provided luxurious shelter.

"Not at all." She lifted her gaze back to his face and as their eyes met, her heart gave an odd little jerk. "Uh, do you live alone? I mean, you don't share the place with a friend?"

He shook his head as his eyes remained locked on hers. "I have an apartment on the north side of town. And the only one I ever shared it with was a dog, but he's not there anymore."

"Please don't tell me something happened to him."

A faint grin cocked the corner of his lips and Sophie felt a breath rush out of her.

"Andy is just fine. He lives with my oldest brother down in San Antonio. I didn't feel right about leaving him alone in the apartment day after day with no place outside to run and play. With my brother, he has a fenced-in backyard and another dog to be his buddy. I hated giving him up, but I wanted him to be happy."

"You did the right thing," she said softly. "We all need companionship."

He cleared his throat, then absently rubbed a hand against his chest. Sophie wondered what he would think if she moved his hand aside and placed hers there. How would it feel to slip her fingers between the pieces of fabric and touch his warm skin?

Shocked by the naughty thought, she tried to focus on Thom and Valentine's Day and all the hopes she'd had for the two of them, but at this very moment, none of that seemed to hold any importance. Had she lost her mind?

Clasping her hands together and resting them on her knee, she forced her gaze to move from Mason and on to something else. Beyond his left arm, she spotted a framed photo on his desk and she peered at it closely, trying to discern if Mason was one of the three men in the picture.

"Is that some of your family in the photo?"

"That's me and my brothers. We'd been fishing that day down at Corpus."

Curious now, she left her chair to pick up the frame. The three men with windblown hair and sunburned faces were smiling and laughing. Mason was only wearing a pair of swimming trunks and Sophie was mesmerized by the chiseled abs and long, muscular limbs.

"You three look like you were having lots of fun."

"We always have fun when we're together."

Sophie wished she could say the same about her own family. Most of the time they were discussing their father's philandering and whether any more of his illegitimate children were going to show up.

"You're so lucky, Mason. More than you could possibly know."

She leaned over to replace the photo on his desk. At the same moment, his chair swiveled toward hers. When the arm made contact with her thigh, the bump knocked her off balance and she teetered toward him.

"Oh!"

She managed to drop the photo onto the desktop without breaking it, but lost her footing in the process. Instinctively she grabbed his shoulder for support and then suddenly she found herself draped across his lap, her face only inches away from him.

"Sophie."

He whispered her name and the sound caressed her like a ray of hot sun on a cold day.

"Mason, I—"

She didn't have a chance to say more. Somehow, someway, their lips had made contact and her senses were rocketing upward with such a force, she couldn't think or breathe.

The taste of his lips was like a rich dessert. The more she consumed, the more she wanted.

Oh, my. Oh, my. This was a kiss. This was paradise! Now that she'd found it, she didn't want to leave. She wanted to let herself be carried away on the shiny stars exploding behind her eyelids, sending shards of tingling heat throughout her body.

But eventually Mason eased his mouth from hers and reality came rushing in like a gust of cold wind.

Scrambling from his lap, she turned her back and

quickly straightened her clothing. Behind her, Mason rose to his feet.

"Sophie, I—" His words broke off as his hands settled over her shoulders. "I can't explain what just happened. I hope you're not angry with me."

Angry? A choir of voices were still rejoicing in her head. She'd never been so happy in her life. She wasn't a chunk of ice! She could feel and want and burn with need just like any normal woman.

But what did this mean? And what could Mason possibly be thinking of her now? That she was a promiscuous two-timer? Oh, Lord, she was making a mess of everything.

Passing a hand over her heated face, she said, "How could I be angry, Mason? You didn't ask me to fall in your lap."

She suddenly realized she was trembling all over and she wondered if their kiss had affected him as deeply as it had her.

"I didn't mean to bump you with my chair. But I—I'm not going to apologize for kissing you. It was nice. Very nice."

The sound of his hushed voice so close made her shiver and for a split second she considered giving in to the wild impulse and throwing herself straight at him. But Mason wasn't the man of her plans! She had to remember Thom and resist the crazy urges that were trying to take control of her senses.

"It was nice for me, too. I—I didn't know that friends could kiss that way. But it's done. So let's forget it and move on." She turned to face him and her heart made a silly leap at the look on his handsome face. There was something very mysterious and sober in his brown eyes. Something she'd very much like to unravel. "Okay?"

He gently touched her cheek and the tender gesture melted Sophie like candy in the hand of a child.

"Whatever you want, Sophie."

She couldn't make any sort of reply to that. She was too busy fighting the urge to kiss him again.

Thankfully, he attempted to break the awkward tension swirling around them. "Let me help you with your coat and we'll walk down to Bernie's. I don't know about you, but I could eat a big bowl of dessert right now."

Trying to ignore the electricity that seemed to be arcing between them, Sophie forced out a light laugh and reached for her faux fur jacket. "I could eat two bowls!"

She handed him the garment and as he held it open for her, she felt a rush of silly tears. Mason made her feel all the right things. But she'd never thought of him as her Mr. Right. Did that make her immature or just down right stupid? And what was she going to do about Thom?

Behind her, Mason switched off the desk lamp and planted a hand against the small of her back.

"Ready?" he asked.

"Sure. All ready."

Her hands trembling, she reached for her handbag. Thankfully, he'd never guess just how ready she was to let herself make love to him.

Chapter 7

Sophie absently rolled a pen between her palms as she sat on the corner of her sister's desk. In fifteen minutes she was going to meet with a local magazine writer, Ariana Lamonte, and Sophie wasn't looking forward to the interview. She supposed there were plenty of people who were interested to read what it was like to be part of the Fortune family. But Sophie couldn't explain what it had been like to go through the name change and learn her father had been living a life of deceit for many years. She'd not totally digested it all yet, so how could she tell anyone what it felt like to become a Fortune?

"I'm not keen on meeting with the woman, Olivia. She didn't exactly put a nice slant on her blog about Keaton. I cringe to think what she might write about me."

Olivia shot Sophie a droll look. "She didn't say anything unflattering about our new half brother."

"Maybe you didn't think so, but I'm sure it made him and Francesca very uncomfortable. Surely you've not forgotten she implied Keaton was a ladies' man—like our father."

Sophie followed Olivia's gaze across the work area to where Thom was chatting with a female programmer. The young redhead was known to be a party girl. Maybe she had her own plans to make Thom her Valentine date. Strange how that notion didn't even make a bleep on the radar of Sophie's feelings.

A few minutes ago, when Sophie had entered the research and development department her first glance had been toward Mason's desk, but to her disappointment, his cubicle had been empty. And then she'd spotted Thom by the water cooler. She'd simply given him a casual wave and continued straight to Olivia's cubicle. No doubt he was probably wondering why she'd not made a point to talk with him. To be honest, she wasn't quite sure why she'd avoided him. Other than the fact that it would be terribly uncomfortable to make conversation with Thom while her mind was preoccupied with Mason's red-hot kiss. Ever since last night, the reckless moments she'd spent in his lap had been looping over and over in her mind, making it impossible to think of little else.

"And like our company lothario," Olivia suggested with a smile.

Sophie let out a frustrated sigh. "Do you have to be so tacky? Thom might like women, but he's hardly a lothario. Unlike our father, he doesn't have illegitimate children popping up here and there."

"Give him time," Olivia retorted.

Was that how people really viewed Thom, Sophie

wondered. Or was her jaded sister simply trying to put Sophie off the idea of making him her guy?

"Really, Olivia," Sophie scolded. "We were talking about Ariana Lamonte and the blog she wrote about Keaton. Not about Thom."

Leaning back in the desk chair, Olivia crossed her arms and gave Sophie a rational look. "Like father, like son. With all that's come out about our family recently, I'm sure most everyone in Austin is thinking about Keaton and Dad in those terms. Which is totally unfair to Keaton. He's not a playboy. But Ms. Lamonte sort of slanted things in that direction. Even so, we can't avoid the media, Sophie. To try to hide from it would only make matters worse. Besides, what could the woman possibly write about you that would be unflattering? You've never done anything wrong or bad or—"

"Interesting?" Sophie finished wryly.

"You're the one who used that word," Olivia pointed out. "Not me. I was only going to say you've not done anything a person could criticize."

"Well, I'll try not to say anything that might reflect badly on our family."

"Easier said than done," Olivia told her. "I'm sure Ms. Lamonte will try to trip you up or put words in your mouth."

Sophie rose and smoothed down her figure-hugging sweater dress. She'd chosen it today because she'd wanted to look sexy and fashionable for the interview. Or so she'd told herself. Deep down, she'd hoped Mason would glance her way and see her as a woman instead of a friend.

"Gee, thanks, Olivia," she said with sarcasm. "That gives me a wealth of confidence."

Olivia laughed. "Let me know how the interview goes."

Sophie sighed. "We'll know the answer to that when Ms. Lamonte's article comes out in *Weird Life Magazine*. See you later, sis."

She left Olivia's cubicle, but before she reached the exit, Thom intercepted her and from the way his brow was arched, she got the impression he was a little confused by her behavior. He wasn't the only one. Sophie was confused by it, too.

"What's up? I thought you'd want to talk with me before you left."

Sophie glanced at her watch while hoping her cheeks didn't appear as pink as they felt. "I'd planned to. But I have a meeting in five minutes."

"Business?" he questioned.

The suspicious note she heard in his voice made no sense. Thom had no reason to be doubtful or jealous. He was the golden boy of Robinson Tech. He could have his pick of women. As for her, she was quite sure he'd not developed any deep feelings for her. Not yet, at least. Perhaps the gossipers in the ladies' room had been right about Thom, she thought. Perhaps he was viewing Sophie as a step ladder to the top of her father's company and he didn't want anything to prevent his climb.

"Uh, yes, the meeting is business related."

She smiled at him even though she wasn't feeling it, but the gesture must have pleased him, because his features softened and he moved a step closer.

"So when are we going to get together again? Tonight?"

Was it only a few days ago that she'd wanted to turn handsprings because Thom had asked her out on date?

How could her feelings about him have changed in such a short time?

"Oh, it's nice of you to ask, Thom. But I have a family engagement tonight. I'll get back with you later. Right now I've got to run."

She hurried out the door, leaving him staring after her.

When Sophie entered the conference room a few doors down from Wes's office, she found Ariana Lamonte standing at a window, staring out at the Austin skyline.

"Ms. Lamonte?"

The tall, shapely woman with long dark hair turned and walked briskly toward Sophie. As she moved, a long printed skirt in orange and green swirled around a pair of brown suede boots. At the same time, the fringe on her leather jacket swayed with a life of its own. Ariana Lamonte rocked the chic bohemian look, right down to the long beaded earrings.

"Yes, I'm Ariana." She offered her hand. "And you're Sophie Fortune?"

"Sophie Fortune Robinson," she corrected. "I was a Robinson for twenty-three years. I'm not yet ready to let go of the name."

Ariana studied her thoughtfully. "And the Fortune name still feels a little strange, I'm sure."

"Exactly. Shall we sit? There should be fresh coffee over on the serving table if you'd care for any."

"No, thank you." She took a seat near the end of the table. "But please go ahead without me."

Sophie eased into the chair across from her and tried

to make herself comfortable. "I'm not very good at this sort of thing—interviews about myself, that is."

"If you'd rather I didn't record our conversation I'm perfectly fine with taking notes," she suggested.

Maybe the woman wasn't only about getting a scoop on the Fortune family, Sophie thought. Or it could be Ariana Lamonte was playing nice to get Sophie in a relaxed enough mood to spill her guts. The notion spurred Sophie's guard to an even higher level.

"I would rather you not have a recorder, Ms. Lamonte."

"Certainly. And please, call me Ariana."

The woman dug a small notepad and pen from her bag and placed it on the table. Sophie crossed her legs and began to slice the air with the toe of her high heel.

"You're very lovely, Ariana. To be honest, I was expecting an older lady with gray hair and wrinkles."

She laughed. "Plenty of people tell me a writer is supposed to be old enough to write from experience. But I don't intend to wait around for old age to set in before making my mark in the business."

"Neither do I," Sophie replied and suddenly she was thinking about Mason and how much that one little kiss had changed her. Just a tiny taste of real passion was all it had taken to reverse her course of action.

Although she hadn't yet figured out how she was going to do that without snubbing Thom and making herself look like a fool in the process.

For the next few minutes, Ariana questioned Sophie about her job, how she'd come to the decision to work for her father's company and how she'd felt when it was discovered that Gerald Robinson was actually Jerome Fortune.

"It's impossible to for me to explain how I felt at that time, Ariana. I'm still trying to digest the revelation." She studied the perfect oval of her pink nails rather than meet the scrutiny of the other woman's gaze. "It's very difficult to accept the fact that the father I knew growing up is someone else. There's that secret part of him that's a stranger to me. And that hurts—more than you can imagine."

Sophie could have gone on to say that unraveling the truth of her father's life had shaken every aspect of hers. At times she felt like a fraud, a person with a phony name who'd lived twenty-four years of lies. So many secrets still swirled around her parents. And though she reminded herself that she was her own person, she couldn't shake the fact that her family was bound together by lies rather than love. But she wasn't about to express those feelings to Ariana Lamonte or anyone. They were simply too deep and disturbing.

"I can only imagine," Ariana said, then hastily scribbled something on the page. "I'm also curious as to how Charlotte—your mother—is handling this whole situation with Keaton Fortune Whitfield becoming a part of the family."

There was so much Sophie could say about her mother. On the other hand, she didn't want Charlotte's problems broadcasted in a magazine article. Her mother had already endured enough embarrassment over the fact that her husband was a repeated adulterer.

"With Mother it's impossible to gauge what she's really feeling."

"Are you saying she hides her feelings from the family? Her children in particular?"

"I think she hides her feelings from everyone. I suppose you could describe my mother as a loner. Although she has a countless number of friends, I don't really believe she shares her private thoughts with any of them. But then, she's from an older generation. Her views on a husband-and-wife relationship are far different than yours or mine."

Ariana leveled a curious look at her. "How do you mean?"

Sophie shrugged. "Well, where Dad is concerned my mother has an overabundance of patience."

Ariana's brows arched upward. "Explain that for me."

"It's just that she…well, seems to look the other way with my father. I could never be as understanding as she is."

"Hmm. I believe there are times when private things go on with our parents that children never discover about them. In this case, I'm wondering if your mother has a reason of her own for not kicking up a fuss about her husband's naughty behavior. Did that notion ever cross your mind?"

Sophie studied the young woman's thoughtful expression and decided she could trust her to a certain point. "More than once," she admitted.

Ariana leaned eagerly forward. "Would you be interested in finding out what's behind your mother's—shall we call it—her blind eye to her husband's womanizing?"

Sophie's lips unconsciously pressed together. If it hadn't been for Rachel's bit of snooping into their father's documents, no one in the Robinson family might ever have learned about Gerald actually being Jerome Fortune, about the nasty way his family had treated him, or how he'd faked his own death just to get away from them. But as much as Sophie would like answers about her mother, she wasn't sure she would feel right playing detective.

"I'm interested," Sophie told her. "But I'm not the person who can give you the keys to Mother's past, or the motives for her behavior. She refuses to discuss Dad and their marriage with me."

A smile crossed Ariana's face. "Sometimes you can pick up clues without even trying. If you keep your eyes and ears open I have a feeling you'll learn far more than you ever imagined."

Sophie wasn't exactly sure what the writer was hinting at, but after the recent events within her family, she doubted there was much left to shock her.

"Are you insinuating that you know something about my mother that I don't?"

The smile on Ariana's face turned suggestive. "Not exactly. But I do believe she has a story of her own. And any writer worth a grain of salt is interested in telling a good story."

And any loving daughter would want to keep the awful truth about her parents safely hidden away. Or would she? Was hiding the truth the best way to deal with a problem?

Sophie didn't know what to think anymore. Not about her parents, herself, or her misguided plans to snare her dream man.

Much later that evening, Mason rubbed his tired eyes and switched off his desk lamp. For the past several hours he'd been working non-stop on the health app.

The new project was a chance to show Wes and Gerald Robinson what he could do.

However, after last night and that wild kiss he'd shared with Sophie, he'd not been able to focus for more than five minutes at a time on his work or, for that matter, anything else. All his mind wanted to dwell on was how soft and sweet her lips had tasted and how eagerly she'd kissed him back. She'd wanted him. He'd felt her desire as much as he'd felt his own. But what did it mean? What could it mean when her heart had seemed so set on Thom Nichols?

Last night, while they'd sat in Bernie's drinking coffee and eating Italian cream cake, both had avoided mentioning the kiss or anything remotely connected to it. But Mason had felt the awkward tension between them and understood the intimate act had changed everything between them.

Groaning at the memory, Mason grabbed his jacket and left his cubicle. One glance at the dark entrance to the HR department told him Sophie wasn't working late tonight. The realization caused his spirits to plummet and he wondered if she'd gone out on another date with Thom.

Why not, Mason? That kiss doesn't make you her one and only. So don't go thinking you're something special to her. The two of you are friends. Not lovers. She wants Thom Nichols. She believes she can drag that little Bantam rooster away from all his hens. She's too blinded by his charm to see how much you adore her.

Maybe she was looking past him right now, Mason mentally retorted to the mocking voice in his head, but he still had time. Valentine's Day was a week away. By then he was going to come up with a plan of his own.

Mason couldn't allow the woman of *his* dreams to spend the special night of love with anyone but him.

Down in the parking garage, he got in his car, but instead of starting the engine, pulled out his phone. Moments later, his oldest brother's voice sounded in his ear.

"Hey, Mason, what's going on in Austin?"

Mason leaned his head back and massaged his aching eyes. "Not much. Are you busy?"

Doug chuckled. "Just going through a stack of depositions. The usual thing."

"Sorry. That was a stupid question, wasn't it? I won't keep you long. I only wanted to see how everyone was doing." Finding Sophie had already left the building had unexpectedly filled Mason with thoughts of his family. Even though it was only eighty miles down to San Antonio, there were times Mason felt like he was a world away from his brothers and parents. "Mom and Dad okay?"

"Busy as ever. Dad's job sent him to New Mexico for a week, but he's back now. And Mom has been trying to set up Valentine's dates for Shawn and me. You know her, she desperately wants grandchildren. Why don't you give her some?"

A wife and babies. At one time Mason had believed he'd be the first of the Montgomery brothers to settle down and start a family. But after Christa had walked out, he'd begun to doubt whether he was cut out for love and marriage.

Groaning, Mason said, "I'm not in the mood to talk about Valentine's Day."

"What's wrong? Don't tell me you're having romance trouble again. After that stomping Christa gave you, I thought you'd sworn off dating."

"I did—I have. Except I—"

"You've met someone and she's turned your head. So what's wrong? She won't give you the time of day?"

Sophie had given him far more than Mason had expected. But he wanted more and he wouldn't be satisfied until she looked at him with stars in her eyes and love in her heart.

"She—uh—likes me enough. But—"

"You want to be more than friends," Doug finished Mason's thoughts.

"You got it. But I'm beginning to think I'm being a big fool—again," Mason said as he glanced around the nearly empty parking garage.

"Why? Don't tell me you've fallen for another flirty blonde with mush between her ears."

Wincing, Mason asked with sarcasm, "Why do I call you? To be reminded of my mistakes?"

Doug chuckled. "We all make mistakes, Mason. And you call me because you want advice from an expert."

Mason sputtered. "On women? I realize you have them lined up on your doorstep, but I'm not ready to call you an expert on the subject."

There was a moment of silence and then Doug said, "Seriously, Mason, are you troubled about something?"

"Troubled. Confused. Dazed. Yeah, I guess I'm a little of all those things. This woman is really out of my league, Doug. Truthfully, I have no business even thinking about her, much less looking her way. She comes from a wealthy family. Extremely wealthy."

"Money doesn't make a man, Mason."

"This is about more than a bank account. Her father owns Robinson Tech."

This time Doug's silence stretched to a point where

Mason was beginning to think the cell signal had dropped.

"Doug? Are you still there?"

"I'm here. I was just thinking that when my little brother picks a woman, he *really* picks one."

"I admit it's crazy. She could never be serious about a guy like me. But—"

"Listen, Mason," Doug interrupted. "This woman could walk the face of the earth and never find a better guy than you."

Mason sat up straight. "You've never said anything like that to me before."

"I haven't? Well, I should have. You've always followed your heart. That's why you're Mom's favorite."

In spite of his doubts, Mason grinned. "You don't have to lay it on that thick, brother."

"Who's laying it on? So when are you coming down to see us? If I can get some of these trials out of the way, we'll go to Padre and do a little fishing."

Mason chuckled. "By the time I get my new project finished and you get the court docket wiped clean it will be the middle of summer."

"Great. Let's mark the calendar. In the meantime, Mason, you keep asking yourself if that girl is good enough for you. Not the other way around. Okay?"

"I hear you. Thanks, Doug."

The two men exchanged goodbyes and Mason ended the connection and started the car. As he backed out of the parking slot, he noticed two cars parked together in the row behind him. One of them was Thom Nichols's sports car. The white economy car parked next to it belonged to a redhead who worked in R&D.

If Thom's car was still here that meant he most likely

wasn't with Sophie. However, Mason had never seen him working overtime. Did that mean he was out with the redhead? The idea caused Mason's jaw to clamp tight. Sophie definitely needed to know about the seedy side of her dream man. But he wasn't going to be the one to tell her. He could only hope that Sophie would learn the truth for herself. Before Thom had a chance to break her heart.

Sophie was sitting in the family room, scanning a stack of work she'd brought home, when she heard footsteps on the Italian tile and looked up to see her mother walking toward her.

Glancing at the tall grandfather clock to the left of an oil painting that Charlotte had paid thousands for at a European auction, Sophie noticed it was only a few minutes past ten.

"Hello, Mother. I thought you'd gone to the theatre. Is the play over this early?"

The older woman dropped her jeweled handbag onto an antique loveseat and slowly eased off her brocade jacket. "I couldn't sit to the end. The whole thing was too boring. But to give the actors credit, no one could have made that dialogue believable. The only saving grace was that the cost of the ticket goes to one of my favorite charities."

That was one positive thing about her mother, Sophie thought. If there was a cause Charlotte felt deeply about, she would generously contribute both her time and money to help it flourish.

"I'm sorry you didn't enjoy it," Sophie told her. "What about your friend Alice? Did she stay to watch the end?"

"No. We left together. Her husband hasn't been feeling well, so she wanted to get home early to check on him."

She wondered if her mother would have done the same.

Charlotte eased into an armchair angled to Sophie's. "I'm glad I caught you," she said. "Olivia informed me that you talked with that magazine writer today. What's her name? Lamonte?"

Sophie nodded. "Ariana Lamonte. She's writing about what it means to become a Fortune."

"Hmmp. Surely the woman could find something more worthwhile to focus on besides the Fortune family."

Sophie frowned at the bitterness in her mother's voice. "Are you forgetting that I am one of those Fortunes? That all your children are now Fortunes?"

"It's a fact I try not to dwell on," she said bluntly, then smoothing a hand over her long, black skirt, she gave Sophie a sidelong glance. "What did you and Ms. Lamonte discuss during your interview?"

What would her mother think if she told her that Ariana Lamonte was more than curious about her behavior? "Just the routine things. Mainly she wanted to hear how I felt about getting a half brother that none of the family knew existed. She also wanted to know what it was like for me to learn how my father had chosen to fake his own death rather than live as Jerome Fortune."

"Sophie! I don't like you speaking about your father in that sarcastic tone."

Sighing, Sophie looked away from her mother's stern face. Drama and secrets seemed to always surround her family. Why couldn't she have been born to regular parents like Mason's? No doubt he'd been conceived in love. Whereas, Sophie could only imagine Charlotte getting pregnant by doing her wifely duty and little more.

"I apologize, Mother. I'm trying to understand what motivated Dad to take on a different identity. But apart from that deceit, some of the things he's done are very… well, disappointing."

"He's your father and he loves you," she said as though that made up for everything.

But did her father, whom she now had to think of as Jerome Fortune, really love her? Or had the affection he'd shown her over the years only been a part of his deception? Oh, Lord, she didn't know what was real or pretense anymore. Not with her parents or with Thom.

"If you say so."

Charlotte's lips tightened, but she didn't issue any more scolding words. Instead, she settled back in her chair and asked, "I'm sure the subject of your mother came up in the interview. What did Ms. Lamonte ask about me?"

Are you asking because you have something to hide?

The question darted through Sophie's mind as she studied her mother's regal features. "I think Ms. Lamonte is like everyone else in this city," Sophie said. "She's wondering how you're dealing with all this scandal about Dad."

"And what did you tell her?"

Sophie frowned. Her mother seemed overly curious about the interview. What could possibly concern her about a simple magazine article? Over the years the Robinsons had dealt with all sorts of bad publicity. Granted, nothing as bad as the recent tabloids, though.

"Don't fret, Mother. I told her how you were standing faithfully behind your husband. And that we're all unified as a family. I'm not so sure she understands your attitude. Frankly, neither do I. But that's another matter entirely, isn't it?"

"Entirely." Clearing her throat, she rose to her feet. "Be advised, Sophie, not to say any more than necessary to this woman. After reading her feature about Keaton I have a feeling she doesn't have any regard for a person's private life."

Not wanting to cause her mother any more distress, Sophie planted a swift kiss on her cheek. "Don't concern yourself about it, Mother. I measured my words carefully. Besides, we're a strong bunch. We can weather any kind of media storm."

In an unusual display of affection, Charlotte patted her cheek. "You're right. I'll say good-night now. I've had a busy day."

As she turned to go, Sophie asked, "When is Dad going to be home? I haven't seen him the past few evenings."

"He called from LA earlier this afternoon. He'll be staying on another day or two. Business, of course."

Of course, Sophie thought sadly. And as she watched her mother leave the family room, Sophie was more determined than ever to make her life different.

She wasn't going to make the same mistake of wasting away in a cold marriage. She was going to marry a man she loved, who would love her in return. A man who would take her into his arms and wrap her in warmth and passion and fill her heart with happiness.

A man exactly like… Mason.

Chapter 8

The next morning, Sophie marched into Dennis's office, dropped a bound folder on his desk and pounded it with her forefinger, while her boss watched on with mild amusement.

"Is something wrong?" he asked.

Folding her arms against her breasts, Sophie stared at him. "Wrong? Have you read this thing?"

"Not yet. All I know is that Ben decided the company needed to save money by changing insurance carriers." He pointed to the folder. "And this is what we have now."

"This is a crock of you-know-what. It's outrageous. As soon as the employees see all the medical procedures being dropped from their coverage, they're going to riot. Ben must have been out of his mind when he decided to go with this provider."

"Health insurance is in turmoil these days and I think

there was a lot of lobbying going on by this company to get Robinson Tech's business," Dennis told her. "And your brother was in a cut-and-save mood."

Sophie snorted. "You know, when a flood of employees show up here to protest, I'm going to send them straight upstairs to Ben's office. He'll be in a different mood then."

Dennis shook his head. "Give your brother a break. He's just become a new father. He has a lot on his mind."

Sophie's expression suddenly softened. "Yes, little Lacey is adorable. I've never seen my big brother so enamored with anyone or anything. He behaves as though he's the first man to ever have a daughter."

"It is a special event when a child comes into your life. You'll learn when it happens to you, Sophie."

Becoming a mother was never going to happen to her unless she connected with the right man. And right now she was trying to decide how she could extricate herself from this mess she'd made with Thom. Perhaps she should just write *FOOL* across her forehead in big letters, take her lumps, and get it over with. But Valentine's Day was less than a week away and she'd gotten a text from Thom this morning hinting that he was already making big plans for the evening.

More wrestling or monster action movies? The mere thought of it made her sick.

"Okay, Dennis, I'll send notices out to all our employees about the change in insurance. Just get ready to hear plenty of howling."

She picked up the folder and left her boss's office. As she walked back to her desk, she spotted Mason. This morning he was wearing black slacks and a plum colored dress shirt that emphasized the faint bronze mix in his brown hair. As she watched him move toward her, she was amazed that it had taken her so long to really see what an attractive man he was. If she'd not been so busy developing such a thoughtless crush on Thom, she might have taken more notice of Mason. And never gotten herself into the embarrassing situation she was in now.

She walked over to meet him. "Good morning, Mason," she greeted with a wide smile. "I hope you're not here in my department to complain."

He grinned. "Me, complain? Never. It's my break time. If you can leave your desk, I thought we might have a cup of coffee together."

Fifteen minutes with Mason would do her a world of good. "That sounds wonderful. Let me just put this away." She held up the folder.

As he followed her into her cubicle Sophie was acutely aware of him standing a few steps behind her. The faint scent of his masculine cologne teased her nostrils while waves of heat seemed to be radiating from his body. That kiss of his had done something to her, she thought. Since then, whenever he got close, her nerves seemed to send up radar that picked up every little nuance about the man.

"What's this?" he asked. "I didn't know you were a hockey fan."

"I'm not." Sophie turned to see him staring at a ticket lying on the corner of her desk. Apparently someone had left it there while she'd been in Dennis's office.

"Someone apparently thinks you are."

"Let me see." She picked up the ticket and found a small note stuck to the back. It read: *We can catch a commuter flight and be in Dallas in time for the game. I'm looking forward to a fabulous evening with you. Thom.*

Sophie wanted to look up at the ceiling and let out a

loud groan. Instead, she glanced at Mason and tried to hide her frustration. "Thom wants to take me to Dallas to see the Stars play tonight."

"Hmm. Rather a long drive to be making on a weeknight. You'd have to leave work early this afternoon to make it in time."

The faint note of disapproval she heard in Mason's voice made her wonder if he might actually be jealous of Thom. But that sort of thinking was farfetched. Even if he had planted that hot kiss on her lips, Mason thought of himself as Sophie's friend. Nothing more.

"He expects to catch a commuter flight," Sophie said, as her mind whirled in search of more than one reasonable excuse to put the man off.

Mason grunted. "His salary must be measurably larger than mine to spend that sort of money on a sporting event."

"Thom loves sports," she said dully. "Of all kinds."

"No doubt," he said dryly.

Sophie looked at him. "What does that mean?"

He shook his head. "Nothing. Just that most men do—love all kinds of sports."

Looping her arm through his, Sophie urged him out of the cubicle. "Well, I seriously doubt Thom's salary is a dime more than yours. His position with the company is not more important than yours. As for this hockey game, I can't go."

"You can't?"

He sounded surprised and Sophie figured he was probably wondering why she would turn down any date with Thom. If she told Mason he was part of the reason, he'd probably think she was joking. And after the big deal she'd made about Thom being the fantasy man of Robinson Tech, she couldn't blame him. Or even worse, he might get the impression that she was, as her mother had implied, a butterfly fluttering from one man to the next, incapable of making a choice.

"Uh—no. It's—well, this evening is not a good time. I have—other things to do." *Like dream about you,* she wanted to say, but didn't.

He slanted her a sly grin. "You can always use the weather as an excuse. There are snow or ice warnings for tonight."

"Oh! Thank you, Mason!"

"For what? Giving you a bad weather forecast?"

She felt a blush slowly creeping over her cheeks. "Well, I don't necessarily like icy weather. But Thom— Sometimes it's hard to make him understand I'm not at his beck and call any given time of the week."

They entered the break room and she was relieved to see that Thom wasn't anywhere in sight. In fact, the room was empty.

"Maybe you should just be honest with him, Sophie. Tell him that you don't like hockey and you'd rather not go."

His suggestion caused her eyes to roll. "What a novel idea. Brutal honesty. You wouldn't like it if a woman told you she didn't like the plans you made for the two of you."

He shrugged. "Maybe. But I wouldn't mind changing my plans to something we'd both enjoy."

"Really? You'd do that?"

"Sure. If the woman was that important to me." He guided her over to a chair and helped her into it. "You sit. I'll get our coffee. Cream and sugar, right?"

"Yes, thank you."

While Mason gathered the drinks, Sophie realized he remembered things about her that Thom had never taken the time to notice. He gave her encouraging words at just the right time and made her laugh when her spirits desperately needed a lift. He inherently seemed to know what she was thinking and feeling. And Sophie was quickly beginning to see just what a rare thing that was to find in a man.

"Here you go." He placed the cup in front of her, then sat to her left. "A boost for the midmorning blues."

Her expression wry, she glanced over at him. "What makes you think I have the midmorning blues?"

"Just a guess. Your shoulders aren't quite as squared as they usually are."

For the most part, she could see that he was teasing, but the remark had her straightening her back anyway.

"I've been so busy I've hardly had time to look up. What about you?"

"This health app is turning out to be much harder than I anticipated. There are so many products out there already. I want this to be fresh and new. Something that will grab the public's attention. I just haven't come up with the right ideas yet. Basically I want to tie sports with health and make the couch potatoes realize that being fit can also be fun. That's been done, too. But hopefully I can put a different slant on it."

She looked at him and the appreciation he saw in her brown eyes made him want to do handsprings. He'd had people praise his work before. Even Gerald Robinson himself. But having Sophie's admiration lifted his ego to another level.

"You will. I have every faith in you. So do Wes and my dad. Or the two of them would've never assigned you the task."

He watched her sip the coffee, while wishing he had the right to lean over and whisper loving words in her ear, to kiss her and call her his own. Perhaps that was crazy thinking on his part, but he couldn't stop himself. Doug had pointed out that money didn't make a person and Mason believed he was right. Even if Sophie was barely scraping by on a pitiful income, he would still be infatuated with her effervescent personality, the caring and warmth that radiated from her eyes.

Mason forced his thoughts back to the conversation. "Pleasing those two men puts me in a pressure cooker," he joked.

Her lips tilted into a soft smile and Mason inwardly groaned. She had to figure out how wrong Thom was for her, he thought desperately. Otherwise, Mason's heart was going to be broken. Along with Sophie's. Because there was no doubt in his mind that Thom was a user and Sophie was just soft enough and vulnerable enough to let him.

"Wes doesn't always put what's on his mind into words, and that makes some people view him as a cold stuffed shirt. But he's really fair minded. Dad is tough and expects everyone around him to be the same. But like I said before, there's a softer side to him if you take the time to look."

To have a father like Gerald Robinson was something Mason wouldn't wish on his worst enemy. He'd noticed that Sophie didn't talk that much about her family, but whenever she did, he got the impression they weren't exactly like the warm, fun-loving groups depicted on a 1950s sitcom. And given the scandals that had recently surrounded the Robinsons, he could certainly see why their family ties might be strained.

"When I left the building last night you were already gone," he told her. "I was going to see how your interview with Ariana Lamonte went. I could tell you were dreading it."

She was carefully clutching her cup and as Mason studied her dainty fingers, he tried to block out the image of Thom sliding an engagement ring onto her left hand.

"It wasn't anything like I expected. She was much younger than I thought she would be. And clever. She certainly knows how to make a person talk. We chatted mostly about Robinson Tech and what made me decide to work for my father. And of course, she wanted to know my feelings about becoming a Fortune." She sighed and shook back her long brown hair. "The woman should know that discovering your father—that you're not really who you thought you were all these years—well, it's something that can't be described in words. It's like the ground has tilted beneath my feet and still hasn't righted itself."

This was the most she'd ever mentioned to Mason about the scandal that had rocked Austin and the business world beyond. The fact that she would share this much with him made him feel special. It also made him want to comfort and reassure her.

Reaching over, he curled his fingers around her slender forearm. "Sophie, no one is accountable for the choices a relative makes. No matter how right or wrong those choices might be."

She turned a rueful expression on him. "You're right, Mason. It's just that when you learn someone you love hasn't been entirely truthful with you—it hurts. A lot."

He gently squeezed her arm. "You can't let it drag you down, Sophie."

"I don't intend to let it," she said with conviction, then glanced at the clock. "I'd better get back to my desk."

"Yeah, I've got to get back to work, too," he said.

Moments later, while they were walking side by side down the busy corridor, Mason dared to ask, "So what do you plan to do about the hockey game?"

She slanted him a look from beneath her dark lashes. "I'm going to give him a weather forecast. He surely can't think I've stirred up a weather storm just to avoid a date."

Mason felt like letting out a loud whoop and making several triumphant fist pumps. Instead he tried to appear as cool as Agent 007 ordering a shaken martini. "He'd never think it in a million years."

At the door of the human resources department, Mason was trying to think up some sort of excuse to see her later tonight, when she suddenly turned and swept him with a demure look.

"Valentine's Day is less than a week away," she said. "Do you have your special date lined up yet?"

He cleared his throat and for one reckless second considered the idea of asking her flat out to be his Valentine's date. But she'd already made it clear she wanted to be with Thom on that special night. And Mason wasn't good with rejection.

"Uh—no. Not yet. I'm still considering."

She frowned at him. "Mason! If you don't quit dragging your feet you're going to end up spending Valentine's alone. And no one should have to be alone on such a special night of love."

"You're right. I'm going to get my act together and show my lady love just how much I adore her."

"Now you're talking," she said, then with a little wave, disappeared through the door.

His mind still on Sophie, he didn't notice Thom until he'd crossed the corridor to his own department. By then, the other man was walking straight toward him and from the tight look on his face, he didn't appear all that happy. Had he seen Mason and Sophie together?

"Hello, Nichols. You need to see someone in R&D?"

"Not exactly. I'm on my way out of the building. For a business luncheon across town."

That was the way with the marketing personnel, Mason thought. They seemed to always get added perks. Especially Thom.

"Better take a coat. Bad weather is moving in," he warned.

"Thanks for the advice, but I don't like coats. Never wear one."

Tough guy. Sure, Mason thought drily. If the truth was known, the man probably wore flannel pajamas and slept under an electric blanket.

"Suit yourself," Mason said, then started to leave.

Thom moved just enough to one side to block Mason's path.

With a smug grin, he said, "I thought you might like to know that Sophie and I are getting on great. In fact, I have a huge evening planned for Valentine's night. The woman loves sports, but this time I've decided to surprise her and blitz her with an evening of pure romance."

Mason suddenly felt ill. The hockey game hadn't impressed her, but the romance would. What in hell was he going to do to stop this from happening? He had to come up with something. He couldn't just sit around and hope that Sophie would get over this crush she had on Thom. He had to come up with a plan to ambush Sophie's heart before Thom could ever get his hands on her.

His mind already preoccupied with options, he muttered, "Sophie will be thrilled, I'm sure."

The grin on Thom's face deepened. "Dinner at the Riverside restaurant, dancing, flowers—the works."

At least he'd not mentioned a ring, Mason thought. But that would be coming soon, no doubt. If he was right, Thom would never let Sophie slip away. Not if he believed she'd be a boost to his bank account and career.

Mason glanced thoughtfully toward the entrance to Sophie's department. She clearly didn't want to go on a date with Thom tonight. Whether that was because she disliked hockey or something else, Mason wasn't sure. But either way, the idea gave him a glimmer of hope.

Mason said, "Sounds look you've put a lot of thought into this Valentine evening for Sophie."

"I've put more than a thought into it. I've already invested a small fortune in it. If this doesn't make her swoon at my feet, then she'd have to be colder than a block of ice."

Ice. Before the day was over, Mason prayed the stuff would fall from the sky in bucket loads. He didn't want Sophie going anywhere for any reason with this man.

"Uh, speaking of ice," he said casually, "did you know Austin is under a winter storm warning for sleet this evening?"

Thom looked stunned before muttering several curse words. "Are you kidding me?"

"I checked the weather site on my computer less than an hour ago. Isn't it weird? We rarely ever have brutal weather like that. The weather gods must have it out for us."

A tight grimace pulled his features. "Or me," he muttered. "Excuse me, Montgomery. I need to go."

"Have a nice lunch," Mason called to the man's retreating back, then whistling under his breath, he headed back to work.

* * *

Later that afternoon, Sophie had just finished speaking with Thom and was on her way out of marketing, when she heard a low hissing noise to her right.

Glancing over, she was surprised to see Olivia trying to draw her attention. Knowing she very well couldn't avoid her sister, Sophie walked over to her.

"What's up?" she asked.

"I'm on my way back to programming," Olivia replied. "Let's step out in the corridor."

Sophie followed her sister into the hall where they found a quiet alcove.

Olivia said, "I just saw you talking with Thom. He looked none too happy. Have you already called it quits with him?"

Sophie frowned. "What are you doing? Did you follow me here just to keep a watchful eye on me?"

Olivia shot her a droll look. "No. I had to confer with someone about advertising. But I should be following you, since you seem to have lost all common sense."

Hoping the mix of emotions churning inside her didn't show on her face, Sophie said, "I hate to disappoint you, but I can still think for myself. As for Thom, he's not exactly your business but I'll tell you anyway. He had this big evening planned to fly to Dallas tonight. I told him I couldn't make it. I explained that Dad would have a fit if I boarded a small plane with the threat of an ice storm looming."

"And Thom didn't take it well, I see. Hmm. Sorry, sis, I take everything back. He's the one lacking common sense. Not you."

Sophie smiled at her. "Thanks. I can use my brain once in a while."

As Olivia folded her arms against her chest Sophie

thought how beautiful her sister looked in the lapis blue dress she was wearing and the way her dark hair waved so perfectly around her face. Olivia was always so poised and sure of herself. She would never get herself into an awkward situation with a man like Sophie had. Olivia was too smart for that. A fact which only made Sophie feel even more foolish.

Olivia asked, "What's the deal anyway? Is flying to Dallas a bit much for the middle of the week?"

Sophie shrugged while wondering how much she could say to her sister without revealing the fact that she was quickly and decisively coming to the conclusion that Thom was a jerk. "Actually, I was thinking the same thing." Leaning closer to Olivia, she lowered her voice. "When I first told you my plans to get Thom to be my Valentine's date—"

"It was more than getting him as your date, Sophie," Olivia interrupted. "The way you were talking, he was the man who was going to slip a wedding ring on your finger."

Perhaps all that gushing she'd done about Thom to her sister had been a bit overboard. Funny, but most of what she'd said, she couldn't even remember now. But at the time Sophie had truly believed she'd been mapping out her very future. Which only proved how quickly life could alter course.

"Okay, so maybe I was letting my dreams get a little out of hand. I'm walking on earth now. And I've been doing plenty of thinking these past few days."

"About Thom?" Olivia prodded with a tad of sarcasm. "Or something more important?"

"About Thom and...other things." Her expression turned sober as she looked at her sister. "Olivia, do you ever wonder about people? The ones who are supposed to be our friends? The ones who are supposed to love us? Sometimes I ask myself if they're close to me simply because I'm me or because my name is Fortune Robinson."

Olivia swatted a dismissive hand through the air. "That's just a part of who we are. Sure, there will always be people who want to use us. But you don't have to be rich to be used, you know. Even a poor woman can be taken advantage of by a man. That is what you're thinking about, isn't it? That Thom or some man might pretend he loves you just so he can get at your wealth?"

Now was hardly the time or place to be getting into such a conversation with her sister. But she couldn't stop herself.

She nodded glumly. "There are times I wonder if I can trust anyone. I mean, we don't even know if our parents are being honest with us."

Olivia frowned. "Our parents," she repeated blankly. "Everyone knows Dad has carried secrets, but you said 'parents.' Mom doesn't have Dad's deceptive ways."

"Do you know that for certain?"

Olivia was shooting her a disgusted look when Olivia's cell phone rang.

Sophie used the interruption to give her sister a departing wave, then scurried toward the elevator. She'd already said more to her sister than she should have.

Chapter 9

Four days later, Sophie was sitting at her desk, wondering how she could finish the day when a smiling Mason suddenly strolled in carrying a foam container.

"What is that?" she asked, gesturing to the object in his hand. "It smells like food."

He pulled up the extra chair she kept in her cubicle and sat a short distance away from her.

"It's a snack. Just for you. I've been to Bernie's."

Excited now, she grabbed the container. "Bread pudding! Oh, you darling man!"

He pulled a plastic spoon from the pocket on his shirt and handed it to her.

"I stopped by to see if you wanted to have lunch, but your neighbor told me you were in a meeting with Dennis."

Nodding, Sophie quickly dug into the rich sweet. "Mmm. That's right. I haven't even had a chance to eat lunch. We've been bombarded over this health insurance thing. I think Dennis and I have convinced Ben if he sticks with this new plan his employees are going to flee like rats on a sinking ship."

Mason grunted with faint amusement. "I have no intentions of running out of the building. If I did that, how would I ever see your smiling face?"

He was so sweet and funny and endearing. And special. How had she worked near him for so long without noticing him? Why had she let Thom's sexy grin and confident attitude turn her head when she should have been looking at a man she could trust?

She playfully wrinkled her nose at him. "I would never allow you to quit Robinson Tech. I'd be lonely without you. And hungry," she added teasingly.

He glanced at a heart shaped box of candy lying on the far end of her desk. "Looks like you've already been given something to eat. Pecan pralines."

She tried not to grimace. "Thom sent me the chocolates this morning. But I can't eat them. I had already told him that I can't eat nuts—especially pecans, but he seems to have forgotten." Or never bothered to pay attention to her in the first place, she thought drearily. Since she'd turned down the Dallas date, Thom had started leaving little gifts on her desk, along with silly little notes that sounded as phony as a three dollar bill. Like she was the only woman he'd ever fallen for, or wanted so much. Who was the man trying to fool?

Who do you think, Sophie? You're the one who thought Thom was a prince on a white horse. You're the one who flirted your way into his life without ever really taking a good, hard look at him. You thought because every other woman in the building wanted him, he had to be

*Mr. Wonderful. Now he's a nuisance. One that you don't
know how to get rid of without making yourself look like
an idiot.*

"I'm sure Thom will make up for the candy on your
Valentine date."

It wasn't only the chocolate that had her mentally
shaking her head. Last Friday she'd found a beautifully
wrapped package on her desk only to find the contents
was a woolen scarf that had looked like something a
lumberjack in the far north would wear. The day before
that, she'd found a DVD of pro wrestling matches in the
seat of her desk chair, along with a note that had read:
In memory of our special night together.

There had been a time when Sophie would have
cherished anything Thom might have given her. Even
the most garish gift would've been appreciated if he'd
given it with genuine sincerity. But these past few days
she'd begun to doubt Thom's motives, not to mention
his integrity.

Sophie took another mouthful of pudding. Why
couldn't Thom have given her something as thoughtful as her favorite dessert?

*Because Thom doesn't know you like Mason does.
Because Thom will never know much about anyone,
except himself.*

"It really doesn't matter," she said honestly. Nothing
about Thom seemed to matter to her anymore.

"I'm sure you know he has big plans for your date
tomorrow night. You must be very excited about that."

Frowning with confusion, she looked at him. "Big
plans? How would you know?"

"He made a point of telling me. A 'blitz of romance'
is the way he described it to me."

She could hardly keep her mouth from falling open. "He told you that?"

He nodded and for a split second Sophie thought she saw a flash in his eyes that looked something like disapproval. Or had it been jealousy? The notion gave her a glimmer of hope. If there was a slight chance that Mason could see her as more than a friend, she had to grab it and hold on for dear life.

He said, "I suppose I shouldn't have mentioned it. He probably wants to surprise you."

Any sort of romance from Thom Nichols would be more than a surprise, it would be a stunner. As far as she was concerned, the man had the romance of a rock.

"It would be a surprise all right," she muttered.

She could feel his eyes studying her closely and she glanced up to see confusion on his face.

Before she could say more, he asked, "What's wrong?"

Everything, Sophie wanted to say. But she couldn't pour her heart out to Mason now. Especially here at work where coworkers might overhear. The gossip mill would spin so fast it would probably catch fire.

"Nothing is wrong," she said, trying her best to sound casual. "I'm just a little tired, that's all. Dealing with this insurance change has been a giant headache."

"Hmm. You normally thrive on challenges. And I've never seen you tired." His eyes narrowed with concern. "I hope you're not coming down with the flu. That would be awful to finally get your Valentine date and then not be able to enjoy yourself."

Sick? Mason was partly right. She was definitely heartsick over her misjudgment of Thom, she thought grimly. "I feel fine, Mason. Really."

She swallowed the last bite of pudding and tossed the container into the trash.

"I'm glad to hear it," he said. "I just thought—"

She glanced around to see him shaking his head with doubt and for one wild second Sophie wanted to leap from the chair and throw herself into his arms. Mason could make everything right. He could fix the troubled thoughts in her mind and the hollow ache in her heart. But he didn't know that. He might not even want to know it.

"I keep remembering back to the night when you first talked about Thom and your hopes to get him for your Valentine date. You were so excited about the prospect. And now that you've accomplished your goal, I figured you'd be dancing around the building in anticipation of tomorrow. Instead you look about as perky as a wet hen."

She wrinkled her nose at him. "I'm not a farm girl. What does a wet hen look like?"

"Droopy. Instead of clucking and running around the chicken yard strutting her stuff, she's standing at the edge of the flock trying to shake the water off her feathers. In your case, you look like you're trying to shake off a flood of tears."

His assessment, corny as it sounded, was so accurate it was eerie. Instead of dancing, she was brooding. And though she was a girl who rarely ever shed a tear, these past few days there'd been several times she'd had to fight them off.

It shouldn't surprise her that Mason could read her so well. He seemed to pick up on her feelings, even when she was trying to hide them.

She straightened her shoulders and leveled him the

most confident look she could muster. "I'm sure I need to freshen my lipstick. But I don't believe I look anywhere near shedding a tear. As for me dancing around the department, Dennis is a very lenient boss, but he might not appreciate the merriment."

A faint smile twisted his lips and Sophie couldn't help but look at them and relive the kiss they'd shared. Tomorrow night he'd surely be kissing his Valentine sweetheart. Each time she'd asked him about his date, he'd skirted the answer. Sophie didn't have a clue as to who he might be dating, but she knew one thing: She fervently wished it was her.

"I'm glad I don't need to drag out my handkerchief and wipe your cheeks." He glanced at the digital clock on her desk. "I've been here too long. I need to get back to work."

He started out of her cubicle. Before Sophie realized what she was doing, she practically leaped out of her chair and blocked his path.

"Mason, before you go, I—" Not knowing how to express her feelings in words, she rose on the tips of her toes and kissed his cheek.

His brow arched in question and she said, "That's for the pudding. And for helping me shake the water off my feathers."

She expected her comment to gain a smile from him, but she couldn't find a speck of amusement on his face. Instead, he gently patted her cheek.

"If I don't see you before tomorrow evening, good luck with your plans. Thom is a lucky man."

As she stood there watching him go and wishing she had the right to run after him, her cell phone jangled with a text message.

Crossing to her desk, she picked up the phone and read the message. The sender was Olivia.

We're waiting on you in the conference room. Have you forgotten?

Oh, Lord, the moment Mason had shown up with the pudding, she'd forgotten all about the family meeting.

Hurrying now, Sophie dashed off a note to anyone who might come looking for her, then grabbed her handbag and left the cubicle.

The last thing she needed today was to listen to Ben talk about digging up more of their father's indiscretions. But Sophie was a Fortune Robinson and she, along with the rest of her siblings, needed to help hold their fractured family together.

Moments later, she stepped into the conference room and felt every eye on her as she sat at the long table where her four brothers, Ben, Wes, Graham, and Kieran sat waiting, along with her three sisters, Rachel, Olivia and Zoe.

"Hi, everyone! I'm sorry," she apologized, her voice breathless from rushing. "I got busy and forgot the time."

"Don't worry about it, Sophie. Five minutes isn't going to kill us," Graham, the cowboy of the bunch, spoke up.

"That's right," Rachel replied. "Since I don't get over to Austin that often, it's given me a little extra time to visit with everyone."

After her older sister had married Matteo Mendoza and settled down in Horseback Hollow, the family didn't see her nearly as often. Sophie missed her sister, but on the other hand, she was very glad that Rachel had found true love and happiness.

Sophie took a seat next to Olivia and glanced around the group. "Have I missed anything?"

Wes said dryly, "Not unless you count hearing Ben describe his baby daughter's burps as big news."

Ben leveled a sardonic look at his twin brother. "Just wait, Wes. Your time is coming. When you and Vivian have a daughter, she'll be the smartest most beautiful child on earth."

Wes chuckled. "Viv wants twins. I can only hope they're boys."

A few teasing shots were passed back and forth between the siblings until Ben decided to get down to business.

"I'm sure all of you have been wondering what I've called this meeting about," he said.

"I think we all pretty much assume you have more news about Dad," Wes said, then added dully, "As if we haven't already had enough."

Ben glanced around the table at each of his siblings and Sophie's stomach clenched in a tight knot. Wes was right. The family had already been forced to accept so many discoveries about their father. She wasn't sure she could bear any more surprises, but from the look on Ben's face, she feared she was about to get one.

Ben continued, "As you all know, Keaton and I have been doing more digging into Dad's—uh, past connections and—"

"Don't you mean transgressions?" Wes interrupted.

Frowning at his twin brother, Ben said, "Call them whatever you like. But the truth is we've discovered we have a half sister and she's living right here in Austin."

Sophie felt as if someone had slapped her across the face. She wasn't just stunned. She was sick to her stomach.

"Ben, you must be joking," Graham spoke up. "How could we have a half sister living right under our noses and not know it?"

Glancing around the table, Sophie noticed that all her siblings, except Olivia, appeared to be shocked.

"This is hardly a joke," Ben retorted.

"Who is she? Do we know her?"

The questions came from Zoe who'd been so instrumental in persuading their father to admit he was actually a Fortune by birth.

Ben answered, "Chloe Elliott. Her mother is Janet Reynolds."

Rachel gasped. "The woman who lived down the street from us? You can't mean her! That's indecent!"

"Indecent or not, it's the truth," Ben assured her. "Keaton and I have covered every angle concerning Mrs. Reynolds and her daughter. Chloe is definitely our sister."

"Illegitimate half sister," Sophie couldn't stop herself from pointing out. "Dear God, when is this going to stop?"

Wes's expression turned grim. "I have a feeling this is just the beginning."

From the very start, Wes had been against digging into the mystery of their father's birthright. He'd believed opening a can of worms would hurt everyone in the family more than help. Sophie could now see just how right her brother had been.

Ben said, "The way I see it if we have more brothers and sisters out there somewhere, then we need to know it."

Ben could think in those terms, but not everyone else in the family had to side with him, Sophie thought.

Glancing to her left she could see that Rachel had

gone pale. To her right Olivia appeared maddeningly indifferent and, if anything, Zoe looked sad. As for Sophie she was so angry and disgusted it was all she could do to keep from scraping back her chair and running from the room.

It was one thing for their father to have had a discreet affair in London years ago, far away from his family here in Austin. But this affair with Mrs. Reynolds had been carried out right under their noses! It was embarrassing and sickening!

From down the table, Kieran asked, "Does Mother know about this yet?"

"I've given her the news," Ben stated. "She looked grim, but for the most part she took it pretty calmly. I tried to encourage her to talk about the situation, but she hardly said a word. So I decided not to press her."

The nauseous feeling in the pit of Sophie's stomach turned to a cold, lead weight.

No one understands your father like I do.

Only days ago Sophie had tried to talk with her mother about her marriage. Charlotte's calm acceptance of her husband's infidelity had both infuriated and puzzled Sophie. But hearing about a second illegitimate child might change her mother's attitude. Would this finally push her to file for divorce?

"Of course Mother didn't say much," Wes muttered. "She was too crushed."

Ben nodded. "Facing the truth isn't easy."

No, it was more like hell. Sophie could attest to that. These past few days she'd had to accept the truth about Thom. She'd had to take a long look at herself and the bad judgment she'd used in thinking he was the perfect man for her. The man she wanted to spend the rest of her life with. Yes, the truth was painful.

"We all need to rally around Mother," Graham said. "She needs to know her children love and support her."

After Graham expressed his thoughts, everyone at the table began talking at once. Except for Olivia. She appeared totally unaffected by the news.

Infuriated by her sister's attitude, Sophie asked, "What is it with you, anyway? How can you sit there so calmly? Saying nothing?"

Olivia shrugged. "What is there to say? We've known for some time now that Dad has been unfaithful throughout his marriage. I'm sure Chloe isn't going to be the last one to show up with a connection to our family name."

Unfortunately, Sophie believed her sister was right. And if more of their father's *other* children started showing up, just exactly what would their mother do?

Even though her parents lived pretty much separate lives, the notion that her mother might actually divorce him shook Sophie deeply. Perhaps because she was the baby of the family, and the last symbol of them ever being connected in a loving manner. Or maybe it was the fact that Chloe Elliott appeared to be so close to her own age; it made her feel even more deceived.

"I'll never trust another man in my life!" Sophie muttered angrily.

Olivia showed more surprise over Sophie's bitter remark than she had over the news about their father hooking up with Mrs. Reynolds. "What about Thom?"

Her jaw set, Sophie snatched up the handbag she'd placed beneath her chair. "Thom who?" she asked sarcastically.

"Sophie! Get a grip," Olivia said. "You can't let this get to you."

"I can't keep sitting here listening to any more of this, either. You can fill me in later!"

Before Olivia or anyone else at the table could stop her, Sophie rushed from the room, hoping she could get back to her desk before she burst into tears.

The next morning Sophie stared glumly at her image in the cheval mirror. The cream and black patterned dress she was wearing looked okay, but it hardly screamed romance. It was Valentine's Day, the day she'd been so eagerly looking forward to. Under any other circumstances, she would've taken great pains in choosing her outfit, especially knowing full well that many of the women at Robinson Tech would be dressed in something red or pink and as romantic as one could get and still be appropriate for office wear.

But after yesterday and Ben's announcement about Chloe Elliott, Sophie was in no mood for Valentine's Day or a special night on the town. The father she'd known and loved had turned out to be a habitual cheater. And Thom's sexy veneer had turned out to be just that. A coating on the surface with nothing substantial underneath.

On the very day she should be feeling on top of the world, Sophie felt like the dregs of a nasty drink. And the day was only going to get worse, she realized. Once she arrived at work, she was going straight to Thom and call off their date. Then she was going to have to sit at her desk for the remainder of the day and wonder about the lucky lady who would be dancing with Mason tonight. Kissing Mason.

* * *

Nadine stared suspiciously at the single pink rose Mason sat on her desk.

"What is this? It's not my birthday, thank God. Forty-six is quite old enough," she told him.

Mason gave her a cheeky smile. "Surely forty-six is not so old that you forgot today is Valentine's Day. Got a date for tonight?"

The platinum blonde picked up the rose and drew it to her nose. "No. What about you?"

"I doubt it. Unless by some miracle things change between now and then."

Nadine continued to hold the rose and Mason could see she'd been touched by his little gift. Too bad he couldn't present Sophie with a rose and make her forget all about that damned Thom Nichols.

Nadine frowned. "Are you still thinking about the boss's daughter?"

"I've never stopped thinking about her. But it looks like she'll be on a big romantic date with Thom. The creep. I'd really like to hogtie him, put him in a dark closet somewhere, and not let him out until tomorrow."

Nadine laughed. "Forget about Thom. Why don't you go to Sophie and persuade her that you're the man, not Thom?"

"Because it won't work. I've tried to make her notice me. But it hasn't seemed to help." He'd even kissed Sophie. And though she'd seemed receptive, she'd certainly not talked about dropping Thom.

"Then you need to use a different tactic. Knowing you, you've probably been too nice. Give her a little alpha-male treatment. Show her you can take the bull by the horns."

"This isn't a rodeo, Nadine."

"No, but this is Texas and we Texas women like our men tough."

"Tough. Gotcha." Mason curled his arm and made a muscle. "How's that?"

Laughing, Nadine left her chair and planted a kiss on his cheek. "Thanks for the rose, sweetie. Now get out of here. Go get your little black book and find yourself another date for tonight. Any woman that would actually want to go out with Thom Nichols isn't worth having."

Mason was back at his desk, trying to get his mind focused on work when he was summoned to a meeting with the director of marketing. Marketing was the last department he wanted to visit today. The thought of seeing Thom's gloating face put a bitter taste in his mouth, but there was nothing Mason could do about it. Except hope that Thom was gone to another part of the building.

"Sophie! Over here! Do you have a minute?"

Sophie paused in the middle of the marketing department to see Elsa, one of Robinson Tech's longtime employees, hurrying toward her. Thin and prematurely gray, the woman always had a weary look about her, but today she appeared completely stressed.

"Is anything wrong, Elsa?"

"Not exactly. I'm just extremely worried, that's all. I've been wanting to talk with you about the health insurance changes."

You and about a hundred others, Sophie thought dismally. "I realize it's a jarring change, Elsa. It has been for most all the employees. Was there something specific that concerned you about the policy?"

She nodded. "My thirteen-year-old son. A part of his face was accidentally burned a few months ago. He's healed now. But once school is out this summer the doctor wants to do another surgery to reduce the scarring. Under this new policy the procedure will be considered cosmetic, which means they won't pay. Sophie, this isn't just a vanity case! My son is disfigured and—"

Sophie reached out and took a firm hold on the woman's shoulder. "You don't have to say more, Elsa. I understand completely. And I want you to quit worrying about this. The new policy won't take effect for a couple of months, so there's still time for the surgery. I intend to talk to my brother about this whole situation. Ben will make the right decisions, I'm sure."

A measure of relief came over the woman's face. "Thank you, Sophie. You've already made me feel better."

Sophie gave her a few more encouraging words, then walked to Thom's desk. When she didn't find him there, she was about to look elsewhere, when he suddenly stepped up behind her.

"Are you here to see me, Ms. Fortune?"

As much as she disliked him leaving the Robinson off her name, she tried to put on a pleasant expression as she turned to face him.

"Yes, actually, you're the man I'm here to see. Elsa sidelined me."

"Yes, I noticed," he said with an impatient roll of his eyes. "She's always whining about something. I honestly wish the woman worked on a different floor."

She could hardly believe his unfeeling attitude. "I wouldn't be saying anything bad about Elsa. She's a good woman and a hard worker."

He must have detected the sharp edge to her voice because his brows lifted briefly in surprise and then he said, "Surely you're not up here to discuss another employee with me."

"No." She glanced around her. People were coming and going; a small group was gathered at the water cooler. It was hardly the perfect spot to cancel a date. "Is there somewhere around here that's more private?"

A leering grin suddenly spread across his face. "By all means."

Taking her by the arm, he led her to a small room that was used for private meetings.

Once they stepped inside and he shut the door, he planted a swift kiss on her cheek. It was the first time he'd ever displayed any sort of affection toward her during working hours and she wondered why she was suddenly seeing a different side to him. Had he been picking up on her discontent?

Feeling worse than awkward, she attempted a pleasant smile. "Do you have a minute? Or am I interrupting your morning?"

"I'm waiting on a few of my coworkers to join me. We're working on an advertising idea to promote Robinson Tech's newest tablet. If things go as planned I may have to fly to California to negotiate the details of a new TV ad."

Too bad he wasn't leaving today, Sophie thought. It would have spared her this uncomfortable task.

"Sounds like you're on an upward climb."

He slicked a hand along the side of his hair. "One of these days your father will realize this company can't exist without me."

If he'd made the statement in a teasing context, she

would've laughed. But he wasn't teasing and his arrogance suddenly made her task far easier.

"Well, Dad has a good business eye," she said. "He instinctively knows when an employee is a true asset to the company."

He glanced over her shoulder, as though he was more interested in who was about to walk through the door than what she had to say.

"Er—so, was there some reason you needed to talk with me?"

She let out a weary breath. Ever since the family meeting yesterday, Sophie had felt as though someone had stomped on her. Now as she moved about the Robinson Tech building, she found herself looking at the employees close to her age and wondering if any of them might be a secret offspring of her father. She couldn't imagine anything being more embarrassing.

"Actually, I wanted to tell you that I'm not up to going out tonight. I'm not feeling very well. In fact, I almost didn't come to work this morning."

Which was partly true, Sophie thought. She was mentally and physically sick. Her spirits were squashed so flat, she could hardly think of putting in a productive day of work. Much less going on a date with this man.

Thom stared at her in shock. "Sophie! Are you trying to be funny? If so, I don't find any of this a bit humorous."

"Look, Thom, I do not feel like joking. Or going out on a date. I'm sorry. You'll just have to give me a rain check."

Clearly outraged, he said, "I've already spent a ton of money for this date! I'll have to cancel reservations and that's going to cost me, too! How can you do this to me at the last minute? Today is Valentine's Day! I thought you wanted to make a big hoopla about the day. Damn it, Sophie, I just don't get you!"

No. He never would *get* her, Sophie thought dismally. That was the whole problem. His lame gifts and phony-sounding messages proved that. "I'm sorry, Thom. Really. I'm just not feeling up to a big night."

His angry gaze swept up and down the length of her. "You look perfectly fine to me. You're well enough to work today. But not well enough for a date with me?"

Sophie had to bite down on her tongue to stop herself from telling him to go jump in the deepest lake he could find. "I'm sorry you don't believe me, Thom. Like I said, you'll have to give me a rain check."

"Sophie—"

Not sticking around to hear more, Sophie turned on her heel and left the room.

She was almost to the elevator when a hand grabbed her shoulder and she whirled around to see it belonged to her sister, Olivia.

"Sophie, what in the world is wrong? You look sick."

"Too bad someone else can't see that," she muttered, then shook her head at the look of confusion on Olivia's face. "Sorry, sis, I'm not having a good morning, that's all."

Olivia's eyes narrowed as she glanced in the general direction of Thom's desk. "Oh. Having trouble with your boyfriend?"

Thom wasn't her boyfriend. He was a jerk, Sophie thought dismally. And she'd been worse than stupid for wanting to date him in the first place.

"I am trying to forget about men. Completely!"

Olivia was stunned. "Today? This is the day for love

and romance! This holiday was tailor-made for a woman like you!"

She shot her sister a cynical stare. "You mean for a woman looking at the world through rose-colored lenses? Or a butterfly flitting around without enough sense to see that men are always thinking about themselves and never to be trusted? Believe me, Olivia, I can do without this day just fine!"

Angry tears threatened to spill onto her cheeks and Olivia quickly pulled her into an empty office, away from any prying eyes that might be looking their way.

"Sophie, this isn't like you at all," she said in a hushed tone. "You've got to get a grip on yourself. Are you still upset over the news about Dad? About him and Mrs. Reynolds?"

Once she'd left the family meeting yesterday, Sophie had avoided speaking with any of her siblings and when she'd gotten home her mother had been nowhere in sight. Which had been a relief. Discussing such a painful issue with her was the last thing she'd wanted to do.

"Upset? Is that how you'd describe it? I'm crushed, Olivia. Totally crushed that our father had no more respect for his family than to consort with our neighbor! Now Chloe Elliott will no doubt want to worm her way into the family. Well, as far as I'm concerned, she's not one of us and never will be!"

"Sophie! You might as well start toughening up that soft skin of yours right now! Dad is no angel. We've all known that for some time now. And you shouldn't allow his behavior to dictate how you feel about men and love and marriage."

Marriage! Dear God, the thought of spending one

night of married life with Thom was enough to put her into a straightjacket.

Swallowing hard, she sniffed and straightened her shoulders. "Don't worry about me, sis. I can see very clearly now. Dad's thoughtless behavior toward Mother and his children proves to me that true love is far more than a handsome face or bulging bank account."

"I don't know what's going on in that pretty head of yours, but you need to clear it." Olivia gave her a brief hug. "I have to get back to work. Now put a smile on your face and have a happy Valentine's Day."

Oh, sure, Sophie thought, as she headed toward the elevator. She'd called off her date with Thom and would be spending the night alone. It wasn't the sort of Valentine's evening she'd envisioned two weeks ago. But so much had happened since, there was nothing she could do about it now.

A part of her wanted to run to Mason and throw herself into his arms. She wanted to pour her heart out to him and hear his strong voice assure her that everything would soon be better. But Mason had his own life. No doubt he was looking forward to a night out with his lady love. Today was not the time to burden him with her father's shortcomings, or her busted dreams about Thom. She was going to have to deal with her misery on her own.

But as she passed the entrance to his department, it took every bit of willpower she possessed to walk on and forget about Mason and the comfort of his arms.

Chapter 10

At the end of the work day, Sophie was the last person to turn off her computer and pull on her coat. She'd purposely stayed behind as her coworkers had left for their dates. Most every female in her department had gotten flowers or candy delivered to their desks. The only thing Sophie had gotten was more complaints concerning the insurance changes.

What are you whining about, Sophie? Thom has been sending you all kinds of gifts. You never appreciated any of them. And if you hadn't feigned sickness and called off your date, you would've probably gotten roses or candy. You're getting just what you deserve.

The accusing voice in her head left a bitter taste in her mouth. She tried to ignore both as she buttoned her coat. She might be down for the evening, she thought as she made her way out of the building and to the parking garage, but by tomorrow she would pull herself together and put on a brave face. If anything, she wanted to show Mason she was a strong woman. Not a whiner.

Darkness had settled over the city more than an hour ago. The dim lights illuminating the garage showed only a handful of vehicles left on this level. Which was hardly surprising. Everyone had been in a hurry to go off on a night of romance.

She had no idea what, if anything, her parents were doing. With the news breaking about Mrs. Reynolds and Chloe, she figured her father had most likely found an out-of-town business meeting to attend.

Trying to shove away the melancholy cloak wrapping itself around her, Sophie hurried to her car. The sooner she got home, the sooner she could sink herself into a hot bubble bath with a glass of wine. By then she might forget she'd wasted all this time pursuing Thom, when Mason was the man she should have set her eyes on.

She was unlocking the door, when she suddenly stopped in her tracks and stared at the cuddly red teddy bear propped against the windshield.

Who could have left the precious stuffed toy? Oh, please, not Thom, she thought. She couldn't bear to deal with him again.

A note was stuffed under one of the bear's arms and Sophie quickly retrieved it.

No one should spend Valentine's Day alone.

Clutching the bear to her breast, she glanced around to see if there was anyone who could tell her who'd left the stuffed animal. And then she spotted a man standing next to a nearby car.

Was that Mason?

Her heart tripping over itself, she took a hesitant step forward. Across the expanse of concrete, the man emerged from the shadows and joyous relief flooded through her.

"So you found Mr. Bear?" Mason asked, a sheepish grin on his face.

Hope spurted through her. She didn't exactly comprehend how or why Mason was standing there in front of her. But at the moment, it didn't matter. The sight of his handsome face sent her spirits soaring.

"You're the one who left this adorable little guy on my car?" she asked.

Nodding, he said, "I thought you might be needing someone to hug about now."

The urge to laugh and cry hit her at the same time, creating a hard lump in her throat. She tried to swallow it away, and her voice came out sounding like a husky whisper.

"I thought—uh—shouldn't you be leaving soon?" she asked in confusion. "Your date must be waiting for you."

He shrugged as a guilty expression crossed his handsome face. "To be honest, I don't have a date, Sophie. I never cared much for going out on Valentine's Day. Everyone has such high expectations—like they're going on a romantic fantasy. Then the reality of the evening sets in and all those hopes fall flat. It's deflating."

Strange how only moments ago the parking garage had felt freezing and spooky, but with Mason standing close to her, she was as warm as if she was standing on the beach of a tropical island.

"Before—well, before things happened I always loved this day," she admitted. "Valentine's Day is a time when a woman can get mushy and flirty and no one will laugh at you for being a romantic. And there's hardly a woman alive who doesn't dream of finding her prince. But today…"

"What about today?" he gently urged.

She glanced down at the bear's fuzzy red ears. "It's not been a good day. I came to work dreading it and I stayed late hoping no one would see I was going home alone. Especially after the way I crowed to you about Thom and how I was going to make Mr. Perfect all mine."

"I don't understand, Sophie. I thought you had your Mr. Perfect right where you wanted him. The big Valentine's date—everything just as you'd planned."

Her head swung back and forth as she lifted her troubled gaze up to his brown eyes. "It was too perfect, Mason. And nothing like I thought it would be. Everything about it—from the very start—was absolutely wrong. *I* was wrong for imagining Thom was the man for me."

He let out a long breath and Sophie had to wonder what he was thinking about her now. That she was fickle and couldn't be trusted? She could hardly blame him. One minute she'd been purring about Thom and next minute she'd given him the boot. The whole thing made her look worse than shallow.

"I confess, Sophie, I was in the marketing department this morning and I overheard you telling Thom you weren't feeling well. Are you feeling better now?"

So that was how he'd known she wasn't going with Thom tonight, Sophie concluded. Sometime after that, he must have purchased the bear with the intention of waiting until she showed up at her car. What did it mean?

"I have a confession, too, Mason. I wasn't really sick.

Not physically sick, that is. Emotionally—well, that's a different matter."

His eyes continued to study her face and it suddenly dawned on Sophie that Mason had given her the benefit of the doubt about being sick, whereas Thom had brushed her off and practically accused her of lying. The two men were as different as night and day. And it had become crystal clear to her as to who was the better man.

He stepped closer and her heart nearly stopped as he smoothed a finger along her cheekbone. "Sophie, it would make me happy to see a smile on your face."

She must truly be standing on a hot beach, she decided, because her heart was melting right into the palm of his hand.

"You don't think I'm awful for cancelling the date with Thom?"

His gaze delved deep into hers. "Sophie—"

Suddenly anything else he might have planned to say went unspoken. Instead, he lowered his head and kissed her.

The sweet contact instinctively caused her eyes to close, her lips to part. The feel of Mason's mouth upon hers sent a shower of hot sensations pouring through her body, prompting her to move closer, to savor even more of the masculine taste of him.

Wild and reckless and oh, so good. That was Mason's kiss and not for anything did she want it to stop. It didn't matter that they were standing in a cold, parking garage or that any passerby could see them. Touching Mason, kissing him, being close to him was taking away all the doubt and misery in her heart. This man was all she wanted or needed.

By the time he finally lifted his head, Sophie was completely dazed and realized she probably looked it.

"Umm—that was quite a Valentine's Day kiss."

He grinned and tugged on one of the bear's ears. "To go with little red here."

She smiled impishly up at him. "Thank you for the bear. And the kiss."

His hand kneaded her shoulder and Sophie felt the heat of his fingers all the way through the heavy coat.

He asked, "Would you like to go out for dinner?"

Not about to play coy, Sophie punched the button to relock her car, then looped her arm through his. "I'm hardly dressed for a night on the town, but I would love to go out to dinner."

"You look perfect to me. Let's go see if we can find a restaurant that isn't booked solid."

Fifteen minutes later, Mason tossed his phone onto the console between the bucket seats and groaned with frustration. "Everything is booked up. I can't find one nice restaurant in Austin with available seating. Looks like we're going to have to settle for fast food. What about pizza?"

Laughing, she fastened her seatbelt. "Sounds wonderful to me. Let's go."

Grateful that she was being so understanding, he said, "There's a pizza joint not far from my place. The food is delicious and the service fast. How does that sound?"

"I'm in your hands."

As Mason drove through the city traffic, he kept glancing over at Sophie and wondering how his luck had managed to change in the matter of one short day.

If he hadn't overheard Sophie cancelling her date with Thom this morning, he would've never known she'd be spending the evening alone and he'd have missed the opportunity to spend this special evening with her. Now, somehow, he had to make the most of it.

A few minutes later, as the two of them sat in the pizza parlor waiting on their order, a group of rowdy kids romped through the tables and yelled across the room. The chaotic atmosphere was hardly the sort of evening he wanted to give Sophie.

"I'm sorry about this, Sophie. This is not the romantic dinner I'd envisioned."

She reached across the table and squeezed his hand. "Don't fret about it. Just spending the evening with you is enough for me. But maybe we should get the pizza to go and find someplace quieter to eat."

Was being with him really enough for her, Mason wondered. These past few days he'd sensed that all was not well between Sophie and Thom. Still, that didn't mean that she'd suddenly fallen head over heels for Mason. He needed to put the brakes on his runaway feelings. He couldn't let his hopes get out of control just because she'd kissed him like she'd never wanted it to end.

"I could take you home," he offered.

She shook her head. "I still live with my parents. And I have no idea if either of them is home."

He nodded, his mind whirling with possibilities, none of which seemed appropriate. Finally he asked, "What about going to my place? It's only about five minutes away. It's nothing fancy, but it would definitely be quieter than this."

She laughed as a plastic fork went whizzing by his

head, while Mason glared at the pair of adults who seemed oblivious to the children's unruly behavior.

"That sounds nice, Mason. I'd like to go to your place."

Minutes later, Mason showed her into a charming, second-floor apartment with a small balcony that looked out at the river.

While he switched on a pair of table lamps and lowered the overhead lighting, she gazed curiously around the living area. "This is so homey and comfortable, Mason. I love it."

He chuckled. "I don't expect it's anything like your home. But I try to keep it tidy and make the most of the space I have." He inclined his head toward a short hallway to his left. "If you'd care to freshen up before we eat, the bathroom is that way."

"Thanks. I would like that. I actually think some food hit the back of my head while we were waiting in the pizza parlor," she said with a laugh.

"Take your time. I'll get our dinner ready. Where would you like to eat? At the table or the couch? You choose."

She glanced at the dark green leather couch with a long coffee table sitting in front of it. "Oh, then I choose the couch. If you don't mind it would feel great to kick off my heels and get comfortable."

Mind? Mason didn't know how many times he'd dreamed of having her on that couch. The fact that she wanted to get comfortable was making his fantasy really come true.

"Then the couch it will be," he told her.

While she was gone, Mason placed the pizza box on

the coffee table, then fetched napkins and paper plates, and just in case she didn't want to use her fingers, added two forks.

When she reappeared a few moments later, he saw she'd freshened her pink lipstick and brushed her brown hair to a sleek curtain against her back. She looked like a walking dream and he could only hope he didn't wake up and find he was actually alone.

"Have a seat and I'll get some sodas. Or if you'd prefer I have beer." He started toward the kitchen, then tossed teasingly over his shoulder, "Sorry, I'd offer you champagne, but I'm all out. I didn't know I was going to be entertaining a beautiful woman tonight."

She called across the room to him, "We don't need champagne to make a Valentine's toast. Soda will do just fine."

"Sophie, did anyone ever tell you—"

"That I'm a good sport? Oh, please, Mason, whatever you do, don't say that to me."

He emerged from the kitchen carrying two chilled cans of cola. As he took a seat next to her, he said, "I wasn't going to say that. I was going to say that I've never seen you behave like a spoiled little rich girl."

She wrinkled her nose at him. "And hopefully you never will. If I ever do act like that I hope someone will bop me over the head. Don't get me wrong, I'll be the first to admit that I've been spoiled. But that doesn't mean I always need to have everything perfect. I want to be able to appreciate the simple joys of life, Mason. Otherwise, I'd be missing out on the things that are the most worthwhile."

He smiled at her. "Like pizza for Valentine's dinner?"

"Exactly," she answered. "I can't think of anything

I'd rather be eating tonight or any other place I'd rather be than here with you."

He handed her one of the sodas, then opened the pizza box.

After serving her a slice, he helped himself and settled back against the couch. She was already eating with gusto and the fact that she appeared to be enjoying herself surprised him somewhat. Partly because she was a Fortune Robinson and could buy the finest gourmet food, even an entire restaurant if she chose to. And partly because he'd never really gotten the hang of how to entertain a woman. At least, not a woman like Sophie.

He said, "I think you actually meant that."

"Mmm. This is delicious and well worth the wait," she said of the pizza. Then she turned to face him. "And why wouldn't I mean it? You didn't twist my arm to get me here."

"I know. But you had such high hopes for tonight. This wasn't the sort of date you envisioned, I'm sure."

"I'm certain Thom had made reservations at one of the ritziest places in town. He might even have given me flowers and taken me dancing. Only because he felt obliged to do those things for me. Not because he actually wanted to." She shook her head. "Believe me, Mason. That's not the sort of date I wanted. I want things to be genuine. And with Thom—I'm not sure that he cares about anyone's feelings. Except his own."

He momentarily forgot about the pizza he'd lifted halfway to his mouth. "When did you come to this conclusion? I thought— well, for the last few days he was giving you gifts and planning this night and you didn't say anything. I thought you were still gaga over the man."

Her face tinged with color, she lowered the plate to her lap and slanted him a rueful glance. "In a way, Mason, I suppose I'm just as phony as Thom. I've been pretending all this time. I didn't want anyone to guess that after our first date I realized he and I would never be the real thing. It was just too embarrassing. My sister Olivia had tried to warn me and I wouldn't listen to her advice. You see, where men are concerned, she has a cynical streak, so I thought she was just being negative. Now I'm going to have to listen to her say I told you so. Not to mention the gossip that will go on at Robinson Tech once the news gets out that I called it quits with Thom. After everyone could see I was chasing after him."

"Sophie, you're being too hard on yourself. You didn't chase after Thom. You merely made him notice you. Which, if the truth was known, he'd already done. You just made it easy for him to ask you on a date."

She smiled at him and Mason wondered why she was the only woman who'd ever made him feel so vulnerable and weak, yet so oddly happy. It didn't make sense. But was love supposed to make sense?

Whoa, Mason, you're getting way ahead of yourself. You don't love Sophie. You're enamored with her, for sure. And you'd like to take her in your arms and kiss her until the two of you end up in the bedroom. But that isn't love. And, besides, this woman is going to move on to a bigger and better man than you.

"You're being way too kind, Mason. But thank you for listening. And for trying to make me look not so much of a fool."

Her comment broke through the warning voice in his head and he glanced over to see her eyes had suddenly clouded with doubts and sadness. In all the time he'd known Sophie, he'd never seen her as she'd been these past few days. It was like her confidence and sassiness had flown out the window. If Thom had caused this abrupt change in her, then he'd like to choke him until he turned blue in the face.

"Sophie, you can tell me if this is none of my business. But is this all about Thom? Or has something else been bothering you?"

Instead of looking at him, she stared at her plate. "I do have other things on my mind, Mason. But I'd really rather not talk about them now. Maybe later." She looked at him, her eyes pleading. "Tonight I just want us to enjoy this time together. Okay?"

Although Mason would've liked for her to open up to him and share her problems, he wasn't about to push his luck. But eventually, if he got his wish, she might want to talk about all the things she'd buried in her heart.

He scooted close enough to wrap his fingers around her forearm. "It's perfectly okay, Sophie. So let's dig in and finish this pizza before it gets cold."

With a look of relief, she began to eat and Mason purposely changed the direction of their conversation to a safer topic. Eventually they began to talk about their college days and the sticky situations they'd gotten into both in class and on campus. Which had them both laughing.

Finally she placed her empty plate on the coffee table, then kicked off her heels and drew her legs up beneath her. She was wearing black lacy tights and Mason could hardly keep his eyes off the shapely calves, slim ankles and dainty feet. Beneath the black stockings there would be smooth creamy skin that would be soft and warm beneath his hand. The need to touch her was growing with each passing minute.

Rising restlessly to his feet, he said, "Uh—I could turn on the TV, or put some music on the stereo?"

"Some music might be nice. If you have something that's not too intrusive."

"I have plenty of elevator music—the kind we listen to all day at work. How does that sound?"

"It sounds like you're trying to pull my leg."

He laughed and her soft chuckle joined in.

"Okay. I'm teasing. I'd really like to take a shotgun to the speaker over my desk."

"I know. If we didn't have to listen to that morbid music, we all might be more productive." She looked at him with raised brows. "We're not at work, so what are you going to play for me?"

He walked over to the stereo and began to dig through a stack of CDs until he found the one he thought she might enjoy. "Something soft and romantic," he said. "For Valentine's night."

Soon the sexy R&B music floated quietly out of the speakers, and he walked back over to the couch.

Holding his hand out to her, he asked, "Would you care to dance, my lady?"

"I would love to," she murmured.

Placing her hand in his, she uncurled herself from the couch and stepped into his arms. His first instinct was to wrap his arm around her and crush her warm body to his. But she viewed him as a friend and a gentleman she could trust. He needed to keep a respectable distance between them, he reminded himself.

Earlier this evening in the parking garage, she wasn't kissing you like a friend, Mason. She was kiss-

*ing you like a lover. Now isn't the time to hold back.
Show her exactly how much you want her.*

He was trying to ignore the prodding voice in his head when she said, "The music is nice. You have good taste, Mason."

"I'm glad you like it," he murmured as he dared to rest his cheek against her silky hair. "But you probably should've put your heels back on. I'm not that good a dancer. I might step on your toes."

"I'm not worried. Besides, dancing barefoot with you feels…very good. Why would I want to stop and put on my shoes?"

As she spoke, he could feel her drawing closer until the tips of her breasts were brushing against his chest, her hips swaying rhythmically against him. The intimate contact filled him with sizzling sensations and before he realized what he was doing, both his arms had wrapped around her, his hands linked at the small of her back.

"We still have time to go to a club—to dance and celebrate. All you have to do is say the word."

"We're dancing and celebrating right now. And honestly, I don't want to be crammed in a crowd." She looked up at him, then brushed a finger against a spot on his chin. "You have a speck of cheese. Right there."

"I'm messy. Thanks." He looked down at her and his gaze focused on the plump, pink curves of her lips. "And you have a tiny dot of sauce at the corner of your mouth."

"I do?" She paused long enough to lick both corners. "Did I get it?"

The only thing she'd managed to do was make his

insides clench with longing. He struggled to keep from groaning out loud. "No. It's still there. Let me."

He wiped the speck of sauce away, but his gaze remained frozen on her lips. Had there been some sort of potion in the soda or pizza? He seemed to have forgotten how to breathe and the temperature in the apartment felt as though it had zoomed up to ninety degrees or higher.

"Sophie, either I'm getting sick or being this close to you is doing something strange to me."

Her hands were suddenly on the middle of his chest, sliding slowly upward toward his collar bone. Mason swallowed and tried to keep his head from reeling.

"It's doing something to me, too. But I don't think it's strange, Mason. I think it's natural and nice and nothing to run from."

Run. Yes, that's what he should do. Run to the balcony or out on the stairs. Anywhere he could breathe and clear his head of this drunken desire that was taking control of him. But he didn't want to move away from her. At least, not until he could taste her lips again.

"I'm glad you think so. Because I—"

The remainder of his words stuck in his throat and, no matter how he tried, he couldn't cough them up or swallow them down.

Her eyes were glowing and her lips tilted in a provocative smile. "Because you want to kiss me?"

The softly spoken invitation was more than Mason could resist. Without a second thought, he drew her in the tight circle of his arms and, with a hungry growl, took her lips with his.

A flash fire roared through him and as his hands roamed her back and her soft curves melted into his body, he recognized this feeling was not just a man wanting a woman. He was holding something precious in his arms. He wanted to cherish and protect everything she was giving him, not take advantage of her vulnerable emotions by asking her for more.

The thoughts in his head continued to wage a war with the very real needs flowing through his body. But eventually common sense won the fight and he gently eased his lips from hers and set her away from him.

"I—I'm sorry, Sophie. This is getting out of hand."

She stared at him, her eyes full of confusion, her swollen lips parted with surprise. He could see words practically forming on her tongue, but they were never released. Instead, she turned her back to him and walked to the opposite side of the room.

As Mason studied her slumped shoulders, he felt sick with loss. Moreover, he felt like a coward. This was his chance to show Sophie exactly how he felt about her. If he let this moment slip away, he might never be given another.

With that desperate thought pushing at his back, Mason took a fateful step in her direction. Then another. And another. Until his hands were on her shoulders, urging her back to him.

Chapter 11

Fighting a wall of stinging tears, Sophie tried to pull herself together and give Mason an understanding smile. But try as she might, her lips refused to do little more than wobble into a half-hearted grin.

"I'm sorry, too, Mason," she said hoarsely. "Maybe you should just drive me home."

"Sophie, I—"

"You don't have to explain, Mason," she gently interrupted. "I understand completely. You've always thought of me as a friend. And that's the way you want things to remain between us—just friends. I can accept that."

An incredulous expression swept over his face and then he shook his head. "You don't understand, Sophie! For ages—from the very beginning I met you—I've wanted us to be more than friends! But with all that's been going on in your life—I'm trying to do the right thing and give you more time. To think about you and me. I don't want to rush you and make a mess of everything."

Relief and joy swirled inside her until she felt as though her bare feet weren't even touching the hardwood floor.

"You're not rushing, Mason. And sometimes a little mess is a good thing. A whole lot better than perfect."

For one anxious second, she thought he was going to argue the point, but then his eyelids suddenly lowered and his lips found their way back to hers.

This time there was no restraint on his part, or hers. She felt no barriers standing between them or had thoughts of escape dashing through her whirling head. The only thing on her mind now was getting closer to the man she wanted.

Wrapping her arms around his neck, Sophie let every guard down, every vulnerable spot inside her show as she lost herself in the magic of his kiss. And almost instantly, she was transported to a place where nothing mattered but the masculine taste of his lips and the achingly wonderful warmth pouring through her.

Over and over he took her mouth in a succession of deep, scorching kisses that stole her breath and had her hands clinging to his shoulders to support her shaky legs.

Finally, he tore his mouth from hers and spoke between long, ragged breaths. "This—isn't—enough, Sophie. I want you. All of you."

Cradling his face between her palms, she whispered up to him, "Oh, yes, Mason. I want that, too. Very much."

His hands pushed into her hair until his fingers

were tilting her face up to his searching gaze. "Are you sure, Sophie? Just because it's Valentine's Day doesn't mean—"

"I don't care if it's the Fourth of July or Friday the 13th," she whispered with conviction. "I'd want you just as much."

His gaze searched her face one last time and then he reached for her hand and led her out of the room. As Sophie followed him, her heart was pounding so hard the noise in her ears was drowning out the soft music playing on the stereo. This morning she'd been miserable and all day she'd told herself she wanted nothing more to do with any man. That all of them were nothing more than low, slithering snakes.

But that hadn't included Mason. No, he was the only man on earth that made her feel safe and wanted. And yes, a teeny bit loved. Thinking like that perhaps made her an even bigger fool than she'd made of herself these past two weeks. But tonight Sophie wasn't going to let herself dwell on all the things she'd rather forget. She was with Mason and for now the world felt right.

At the end of the hall they turned left and the next thing Sophie knew they were standing in his bedroom.

Mason clicked on a bedside lamp, shedding a pool of light across a bed with tumbled navy blue bedcovers and pillows stacked against a brass headboard.

"Sorry, Sophie," he voiced the husky apology. "The bed isn't made, but the sheets are clean."

She laughed softly as she curled her arms around his waist and hugged him. "Who cares about bedcovers? We're just going to mess them up anyway."

His hands slid down her back until they were cupping her rounded bottom and drawing her hips toward his. "Sophie, why did it take so long for this to happen? Why didn't we figure this out sooner? I think I've wanted you forever."

Desire was already simmering deep within her. It was impossible to imagine how it was going to feel once their bodies were united. The mere thought of it was sending shivers of anticipation through her.

"I thought you only wanted me as your friend—someone to talk to. I didn't know." She stroked the pads of her fingers along the strong line of his jaw. He felt so strong and warm. And with each breath she drew in, the male scent of his skin and hair filled her head like a strong drink of wine.

His head dipped alongside hers until his nose was nuzzling her neck. "Yes, we're friends. And we talk as friends. But tonight we've done enough talking. Don't you think?"

Her fingers reached for the buttons on his shirt. "I think we can figure out plenty of other things to keep us occupied," she whispered.

He planted another long, breathtaking kiss on her lips, but once the erotic contact ended they began shedding their clothing, each assisting the other with zippers and buttons, until finally Sophie was stripped down to a lacy pink bra and panties and Mason a pair of dark printed boxers.

Sophie's hungry gaze barely had time to scan his hard, muscled chest and arms and slip to his corded abs, before he picked her up and laid her on the bed.

With a breathless laugh, she reached for his hand and tugged him beside her. They turned toward each other, until the front of her body was pressed against his.

To feel his bare skin rubbing against hers was as

erotic as the touch of his fingers sliding down her breastbone until they reached one plump little breast. His fingers teased the nipple, until the offending barrier of her bra became a frustration.

He quickly removed the scrap of fabric and tossed it to the floor with the rest of their clothing, then turned his attention back to her breasts and the budded nipples just waiting for his touch. He didn't disappoint as he bent his head and suckled first one and then the other.

White hot fire shot straight to the core of her, causing her lower body to involuntarily arch toward his.

Moaning, she thrust her fingers into his hair and held his head fast against her. Too soon the exquisite pleasure turned into needy pain and she tugged on his hair to signal her need for relief.

He lifted his head and in that split second when their eyes met, Sophie felt a connection so deep and real that tears stung the backs of her eyes. This was the special thing she'd been searching for. And now that she'd found it, she had to hold tight and cherish every second of passion that Mason was giving her.

"Oh, Mason, I want you," she whispered. "So much that it's scary."

Groaning, he brought his lips back to hers. "That's the way it's supposed to be. Wild and scary and special."

As the last word was spoken against her lips, Sophie circled her arms around his neck and opened her mouth to his. In a matter of seconds he was kissing her with a need so deep it rocked her senses. And when his tongue slipped inside, she eagerly responded, reveling in the taste of him, while wanting more and more.

Somewhere in the back of her spinning mind, she recognized his hands were tracing her heated skin, exploring the hills and valleys, pausing at her breasts and belly, before finally moving downward to the juncture between her thighs.

He quickly stripped away her panties and when his fingers found her most intimate spot, she moaned with need, her hips arching toward the pleasure he was bestowing.

Incredible. No one had ever touched her like this, she thought wildly. No one had ever turned her whole being into one aching flame. It was carrying her away and the helpless feeling had her frantically grabbing his shoulders and crying out.

"It's okay, Sophie," he whispered in a voice rough with passion. "Just ride it out. Let yourself feel everything."

The sound of his masculine voice urging her onward was all it took for Sophie to surrender to everything he was giving. And all at once she was spinning out of control, her body writhing against his hand, her cries of pleasure like music to his ears.

Before the quaking aftermaths subsided, his mouth was back on hers, his tongue thrusting deep as it searched the ribbed roof and the sharp edges of her teeth. After the explosion that had just gone off inside her, she'd not expected to feel more. But she'd been wrong. Hot passion was throbbing inside her once again, driving her hands to move over the hard muscles of his torso, her legs to wrap invitingly around his.

Eventually, he tore his mouth away from hers and by then they were both gulping for air and Sophie wondered if he was just as dazed as she was by the urgent need that had suddenly and completely combusted between them.

"Sophie, I think you want this as much as I do, but what's going on with us—it's happened so fast. If you're uncertain, tell me. Because when this is over I don't want you to look at me with hate or regret."

Her throat was so tight with raw emotions she could barely force her words out. "Yes, Mason! Yes, I want this. I want you. There will be no regret. Not now. Not ever."

He pressed his lips gently to hers, then eased away to open a drawer on the nightstand. "I'll get some protection."

Even though Sophie could count on one hand the times she'd had intimate relations with a man in the past five years, she did take the Pill. But she didn't bother explaining this to Mason. She wanted him to feel safe and protected.

Moments later, he returned to her and as he positioned himself over her, Sophie shivered with a need that went far beyond the physical. She wasn't just giving her body to this man. She was trusting her heart to him.

As he hovered over her, his hands gently cradled her face and the tender touch overwhelmed her with sweet emotions, the sort she'd dreamed about.

"You're my Valentine, Sophie. My sweetest Valentine." His head shook back and forth as though he was trying to wake himself from a dream. "I didn't know we were going to be making love. I never thought this would happen. But now that we are— Oh, Sophie, I'm shaking."

Linking her hands at the back of his neck, she drew him down to her and whispered against his lips. "I'm shaking, too. But it will be special. So special."

"Yes. Oh, yes."

She opened her legs to him and then slowly, gently, he entered her warm, welcoming body.

The intimate connection was even more incredible than she expected and for long moments, she could scarcely breathe. But then he began to move and suddenly hot vibrations were radiating through her body, filling her with a need so reckless and wild she couldn't contain it.

Before long, she was matching the rhythm of his movements, straining to give him everything he was giving her. Over and over their bodies crashed together in mindless ecstasy.

Sophie lost all awareness of time and place. All she knew was Mason's hot body pushing her, driving her to a place she'd never been before. Her heart was racing, pounding in her ears like a frantic drumbeat, while her breaths had turned into little more than raspy gulps.

This white hot passion was everything and more than she'd been searching for, but never found until tonight. Until she'd stepped into Mason's arms. This couldn't be a one-time thing. No, this fire between them had to be the kind that never died. Never turned cold.

Just as the desperate thoughts rolled through her mind, she could feel his strokes growing faster and faster. The speed tugged her along and before she realized just how far she'd climbed, she was standing on the edge of a star, where moon dust was showering over her, and her heart was overflowing with warm, precious love.

"Sophie, Sophie."

As she floated through the starlight, she heard him call her name, but she couldn't utter a word. All she could do was cling to him and wait for her whirling senses to return to her body.

Long moments passed before she slowly became aware of Mason's torso draped over hers, his damp cheek resting upon her shoulder. She could feel his heart thudding rapidly against her breast, his warm breath fanning her arm.

She threaded her fingers through his damp hair, loving the way the waves felt against her skin.

"I'm heavy. I need to move." He rolled to one side and reached for a pillow. After he'd stuffed it beneath her head, he lay beside her and she shifted so that her face was aligned with his.

"I never expected my Valentine's evening to be like this." She reached over and slid her hand down his muscled arm. "Thank you, Mason, for not wanting me to be alone."

He smiled. "I'm the selfish one, Sophie. I wanted you to be with me tonight. So I'm thanking you for being here—next to me." He cupped her face with his hand. "You're so beautiful, Sophie. Inside and out. Have I ever told you that?"

Her heart swelling with emotions, she caught his hand and drew it to her lips. "Not exactly," she murmured. "But the lighting is bad in here. You might change your mind tomorrow."

Chuckling, he drew her tight against him and buried his face in the damp curve of her neck. "Are you trying to be as funny as me?"

"I'm trying to be real."

He eased his head back and Sophie could see the humor in his eyes had disappeared.

"Sophie, please, don't ever doubt me. Maybe it

sounds like I'm just mouthing words that I think you want to hear. But I'm not. Eventually, you're going to see that I'm being honest with you."

Curling an arm around his waist, she pressed her cheek against his chest and closed her eyes. "You're a good man, Mason. And if it seems like I'm being mistrustful, well, I—I'm having trouble hanging on to my trust in anyone. I'm having trouble keeping my faith about anything—especially love and marriage."

"Sophie," he gently scolded. "That's not like you. Has Thom done something unforgivable? I know you said you'd rather not talk about it. But maybe talking about it now would help."

His fingers were making gentle, soothing circles upon her back and the sound of his steady heartbeat beneath her ears was lulling her into a safe cocoon. One that she never wanted to leave.

"It's not Thom. Yes, he was a big disappointment. That's not exactly right, either. I'm very disappointed in myself for being so stupid about him. No, this is something else. It's—" She tilted her head back so that she could see his face. "It's about my family, Mason. Things are so—I'm so mixed up. I don't know what to think anymore. Yesterday we had a family meeting—just us siblings. And Ben has discovered that we have a half sister we never knew existed. An offspring of one of my father's numerous affairs. This young woman lives right here in Austin. Actually, her mother was our neighbor! Oh, Mason, can you imagine your father having an affair with your neighbor? And having a child from it? I don't know what to believe anymore. Who to trust."

His hand smoothed the tangled hair from her brow. "Honestly, Sophie, I can't imagine any of it. My dad has always been rock solid for his family. To learn otherwise would really shake me. You've already had to deal with his fake identity. That should be enough. And then the half brother from London. I thought surely that would be the end of things."

She bit her bottom lip as tears threatened to slip from her eyes. "I shouldn't be telling you any of this. My father's your boss. But I—oh, Mason, you're the only one I can really talk to about this. My sisters— well, Olivia, is just plain indifferent. I can't understand where she's coming from. And Zoe, she's always been in Dad's camp. Then there's Rachel. She's the one who sort of unearthed all of this about Dad in the first place. I think she's been pretty shaken by it all, too. But she's married and lives in Horseback Hollow now. She's not always around for me to commiserate with."

He continued to stroke her hair and the strong rhythmic feel of his fingers helped to ease her troubled mind.

"As far as I'm concerned, you don't have to worry, Sophie. What you tell me in private will stay private. But I'm curious about one thing. What does your mother say about all this? Do you think your parents might get a divorce? Is that what's troubling you?"

His questions pulled a long groan from Sophie's throat. "I'm clueless about my parents, Mason. When Mother found out about Keaton it was like she just turned the other cheek. Not long ago I tried to talk with her about it, but she doesn't want to discuss it. Maybe she doesn't want to go through a messy divorce and split up millions of dollars of assets. Or maybe she still loves Dad in spite of everything. I just don't know. But if more illegitimate children start to appear, I can't fathom her just turning a blind eye to the awful truth.

Oh, Mason, don't you see? My family isn't real to me anymore. Everything is fake and cloaked in secrecy."

He wrapped his arms around her and pulled her tight against him. "Sophie, there's nothing fake about you. You're one of the most real people I've ever known. You can't let any of this drag you down or make you doubt yourself."

All of a sudden she wanted to tell him how very much she adored him. She wanted him to understand how making love to him had been so perfect and right. But this was the first time they'd been together as a real couple. She didn't want to spoil things by going too fast.

"Being here with you is the most real thing that's ever happened to me, Mason," she murmured. "Is it too late to say Happy Valentine's Day?"

"It's not a bit too late. The night is just starting."

It was the wee hours of the morning when Mason drove Sophie back to the parking garage to pick up her car. Although he'd wanted her to stay overnight at his place, she'd reasoned that it wouldn't be smart for the other Robinson Tech employees to see them arriving at work together. At least, not yet. Not until everyone could see that Sophie was no longer dating Thom. She hardly needed to add more gossip about her family to what was already going around the office.

Mason had been none too happy about Sophie's desire to keep their relationship a secret. But he'd understood her reasons and had finally promised to go along with her wishes. The fact that he was willing to do that for her made her love him even more.

Love. Had she already fallen in love with Mason?

One session of hot, mind-blowing sex shouldn't make her heart fall in love.

No, it was more than sex that was making her heart want to sing with joy, she thought. Making love to Mason had been perfect. More perfect than she could've ever imagined. But the truth was, she'd been falling in love with him for some time now. She'd just been too blind to see it.

She was walking through the house on the way to her bedroom, thinking about Mason and how her life had taken an abrupt change, when she spotted a dim light filtering from the partially opened doorway of her father's study.

Even though Gerald Robinson was a workaholic, she'd never seen him in his study at nearly four in the morning. Or was that her father burning the midnight oil? As far as she knew, he was still out of town.

With the red bear Mason had given her clutched beneath one arm, Sophie silently tiptoed to the door. She peered in and stared in complete confusion. Her mother was sitting at the desk, carefully studying papers scattered in front of her. Her mother never involved herself in Robinson Tech business. Nor in the household accounts; a private secretary took care of them. So what was she doing? Digging into her husband's secret transactions? Or perhaps it was love letters?

A part of Sophie wanted to barge into the room and demand answers. She wanted to scream at her mother that she was sick of the lies and secrets. But that wouldn't be a particularly smart move. Knowing Charlotte, she would simply dismiss Sophie's confrontation as childish and order her out of the study. No, if

Sophie wanted to discover the truth, she'd have to be far more patient and subtle about going after it.

Sophie, there's nothing fake about you. You're one of the most real people I've ever known.

Mason's words suddenly returned to her and Sophie glanced down at the bear she was clutching tightly to her breast. For Mason's sake, for her own sake, she couldn't hide from the truth about her family. Nor could she hide from these newborn feelings in her heart.

Her faith in her family had been shattered, but she had to trust Mason. She had to believe that their relationship would grow into something strong and unbreakable. She had to keep telling herself that her life, her marriage was going to be real and filled with love. She was not going to be a cold woman sitting alone at her husband's desk at four in the morning.

Chapter 12

Three days later on Friday morning, Mason got a call from his brother, Doug. Because it was unusual for him to be phoning him at work, Mason answered rather than let it go to his voice mail.

"Don't worry, I'm still able to tell time," Doug joked. "It's ten in the morning and we're both busy, so I'll just keep you a minute. I wanted to see if you'd like to drive down and go to the Spurs game tonight. Shawn's going, too. They're playing the Grizzlies, so it should be good."

Normally, Mason wouldn't hesitate. Basketball and his brothers' company would make for a great evening, even with the eighty mile drive down to San Antonio. But it wouldn't be worth missing a chance to be with Sophie.

"Sounds good, Doug. But I think I'm going to be busy tonight."

"You think? You mean you don't know yet? Don't

tell me you're working late. I'm the one who's supposed to be chained to my desk. I shouldn't keep the scales of justice waiting and all that. But if I can put off a case, then you can put off an app."

Mason settled back in his chair. "It's not work. It's a woman."

There was pause, then Doug said, "If that's the case, then I can hardly blame you."

Since the night of Valentine's Day, Mason and Sophie had been together every night at his apartment. Normally, that much time with any woman, including Christa, would have cooled his ardor. But with Sophie the time together had only kindled his desire. If possible, the sex between them had grown even hotter. And as good as that was, Mason couldn't help but feel uneasy.

Tonight he wanted to take her out to a nice dinner, but he doubted she would agree to such a date. She'd be afraid the two of them would be seen together, he thought grimly. He could understand her wanting to keep their relationship a secret, up to a point. But the more he dwelt on the problem, the more he recalled how she'd seemed quite proud to be seen sitting with Thom in the break room. But Thom Nichols was Mr. Dreamboat, the marketing strategist. Being seen with him had been different than Mason, the computer geek.

"Mason? Are you still there? Can you hear me?"

Mason wiped a hand over his face. "Sorry, Doug. I was thinking."

"Is that what you call it?"

His brother's wry question caused Mason to groan. "Doug, do you remember me telling you a few days back about a woman? The wealthy one?"

"Vaguely," he teased, then added in a more serious

tone, "Yes, I remember. The boss's daughter. Don't tell me she's the one who'd make you turn down a night of basketball."

"That's what I'm saying."

Doug whistled. "Damn, brother, you're playing with fire."

"Yeah. I'm standing close to the flames all right. But she's worth it."

"Worth losing your job?"

These past years his work at Robinson Tech had been the most important achievements he'd made in his life. The thought of putting his job in jeopardy was unnerving, but not nearly as much as losing Sophie.

"If it came to that," he said bluntly.

"Wow! Mason, you sound like you've fallen hard for this woman."

Had he fallen in love with Sophie? The question sent uncertainty drifting through him like a cold, dark fog. Sophie was so out of his league it was ridiculous. She could have most any man she set her eyes on, a man far wealthier and accomplished than Thom Nichols or anyone working for Robinson Tech.

"It's too early for that kind of thinking."

Doug responded with an amused grunt. "What about all those people who fall in love at first sight? Or believe they do."

Mason grimaced. "It doesn't last."

"Hmm. It takes work to make a relationship last, Mason. That's why you don't see me in one. I'm too lazy."

"Hah! Why not just admit that you're about as flexible as an iron rod? You really should be aiming for a judge position, my brother. You always did want to rule everybody."

Doug laughed, but the happy sound quickly sobered. "Mason, being flexible and giving is good. I just hope you don't end up doing all the bending and sacrificing. Okay?"

Mason let out a long breath. "I hear you."

The two talked for another minute before both agreed they needed to get back to work.

Mason scrubbed his face with both hands and tried to refocus his attention on work, but his conversation with Doug continued to prod at him.

Where Sophie was concerned was he doing all the bending? True, they'd not been together as a couple long enough to really weigh the situation. But so far, Mason was the one who'd given in and gone along with her request to keep their relationship hidden. When would it be time for her to start giving in and showing her family and friends that she cared about him? Would she ever want them to know?

That afternoon, as soon as Sophie found a stopping point in her work, she made a beeline to Mason's desk, only to find it empty.

"Mason and Nadine left on break a few minutes ago."

Sophie turned to see a young woman with short black hair and a calculating smile. Sophie recognized her voice. She was one of the gossiping women from the bathroom. Although she'd not gotten a look at the two gossipmongers that morning, she hadn't forgotten their pompous tone.

"Oh. I see. Well, I needed to speak with him about a work matter."

The smile on the woman's face grew even cattier and Sophie could only wonder what she'd ever done to deserve this kind of treatment. Being born a Fortune? Was that enough cause to be despised?

"Work. Yes. Maybe you should go upstairs and see Thom. I'm sure he'd love to talk about work."

Sophie would've thoroughly enjoyed telling this woman to keep her warped tongue to herself and to mind her own business. But in the long run, lowering herself to such a demeaning level wouldn't help her. No more than it would help this woman improve her behavior.

"Thanks," Sophie told her sweetly. "You've been more than helpful."

The woman lifted her nose, then turned on her heel and walked off. Sophie's teeth ground together as she turned back to Mason's desk and began to search for a scrap of paper to write a note.

"Hey, beautiful! Are you on a secret mission?"

The voice caused her to jump and she whirled around to see Mason entering the cubicle.

"Mason! I was writing you a note. Don't you keep a pencil and paper around here?"

"I rarely use the things," he said wittily. "We have these new gadgets now called cell phones that actually send text messages."

She shot him a sardonic look. "Smarty. Sometimes a handwritten note is nicer."

"Nicer," he repeated in a voice somewhere between a growl and a whisper. "Finding you here is the highlight of my day."

As he moved toward her, a sexy glow lit his brown eyes and, even though Sophie was a bit miffed with him, she couldn't stop a wide smile from spreading across her face.

"Nadine and I have been in the breakroom."

"Yes, I know. A little mockingbird told me."

"What?"

She shook her head, then glanced around to make sure Miss Nosey had left the area. "Nothing. Did you forget that I told you I'd be by to talk about tonight?"

"No. I didn't forget. But you didn't say exactly when. If you knew I was in the breakroom, why didn't you come down there to see me?"

She shot him an impatient look. "Mason! You know why," she muttered in a hushed tone. "People are already starting to talk about us. I don't want to add fuel to the fire."

"How do you know they're starting to talk? Have you been eavesdropping?"

Shaking her head, she let out a long breath. "I just had a nasty visitor drop by here. She suggested that I go upstairs and talk to Thom instead of you."

He glanced around him as though the gossiper might still be lurking nearby. "Are you serious? Who was it?"

"I don't know her name. I think she works in marketing. Which probably means that Thom and the whole marketing department know about us now."

He frowned. "So what if they do? It's none of their business. This need you have to hide everything doesn't make sense, Sophie. Before, when we were just friends, you never worried about us being seen together."

"That's because—" She broke off as red heat swept up her face. "Well, it's different now. We can't be close together and keep our hands off each other. You know that!"

Grinning now, he stepped close enough to wrap his hand around her upper arm. "I'll tell you what I know. Right now I'd like to kiss you and carry you off to the broom closet."

The idea of being locked in any closet with Mason was enough to make her whole body tingle. But rather than admit it, she arched an innocent brow at him. "Broom closet?"

His head dipped close enough to whisper in her ear. "It's dark and we could lock the door."

Even though his rough, masculine voice sent shivers of desire over her skin, she forced herself to step away from him. "I hate to tell you this, but the janitors have keys. They can unlock the broom closets anytime they please."

He feigned a look of disappointment. "Our luck and one of them would come along and want a push broom right when things were getting…delicious."

She shot him a sexy, sidelong glance. "I need to get back to my desk. Are we still on for tonight? I can be at your place by seven."

He cleared his throat. "Yes, we're still on. But I thought I'd take you out to dinner tonight. To Pedro's. I know how much you like Tex-Mex and he dishes up some of the best in Austin."

Pedro's was a quaint little café situated in the old part of town. It still had a real screen door on the front entrance and scrubbed plank floors. The round tables were just large enough to hold two plates, two drinks and a candle in between and the scents coming from the kitchen were enough to make a person's mouth water. To be there with Mason would make the place even more special.

"I would love to go to Pedro's, Mason. Really, I would. But I—I just don't think it would be wise—yet. What if some of our friends or family saw us?"

"That's right, what if? Would the sky actually fall

in, Sophie? This is getting ridiculous, don't you think? You're a grown woman. You should be able to date whomever you choose without worrying about what people are going to say."

Sophie looked away and swallowed the lump of pain in her throat. Although it had only been a few days since they'd started seeing each other, already Mason was getting weary of the subterfuge. And she could hardly blame him. It wasn't his fault that things had played out so swiftly and unexpectedly. Nor was it his fault that she'd made a fool of herself over Thom Nichols.

"I understand you're not exactly happy about this secrecy, Mason. But I'm not asking you to do it forever. I don't want people saying I dumped Thom for you. Or that you got me on the rebound."

His hand gently tugged her arm, prompting her to look at him.

"Sophie, no matter how much time passes, people are always going to talk. Especially because of who you are. You're a Fortune Robinson. Everything you do is under a microscope. That isn't going to change."

"I realize that. But, oh, Mason, I admit I'm responsible for this…situation. If I hadn't been so stupid about Thom none of this would be happening. I just don't want to look like a two-timer or schemer! Especially after the things that have come out about Dad. Everyone is going to think our family is not to be trusted!"

His expression softened. "Sophie, I understand you've been having a rough time of it lately with your family. I just want—well, I just want us to be together. Out in the open. Like a real couple."

"And we will be, Mason. I promise. Just give it a little longer. In the meantime, I'd still like to be with you tonight. Am I invited to your place or not?"

Slowly, the tension on his face began to ease and then he chuckled under his breath. "Just try to stay away and I'll come after you."

Late that evening, Mason was getting ready to shut down his computer for the day when from the corner of his eye, he saw someone enter his cubicle.

He was more than surprised to see Thom sauntering up to his desk.

"What's wrong? Lost your way? Wes's office is down the corridor," Mason said with a heavy dose of sarcasm. He'd never liked the man in the first place and the feeling had only intensified. "You wouldn't be down here to see anyone but the boss, would you?"

One corner of Thom's mouth lifted in a sneer that assured Mason there was no love lost between them.

"Actually, I'm on my way out. I never did feel the need to work late just to try to impress anyone."

Anyone as in Sophie? Or anyone like Gerald Robinson? The questions rolled through Mason's thoughts as he studied the man that many women in the building had dubbed Mr. Dreamy. As far as Mason was concerned Thom Nichols was a walking nightmare.

Mason cast Thom a smug smile. "I'm not working late this evening. I happen to have a date. And I don't want to be late," he added pointedly.

The sneer on Thom's lips grew more twisted. "With Sophie, no doubt."

"I didn't say anything about Sophie."

Thom folded his arms against his chest. "Of course you didn't. The rest of the building is saying it for you."

So Sophie was right. The gossip had already started. Mason didn't care what anyone said, especially this pompous jerk. But he didn't want Sophie hurt. Not for any reason.

"Is there some reason for your visit, Nichols? If not, I'm out of here."

"No reason. I just thought I'd stop by and give you a bit of friendly advice."

"I don't remember asking you for any."

Thom shrugged and Mason thought how the guy was exactly like the taunting bully on the school playground. A fist to his mouth would definitely shut him up. But in the end Gerald Robinson would probably fire both of them. Especially because the fight revolved around his youngest daughter.

"Well, a man needs to know his limitations. I certainly learned that lesson the hard way. Think about it, Montgomery. I barely managed to hold on to Sophie for a few days and then her interest in me went south. What makes you think you can do better? The woman is a rich butterfly. She's never going to stay in one place long." With a short, mocking laugh, he started out of the cubicle. "All I can say is good luck. You're going to need it."

Biting back several choice curse words, Mason jerked on his jacket and flipped off the light. On his way out, he very nearly knocked Nadine off her feet.

Snatching a steadying hand on her shoulder, he quickly apologized, "Nadine, I'm sorry. Did I hurt you?"

She answered his question with a scoffing laugh. "It takes more than a little bump to knock this woman off her feet. Now, a kiss might do it. If only you were fifteen years older you'd be the perfect man for me."

Laughing with her, he gave her a little hug. "Ready to go? I'll walk with you to your car."

"I'll be ready as soon as I get my purse. Right now, I want to know what Mr. Phony was doing here. And yes, I'm being nosey. But I just happened to glance over here a minute ago and it looked like you had murder on your mind. Do I need to start saving money for your bail bond?"

Mason let out a weary sigh. "Thom thought he should come by and give me fair warning. Sophie will dump me just like she dumped him—swiftly and painfully."

Nadine scowled at him. "Don't listen to the man. He's obviously jealous."

"And he could be very right," Mason mumbled. "Think about it, Nadine. I'm just a regular Joe. I can't give Sophie what she's used to having."

Nadine patted his cheek. "You can give her the very thing her daddy can't buy her. Love. So there. Think about that while I fetch my purse."

Love. Yes, Sophie talked about love. About how very much she wanted her marriage to be full of warmth and love instead of the cold arrangement between her parents. But she'd never so much as hinted that she was falling in love with Mason. She'd never brought up their relationship in a long term context. She was living day to day, enjoying their time together. But that wasn't enough for Mason. Not nearly enough. And deep down, he was afraid Thom was right. Neither of them were good enough for Sophie Fortune Robinson.

By Sunday morning, the weather had turned spring-like and after much persuasion, Mason was able to talk Sophie into driving down to San Antonio to spend a day on the Riverwalk. With the sun shining brightly and the birds chattering in the trees, the day couldn't have been more beautiful. And having Sophie stroll alongside him made it even more heavenly.

Sophie had called on her inner cowgirl and donned a blue chambray shirt with a pink skirt and a pair of fancy cowboy boots. Her hair was pulled up in a high ponytail and the casual style made her look very young and very adorable. Mason found himself looking at her instead of the Riverwalk.

"Do your parents live downtown?" she asked, as the two of them meandered along the narrow river's edge.

"No. They live on the west side, in the same little stucco house they lived in when we boys were born. If you offered them a mansion right on the river, they'd just laugh and say they're happy where they are."

She looked at him with a faintly wistful expression and Mason wondered if she'd been expecting him to take her to meet his family today. Since she was still on this quest to keep their relationship a secret, he figured she would hardly want to announce it to his family. And to be honest, he wasn't yet ready to take Sophie to meet his parents. For a long time now, the Montgomerys had wanted to see their sons settle down and start producing grandbabies. Mason didn't want his parents, especially his mother, getting the idea that he and Sophie were getting serious about each other. Not when there was the very real possibility that in the next few weeks she'd be giving him the cold shoulder.

"Sophie, you didn't think you were here to meet my family, did you?"

The awkward question caused her cheeks to turn pink and she swiftly diverted her gaze to a passing tourist boat. "No. I don't expect that sort of… commitment from you. Meeting your parents would be a serious step. And you and I—well, we're just getting started with this dating thing."

She looked at him through lowered lashes and gave him a wobbly smile. Mason took her by the arm and led her over to a park bench which was partially shaded by a live oak.

Once they were seated, he took her hand and folded it between his. "Sophie, are you getting tired of me?"

"Tired? That's a silly question, Mason. We've been together every night since our Valentine's date. Why would you think such a thing?"

Not about to reveal the doubts he'd been feeling, he simply shrugged. "I don't know. You just seem a little withdrawn. Especially when we started talking about my parents."

Sighing, she said, "I'm not hurt about that, Mason. It just made me think of my parents and all that's going on with them. I wish to heck Ben would just leave it all alone! At least, that's what I think some of the time. Other times, I believe he's doing the right thing. If we have other siblings out there, we should probably know about them." She looked at him, her brown eyes swirling with dark shadows. "But then I think about Mother and what must be going through her mind. It's all so hard to deal with, Mason. And now something else has come up."

He cast her a questioning glance. "Oh. What now?"

"This coming Thursday night, we've all been invited to the Fortune Ranch for a family dinner. Kate Fortune wants to get to know the Fortune Robinsons better. Which I suppose is a nice thing. But I'm not sure I'm ready to mix and mingle with that side of the family. After all, they treated Dad so badly he faked his own death to get away from them. If that isn't an awkward setting, then I don't know what is."

Mason shook his head. "But that happened years ago. From what you've told me, Kate is trying her best to make amends for the brutal way your father was treated by his parents. You shouldn't feel awkward. If anything you should feel grateful that she's being so welcoming."

"Yes, I suppose so. And she's kindly encouraged each of us to bring along a guest. But I—I'm planning on going alone. I just want to get the whole evening over with."

In spite of the warm sun filtering through the tree limbs, Mason felt chilled. She could have invited him to the family dinner, but she was going alone. That proved just how much she thought Mason would fit into her highbrow family.

What are you carrying on about, Mason? You're less than twenty minutes away from your parents' house and you have no intention of taking Sophie to meet them. Is that because you don't think she'd fit in? Because you think she's too good to ever be a Montgomery?

Yes! He wanted to scream the word at the accusing voice in his head. Sophie was too good for him. That was the whole crux of the matter. And the sooner he realized it, the better off they'd both be.

The gentle pressure of her fingers on his claimed his attention. She was studying him with a faint frown and Mason only hoped she couldn't read his thoughts.

"Mason, a few minutes ago you were asking me if something was wrong, but I'm thinking it's you who has a problem. You seem preoccupied. Has something happened to upset you?"

Only that you've made it clear that your family and I don't mix.

Giving her his best smile, he said, "Not at all. It's a warm, gorgeous day. I have a beautiful woman to enjoy it with. What could possibly be wrong?"

Leaning forward, she kissed his cheek and in that moment, Mason realized his heart was lying right in the palm of her hand. No matter how hopeless it all seemed, he had to stick it out to the bitter end.

"You don't want fried chicken for lunch. That's it, isn't it?" she teased.

He grunted with amusement. "Fried chicken? Who said anything about that?"

She snuggled closer and Mason's gaze focused on her soft lips. If the two of them weren't sitting on a public bench, he'd kiss her until his mind was blank of worries. Until nothing mattered except making love to her.

She said, "I did. It's my favorite meal. Do you think we could find any around here?"

On this perfect Sunday the heiress wanted fried chicken. Maybe there was still hope for a future with her, he thought wryly. Could it be that deep down she was just a regular girl looking for a regular guy? For today he was going to let himself believe just that.

"This is the best news I've heard since my daughter and her husband decided to call off the divorce." Dennis grinned happily at Sophie, who was standing in front of his desk. "And this is all your doing, Sophie. I'm proud of you."

Any other time Sophie would've felt like dancing

around her boss's office. But not today. The satisfaction she felt over her worthy accomplishment was dimmed by the reality that she'd be going to the Fortune Ranch tonight instead of spending it making love to Mason.

"I really didn't do anything special, Dennis. Once I pointed out all the gaps in the new insurance coverage, Ben was in agreement to come up with an improved plan. That's why he's a sharp businessman. He realizes happy employees are much more productive."

"Well, I only hope that your family and everyone in this building can see what a conscientious person you are. How hard you work for everyone's benefit, not just your own."

Yes, Dennis would praise her. As for her family, she wasn't sure any of them took that much notice of her work or what she hoped to do with her life. Her mother considered her flighty and Olivia thought she was foolish. No telling what the others were thinking, especially now that gossip about her ditching Thom and picking up Mason was circulating around the building.

"Thanks, Dennis. Coming from you that means a lot."

He started to say something else when the phone on his desk rang. "Excuse me, Sophie. I'd better get this. It's a call I've been waiting on."

Once she left Dennis's office, she spotted Olivia waving an arm to catch her attention.

The two women met near the alcove where Mason had comforted her the day she'd overheard the nasty talk in the restroom. He'd made her feel special and given her the extra strength she'd needed to keep her chin up. Had she been falling in love with him then? Or had the love she felt for him as a friend suddenly blossomed like a seed in springtime? She didn't know. She only knew that her feelings for Mason were growing so big they were scaring her.

"What's up?" Sophie asked her sister.

"I wanted to see what you're wearing to the dinner party tonight. I went out on my lunch hour today and bought a new gown. I hope it'll be okay."

Sophie shrugged. "I haven't thought about it. I'm sure I can find something in my closet to impress the Fortunes."

Olivia rolled her eyes. "Sophie, we are the Fortunes, too."

"How could I forget?" Sophie asked sardonically. "We're getting new Fortune relatives every day."

Olivia regarded her skeptically. "Is that what's eating at you? You're afraid Ben is going to use the setting tonight to announce another one of Dad's illegitimate children? Forget it. He wouldn't do anything that crass. Not in front of Mother."

Sophie hoped not.

Sighing, she said, "I really don't want to go to this party tonight."

Olivia frowned at her. "Why? It will be fun to go to the Fortune Ranch. Maybe Kate will give us some of her fabulous cosmetics. Especially her famous Youth Serum. And it will give you an opportunity to show Mason our side of the family. You have invited him, haven't you?"

Olivia's question caught her by complete surprise. "No. I haven't invited him. I'm going alone."

Olivia's big brown eyes grew even wider. "Alone! But why? I understand that things ended rather quickly with Thom and developed even faster with Mason, but that's nothing to be embarrassed about. I'm just happy that you came to your senses and latched on to a nice man. And tonight would give you a chance to show Mother and Dad that you're serious about Mason. You are, aren't you?"

Sophie's mind was suddenly whirling. Not only with thoughts of Mason, but also about Olivia, and how her sister appeared to know so much about Sophie's personal life. She hadn't told anyone in her family about Mason yet. She'd been waiting for the right time. And waiting, too, for Mason to show some sign that he wanted their relationship to be the permanent kind. But so far he hadn't mentioned anything about love, much less forever.

"How did you know about Mason?"

Olivia rolled her eyes. "Sophie, I'm not blind. I've seen the two of you at Bernie's with your heads together. And Mother tells me you've been staying out late every night. It's not hard to put two and two together."

Sophie felt her cheeks turning red. "Mother has noticed me being gone? That's surprising. She hasn't mentioned it to me. I wonder why she said something about it to you."

Olivia shrugged. "Who knows? She probably thinks you'll get defensive and clam up."

The same way that she did? The suspicious thought raced through Sophie's mind, but she kept it to herself. Just as she'd kept to herself the image of Charlotte sitting at Gerald's desk in the wee hours of the morning.

"Maybe so," Sophie murmured. "And considering everything, she does have a lot on her mind."

"That's putting it mildly," Olivia said. "Well, I need to get back to my desk. I'll see you tonight. Since you're not taking Mason, are you riding out to the ranch with Mother and Dad?"

Cooped up for miles in the frozen atmosphere of her parents' car would be more than Sophie could endure for one evening. "No. I'll be taking my car. Why don't you ride with me?"

"Thanks, Sophie. I'll come out early. We'll get ready together and make it a real sister night." Olivia dropped a swift kiss on her cheek, then walked away.

Tonight would give you a chance to show Mother and Dad that you're serious about Mason.

Olivia's words continued to nag at Sophie and by the time she passed the entrance to R&D, she was very nearly ready to walk straight to his desk and beg him to go with her to the Fortune bash.

But then she remembered how forward she'd been with Thom and how quickly it had all blown up in her face. No, she wasn't going to press Mason into attending the family outing with her. If he ever decided he was ready to take that serious step, she wanted him to do it on his own. Not because she was pushing and prodding him toward a proposal of marriage.

But would he ever want to take such a step with her?

Her throat aching with raw emotions, she hurried down the corridor and wondered why love had to surround itself with so much pain and worry.

Love? Is that the reason she felt so melancholy? Because she was finally and truly in love?

She was going to have to answer that question and soon. Because something was telling her that Mason was about to demand the truth of her feelings. About him and her, and what she wanted for the future.

Chapter 13

Her petite curves draped with an organza gown of pale peach, and her long hair twisted into an elaborate chignon, Sophie glanced over the rim of her cocktail glass at the guests gathered in the grand room of the Fortune Ranch house.

The men were all dressed in dark, elegant suits, while the women wore long, bejeweled gowns, the cost of which would've fed a family of four for months.

"I used to think our home was elaborate, but this place is unbelievable." Olivia shook her head with awe. "Makes me wonder how long it took Kate to put her stamp on the place. I doubt it looked like this when it was the Silver Spur Ranch. Look at those drapes. There's enough material there to open a fabric store. And every room seems to have a bar. I suppose Kate wants to make sure she keeps her guests relaxed."

The place was more than elaborate, Sophie agreed.

It was like stepping into a fairy tale where everything was too beautiful and lavish to be real. Wide archways on three sides of the room made the area appear even more spacious. Instead of artificial lighting, the middle of the incredibly tall ceiling was lit by the stars shining through an enormous skylight. To the right, several feet away from Sophie and Olivia was a marble fireplace with an elevated hearth. Presently, mesquite logs crackled and simmered, throwing off enough heat to make the room comfortable for the women with bared shoulders.

"Well, I'll say one thing, everything is done tastefully. The western accents are just enough to let a person know they're in Texas. But not enough to be ostentatious."

A young male server paused in front of the two women. Sophie chose a canapé made with gulf shrimp and cream cheese. Olivia placed her empty cocktail glass on the man's tray and picked up a fresh one.

Maybe that was what she needed, Sophie thought ruefully. A bit of alcohol to numb the raw edges of her nerves. But she'd never much cared for the stuff. Besides, a cocktail wasn't going to make her forget about her parents' sham of a marriage, or the real idea that Mason only wanted her for a lover.

"Mother looks especially nice tonight," Olivia commented as she sipped her drink. "That pale blue dress flatters her."

"She'd look even better if she would smile," Sophie said dully. "But in her situation I suppose she's forgotten how."

Olivia slanted her a disappointed look. "Sophie, what in the world is coming over you? I'm the cynical one. Not you. Where's that cheerful attitude of yours?"

Sophie let out a long sigh. "You're right. I'm going to go mix and mingle and try to lift my spirits."

For the next hour, she moved around the crowd, greeting other family members, including her new stepbrother, Keaton Fortune Whitfield. Eventually she found herself face-to-face with Kate Fortune and her husband, Sterling Foster. Expecting the woman to be austere, Sophie was pleasantly surprised when Kate greeted her with sincere warmth.

By the time their short chat had ended, Sophie had to admit that Kate Fortune was an incredible woman. At ninety-one she looked years younger. Her slim figure remained straight and spry and her skin as dewy and fresh as a first rose in spring. No doubt a result of using her famous Youth Serum cream.

However, Kate's appearance was only a part of her dynamic presence. She had a razor-sharp mind, especially concerning business. The billionaire matriarch obviously had the knack to accurately gauge the needs of the consumer and to come up with the perfect product.

Yet as impressed as she was with Kate Fortune, it was her husband that touched Sophie in an emotional way. The suave, elderly gentleman was clearly very much in love with his wife. Each time he looked at her or lightly touched her hand, it was like he was touching an angel.

Was it crazy for Sophie to want that same thing for herself?

Sophie was standing at the back of the room, mulling over the question as she watched her mother and father interact with the other guests. So far tonight, the only time she'd seen them together was when they'd first arrived.

That sad fact shouldn't be bothering Sophie so much. It wasn't like her parents had been all lovey-dovey and then, all at once, everything had gone cold. But since she and Mason had become intimate, Sophie had started to look at everything differently. And she was seeing more and more how love, and nothing else, mattered in this world.

"It's a nice party, don't you think?"

The soft, feminine voice had Sophie turning to see a petite woman with wavy blonde hair that barely touched her shoulders. Her dress was a romantic floral with a delicate ruffle edging the neckline.

Until this moment, Sophie hadn't spotted this pretty young woman in the crowd of guests. And though she didn't immediately recognize her, something about her face seemed vaguely familiar.

Sophie said, "Yes. Ms. Fortune and her husband have certainly gone all out."

The woman, who appeared to be around Sophie's age, moved closer and thrust out her hand in greeting. "I don't think we've met before. I'm Chloe Elliott. And you are?"

Even though the woman was smiling warmly, the only thing Sophie could feel was icy shock. This was her father's illegitimate daughter! What was she doing here? Why did she think she could come here and mingle with Sophie and her brothers and sisters as though she were one of them?

Ignoring her outstretched hand, Sophie's expression turned as cold as the sick feeling inside her. "I'm Sophie Fortune Robinson. And don't ever think of calling me sister! Because you're not my sister! And you never will be!"

Chloe Elliott appeared totally stunned, but not nearly as much as Sophie. Horrified by the words that had come out of her mouth, she hurried across the enormous room and snatched up a glass from a tray full of drinks.

Not bothering to determine what the amber tinged drink might be, she took a giant swig and instantly choked on the fire sliding down her throat.

"Sophie! Are you all right?"

Glancing up, Sophie saw her mother frowning at her with a mixture of concern and admonition.

Careful to keep her voice hushed, Sophie answered, "No! I am not all right! I really want to leave!"

Thankfully, Charlotte didn't ask her why. Instead, she took a firm hold on Sophie's shoulder. "Leaving is out of the question. You're not going to embarrass yourself or your family. There are times, Sophie, when we women have to be strong and plaster a happy smile on our faces. This is one of those times. So don't disappoint me—or your father."

Sophie looked at her in amazement, while fighting the urge to laugh hysterically. Disappoint her father? Hadn't Charlotte already noticed her husband's illegitimate daughter walking among the guests? Didn't she care?

After downing a second, more careful sip of her drink, Sophie said, "All right, Mother. I'll pretend—for tonight. But don't expect me to keep pretending. I simply can't be like you."

By the next afternoon, Mason was more than smarting over Sophie's decision to go to the Fortune party without him. It wasn't that he was all that keen to rub elbows with wealthy society. To be honest, he would have probably felt uncomfortable during the whole affair. No, his feelings went deeper than that. Sophie had dismissed him as though he was the last person she would consider good enough to mix and mingle with her family.

All last night, he'd sat in his apartment alone, brooding and calling himself all sorts of a fool. It was plain he was headed down a dead-end path with Sophie. The two of them came from entirely different worlds. Just the thought of asking her to marry him, to live with him in a home he provided her, was laughable. And in the end, that was most likely what he'd get from her. A laugh. The sort of home he could give Sophie would never measure up. The sort of life he could afford to give her would always fall short. It would never work. No matter how much he dreamed and hoped and tried.

"Hey, handsome. Ready for a coffee break?"

The sound of Sophie's sweet voice shot right through his churning thoughts as she walked into his cubicle.

A red knit dress clung to her perfect little curves while her long hair was swept behind her ear on one side. She looked good enough to eat and it was all Mason could do to keep from pulling her into his arms.

Steeling himself against her charming smile, he raised his brows with faint surprise. "A coffee break? Aren't you worried that someone will see us talking, or God forbid, touching one another?"

His sarcasm clearly stunned her. Well, it had stunned Mason, too. He didn't want to be mean. Nor did he want to hurt her. But he was tired of giving in to her without getting any sort of reassurances that their relationship meant more to her than jumping into bed together.

Her smile faded as she walked over and leaned a hip against the edge of his desk.

"Actually, I'm not worried. I don't give a damn about gossipers anymore."

"Really? You couldn't prove it by me."

She frowned at him in confusion. "Mason, what's wrong?"

You're breaking my heart and you don't even know it. That's what's wrong.

The words were silently screaming inside him as he turned the chair so that he was facing his computer screen instead of her.

"Nothing. I'm way behind on my work."

A long stretch of silence passed till she asked, "What about tonight? Maybe we could go to Pedro's."

A few days ago, he'd have felt like she'd handed him the moon. Now her offer felt like too little, too late.

"Sorry. I've promised my brothers to go with them to a Spurs game. So I'm going to San Antonio tonight. I won't be home."

She let out a groan of disgust. "Basketball," she muttered. "I've never been so sick of hearing about sports events in my entire life!"

Anger had him whirling the chair so that he was facing her once again. "And I'm sick of hearing how hard it is for you to be a Fortune!"

She stared at him in disbelief. "Did I hear you right?"

"Every word," he said coolly. "You act as though no one else has family issues. No one else has been betrayed or lied to or hurt. Well, grow up and open your eyes, Sophie. You're just one of many."

Tears flooded her eyes and for one second Mason weakened to the point where he almost reached for her.

He almost asked her to forgive him for being such a heartless bastard. But deep down, his pride and every ounce of common sense urged him to hold his ground.

She stepped away from the desk and Mason could see her hands had balled into tight fists at her sides. "If that's what you think of me, then I'm glad I found it out now. I wouldn't want to keep torturing you with my monotonous problems."

Swallowing the ball of pain in his throat, he said, "It was fun for a while, Sophie. But I've been thinking and I believe it's time we broke things off. For both our sakes."

Sniffing, she tossed her hair back over her shoulder. "Are you doing this because of last night? Because I didn't invite you to the Fortune dinner party?"

"No," he said and realized he truly meant it. This wasn't just about a party. This was about the fundamental differences in their lives. One day soon she would realize they were wrong for each other and move on to a man who would really be her Mr. Perfect. As for him, he expected he would spend the rest of his life trying to forget her. "I'm doing this to save us both a lot of heartache. Now if you don't mind, I'm busy. I need to get back to work."

She gave him one last look, then turned and walked stiffly out of the cubicle. The moment she was out of sight, Mason slumped forward in his chair and dropped his head in his hands.

Minutes later he was still sitting that way when Nadine poked her head into his work space. "Ready for some coffee, honey?"

He lifted his head and by then Nadine must have realized something was amiss. She hurried over to him.

"Mason, you look like hell! What's wrong? What's happened?"

Pushing himself to his feet, he shook his head. "Nothing's happened, Nadine. Except that I've just given up the most important thing in my life."

Nadine's lips pressed to a thin line of disgust. "Don't tell me. Ms. Fortune just gave you the shaft."

"No," he said, barely able to speak around the bitter gall rising in his throat. "I'm the one who called it quits."

Nadine shook her head. "You! But, Mason, why? I don't understand. You were crazy about the woman!"

"That's exactly why, Nadine. I want her to be happy. Not just for now. But for the rest of her life. And I'm not the man who can keep her happy."

"Oh, Mason, you're letting talk around the office get to you. You've let Thom get to you."

Mason slung his arm around Nadine's shoulders and urged her out of the cubicle. "Right now you're getting to me, Nadine. So let's go have some coffee. And all I want to hear from you is something about getting your roots done or work on your mother/baby app."

With a mirthless laugh, she wrapped an arm across his back. "Oh, hell, if I were only a few years younger."

For the next three days Sophie's feelings alternated between anger, sadness, and confusion. Anger, not just at Mason for suddenly picking a fight and ending things, but at her family and the whole world for being so messed up and wrong. Confused because she still didn't exactly understand what had come over Mason so abruptly, and sadness for the utter loss of something she'd believed had been strong and true.

Sophie had never been one to sit around and cry and mope over what could have been. She'd always been the sort to look toward the future and fight on. But losing Mason had hurt her so deeply that the world around her was like a strange and scary place. She was afraid to take any sort of step. Afraid that whatever direction she took, it would be wrong.

For the past few nights she'd sat in her bedroom and stared at the little red bear Mason had given her on Valentine's Day. The little bear had reflected all her hopes and dreams. It symbolized everything she'd ever wanted in her life. A man to love her, a marriage that was genuine, a life that would be filled with happiness and children. Money couldn't buy her those things. And, in Mason's case, she feared her wealth had actually worked against her.

Oh, Lord, he'd been wrong, she thought sadly. Mason had no idea just how hard it was to be a Fortune. To be so insanely rich that a regular guy was too afraid to come near her. And the others were simply cons after her money. He didn't know how it felt to go home to a palatial estate where there was no love or laughter.

Somehow her brothers, Ben and Wes and Graham, and her sisters Rachel and Zoe had found their soulmates. And for a few short beautiful days Sophie had believed she'd found hers. Now, she was beginning to think that men were nothing but selfish creeps. She was trying to convince herself that she'd be better off if she marked love completely off her future plans.

Glancing to the far edge of her desk, she groaned at the sight of the latest little gift Thom had dropped on her work space. A small picture of himself inside a gaudy gilded frame. Could the man get any more narcissistic? And why did he think just because she was no longer seeing Mason that she'd be willing to date him again? It was insane.

The office gossip machine must have been working overtime to spread the news about her bust up with Mason. One day hadn't passed before she'd found a flower on her desk. A card with nothing but Thom's name had been attached. Sophie had tossed the card in the trash and given the flower to Dennis's secretary.

Yesterday, a text message from Thom had popped up on her phone, suggesting the two of them meet for drinks. She'd promptly blocked his number. Now today, the photo had arrived, but rather than toss it, she'd decided she was going to return it personally, along with firm instructions to leave her alone.

"Great! You're back at your desk. I stopped by earlier, but you weren't here."

The sound of Thom's voice made her want to scream with frustration. Instead, she swiveled her chair and asked bluntly, "Do you have a problem you need to discuss? A human resource problem?"

A smug smile crossed his face. "I do have a problem. You won't say yes to another date with me. But I intend to change your mind. We can start over, Sophie. And this time you'll see I'm serious."

He was serious all right, Sophie thought. Seriously self-absorbed.

Leaning back in her chair, she leveled a sharp look at him. "Doesn't it bother you that I've been seeing Mason?"

He shrugged and his indifference amazed her. "Why should it? He's out of your life now. A fact that I knew would happen sooner rather than later."

The man's insolence was beyond measure and though Sophie was trying to hold on to her temper, her stomach was simmering with anger and resentment.

"I'm sure," she practically sneered. "The last time I looked, I didn't see a crystal ball on your desk."

He let out a short laugh. "I hardly needed a crystal ball to tell me your little hookup with Mason wasn't going to work. The man isn't nearly good enough for a woman of your class. I pointed out that very thing to him a few days ago. And I'm sure you're relieved he took my advice. Apparently he saw the light and was smart enough to save himself a lot of awkward embarrassment by letting you dump him later."

Her mouth fell open as her tangled thoughts tried to unravel enough for her to see the whole picture.

"Are you saying that you told Mason he wasn't good enough for me?"

Grinning, he moved closer and Sophie immediately jumped to her feet and stepped back.

"Why not? It's the truth. Better that you both face facts now, rather than later. Long, pointless affairs can often get messy at the end. You both saved yourself from an ugly situation."

Furious, Sophie picked up the photo and practically threw it at him. "You're not half the man that Mason is, Thom Nichols! You never will be!"

"Really? If he's so wonderful, then why did you break up with him?"

She hadn't broken up with him, she thought miserably. Mason had broken up with her. He'd suddenly picked a fight, as though he'd deliberately wanted to push her into ending their relationship. But why? And why hadn't she stood her ground and fought to keep everything they'd built together?

Because she'd been terrified. Afraid to trust. Afraid to open her heart and admit to Mason how very much she loved him. Could the same thing have been going through his mind, she wondered frantically. Could he have been having those same doubts and fears? She had to know! She couldn't just let the best thing she'd ever had slip through her fingers without putting up a fight to hold on to him.

"Take that ridiculous picture and get out of my work space!" she said to Thom in a low, gritty voice. "Before I call security and have them throw you out!"

He lifted his nose as though he couldn't believe she could utter such a threat, much less go through with it.

"Oh, Sophie. You wouldn't do that in a million years."

"Try me," she challenged. "And you'll see I'm no longer that starry-eyed young woman who looked blindly past your faults."

His face hardened like a piece of granite. "You're going to be sorry about this, Sophie. One of these days you're going to be begging me to notice you."

Thom's parting words were laughable. But Sophie didn't laugh, even though she was silently rejoicing. Because in his own conceited way, Thom had just opened her eyes and given her hope.

Turning back to her desk, she reached for the phone. She was going to put a plan in motion and pray it worked.

"Mason, you look drained. I honestly don't think you should work anymore this evening," Nadine advised as the two walked back to the office after having burgers at Bernie's. "Your health app won't get finished if you fall over from exhaustion."

"I'm not going to fall over from exhaustion." A broken heart, maybe, Mason thought ruefully. And that was something that bed rest wouldn't fix. Unless Sophie was lying in the bed with him. And that wasn't going to happen. Not after the way he treated her.

"How do you know?" Nadine asked. "I've heard of people falling into comas from extreme fatigue."

He looked over at his friend and gave her the best smile his wounded spirits could generate. "I appreciate your concern. But even if I went home right now, I wouldn't rest. I don't think I've slept three hours in the past three nights."

"And whose fault is that?" she shot back at him. "I just don't get you, Mason. You go gaga over a woman and then deliberately break up with her. Because you want her to be happy. Well, do you think you've made her happy? I don't. I saw her this afternoon at Olivia's desk. She looked horrible—like you."

"Sophie came into research and development?" he asked with surprise. "I didn't see her."

"No. You were too busy staring at your computer screen while trying to make everyone believe you weren't somewhere in outer space."

It was just as well that Mason hadn't been aware that Sophie was close by. Each time he'd caught a glimpse of her, it had felt like someone was stabbing him with a double-edged knife.

Since their breakup, he'd felt like Austin had suddenly moved within the Arctic Circle and the days had all turned dark. Without Sophie in his life nothing felt right or good. And he'd been asking himself over and over if he'd been an utter fool to let her go.

Maybe she hadn't said anything about love. And maybe she had wanted to keep their relationship a secret. But all of that could've changed if he'd been willing to give them a chance. And now? Well, he'd said some awful things to her. Things that had cut him just to speak them aloud. How could he ever expect her to give him another chance?

"Uh, Mason, beam me up, would you? I've lost my friend and maybe I'll find him out there somewhere in a galaxy far, far away."

Nadine's sardonic voice suddenly got through his deep thoughts and he slanted her a wry glance, then glanced around to see they had reached the Robinson Tech parking garage. The same spot where everything had started between him and Sophie. If only he could turn back time.

"Sorry, Nadine. I was thinking."

"Obviously. Do you think you can make it back into the building without me? Or do I need to guide you to your desk?"

Leaning down, he planted a swift kiss on her cheek. "Thanks. But I think I can find my way back. See you in the morning."

Nadine wished him a good night then slipped into her car. Mason watched her drive safely away before he headed inside the building.

Since the work day had ended hours ago, the corridor was eerily quiet. As he approached the entrance to Sophie's department, he noticed there were no lights coming from that area.

And what if there was, Mason? Would you finally

gather enough courage to face her? To beg her to give
you another chance?

Tormented by the voice in his head, he wiped a hand
over his face and trudged on. A part of him wished
Nadine was right and he would fall into a temporary
coma. At least then, he'd get a reprieve from the agony
of losing her.

He was thinking about all the things he wished he'd
done differently and how good it would feel to pull her
into his arms and kiss her, when he walked into his cubicle and stopped in his tracks.

Seconds ticked away as Mason stared in stunned fas-
cination at a little stuffed bear sitting in his chair. The
animal's shaggy golden brown hair resembled that of a
grizzly. An educated grizzly, no doubt, since his paws
were resting on the computer keyboard.

His heart racing madly, Mason stepped forward and
discovered a note attached to the bear's leather collar.

No one should have to spend February 27th alone.

He was staring at the note, trying to tamp down the
ridiculous hope that was rushing to every cell in his
body, when Sophie's voice sounded behind him.

"You've been gone so long I was afraid you'd left
for home."

He slowly turned to face her and his heart began to
beat so hard he thought his breastbone would surely
crack down the middle.

"Sophie! What are you doing here?"

Like a beautiful dream, she glided toward him.

"Waiting for you," she answered quietly.

"I don't understand." His voice closed around his
words making it sound as coarse as gravel. "The bear—
are you trying to say—"

She reached for his hands and as Mason wrapped his fingers tightly around hers, his gaze was riveted on the emotions flickering in her eyes. The feelings he saw in the brown depths were so soft and tender and pleading, they smacked him right in the middle of his chest.

"Mason, I don't know what happened with us. Or why you—"

Shaking his head, he interrupted her before she could say more.

"Sophie, listen to me. I've been a damned fool. These past few days I've been wanting to come to you—to try to explain—to beg you to forgive me. I was a bastard, a jerk, and all kinds of a fool for saying those things to you. But I—"

All at once her forefinger was pressed against his lips. "You had a right to say those things. I've been an idiot, Mason. More than that, I've been a big coward. I was afraid to show everyone how much I cared about you. Most of all I was afraid to show you—to tell you how very much I love you. Everything was so good with us I kept thinking it couldn't last. My parents' marriage is nothing about love, and Thom—he doesn't fathom the word. When you and I started getting close—well, the closer we got the more afraid I was to believe you could ever truly love me."

Relief washed through him, leaving his insides trembling with weakness. "Sophie, if you've been an idiot, then I've been an even bigger one. I kept thinking there was no way you could ever love a man like me. That's why I went off on you like I did. Because I believed you were going to eventually drop me anyway. That you'd move on to some man more fitting to a woman of your status."

A tentative smile tilted her lips. "Fitting? Oh, Mason, you should know by now that you fit me perfectly."

Slipping his arms around her waist, he pulled her toward him until she was pressed tightly to him. Then burying his face in the crook of her neck, he murmured in her ear, "I love you, Sophie. I should've told you that from the very start. But I was afraid you'd think I was a sap. I was even more afraid to believe I could ever have a future with you."

She eased her head back and the love he saw on her face swelled his chest until he could scarcely breathe.

"Do you want a future with me, Mason?"

"Only for the rest of our lives. Is that too long?"

Joy spread her lips into a radiant smile. "Forever isn't nearly long enough, but I'll take it."

He kissed her then and in a matter of a few seconds, desire began to sweep them both away.

Finally, he lifted his head and said in a voice rough with desire, "Let's go home—to my place. If you can call that home?"

Her arms tightened around him. "My home is going to be wherever you are, Mason. Now and always."

Early the next morning, Sophie carried a steaming mug of coffee into the bedroom and with her free hand reached down and touched Mason's bare shoulder.

Groaning, he lifted his head and opened his eyes to see her standing at the side of the bed. His navy blue robe swallowed her small curves and her face was bare of makeup, but she didn't feel self-conscious about letting Mason see her this way. During the past twelve hours she'd learned that Mason loved her for the person she was inside, not for her looks, or name, or bank account. And that fact made her so deliriously happy she was certain she was walking on air instead of a hardwood floor.

"Sophie, honey, what are you doing up already?" he asked with a sleepy smile. "And you made coffee, too?"

Laughing softly, she said, "I know it's hard to believe, but I can do one or two things in the kitchen."

He quickly propped a pillow against the headboard. Once he'd scooted up to a sitting position and settled back against the pillow, he took the coffee from her.

She watched him take a sip, then his brow arched with surprise. "Mmm. This is delicious. What did you do to it?"

She cut him a saucy glance. "I put in water and coffee grounds and turned the switch to ON."

Chuckling, he took another sip, then set the mug on the nightstand and reached for her. Sophie let out a happy squeal as he pulled her down onto his lap.

"Good morning, beautiful," he whispered against her lips.

She kissed him deeply, then eased back to look at him. With his dark hair rumpled and a shadow of a beard covering his face, he looked incredibly handsome and terribly sexy. Yet to know that he loved her—not because she was a Fortune, but because she was simply Sophie— filled her heart with a joy that was almost impossible to contain.

"Good morning, my darling. How does it feel to wake up to a woman and a cup of coffee?"

His eyes narrowed to a provocative slant. "I think this is going to be pretty darn easy to get used to. Uh—what do you think your family is going to say when I slip an engagement ring on your finger?"

She held up her left hand and imagined a ring sparkling back at her. "When is that going to happen?" she asked coyly.

"Today. That is, if I can find a stone that suits you and one that I can afford."

Shaking her head, she cradled his face with her hands. "Mason, I don't care if it's a tiny chip of a diamond or a plastic ring out of a toy machine. As long as it means that you love me. And as for my family, I'm sure my siblings will be very happy for me. As for my parents, they're in no position to give me advice about marriage."

His expression turning sober, he threaded his fingers through her long hair. "Sophie, the other day—when I said all those awful things about you being a Fortune—I was wrong. And I'm sorry. I said them out of frustration."

"It doesn't matter now, honey. Really, it doesn't."

"Yes, Sophie, it does matter. I want you to know that I do understand that being a Fortune can't be easy for you. In fact, I can see how hard it is for you to deal with your father's infidelity and illegitimate children."

"I feel like I've gone through an earthquake and I'm still searching for solid ground," Sophie admitted. "But in a way it's helped me see exactly what's most important in life. Wealth, social position, gossip and reputations, none of that means anything compared to having someone to love and share your life with. That's all I want for us, Mason."

She glanced away from him and let out a rueful sigh and Mason quickly touched a hand to her cheek.

"You're not still worried, are you? About us?"

Smiling wanly, she turned her gaze back to his. "No.

But now that we're so happy and I feel so blessed, I'm beginning to see how wrong I've been about Chloe Elliott. She was at the Fortune dinner party the other night and I'm ashamed to admit I said some very nasty things to her. I was so outraged to see her there acting like family. But now—well, I've come to realize she can't help the circumstances of her birth any more than I can. I'm going to do my best to make amends with her as soon as I can."

He patted her cheek. "That's my sweet Sophie. The one I love."

A while later, after they'd eaten a quick breakfast of toast and jam, Mason headed to the shower, but Sophie wasn't in a hurry to leave the little breakfast table. Instead, she picked up her cell phone and scrolled through her contact list until she reached the name Ariana Lamonte.

The woman answered on the third ring and as Sophie responded, she turned her gaze toward the bright morning sunlight streaming through the kitchen window. Today was a new beginning to the rest of her life, she thought. From now on things could only get better.

"Ariana, this is Sophie Fortune Robinson. I hope I'm not calling too early."

"Not in the least," Ariana replied. "I'm already at my desk. Is there something I can do for you?"

Sophie took a deep breath. "As a matter of fact, there is. I'm ready to help you find out my mother's real story."

"I'm so pleased you've decided to go after the truth, Sophie. So when will you be free to meet?"

A few minutes later, Sophie had scheduled a meeting with Ariana and ended the phone call just as she felt Mason's hands settle gently on her shoulders.

Already dressed in black slacks and a pale blue dress shirt with a tie tossed around his neck, he'd clearly overheard the end of her conversation with Ariana and couldn't keep the concern from his voice. "What if you find something unpleasant about your mom? Will you be able to handle more bad news about your family?"

Their gazes met and the love she saw in his brown eyes filled her with courage and strength. "As long as you love me, Mason, I can face anything."

Bending his head, he kissed her thoroughly, then whispered against her lips, "And I'm going to love you for a long, long time. Like forever. So hurry and get ready. We have some engagement ring shopping to do."

"I'll be ready in a flash," she promised.

Ready to start their new life together.

* * * * *

Nationally bestselling author **Nancy Robards Thompson** holds a degree in journalism. She worked as a newspaper reporter until she realized reporting "just the facts" bored her silly. Now that she has much more content to report to her muse, Nancy loves writing women's fiction and romance full-time. Critics have deemed her work "funny, smart and observant." She resides in Florida with her husband and daughter. You can reach her at Facebook.com/nrobardsthompson.

Books by Nancy Robards Thompson

Harlequin Special Edition

The Savannah Sisters

A Down-Home Savannah Christmas
Southern Charm & Second Chances

Celebration, TX

The Cowboy's Runaway Bride
A Bride, a Barn, and a Baby
The Cowboy Who Got Away

Celebrations, Inc.

Celebration's Family
Celebration's Baby
A Celebration Christmas
How to Marry a Doctor
His Texas Christmas Bride

Visit the Author Profile page
at Harlequin.com for more titles.

FORTUNE'S SURPRISE ENGAGEMENT

Nancy Robards Thompson

This book is dedicated to
Susan Litman and Marcia Book Adirim,
the heart and soul of the Fortunes.
And to Melanie Ashman for naming the signature
drink Olivia served at Sophie's bachelorette party!

Chapter 1

"It's time to break out the Fuzzy Handcuffs, Mike." Olivia Fortune Robinson gave the sexy bartender her most flirtatious smile.

He cocked a brow and grinned. "It's my pleasure to hook you ladies up."

"Excuse me?" Her sister Sophie frowned at him and then her eyes went wide as realization seemed to dawn. "Oh, no." Sophie held up her hands as if to ward off Mike. "Please tell me you are not a stripper." She pinned her panicked gaze on her sister. "Olivia, Dana and I specifically told you we didn't want strippers at our bachelorette party. No offense, Mike. I'm sure you're very good at what you do. You just can't do it here. Not tonight. Not for us."

She looked at her sister-in-law-to-be, Dana Trevino, and the other Fortune Robinson sisters seated on the plush love seats and overstuffed armchairs grouped around a glass cocktail table in a cozy corner of the Driskill Hotel bar.

Sophie's brown eyes were huge and color blazed high on her cheekbones. By contrast, Dana seemed to have gone pale as she perched hesitantly on the edge of her seat, as if weighing whether or not to bolt. Watching the pair of them squirm was worth all the effort Olivia had put into planning this sisters' weekend. Olivia almost hated to burst their horrified balloons.

"Unfortunately, Mike is not a stripper," she said, pausing to let them sit with thoughts of what they would be missing.

Her sister Rachel sighed. "Aw, that's too bad. For one glorious moment, I thought we had our very own Magic Mike."

Zoe, another sister, nodded in agreement.

Mike laughed. "Sorry, ladies. It's true, I'm not a stripper. Although I will be tending to your every need tonight."

The innuendo was thick.

"Does that mean you're a gigolo then?" Rachel asked, her eyes sparkling with mischief.

Mike laughed. "No, not a gigolo, either. I am your personal bartender and I am happy to be at your service."

Sophie's mouth formed a perfect O before her brows knit together. "And exactly what were you planning to do with the fuzzy handcuffs?"

Olivia and Mike exchanged a conspiratorial look.

"Forgive them," she said. "They don't get out much."

"There is nothing to forgive," he said. "Would you like to tell her about the Fuzzy Handcuffs or shall I?"

"Please, do the honors," Olivia said.

"Your sister commissioned me to create a signature

cocktail for your bachelorette party." He stopped and looked at Sophie. "I'm guessing you are one of the brides."

"Yes, I'm Sophie."

He took her hand and lifted it to his lips before he asked, "Which one of you is Dana?"

"That would be me." The pretty redhead gave a hesitant wave before she tucked her hands into the fabric of her flowing gypsy skirt. Mike winked at her. Rachel and Zoe promptly introduced themselves, laughing as they made a dramatic show of extending their hands for a kiss. Mike didn't disappoint them.

Mike was a very good sport. As Olivia made a mental note to tell the manager how he'd gone above and beyond, her gaze was snared by a tall, dark, good-looking man walking into the bar. Though she only caught his profile before he turned and sat down with his back to her, he reminded her of someone. Who, she couldn't place, but Olivia hadn't gotten a very good look at him.

"Congratulations, ladies," Mike said. "I'm honored to serve you on your special night. I understand you're staying at the Driskill?"

"We are," Sophie said. "We checked in this afternoon. Olivia has planned a fabulous weekend for us."

"Nothing but the best for my sisters," Olivia said.

"When is the wedding?" he asked.

"Next weekend," Dana said. "Right here in this hotel in the ballroom. But there will be a full week of events leading up to the ceremony. This girls' get-together is a nice way to kick off the festivities."

"Well, don't let me hold up the party," Mike said. "One round of Fuzzy Handcuffs coming right up."

"Fuzzy Handcuffs." Rachel shook her head. "Only you would come up with a name like that, Olivia. Only you."

They all laughed.

"Originally, Mike wanted to call the drink the Bride's First Blush, but that was boring."

"No it's not," Sophie said. "It's pretty."

Olivia resisted the urge to roll her eyes. The name Bride's First Blush was too sweet for such a potent cocktail. The drink itself was perfect. It was festive and fizzy, but it also had just the right amount of something stronger to pack a pop. It needed a name that was just as strong, not one that sounded like a virgin cocktail. Fuzzy Handcuffs was perfect.

Olivia had gone to the ends of the earth to ensure that every single detail of this sisters' weekend was perfect. And of course, it had been perfect so far. She may have been a computer programmer by trade, but if she ever found herself in need of a career change, she did have a knack for event planning.

Sophie and Dana weren't party girls, so they'd been ecstatic with the plan of a weekend of pampering. After they'd checked into the suite at the Driskill, a limousine had whisked them away to the spa where they'd enjoyed hot stone massages, facials, seaweed wraps, special conditioners that had brought out the shine in their tresses and luxurious aromatherapy soaks in jetted tubs. At noon, they'd taken a break from the pampering to enjoy a light lunch complete with mimosas. Afterward, they'd returned to the spa for mani-pedis before adjourning to the pool to sip fruit-infused reverse-osmosis water while they relaxed and soaked up just enough sun so not to burn, but to give them a healthy glow.

"I wanted my sister and sister-to-be's last weekend of freedom to be something you two will never forget. Since you nixed the strippers, I had to sneak in something edgy somewhere else. Voilà—Fuzzy Handcuffs. At least I didn't call it the Ol' Ball and Chain."

"No, that'll be the name of the drink we serve at your bachelorette party," Zoe quipped.

"Hell Froze Over might be a more apt name for my bridal cocktail, since that's what would happen if I ever got married."

"Don't be so cynical," Zoe said. "You reap what you sow."

"I beg your pardon?" Olivia knew exactly what her sister meant, but she wasn't going to give in that easily. Zoe was the consummate Pollyanna when it came to love and romance—despite every bad example their parents' screwed-up relationship and sham of a marriage had set for them.

"You know exactly what I mean." Zoe sighed and looked at Olivia as if she was hopeless. "You draw to you exactly what you put out into the world."

Olivia blanched, but now wasn't the time to get into a philosophical discussion about the realities of love and happily-ever-after. Besides the fact that this was supposed to be a happy occasion celebrating Sophie and Dana's imminent wedding, her other two sisters were newly married. Zoe was still in the honeymoon phase of her own marriage, having just wed Joaquin Mendoza last year. Rachel was married to Joaquin's brother Matteo.

Wait a minute—

Olivia's gaze found the tall guy at the bar. Was that the other Mendoza? The single one—what was his name?

She turned to her sisters. "See that guy over there? Isn't that your brother-in-law?"

They turned in unison and looked.

"Is that Alejandro?" Rachel said.

"I think it is," Zoe said.

"I didn't realize he was coming to town early," Sophie said. "We should say hi and invite him to join us for a drink." She started across the bar toward him and the next thing they knew, she was walking back arm-in-arm with him.

"Look who I found," Sophie said, triumphantly. "Alejandro, I'm sure you remember my sisters, Olivia, Rachel and Zoe. And this is Dana, the other bride-to-be."

They exchanged hellos.

"When did you get in?" Rachel asked.

"A couples of hours ago. I came in early to take care of some business before the wedding."

All of the Mendoza men had been blessed by the tall, dark and handsome Latin gene, but Alejandro seemed to have gotten an extra helping of good looks. Olivia wondered how she'd failed to notice that before now. Of course, she'd only seen him on two other occasions: Rachel's and Zoe's weddings. She'd brought dates both times, so she hadn't exactly been looking.

"You came in from Miami, right?" Olivia asked. She did remember that much.

He turned his sultry gaze on her.

"I did."

"I didn't realize you had business ties to Austin," Sophie asked. "What do you do, Alejandro?"

"I'm in the wine business," he said. "I'm a wine sales rep, but I'm in town because I'm in the process of buying a small vineyard about twenty miles west of here."

Zoe's mouth fell open. "Your very own vineyard? That's so cool. Why hasn't Joaquin mentioned it?"

Alejandro shrugged. "Until last week, it was still

up in the air, but everything finally fell into place. I'm going to meet with the owners tomorrow and do one last walk-through before we finalize the deal."

"Which winery?" Rachel asked.

"It's called Hummingbird Ridge." He kept stealing glances at Olivia.

"I've never known anyone who's actually owned a winery," Sophie mused. "I'd love to see it. Can you give us a tour?"

Alejandro's brows shot up as he considered the possibility. "I'm sure I can arrange a tasting for you. Is there time this week?"

Everyone looked at Olivia as if she was the keeper of the schedule. There were events and outings scheduled for every day of wedding week—tours of Austin for those from out of town, rounds of golf, tennis matches, couples' massages, luncheons, teas and dinners. But with a guest list close to five hundred people, the only activity they would all be doing as a group was watching the couples exchange their vows and celebrating at the reception afterward.

"How many people could you accommodate?" Olivia asked him.

"I'd say about two dozen," he told her. "Of course, I'll have to check with the winery and see how their availability looks. But this is their slow time of year when they don't get many large groups. It shouldn't be a problem. Maybe you can start organizing on your end and we can touch base and coordinate. Give me your number."

Out of the corner of her eye, Olivia saw Sophie elbow Zoe. The only reason she didn't make a face at them was because she didn't want to draw Alejandro's attention to their antics.

Olivia rattled off her cell number and Alejandro put it in his phone, calling her to make sure he'd input the right digits. When her phone rang, Olivia entered his name.

"There," she said. "We should be all set."

Mike reappeared with a tray full of hot-pink cocktails. True to the drink's name, a pink-and-black fuzzy handcuff graced the stem of each frosted martini glass. A drink stirrer that seemed to be exploding silver tinsel decorated the top. The tray looked like a mini Fourth of July fireworks display.

As the five women expressed their delight, Mike looked pleased, but Alejandro took a step back.

"Why don't you join us for a drink, Alejandro?" Rachel said.

"Actually, he's welcome to mine," said Dana. "As much as I hate to leave this fabulous soiree, I have to go pick up my maid of honor from the airport. It's a pretty long haul out there. I really shouldn't drink and drive. I'm so eager to hug Monica. It's been ages. And she's bringing my wedding dress. She's letting me borrow an antique dress that belonged to her grandmother. I've seen pictures, but I haven't had a chance to try it on yet. I'm a little anxious about it. That's one of the reasons I need to go. I hope you understand."

Their future sister-in-law's early departure wasn't a surprise. Monica had made her reservations nearly simultaneously with Olivia finalizing the plans for the bachelorette party. While they wanted her to stay, they understood. Monica was like family to Dana, who had lost her parents in an accident when she was twelve and had grown up in foster care. While the guardianship had been adequate, it hadn't been warm enough to warrant keeping in touch or inviting them to the wedding.

The redhead, whose style was more boho-vintage than traditional, would look perfect in an antique gown. She twirled a long strand of copper hair around her index finger and drew in an audible breath.

"Wow. My maid of honor is arriving and I finally get to try on my dress. I guess that means this wedding is really happening." She put a hand on her heart. "I can't believe it's finally here."

The look of love was so evident in Dana's sparkling blue eyes that for the briefest moment, a pang of envy stabbed at Olivia's insides. It was an odd feeling. If given the chance, she wouldn't change places with her sisters. She cherished her independence. Even though the thought of tying herself to one man for the rest of her life made her feel claustrophobic, she was happy for her sisters. It was the happiness that she envied.

"I know." Sophie swooned. Feeling like an outsider, Olivia watched Rachel and Zoe coo right along with Dana and Sophie.

Her little sister, Sophie, and Mason Montgomery had gotten engaged in February, and just last month her brother, Kieran, had asked Dana to be his wife. Her siblings were certainly falling like flies bitten by the love bug. Olivia was the only one who hadn't succumbed. Even so, just because she didn't believe in the institution of marriage, it didn't mean she couldn't be happy for them.

That's precisely why she'd decided to go all out for Sophie and Dana's bachelorette party. Olivia couldn't resist a good party, especially when the guests of honor were women she adored and it gave her a chance to get together with her sisters Zoe and Rachel. Who, other than herself, could she trust to make sure that every detail was perfect?

"I'm so sorry you can't stay," said Sophie. "Why don't you pick up Monica and bring her back here? She could join us for dinner. As far as we're concerned, the more the merrier. Right?"

The sisters nodded. But Dana's left shoulder rose and fell. "As much as I'd love to, I can't. Monica is bound to be exhausted. But we will definitely come for brunch tomorrow, if that's still okay."

"We wouldn't have it any other way," Rachel said. "I'm sure you want a chance to catch up with Monica before everyone gets swept away by the festivities leading up to the wedding. It's going to be a busy week. And I know you want to try on your dress. I wish we could be there for that."

Sophie reached out and squeezed Dana's hand. "Of course, we completely understand. Monica needs to be rested up for the wedding. This really is the calm before the storm hits."

Something that sounded like a cross between a squeak and a squeal escaped from Sophie and she covered her mouth with both hands. She shook her head and wrung her jittery hands, excitement rolling off her in waves. "Oh, my gosh. You're right. It just got officially real. This time next week we will be married and dancing at our wedding reception. Maybe I should make my next Fuzzy Handcuffs a double."

"Good, that means you can have one for me," Dana said. "On that note, I'd better say good-night."

As the four Fortune Robinson sisters took turns hugging Dana, Alejandro, who had been silent since all the wedding talk started, spoke up. "I have some work to catch up on. I, too, will leave you ladies to your festivities."

His gaze caught Olivia's and lingered long enough

to cause a slight shift in the room's temperature. It was like wading into a warmer current of water.

"Have fun," he said. "Olivia, I'll be in touch."

In reverent silence, the sisters watched Alejandro walk away.

"Gotta love those Mendoza genes," Rachel said under her breath.

"Oh, yeah. Highly recommended," Zoe said and sipped her drink. "Olivia, I think Alejandro is into you. You should go for him this week. Isn't it a lovely coincidence that he's Joaquin's last single brother and you're my last single sister?"

Sophie squealed. "I think Alejandro would be a perfect match for Olivia."

Olivia could think of many worse things than "going for" Alejandro Mendoza. A wedding fling with a gorgeous Latin man? *Hell, yeah.* It didn't get much better than that. Especially since he lived in Miami and she lived in Austin. That was just enough distance for a no-strings-attached fling.

A slow heat burned deep in her belly. She threw back her drink to cool herself off. The Fuzzy Handcuffs went down way too easily.

Yeah…but, no. Hooking up with Alejandro wasn't a good idea. He was family. Sort of. But not really. There was no blood relation. Her sisters were married to his brothers. That in itself was a problem. If she didn't handle the fling just right, it could get awkward at future family gatherings. And really, when was the last time she'd had a fling? Olivia liked to talk a good game, but she wasn't into casual sex. Anyway—

She plucked another drink from the tray and took a healthy sip.

"This night is not about me," she said. "It's about our

sister and her happiness." She raised her glass high before she threw the drink back.

"Hear, hear," said Zoe. "I have an idea. Rather than a traditional toast, I think we should each take turns offering sweet Sophie our best words of sisterly advice for a long and happy marriage."

"Olivia, you go first," Zoe said.

Olivia frowned, already feeling the effects of the alcohol. "Marital advice is not exactly my department."

Zoe batted her words away. "Don't be a killjoy, Liv. You know what I mean. Give her your best sisterly advice."

Run! Run for your life. Get out now while you can still save yourself.

She chuckled at the thought. It was what she wanted to say, but even as tipsy as she was, she had enough good sense to know the reaction that comment would inspire in her sisters. Then she really would be the killjoy that Zoe had accused her of being. That wouldn't do. She'd have to dig deep to come up with something.

Of course, Zoe and Rachel and their husbands could be the poster couples for happy marriage. "You two go first. Come back to me."

As Rachel and Zoe spouted pearls of matrimonial wisdom, Olivia searched her soul to find something to offer—*anything*—that didn't sound jaded or bitter. But her head was spinning. Either she was a lightweight or these Fuzzy Handcuffs really did pack an über-potent punch.

That's when she realized three sets of sisterly eyes were focused on her, waiting expectantly.

"Guys, come on." Was she slurring her words? *Nah*, she was just thirsty. Water, she needed water. She looked over and signaled for Mike to come over. He gave her a thumbs-up, which Olivia took to mean he would be there as soon as he was free. He had a couple of customers at the bar, including Alejandro Mendoza. God, he was one sexy Texan—no, wait, he was from Miami. With a vineyard in Texas. So he was sort of an honorary Texy sexan...uhh, a *sexy Texan*. Whatever. He certainly was the best of both worlds: a head for business and a body for sin.

A body she really wouldn't mind taking for a test drive, she thought as she watched him sitting at the bar sipping his beer and doing something on his phone.

"Olivia!" Zoe demanded. "Earth to Olivia. We're waiting for you."

"Come on, Zo. You know I'm the worst person to ask about this. I don't believe in love."

She tried to wave them away, but realized that gesture probably looked as sloppy as she felt right now.

"How can you not believe in love?" Sophie pressed. Her voice went up an octave at the end of the sentence. "Everyone believes in love. I mean, what kind of a world would this be if people didn't believe in love?"

Rachel, who was still holding her first drink, shot Olivia a look. "You might want to slow down a bit, too. You're starting to be a bit of a buzzkill, Liv."

Oh, first she was a killjoy. Now she was a buzzkill?

"You want a buzzkill? I'll give you a buzzkill. I'm happy for the three of you, that you think you've found your soul mates. How fabulous for you. But just because it works for you, doesn't mean love and marriage are for me."

"It's because you're too guarded," Zoe said. "Of course you're not going to find love with that attitude. You have to open your heart before love can find you."

Rachel and Sophie nodded earnestly.

Olivia snorted. "Please tell me you're not going to start singing 'Kumbaya' in three-part harmony."

She rolled her eyes and when she did, she saw Alejandro looking in her direction. She looked away fast.

"I just don't understand why you feel that way," Sophie said in a small voice.

Olivia should've left it alone. She should've just made up something that sounded warm and fuzzy. Grabbed the first thing off the top of her head, something about love being the merging of two souls and blah, blah, blah, and tossed it at her sisters.

But they kept pressing her about *why*.

Why? Why? Why?

"You want to know *why* I don't believe in love? I'll tell you. Love is a crock. Every single guy I've dated has had some ulterior motive for dating me. They've wanted money or wanted a job or thought our father could make them rich by buying the app they've designed. They didn't want me as much as they wanted a piece of Robinson Enterprises."

"Sounds like you've been dating the wrong guys," Rachel said.

It was probably true, but there was something in Rachel's tone that sounded so judgmental. It was the last straw.

"And that's only half of it." Olivia leaned in and set her empty glass on the cocktail table. "The other reason is our parents. Their marriage is a mess. It's a phony sham of a relationship. I don't know why they stay together, because they hate each other. They are slowly but steadily eating each other alive. Anyone with good sense would take a clue from them and realize all relationships are doomed."

"But they're still together," Sophie said.

Olivia shrugged. "Why *are* they still together? They don't love each other. Even if they did, what about the general state of society? Fifty percent of all marriages end in divorce and the other fifty percent—like our parents—make each other so miserable that divorce probably seems like a preferable option. And that's why I can see no reason to yearn for a doomed institution. On that note, why don't we go get something to eat?"

Her sisters sat stock still, silently staring at her. Rachel looked irritated. Zoe looked shell-shocked and Sophie looked like she was about to burst into tears.

Uh-oh. Obviously she'd gone too far.

"Look, you asked." She softened her tone. "That's why I didn't want to get into it."

All three were still frozen in their seats. The only thing that moved was the tears meandering down Sophie's cheeks.

Crap.

"Okay. I'm sorry. I understand that y'all are newlyweds—even you, Rach. So your relationships are still shiny and new—"

Now Sophie was shaking her head.

Sometimes it was as if she was the only one in her family who didn't have their head in the clouds. Maybe being the one with a clear head and common sense was her burden. If so, she could deal with it more easily than she could deal with a broken heart. She was a realist when it came to love—it never lasted. Her parents were living proof. Why should she fool herself into believing it would turn out otherwise for herself? Nope. She would save herself the heartache and focus on her career, which was in her control.

"I'm really sorry," Olivia said. "I didn't mean it the way it came out."

"Yes, you did." Sophie's voice broke and she stood up abruptly. "I'm tired and I want to go to bed."

"No, Soph. Come on. We need to get something to eat. I've made us a reservation at the Driskill Grill. I'm sure they can seat us early. Come on—"

"No." Sophie took off.

Her sister had barely cleared the bar when Zoe said, "I'll go check on her."

"I'll come with you," Olivia offered.

"No," Zoe and Rachel said in unison.

"Stay here," Zoe said.

"Bring her back," Olivia said. "It's Saturday night. It's her bachelorette party. We're supposed to have dinner. And then right after dinner, we're supposed to have fun."

"And clearly not a minute sooner," Rachel said under her breath, but Olivia heard her loud and clear.

"That wasn't very nice," she said.

Rachel shrugged. "Look, Olivia, I know you mean well, but why did you do that?"

"What?"

"Your down-with-marriage campaign was harsh. Even you have to admit it wasn't your best moment."

She covered her eyes with both palms. "I know. I already said I'm sorry. These Fuzzy Handcuffs are stronger than I realized. I think I'm a little drunk."

"Ya think?"

As if right on cue, Mike delivered another round of five Fuzzy Handcuffs.

"Who ordered these?" Olivia asked.

"I thought you wanted another round when you signaled me a few minutes ago."

"No, I need water."

"Oh, sorry," he said. "Well, these are on the house. I'll bring you some water."

Rachel stood.

"Where are you going?" Olivia asked.

"I'm going to go check on Sophie and Zoe."

"I'll go with you."

"No, stay here and drink some water."

"Will you please bring them back so we can go to dinner? I think we're all hungry. That's probably why the drinks hit us so hard."

Rachel sighed. "I'll try. I'll text you and let you know what Sophie is up for. Okay?"

As her sister walked away, Olivia sat down on the love seat. She'd already said too much tonight. The best thing she could do was give her sisters some space.

Fifteen minutes later, Rachel texted:

Sophie's asleep. Zoe is on the phone with Joaquin and frankly, I'm exhausted. I think it would be best if we call it a night and start fresh with the brunch tomorrow morning.

I'm sorry I ruined the night. I feel so bad.

Not your fault. I think the reality of the wedding is finally hitting Sophie. She'll be fine tomorrow.

Olivia wasn't mad; she was frustrated. This wasn't the way tonight was supposed to turn out—her sister in tears and the evening going up in flames.

Okay, maybe she was a little bit irritated. Why had they pushed her? Why had she been so weak as to give in? Sophie'd get over it. They'd be fine, but she needed to stay away until they all cooled off.

Olivia texted her again:

I'll be up after I get something to eat. Want me to bring you something?

Thanks, but no. I'm going to talk to Matteo and then I'll call it a night. Are you okay? Do you just want to come up to the suite and order room service?

It dawned on Olivia that her married sisters missed their husbands. Melancholy pushed at Olivia's heart. As she looked up from her phone, thinking about how to answer, she caught Alejandro Mendoza looking at her. This time she didn't look away.

She had plenty of drinks in front of her and a reservation for dinner for four that was about to become dinner for two. Olivia texted: I'm fine.

And she was about to get a whole lot better.

Alejandro couldn't hear what the Fortune Robinson sisters were talking about on the other side of the bar, but one minute they'd been toasting, raising their Fuzzy Handcuffs high, and the next it looked like they were arguing.

He shouldn't have been watching them. They were out for a girls' night, which appeared innocent enough, but what man in his right mind could've kept his eyes off such a collection of beauties? They were like magnets. He couldn't help but steal glances their way. His brothers were lucky men. Sophie would soon be married. What about Olivia? No doubt he'd meet the fortunate dude who'd claimed her heart at the wedding.

They'd seemed oblivious to him even as one by one they'd gotten up and left the party. First, Sophie left looking upset, followed by Zoe looking concerned. And finally Rachel, looking like a mother hen.

Olivia was the only one who remained. She'd been sitting alone for a solid five minutes staring at the tray of drinks the bartender had delivered shortly before the mass exodus. Maybe her sisters were coming back? Maybe she could use some company until they did. Alejandro stood, slid his phone into his shirt pocket and went over to Olivia.

"Is the party over already?" he asked.

She blinked up at him as if he'd startled her out of deep thought—or deep, stubborn brooding, based on her irritated expression. That full bottom lip of hers stuck out a little more than he remembered from when he saw her at his brothers' weddings.

As she gazed up at him, she pulled it between her teeth for a pensive moment before she spoke.

"May I ask you a question, Alejandro?" She slurred her words ever so slightly.

"Sure."

"Do you believe in love?"

"Is that a trick question?" He laughed and cocked his right brow in a way that always seemed to get him out of tight spots and trick questions like this one.

Answering questions about love qualified as a very tight spot, because the last thing he wanted to do right now was get into a debate about affairs of the heart with a woman who'd had too many Fuzzy Handcuffs. In his experience, drunk women pondering love were usually vulnerable women, especially when their sisters were all married or in the process of getting hitched.

"No, it's not a trick question," Olivia said. "In fact, it's a fairly straightforward yes-or-no query. You either believe in love or you don't. So what's it going to be, Alejandro? Yes or no?"

Wow. Olivia Fortune Robinson was a force. An intense force. And he could see that she wasn't going to let him off the hook without a satisfactory answer. The problem was, he didn't want to talk about love.

He'd been a believer once—but that was a long time ago. Another lifetime ago, when things were a lot simpler. So simple, in fact, that he'd never had to ponder love's existence. He'd just had to feel; he'd simply had to *be*.

He hadn't thought about love for a very long time. It had been even longer since he'd felt any emotion even remotely resembling it. In fact, these days he didn't feel anything. But he definitely didn't want to conjure ghosts from the past, because they haunted him randomly even without an invitation.

"You're not going to answer me, are you?" Olivia said.

He smiled to lighten the mood. "That's some heavy pondering for such a festive occasion. Where did everybody go? And more important, are you going to drink all those Fuzzy Handcuffs all by yourself? Because if your sisters left you to your own devices, what kind of gentleman would I be to let you drink alone?"

She gestured with an unsteady wave of her hand.

"Don't worry about me. I'm used to drinking alone." She grimaced. "And even though I might be a little tipsy, I'm not so drunk that I don't realize how pathetic that just sounded. Please, sit down and save me from myself."

"If you insist," he said and lowered himself onto the cowhide-patterned love seat that was set perpendicular to her chair. As he made himself comfortable, she shifted her body so that she was angled in his direction and crossed one long, lean, tanned leg over the other.

Damn.

If he'd been a weaker man he might have reached out and run a hand up the tempting expanse, past where skin disappeared under that sexy little black slip of a thing that was riding a little too high on her toned thighs—not in a trashy way, because there wasn't a trashy thing about her. Olivia Fortune Robinson seemed to have mastered the art of classy-sexy, which was a very beautiful fine line to walk.

And he was also treading a very fine line, because Olivia Fortune Robinson was so very off-limits, since she was practically family.

He lifted a drink off the tray and handed it to her, then he took one for himself and raised it to hers. She looked him square in the eyes as they clinked glasses.

"You know, they say you'll have seven years of bad sex if you don't look the person you're toasting in the eyes as you say cheers," she said.

"I guess that means we'll have good sex," he said, still holding her gaze.

"Will we?" She sipped her drink.

He knew she was baiting him and he also knew she was probably drunker than she realized. The drinks were more powerful than they looked. The kind that went down easily and, before you knew it, knocked you flat on your ass. Probably not so dissimilar from the effect that Olivia Fortune Robinson had on men.

"Are you hungry?" Olivia asked.

"For food? Or did you have something else in mind?"

She tilted her head to the side. "You're a naughty boy, aren't you, Alejandro?"

Her words were unwavering and unabashed.

He shrugged.

"I made a dinner reservation for four at the Driskill Grill," she said. "It seems my sisters can't make it. The only thing worse than drinking alone is dining alone in a fancy restaurant. What do you say, Alejandro? Will you let me take you to dinner?"

"That depends on what you expect in return," he said. "Are you going to feed me and then try to take advantage of me?"

"Absolutely."

This was fun. Much more fun than poring over facts and figures of the Hummingbird Ridge purchase.

When he was fresh out of college, would he have found bantering with a clever woman preferable to dotting the *i*'s and crossing the *t*'s on the details that would make his hard-won business dream a reality? Then again, he hadn't eaten and he was starving.

"In that case," he said, "how can I refuse?"

He knocked back the last of his drink. It was a lot stronger that it appeared.

"Good," Olivia said, handing him another drink from the tray. "The reservation isn't until eight o'clock. We have time to finish our cocktails."

They clinked glasses, locking gazes again before they sipped and settled into an uncomfortable silence. Alejandro was way too aware of how damn sexy she looked in that black dress, too intent on that full mouth that kept commanding his attention, speaking to the most primal needs in him.

He didn't do well with silence.

"Is this your favorite kind of drink?" he asked.

"Me? No. I'm all about champagne. This drink was made especially for the brides-to-be."

"I don't mean to be nosy, but is everything okay with your sisters?"

She shrugged. "I'm sure they're fine. That reminds me. You didn't answer my question. Do you believe in love? I'm guessing you do. Because what else would possess you to tattoo a woman's name on your arm? Who is Anna?"

Reflexively, his right hand found his left forearm, covered the ornate script.

"Anna was someone who made me know that love is very real. But I also learned that love can be a total SOB, too."

Olivia leaned in. "You said 'was.' So I'm guessing that Anna is no longer in the picture?"

The curtain of dread that always closed around him when he remembered Anna started falling. "No, she is no longer in the picture."

That's all he was going to say. He was opening his mouth to change the subject when Olivia got up from her chair and sat down next to him on the love seat.

"That's what I was hoping you'd say," she slurred. "People accuse me of a lot of things, but no one can ever say I go after another woman's man. You don't have a girlfriend who isn't named Anna, do you, Alejandro?"

He shook his head. His gaze fell to her lips. She was sitting enticingly close to him. Suddenly, the room temperature seemed to spike.

"Good," she slurred again as she slid her arms around his neck. "Because I'm going to kiss you. You don't mind if I kiss you, do you, Alejandro?"

Before the words *hell no* could pass his lips, her lips closed over his and smothered the reply.

At first, the kiss was surprisingly gentle, tentative. She tasted like the cocktails they'd been drinking and fresh summer berries and something else he hadn't realized he'd been craving for a very long time. When she opened her mouth wider, inviting him in, passion took over and the gentle kiss morphed into wild, ravenous need, feeding a hunger that he didn't realize was consuming him. He reveled in it, wallowed in it, until it blocked out everything else.

She moved against him, sliding her hands over his shoulders and down his back.

A rush of hot need surged through him. His hands followed the outline of her curves until he cupped her bottom and pulled her closer. Damn. She felt good. Keeping one hand on her, he found the hem of her dress with his other and dipped his fingertips beneath the silky barrier that stood between them.

When she moaned into their kiss, he wanted to pull her onto his lap.

But she was drunk and they were in the bar of the hotel where her sister was getting married next weekend. He had enough of his wits about him to know that if she wasn't in the shackles of too many Fuzzy Handcuffs, she probably wouldn't be doing this. She'd probably be mortified tomorrow.

"Alejandro, take me to your room." Her words were hot on his neck and his body was saying *Let's go. Now.*

But he couldn't. And not for lack of want or interest. It just wasn't right. Not when she was like this.

He stood up and gently tugged her to her feet.

"What's your room number?"

Chapter 2

"Olivia, wake up."

The soft voice bounced around her dreams, beckoning her to open her eyes. Maybe if she ignored it, it would go away and she could go back to the dream of kissing Alejandro… His hands in her hair, pulling her mouth to his; him slowly but firmly guiding her in a backward walk, until he'd pinned her against the wall… His fingers lacing through hers, then pushing their joined hands out and up over her head so she could feel the length of his body pressed into hers.

It was glorious and she wanted more of him, all of him.

"Olivia. I'm not kidding. Wake up. It's an emergency." Why was Rachel's voice in her dream? She was intruding again. Only this time she was being more insistent and it seemed like she wasn't going away. Olivia tried to force her eyes open…to no avail.

"Olivia." Something was shaking her body in a way that didn't mesh with Alejandro's tender caresses. She managed to force one eye open. She saw Rachel's and Zoe's anxious faces staring down at her as searing pain shot through her head.

She felt as if someone had clocked her.

As she pressed the palms of her hands over her eyes, everything came back to her. She'd been clubbed by one too many Fuzzy Handcuffs. Okay, maybe a few too many. And then there was Alejandro. She'd all but had him for dinner. Kissing him hadn't been simply a dream. It had been very real—

Oh, no.

"Olivia, wake up!" It was Rachel shaking her. "We have a situation."

At the sound of her sister's no-nonsense tone, Olivia removed her palms from her eyes and forced her eyes open. For the love of God, her head was about to split wide open.

"It's Sophie," Zoe said. "She's missing. We can't find her anywhere."

It took a moment for Olivia to piece together last night's events: the drinks, her spilling the beans to her sisters about how she felt about their parents' relationship—or lack thereof—Sophie getting upset and running off.

"What do you mean she's missing?" Olivia asked. "Maybe she went out for coffee?"

Every word was a nail in her brain. Her mouth was so dry her lips stuck to her gums like they'd been pasted together. She needed water. It probably wouldn't be a good idea to ask them if they could go look for Sophie and bring her back a bottle of ice-cold water.

"Do you think she's in danger?" Olivia asked.

Rachel and Zoe looked at each other.

"No," Rachel said. "Otherwise we would've called the police."

"All of her stuff is gone," Zoe said. "She must have packed up and taken it with her. And I must've been sleeping deeply because I didn't even hear her moving around."

Zoe and Sophie had shared one room in the two-bedroom suite. Olivia and Rachel had shared the other one.

"Personally, I think she's freaked out over what you said last night and has cold feet," Zoe said. "You know, prewedding jitters. I get it. I totally understand. It happened to me. That's why we need to find her and let her know the way she's feeling is perfectly normal and everything will be all right."

"Have you talked to Mason?" Olivia's voice was scratchy. "I'll bet she's with him."

Again, Rachel and Zoe exchanged a look.

"He just called. In fact, his call woke Zoe up," Rachel said. "He was looking for Sophie."

"Did you tell him she's at her bachelorette party and that means no boys? He can live without her for a weekend."

Zoe sighed. "Normally, I would've told him that, but he said she'd left him a distraught message last night after he'd gone to bed. Apparently she said she needed to talk to him as soon as possible and he should call no matter the hour. Now she's not picking up, and she hasn't returned any of his calls or mine. We're worried about her, Liv."

Olivia regarded her sisters, who were still in their

pajamas. "I'm guessing you haven't gone out to see if she's down in the café? She might've just gone out for some breakfast or some fresh air."

Olivia could have used both right about now.

She forced herself into a sitting position, trying to ignore the daggers that stabbed at her brain and filled it with a soup-like fog that refused to let her think straight.

As if reading her mind, Rachel produced a bottle of cold water and a wet washcloth.

"You look like hell," she said. "You're positively green. Drink this and wipe your face with this cool cloth."

Olivia did as she was told. Only then did she realize she was still fully dressed in the outfit she'd worn last night. At least she was dressed. She might have smirked at the thought, if the reaction wouldn't have hurt so badly. Of course she was dressed. She'd only kissed Alejandro. She hadn't slept with him. The memory of him walking her up to the suite and the two of them indulging in a delicious good-night kiss right outside the door flooded back. Her sisters didn't need to know about that. Besides, they had more important things to worry about with Sophie going AWOL.

"What time did you get in last night?" Zoe asked.

Olivia took a long drink from the water bottle. When she was finished, she said, "I don't know. Late. You all jumped ship and left me with a tray full of drinks to polish off. It took a while."

Zoe frowned. "I'm sorry we left. We were concerned about Sophie after your little down-with-love tirade."

Tirade?

It hadn't exactly been a tirade. It'd been honesty.

"Yeah, well, I wish you wouldn't have kept pushing

me to offer love and marriage advice. I felt like you backed me into a corner."

The sisters sat in silence for a moment.

"Of course, the drinks didn't help matters," Olivia said. "They sort of greased the hinges on propriety's trapdoor and once the words started spilling out, there was no stopping them. I feel bad that Sophie was so upset. It wasn't what I intended."

The washcloth had warmed up. Olivia held it by the corners and waved it back and forth to cool it off before pressing it pressed to her eyes again.

Visions of kissing Alejandro played out on the screen in her mind's eye. She was so glad her sisters hadn't pressed her about whether or not she'd polished off the remaining drinks alone. The thought of those Fuzzy Handcuffs made her stomach churn, and the thought of trying to explain what happened with Alejandro tied it up in knots.

Olivia looked at her sisters. "Was Sophie here when you went to sleep?"

"She was," said Zoe.

"In fact, I thought she was out like a light when I finally turned in. I tried to talk to her before she went to bed, but she said she was fine and just wanted to go to sleep. So I went in and took a shower and then I was on the phone with Joaquin for a while. When I came out of the bathroom, she was snuggled down under the covers. I thought she was just missing Mason."

"Me, too," said Rachel. "But that's why we're concerned that he can't get in touch with her. Where do you think she would go?"

"So obviously you two haven't even been out of the room," Olivia said.

"No, not yet," Zoe said. "We hated to wake you since you obviously played a little hard last night." She gestured to Olivia's outfit.

"Not really. It's not as if I did the walk of shame this morning."

But she had kissed Alejandro. The thought made her already knotted, churning stomach clench a little bit more. She put her hand on her belly to quell it.

It would've been easy to give in to lust and do a lot more than kiss Alejandro last night, but she hadn't. Actually, she'd tried, but he'd been the gentleman.

Even so, the essence of him clung to her. Like he had gotten into her pores. If she shut her eyes, there was Alejandro invading her thoughts the same way he had invaded her dreams. Her fingers found their way to her lips as she remembered every delicious detail about their kisses.

Olivia had a lot of faults, but getting blackout drunk wasn't one of them. No matter how much she had to drink, she was always in control of herself. Sometimes it made her a little looser. She paused. Maybe *looser* wasn't the best word in this particular situation. The Fuzzy Handcuffs had unshackled her inhibitions. That was a more apt description. The drinks had simply allowed her to experience a pleasure in which she might not have otherwise allowed herself to indulge. Yes. That was what'd happened.

She was more than willing to own her actions.

And in owning them, she had enough good sense to know kissing Alejandro last night was as far as things would go. She'd gotten him out of her system and it wouldn't happen again. Of course not. She would be far too busy focusing on her bridesmaid's duties this wedding week.

As fractured as the night had been with her sisters, it was still a girls' weekend. Never mind how gorgeous Alejandro Mendoza was. She'd resisted him. She hadn't bailed on her sisters to spend the night with him.

Even if her sisters had bailed on her.

With great care, Olivia swung her legs over the side of the bed. She put her feet flat on the floor, hoping that the effort would ground her and help her regain her sense of equilibrium. Instead, the room spun. She hated being hungover, but she'd done this to herself. She had no choice but to power through. Do the crime, do the time.

"You do look like hell," Zoe said.

"I'm fine," Olivia answered, pushing to her feet.

"I'm going to get dressed and head downstairs to look for her," Rachel said. "Will you help me look, Liv? I think Zoe should wait in the room in case she returns."

She considered asking, *What if she doesn't want to be found right now? What if she just needs a little time? I'm the one who has a pounding headache. Why can't I wait in the room?* But she knew this was their way of nudging her to make amends with Sophie. To go look for her and find her so the two of them could talk this out and make up.

Of course, that's what she intended to do. She took a deep breath and tried to shake off the irritation that prickled her. How had this suddenly become her fault?

Olivia knew her sisters meant well. This was simply their sister dynamics in play: Zoe was the hopeful one; Rachel was the strong one; Sophie was the baby;

Olivia was the one who fixed problems and rallied everyone to take action.

Often, Rachel and Zoe formulated a plan and Olivia made sure it got done.

Olivia cleared her throat and shook off the cobwebs from last night the best she could. It gave her a little more clarity. She made a mental note to have someone kick her if she ever felt compelled to finish off a tray of drinks. Though it would surely be a while before she imbibed again.

Her sisters were chattering at her. As their words bounced off her ears, she pulled jeans, a black blouse and fresh undergarments out of her suitcase and disappeared into the bathroom.

"I have to take a shower before I do anything," she said.

"We can go down to the lobby together," Rachel said. "I'll talk to the bellhops and ask if she called for a cab or if they remember her taking an Uber. Since we all rode here together, we know she didn't drive away and I doubt she walked. We can split up and have a look around the hotel."

Minutes later, after they'd dressed, Olivia grabbed her cell phone and room key and said to Zoe, "Let us know if you hear from her and we'll do the same."

When they got down to the lobby, Olivia looked around as if she might see Sophie standing there waiting for her. She wasn't there, of course. Next, they pulled up a picture of Sophie that Olivia had taken last night with her cell phone and asked the attendants at the porte cochere if they'd called a cab for her or seen her this morning. They hadn't. Next they decided to split up and each search a different half of the hotel.

Had Sophie really taken her words to heart? Regret churned in Olivia's stomach, adding to last night's bile, making her feel sick again. Only this time it had less to do with the Fuzzy Handcuffs and more to do with her big unfiltered mouth and how it had shoved her sister down this spiral of doubt on the eve of wedding-week festivities.

She had to fix this. She would fix this.

She decided to check the café first since it seemed a likely place to find Sophie.

Olivia pulled open the beveled glass doors of the 1886 Café & Bakery and stepped inside. The place was buzzing with families and couples and individuals sitting at the dark wooden tables and booths enjoying Sunday breakfast. She scanned the room with its white honeycomb tile floor and kelly green accent wall that separated the open kitchen from the dining room, and the flagstone archways that partitioned the dining room into smaller, more intimate sections. She fully expected to see Sophie sitting at one of the tables, noshing on a warm chocolate croissant and a café latte.

The place was crowded so Olivia had to walk around. As she did, she breathed in delicious breakfast aromas. Maybe, she thought, a good breakfast would be the cure for her hangover. Or at least the start. But first—Sophie. She would locate her sister—it couldn't be that difficult, even though she clearly wasn't in the café—and then she would treat herself to something delicious. In fact, it would be a good idea to treat Sophie to breakfast too, so they could talk things out and settle this once and for all.

Speaking of delicious…

As if she'd conjured him, there sat Alejandro Mendoza, at a small table tucked into a corner of the restaurant. He was enjoying a hearty omelet that looked like it could feed three people. As if he sensed her watching him, he looked up from the piece of the Sunday *New York Times* that he had folded neatly into quarters, allowing him to read while he dined. He snared her with his gaze before she could turn away and pretend she hadn't seen him.

That sexy, lopsided smile of his that crinkled his coffee-colored eyes at the corners made her breath catch. Visions of kissing him last night—of how perfectly their mouths and bodies had fit together—flooded back, swamping her senses and throwing off her equilibrium.

Get it together, girl.

"Good morning," she said, trying her best to appear nonchalant, to act as if it hadn't taken every fiber of her willpower to go to bed alone last night rather than give in to the chemistry that pulsed between them. She could still feel his kisses on her lips. Her mouth went dry at the thought and she bit her bottom lip to make the memory go away. As if.

He looked her up and down and smiled as if he approved of what he saw. She was acutely aware of the fact that her face was scrubbed fresh and makeup free. She'd pulled her long dark wet hair into a simple ponytail. She felt exposed and vulnerable, but he didn't seem to be turned off by her appearance. Not that it mattered. In fact, maybe it would be better if he was turned off because she would want nothing to do with someone that shallow. Still, she sensed that Alejandro Mendoza might be something of a player.

Maybe he was playing her right now.

"Good morning," he said as he stood. "You're up early."

"So are you," she returned.

He laughed, a deep sound that resonated in her soul and wove its way through her insides.

"Please sit down and enjoy your breakfast," Olivia said. "I don't want it to get cold."

He waved her off and remained standing.

"I have to drive over to Hummingbird Ridge for a business meeting later this morning," he said. "I wanted to grab a bite before I go. Join me. You know what they say about breakfast. It's the most important meal of the day."

The thought of having breakfast with Alejandro conjured all kinds of other possibilities—of what might have happened after the kiss and before the eggs and bacon if she hadn't said good-night—but Olivia blinked away the naughty thoughts.

"Thanks, but I'm looking for Sophie. You haven't seen her, have you?"

He looked confused. "Not since last night before she left the bar."

"So she hasn't been here this morning?"

"Nope. Please join me until she comes." He pulled out the other chair at the table for two.

Needing an ear, she sat down and he helped her scoot in her seat, and he motioned for the server to bring another cup of coffee.

She appreciated his gentlemanly way. Of course, she was perfectly capable of scooting in her own chair, but she had to admit the gesture was nice. It said a lot about him. She thought that chivalry had become a dying art these days. It was nice to meet someone with such good manners.

She bit her bottom lip again as she weighed how much to tell him. He already knew that Sophie had left last night's party upset and that Olivia's blunt words about love had offended her. They'd kissed and shared that secret. She might as well share this, too.

"I can trust you, right?"

He leaned in and studied her, as if he was trying to figure out what she meant, but he nodded. "Of course."

The server delivered a cup of coffee. After adding cream, she took a sip and felt some of the fog lift from her brain. She leaned in and rested her chin on her left hand, toying with the handle of the mug with her right.

"When my sisters and I woke up this morning, Sophie was gone."

"Gone? As in...?"

"Gone. As in packed up her things and left."

"She's not in any danger, is she?"

"We don't think so. Well, not physical danger, anyway. Maybe in danger of calling off the wedding because of my unfiltered tirade on love. I need to find her and fix this."

Alejandro looked concerned. "Have you called her fiancé?"

"He called us, saying he couldn't get in touch with her. That she'd called him last night while he was sleeping and left a couple of messages, and when he tried to call her this morning he couldn't reach her. She wasn't picking up. I've looked all over the hotel and she's not here. The best I can figure is that she called an Uber and left."

"Where would she go?"

Olivia thought for a moment, changing gears from likely hiding places in the hotel to where Sophie might go outside of the place. She had an idea.

"We know she's not at Mason's. He said he'd call if he heard from her. I can think of a couple of places I'd look to start. She probably went home to her condo."

She shook her head. "I'm going to have a lot of explaining to do when I find her."

"Don't jump to conclusions," Alejandro said. "Maybe it's not as bad as you think."

Olivia shrugged. "My sisters and I think that last night sent her spiraling into a case of prewedding jitters. You know, cold feet."

Alejandro opened his mouth as if to say something, but sighed instead.

"What?" Olivia asked.

"Nothing."

"No, it's something. Tell me, please."

"If she's so easily spooked, maybe she knows something we don't."

"Such as?"

"Maybe she's questioning whether she should get married or not. If so, that's not your fault. In fact, maybe you did her a favor. Maybe what you said made her think. If she's having second thoughts, isn't it better to call off the wedding than to get a divorce?"

"We can't call off the wedding, because it's Dana and Kieran's wedding, too. And if Sophie opts out, it will certainly put a damper on their day."

"So you're saying truth be damned? She should just suck it up for propriety's sake? Because if so, maybe you're not as antiestablishment as you think you are."

She squinted at him. "That is *not* what I'm saying. This has nothing to do with me and everything to do with my sister's happiness."

"But you're making it sound like this is all about you.

You must think you have some kind of power over her if you think your feelings about love and marriage can change her mind."

"I'm not saying I changed her mind. I'm saying I've spoiled the mood, cast a black cloud and now she's got cold feet."

Cocking a brow that seemed to say he wasn't convinced, Alejandro sat back and crossed his arms. He looked at her as if the judge and jury resided inside his head and they'd already come to a verdict on the matter. "You're saying all you have to do is talk to her and you can change her mind."

It wasn't a question. It was a statement, and Olivia didn't like the implications. She stood.

"Look, you don't know me or my sister. I don't know why it seemed like a good idea to burden you with the details. So please forget everything I told you. Sophie will be fine. The wedding will be fine. Good luck with your meeting."

As she turned to walk away, something made her turn back. He watched her as she returned to the table. "I hope it goes without saying, but please don't mention this to anyone. Okay?"

"Of course. And I won't mention the kiss, either."

He had the audacity to wink at her. All cheeky and smug-like. That's what he was—cheeky and smug. And a player who took advantage of drunk women.

Okay, so maybe the kiss wasn't so bad.

Olivia flinched and waved him off. Her stomach remained in knots even as she made her way into the majestic Driskill's lobby, away from Alejandro Mendoza. The guy was a piece of work. A smug, cheeky piece of work who called it as he saw it no matter how awkward it rendered the situation. In fact, he seemed to get some kind of pleasure out of making her uncomfortable.

She'd do her best to steer clear of him for the duration of the wedding.

She hated the disappointment that swirled inside her. Because she wanted another taste of Alejandro's lips— she wanted more than just another taste of his lips, if she was honest. But she also knew that the only thing she should be focusing on this week was making sure she got Sophie to the wedding and down the aisle. The conflict tugged at the outer reaches of her subconscious, and she shoved it out of her mind.

She stared up at the gorgeous stained-glass ceiling, taking a deep breath and trying to ground herself. She took her cell phone out of her pocket and checked the time. It was almost eight thirty. There were no calls from her sisters. Dana and Monica were supposed to join them for brunch at eleven, which gave Olivia two and a half hours to find Sophie and make amends.

She called Sophie's cell again. After one ring, the call went directly to voice mail.

She did not leave a message. Instead, she texted her.

Where are you, Sophie? We're worried about you. I understand why you're upset and I'm sorry. I really am, but please let us know where you are...that you're safe.

Fully expecting the message to sit unanswered, Olivia shoved her phone into the back pocket of her jeans and made her way toward the elevators. As she waited for the doors to open in the lobby, her cell phone dinged.

Olivia's heart leaped when she saw that Sophie had replied.

I'm safe.

With shaking hands, Olivia typed:

Where are you?

She stared at her phone as if she could will her sister to answer. But by the time the elevator arrived, Sophie still hadn't replied.

Olivia tried to pacify herself with the thought that maybe there was no cell service in the elevator hallway. She walked back into the lobby and typed another message.

Thank you for letting us know you're okay. Will you please meet me for a cup of coffee before the brunch so we can talk about this?

There's no need. I'm going to pass on brunch. Please give my regrets to Dana.

She was going to pass on brunch?

What am I supposed to say to Dana?

Tell the truth. Tell her I'm not getting married.

I'm going to call you. Please pick up.

There's nothing to talk about.

Are you kidding me? I worked my butt off to give you and Dana a nice weekend. You can't just opt out without so much as a phone conversation. I don't care if you thought I was a little harsh last night. Sophie, you need to grow up. Your deciding not to get married affects others besides yourself.

Seconds after she sent the message her phone rang. It was Sophie.

"Hi," Olivia said. "Thank you for calling me."

"Say what you need to say." Sophie sounded like she was crying and Olivia's heart broke a little more.

"Sophie, please, you can't take to heart what I said last night." She moved out of the lobby and into the bar area where they were last night, looking for a quiet corner where she could talk to her sister privately. "Please don't let my cynical drunken words cause you to make the worst mistake of your life."

"Those weren't just liquor-inspired words, Liv. It's the truth. Every single word of what you said is true. Are you trying to tell me it's not?"

It was true. Her parents had a terrible marriage. If you could even call it a marriage. They led separate lives because they couldn't stand each other.

"I thought so," Sophie said on a sob when Olivia didn't reply. "Look, I need some time to figure out what I'm going to do. I appreciate all the time and hard work you put into the bachelorette party, but I need some space right now. I hope you understand."

"What do you want me to tell Dana?"

Sophie was inconsolable. It killed Olivia to hear her sister in so much pain. Especially since she was the one who'd caused it.

"Tell her whatever you want, Liv. I have to go."

"No, Sophie. Please tell me where you are—"

But it was too late. Her sister had already disconnected the call.

Olivia stood there trying to get her bearings, trying to figure out how to fix this mess—and quickly. It was best not to push Sophie about the brunch. Olivia kicked herself for scheduling the bachelorette party the weekend before the wedding. She should've done this last month. Sophie wasn't a partier and she was probably exhausted and overwhelmed by all the hoopla leading up to her wedding day. The best thing Olivia could do right now was to show her sister some compassion, give her the space she so clearly needed.

They'd simply tell Dana and Monica that Sophie was under the weather. Given the Fuzzy Handcuffs, that wouldn't be such a stretch.

As Olivia made her way upstairs to tell Zoe and Rachel that she'd talked to Sophie, she saw Mason at the front desk.

She called out to him and steeled herself for a frantic response from the bridegroom, but Mason smiled at her, appearing remarkably calm.

"Hey, Liv. What's the latest?"

Good old Mason, the calm to Sophie's occasional dramatic storm. She said a silent prayer that they would be able to weather this Category Five. How, exactly, did one explain that his fiancée was possibly backing out of the wedding? Then, in a moment of clarity, Olivia realized that even if her careless words had set off Sophie, it was Sophie's responsibility to tell Mason she wanted to call things off, not hers.

Olivia put on her bravest face. "I just got off the phone with Sophie. Have you spoken to her?"

"Not yet." Mason pulled out his cell phone. "I'll text her and tell her I'm talking to you."

Olivia waited and watched as Mason sent a message. Sophie responded immediately but it was a good two minutes before Mason finally looked up and said, "What we have here is a good old-fashioned case of cold feet. She'll be fine. Just give her a little bit of time."

Mason's calm was rubbing off on Olivia. Still, she made sure she had her filter firmly in place before she spoke. She had learned her lesson after last night. The less said the better.

"I figure until she feels better, we can simply tell people she's got a bug," Mason said, looking so confident. "That's all they need to know."

"Sure," Olivia echoed. "That's all they need to know."

In the meantime, Olivia silently vowed, she would fix this mess.

She uttered a silent prayer that she could pull it off.

Chapter 3

On Monday evening, Alejandro handed the rental car keys to the valet parking attendant outside the Robinson estate and accepted his claim check. He'd been to functions at the sprawling estate when his brothers, Matteo and Joaquin, had married Rachel and Zoe, but the magnitude of its grandeur still rendered him awestruck.

The place made a statement about who Gerald Robinson was and what he stood for: a man who had started with nothing and built himself an empire with his brainchild, Robinson Computers. The man was brilliant. Alejandro might have found him intimidating if he hadn't been so intriguing. As an entrepreneur himself, Alejandro devoured biographies of successful businesspeople. Seeing how someone else created an empire was better than any business course he could take.

He would've been lying if he'd denied wanting all of this for himself. He wanted it so badly he could taste it.

Someday, he thought, as his shoes hit the pavers of the cobblestone path that was lined with tiki torches and directed people to the back of this castle of a house.

"Aloha. Good evening." Two attractive women dressed in loose-fitting Hawaiian-print dresses greeted Alejandro with warm smiles. Both had tucked a white flower into their long, dark hair. The print of their matching dresses reminded him of a shirt he used to wear back in his college days—only it looked much classier on them.

"Welcome to the wedding luau," the one holding a lei said.

She stepped forward and placed it around his neck and her dark hair glistened in the golden tiki-torch light, reminding him of Olivia and the unfortunate way they'd parted. He regretted grilling her the way he had yesterday morning. As soon as she'd walked away, he'd been planning his apology. He'd been out of line debating her sister's obviously fragile state. He knew it, he owned it and he would apologize for it. He didn't want anything to detract from the wedding festivities—certainly not bad blood or resentment stemming from yesterday's disagreement. Or Saturday night's kiss, either.

All day, the two events had played tug-of-war in his mind. He'd had to hyperfocus during his business meeting at Hummingbird Ridge. It was a rare occasion when he allowed anything to distract him from business. But he hadn't exactly invited Olivia into his brain. She'd barged in unbidden, as strong a presence when she wasn't in the room as when they were standing face-to-face.

As soon as the woman who had presented him with the lei stepped away, her cohort stepped forward and offered him a drink served in a hollowed-out pineapple. The beverage was adorned with exotic flowers, a blue plastic straw and a tiny umbrella.

He took a sip. The rum and tropical fruit juices combined for a delicious drink. The Fortune Robinsons seemed to have cornered the market on signature cocktails. He certainly wasn't complaining since he was on the receiving end of all this libation creativity.

But since signature cocktails and Olivia Fortune Robinson had proven to be a rather explosive combination, he decided he needed to exercise the utmost caution tonight. Then again, given Olivia's demeanor the last time he saw her, he probably didn't have to worry.

The woman who had handed him the drink gestured to her right. "Please follow the torch-lined path around to the tent on the rear lawn and enjoy the festivities."

"Thank you," he said, raising his pineapple in an appreciative toast.

He followed the path and the sound of music. As he rounded the corner and the tent came into view, he took a deep breath and inhaled the sweet scent of gardenias mingling with delicious, smoky BBQ and firewood burning in outdoor fireplaces. A crowd of people mingled on the manicured lawn as a country band played on a stage in front of a parquet dance floor that had been laid out on the grounds.

Alejandro's gaze scanned the crowd for familiar faces. His stomach growled and he realized he hadn't eaten since breakfast. The meeting with the fine folks of Hummingbird Ridge had lasted through the lunch hour. He'd taken some time to drive around the area to get a feel for the town, which was located about a half hour west of Austin. Once he'd returned to the hotel, he'd been tied up on calls with investors, bankers and his partners—his cousins Stefan and Rodrigo Mendoza. Before he knew it, he'd had just enough time to shower, shave and get dressed for tonight.

Skipping lunch was a small price to pay because today he had taken another step toward creating his own empire. The trip out to Hummingbird Ridge had proven that the winery and its acres of thriving vineyards were, indeed, a good investment. The Texas Hill Country was one of the country's upcoming wine destinations.

Alejandro's interest in the wine business had started as a fluke. When he was in college at the University of Florida, he used to come home for the summer. Between his freshman and sophomore years, he'd taken a summer job at a South Beach wine bar to save money for tuition. What he'd thought would be a fleeting means to an end had sparked a passion in him, triggering him to change his major to agricultural operations and eventually get a master's degree in viticulture and enology. Not only had he learned the complexities and distinctions the different grape varietals lent to the bottled end product, he'd become educated on theories such as *terroir*—how the climate and land of an area worked together to make wines unique. He had spent a summer in France interning at a vineyard and another summer at a winery in the Napa Valley. Winemaking fascinated him, but he'd known if he wanted to make enough money to one day buy his own vineyard, he needed to be in sales. After scrimping and saving and working his ass off for a decade, his dream was close to becoming a reality. In fact, it was so close he could almost taste the wine.

Alejandro accepted a bacon-wrapped scallop off an hors d'oeuvre platter passed by a server dressed in Polynesian garb. As he bit into it, he continued to scan the crowd for familiar faces. Hundreds of friends and relatives had started to trickle in for the week of prewedding festivities outlined in the itinerary he'd received when he'd checked in at the Driskill. The information packet had included a schedule of events with dates and times for romantic couples' massages, rounds of golf and dinners. If nothing else, they would be entertained and well fed while they were here.

He hadn't forgotten his promise to check into the logistics of an informal wine tasting at Hummingbird Ridge. Even if the wedding party couldn't fit it into their schedule, which was pretty packed, it would be a great opportunity to spend some time with his father, his brothers and their wives. The Mendozas were a close-knit bunch and he didn't get a chance to see his siblings much now that they were married. His three brothers, Cisco, Matteo, Joaquin, their sister, Gabriella, and their dad, Orlando, had traded in Miami and moved to Texas. If everything panned out with the winery, Alejandro might be following suit, or at the very least visiting more often.

Before Alejandro could locate his family—his brothers and father were there, but his sister, Gabi, and her husband, Jude Fortune Jones, would arrive Saturday morning for the wedding—Kieran Fortune Robinson and Dana joined the band onstage. Kieran accepted the microphone from the guitar player.

"Good evening, everyone," Kieran said. "On behalf of my beautiful fiancée, Dana, my little sister Sophie and her fiancé, Mason, I'd like to welcome you to the start of our wedding week celebration. We are so glad you could join us as we count down the days leading up to the big event. Unfortunately, Sophie is a little under the weather tonight. She stayed home to rest up so that she'll be back to one hundred percent for Saturday."

Alejandro flinched as he recalled Olivia's frantic search for Sophie yesterday morning. Olivia had been so certain that her sister would be fine that Alejandro hadn't even considered the possibility that Sophie might not be here this evening. Was she still having second thoughts about the wedding?

Obviously Kieran and Dana's nuptials were still on. Alejandro watched the couple kiss when the crowd interrupted Kieran's welcoming remarks with chants of "Kiss her! Kiss her! Kiss her!" Kieran grabbed Dana and rocked her back as he planted a smooch on her lips.

The spectacle reminded him of kissing Olivia Saturday night at the Driskill Hotel. He immediately shook away the image, because thoughts like that could only lead to trouble.

Instead, he trained his focus on Kieran and Dana, who looked so happy together. Alejandro understood how they felt; he'd been there before, a long time ago. Were they so caught up in their own happiness they didn't know that Sophie was having second thoughts? Then again, for all he knew, maybe Olivia had found her sister and everything was just fine. Maybe she really was under the weather and the illness was what had driven her away from the Driskill Sunday morning.

Obviously he needed to find a friend here at the party if he'd been reduced to standing here alone pondering situations that had nothing to do with him.

"Please, help yourself to some barbecue and the open bar," Kieran said once he and Dana had come up for air. "In fact, if everyone could grab a drink, I would like to make a toast."

* * *

Olivia had groaned when Kieran had dipped Dana back in that shameless public display of affection. She'd groaned and then she'd been ashamed of herself. She'd wished she could take back the ugly sound as she'd glanced around to see if anyone had heard her.

They hadn't.

Of course not. Everyone was too busy *oohing* and *ahhing* over the blithe display of love. Good grief. Her brother had no shame.

As inappropriate as the groan had been, what she'd really wanted to do was shout *Get a room!* She'd been tempted, but she'd never actually do it. The groan had been the slightly less inappropriate compromise. Her attempt at good party manners.

Right.

She wanted to be happy for Kieran and Dana—and she was. Really, she was. But she was so wrecked over Sophie not being here tonight that her guilt was pretty much all-consuming.

She wished she could borrow some confidence from Mason. He loved Sophie so much and he was determined to stand by her while she figured out her heart.

Mason was willing to fight for Sophie's love—even if that fight entailed him attending the barbecue solo and keeping up the cover that Sophie was home sick with the flu and would be good as new by Saturday. His resolute love made Olivia do a mental double take. No one had ever been willing to fight for her like that. Every person she'd ever allowed herself to feel anything substantial for had walked away when the going had gotten tough. Most of the men who had hurt her— two of them in particular—had been more interested in cozying up to her father, who they'd believed could help them get ahead. When that didn't pan out, they'd left. No one had ever fought for her or believed in her the way Mason believed in Sophie. Sophie and Mason had something special and while it didn't alter Olivia's own thoughts on love, she was willing to concede that her little sister might have actually lassoed the unicorn.

Men like Mason were rare, almost mythical, and Olivia wasn't about to let Sophie make the biggest mistake of her life by letting Mason get away.

Even so, with Sophie refusing to attend the party tonight, Olivia was enough of a realist to know that nothing short of a miracle was going to change her sister's mind. Nothing less than Olivia being struck by lightning…or cupid's arrow. But that wasn't going to happen. She needed to come up with another plan.

Olivia racked her brain, but she kept coming back to one thing. Cupid's arrow. She had a feeling that the only way she was going to make amends with Sophie was by convincing her that she believed in love, that somehow, overnight, she'd had a total change of heart. It was crazy, but it might work. What did she have to lose? Olivia had to take action or otherwise risk earning the title of Prewedding Homewrecker—and carrying around the guilt from being responsible for ruining Sophie's life.

But how in the world could she pull it off? How could she make her sister believe she thought true love was possible?

Olivia was in full panic mode as she scanned the crowd of guests who had gathered for the barbecue, as if the answer lay in the midst of people—both familiar and those she'd never met—who were enjoying the hors d'oeuvres and raising glasses in anticipation of Kieran's toast and in honor of the soon-to-be newlyweds.

Her gaze lit on her sister Rachel, who was talking to her husband, Matteo. Next to them, Zoe was flirting with her husband, Joaquin. There, like a very handsome third wheel, stood Alejandro, bedecked in an orchid lei and holding his pineapple cup.

The last single Mendoza.

Olivia's mind replayed the kiss they'd shared on Saturday night. In an instant her lips tingled as the feel and taste of him came flooding back, as if he'd kissed her only a moment ago.

That kiss... That. Kiss.

Suddenly, she was struck by a bolt of sexy inspiration. The idea was crazy—and a little bit naughty—but it just might work. As long as Alejandro went along with her plan.

Servers appeared with trays of champagne flutes. As Kieran gave the guests a moment to arm themselves with libations, Alejandro sensed someone standing too close behind him, invading his personal space. Before he could turn around a pair of feminine arms encircled his waist and a sultry voice that sounded a lot like Olivia's whispered in his ear.

"I know this sounds crazy, but I need you to kiss me right here, right now, and make it look real. Please just go along with it and don't ask questions."

Was this some kind of a joke?

"What?"

She didn't answer him. She simply moved around so that she was standing directly in front of him. She took the pineapple drink from his hand and set it on the tray of a passing server then she cupped his face in her hands and laid one on him with the same ferocity she'd shown Saturday night.

As she opened her mouth, inviting him deep inside, he obliged. And the rest of the world—and all the questions that had popped into his head as Olivia had whispered her request—faded away. Alejandro pulled her in flush with his body and did exactly as she had asked. There would be plenty of time for questions later. Right now her wish was his command.

The kiss was a lightning bolt that seared Alejandro to his core. He wasn't sure how long they'd stood there, lip to lip, locked in each other's arms, breathing each other's air, but he was vaguely aware of distant cheering as he and Olivia slowly broke the kiss and separated. People were, in fact, cheering, and it wasn't for Kieran and Dana. Everyone who was standing near them was looking at them.

Everyone except for his brothers. Cisco, Matteo and Joaquin weren't cheering; they were piercing him with looks that screamed *What the hell are you doing?*

What the hell *was* he doing?

That was all it took to sober him up. But then Olivia, who still had her arms draped around his neck, leaned in and whispered, "Thank you. Please just keep up the act. I'll explain as soon as we're alone."

Alejandro understood that her version of being alone probably wouldn't include more kissing. But that wasn't the most pressing problem at the moment.

"Quiet down, everyone," Kieran instructed the buzzing crowd. "Olivia, is there anything you'd like to tell us?"

All eyes turned to Olivia, who still had her arms

draped over his shoulders. She just smiled sweetly and made a show of shrugging in a noncommittal way that only fed the fire of speculation.

What *was* she doing? She seemed too smart and sure of herself to be unstable. Olivia clearly knew what she was doing. She was up to something and she was pulling him into it. Yesterday, she was arguing with him and asserting that they needed to act like the kiss had never happened, that everyone would be better off if they kept their distance from each other. Then today she was stealing her brother's thunder and making a spectacle of kissing him senseless.

"Should we start making plans to accommodate a third bride and groom?" Kieran said into the microphone.

As Olivia turned toward her brother, her arm dropped to Alejandro's waist and she held on. He followed suit, putting his arm around her.

One of the servers appeared in front of them with a tray of champagne flutes. They both took one.

"This is your night, my dear brother. Yours, Dana's, Sophie's and Mason's," she said. "To you and to your love and happiness."

The crowd cheered again and raised pineapple drinks and champagne flutes in tribute. The collective attention shifted back to Kieran and Dana.

"Thanks, sis," Kieran said. "That was a perfect toast. I couldn't have said it better." He sipped his champagne. "We hope everyone enjoys this magical week with us. Obviously we're off to a great start." He gestured with his head toward Olivia.

Alejandro felt a little uneasy being dragged into the spotlight. He was happy helping Olivia with whatever she was trying to accomplish—especially if it involved kissing her—but he'd prefer to know what he was working toward.

As everyone settled back into their groups and others made their way toward the food, Rachel, Matteo, Joaquin and Zoe cornered them.

"Hello?" Zoe said. "I think the two of you have some explaining to do."

"What do you mean?" Olivia asked. Alejandro both admired and resented her poker face. He wanted an explanation, too.

"Um, this?" Zoe gestured back and forth between Olivia and Alejandro with her manicured fingers. "When did this happen? What exactly is happening? And when were you going to tell us?"

Alejandro gazed down at Olivia. This was all her show. He smiled the message to her when she glanced up at him, looking every bit like the smitten lover.

Without missing a beat, Olivia said, "Surprise! We just sort of fell into this. Isn't it great?"

As the quartet uttered sounds of confused surprise, Alejandro said, "Yes, we just couldn't resist each other."

Spoken aloud, the sentiment didn't quite sound as convincing as it had in his head.

"Will you excuse us for a minute?" he said before he could say anything else inane. "Olivia and I were getting ready to—"

Getting ready to what?

"We were getting ready to take a tour of the house," Olivia said. "Come on, sweetheart. Let's do that now so we can get back and have dinner."

As Olivia slid her hand into his, Alejandro said, "Excuse us. We'll be right back."

They walked hand in hand in silence, across the lush green lawn to stone steps that led past the pool to a travertine porch. Alejandro looked back at the grounds and the lake that bordered the massive property.

"Is that Lake Austin?" he asked.

"It is," she said as she opened the back door and they stepped inside the house. Alejandro thought they'd be alone once they were inside, but staff milled about everywhere, carrying platters of food and drink and working purposefully. The buzz inside the house, coupled with the sheer grandeur of the place, stunned him into silence.

Alejandro did not speak another word until Olivia had shut them inside a room on the second floor. It was larger than his first apartment.

He blinked as Olivia flicked on a light. The expensive-looking feminine decor registered on him. "Is this your bedroom?"

"It is," she said. "Or it used to be. I have my own place now."

"It's nice that your folks kept it the way you left it. You know, that they didn't turn it into an exercise room or a man cave."

Olivia shrugged. "The house has always had a gym and my father has three man caves. My parents aren't sacrificing anything by keeping my space intact. It's not as if they kept it like this as a shrine to me. It's just not beneficial for them to change it. You know, it was easier to just shut the door. But that's not why I dragged you up here."

She bit her bottom lip again, pulling it into her mouth, a gesture he was beginning to associate with her pensive side.

"Did you bring me in here to make out?" he joked.

"No, I didn't." The sharpness of her tone shouldn't have surprised him, but it did.

He crossed his arms. "Would you care to share why you felt compelled to put on that display out there? You made it look like you couldn't wait to jump my bones."

She looked visibly deflated, but she nodded toward a black chair situated across from a plush sofa and a glass coffee table. The decor looked like it could've been featured in one of those designer house magazines. The sleek, sophisticated, expensive look of it perfectly reflected Olivia's own style.

After they'd seated themselves, she confessed, "I do owe you an explanation and a debt of gratitude. I just don't quite know how to say this. And before I say anything, I need you to swear on your family's life that you can keep a secret. Because if one word of this gets out, it would be very hurtful to certain members of my family."

He made a cross over his heart with his right hand. "I would offer to stick a needle in my eye, but I don't like needles."

She cocked a dark brow. "What? A big, strong, tough guy like you is afraid of needles? I don't believe it."

He wanted to say that needles didn't scare him nearly as much as she did. It was becoming clear that she addled his brain so much that she was able to lord some kind of power over him.

"Look, this has nothing to do with needles," he said. "Why don't you just tell me what's going on? Why did you kiss me like that out there?"

"I did it because I need everyone to believe we're in love—or that I'm in love with you. No, it would be better if they believed that we love each other, you know, mutually."

"But, Olivia, you don't love me. Why do you want everyone to think you do tonight, when yesterday you made it clear that me kissing you again was strictly forbidden? Because it would detract from the wedding, take the focus off the brides and grooms?"

When she didn't answer him, he said, "You're a beautiful woman. You're smart and funny and you're a hell of a good kisser, but I'm starting to think you're off your rocker."

"Oh, well, there you go," Olivia said. "For a second there I was tempted to think you were paying me a compliment. You know, calling me a beautiful woman."

"I was. You are. But I'm a little confused here. I was prepared to make the sacrifice of never kissing you again—for the greater good, for your sister's happiness, but—"

"You wanted to kiss me again, Alejandro?"

"Of course I did."

"Oh. That's good. Then how do you feel about being my pretend lover for the duration of the wedding? You know, my boyfriend—or my intensely romantic date. No, it needs to be more than just a date. I need for Sophie to believe that I've fallen in love with you. I messed up big-time Saturday night. Because of my big mouth, my sister has lost all faith in love. I figure the only way to undo the damage I've caused is by making her believe that I've had a change of heart about love. It's the only way to renew her faith. Would you be willing to do that for me…for my sister?" She suddenly looked very small and fragile, but she looked at him intently. "I promise I will make it worth your while."

Now it was his turn to cock a brow and mess with her. "And just how would you make it worth my while?

Can you please be more specific? I'm talking details. The more vivid the better."

His mouth crooked up on one side and she obviously caught his drift because her cheeks flushed the same color as the hot-pink area rug under their feet.

"Certainly not in the way I think you're implying. You have a dirty mind, Alejandro."

"Hey, I didn't say a word. I was thinking along the lines of dancing and being dinner partners. So the hordes of adoring women will think I'm taken and leave me alone." He was smiling so that she would know he was joking. "That's what I was thinking. However, I am not responsible for whatever that mind of yours conjures up. If you'd like to try out your thoughts and see if it works for you, I'm happy to be at your service."

Her mouth fell open and he could tell she was trying to feign disgust, but the pretense hadn't reached her eyes. "Why are you making this so difficult?"

"Because watching you squirm is so much fun." He held her gaze as he grappled with a peculiar feeling in the pit of his stomach. Something he hadn't felt in ages. Interest and attraction. Maybe this wedding was going to be more interesting than he'd thought. At the very least, it would be fun.

He'd go along as her pretend boyfriend. It wasn't as if he was agreeing to marry her.

He shrugged, to appear not too eager. "I guess I've had worse offers," he said. "I'd be happy to play the role of your lover for the duration of the wedding." But he couldn't resist needling her a bit. "Just how deeply into character would you like to go?"

Chapter 4

"You pride yourself on being the king of the innuendo, don't you?" Olivia said, exercising great restraint to resist adding another layer to his insinuation. The chemistry between them begged her to keep the banter going, to tell him she was all about method acting and she was at his service for any research he needed in order to deliver a convincing performance.

Actually, her body was all in for the research, but her brain knew better. They needed to keep this strictly aboveboard.

"That's the thing about innuendo," he said. "You can interpret it however you choose."

"Okay, since you put it that way, I'd love an Oscar-winning performance, but we need to keep this act strictly PG."

He frowned. "That's disappointing. I was thinking an R-rated production would be so much more convincing."

"Sorry to disappoint you, Romeo, but let's not get carried away. Need I remind you that while this show we're about to put on is a limited engagement, we'll still have to stage a breakup and coexist at future family functions."

He frowned.

"It's not like we'll have to sit across the dinner table from each other every Sunday," he said.

"True."

Maybe this wasn't a good idea. Was it fair to ask a guy she barely knew to pretend to be her lover? To play the part convincingly without giving him all access? For a fleeting moment, she let herself go there. What if for one careless week she allowed herself to go off the rails and immerse herself in the part—onstage and off?

"What are you getting at, Alejandro? Do you expect me to sleep with you?"

After she set the words free, released them from the cage in her mind, the prospect of letting go like that was petrifying. She might not believe in love, but she did believe in feelings. And feelings, when you allowed them to meander unchecked, made you susceptible to hurt.

No. If there was ever a time that she needed to stay completely in control it was now. This was about Sophie. It wasn't about her. It was a means to an end to fix what she had nearly broken.

"You make it sound so romantic," Alejandro said.

When she didn't jab back, he seemed to ease up. "It's clear that's not what you want. So, no, I don't expect you to sleep with me. I would never use sex as a bartering chip. Don't worry, Olivia. You're safe with me."

She should've been relieved, but the most primitive part of her was disappointed that sex was off the table.

But she reminded herself that she needed to set the ground rules up front and they needed to stick to them. For their own good. Hadn't the Sophie disaster been enough of a cautionary tale of what happened when she got careless?

"That's good to know," she said. "I'm glad we're on the same page."

He nodded, but things still felt off-kilter. Before they left this room, she needed to make sure everything was as right as it could be.

"Please know that I do appreciate you helping me," she said. "It's good of you, Alejandro. I realize you don't have to do this. I mean, Sophie is my sister. I'm the one who opened my big mouth and set everything spinning out of control."

Olivia clamped her mouth shut. She was talking too much. She always did when she felt out of control. Obviously she needed to admit to herself that Alejandro Mendoza made her feel that way. *Yes, just acknowledge it—look the problem in the eye, stare it down—and move on.*

She locked gazes with him. Looked deep into those brown eyes, straight into the lighter brown and golden flecks that she hadn't noticed before. He was the first one to blink, breaking the trance, but she still didn't feel any more in control than before she'd tried to stare down the dragon. She needed to try another tactic.

"Even though I'm appreciative and I shouldn't question your motives, I'm wondering why you would do this for me."

There. She'd said it. And it needed to be said.

He was frowning at her again. Not an affected frown this time, but a genuine look of consternation. Still, she was glad she'd said it. Knowing what he was expecting in return for helping her might put things on a bit more of a level playing field.

"What's in this for me." It wasn't a question. The way he repeated her words was more like he was turning them around, looking at them from all angles. "What's in this for me. I don't know, Olivia. Should I expect personal gain? Because I wasn't, other than maybe the satisfaction of helping you out."

"Look, Alejandro, I didn't mean that in the way you seem to be taking it. I just wanted to make sure we're both laying all our cards on the table before we go any further."

"Is everything a business venture to you? I get the feeling you're about to whip out a contract for me to sign."

She wished it was that easy. For a terrifying moment, she feared that her plan was a mistake.

She stood. "I'm sorry. Let's just forget about this whole thing and proceed with business as usual between us. It's not you…it was a bad idea."

He reached out and took her hand, tugging her gently to get her to sit back down. And, of course, she did. Because it was clear that her better judgment, which was telling her to run away and save herself, went belly up when Alejandro did so much as breathe near her. With this man she felt totally out of control. And it was petrifying.

"I hate to be the voice of reality, but after that show we put on before the toast, people are going to have questions. And even though I don't know your sister very well, if everything you said is true—and I have no reason to believe it's not—do you think it will restore

Sophie's faith if word gets back to her that it's 'business as usual' between us again?"

The guy was more insightful than she'd given him credit for. And he was absolutely right. Sophie would be completely disheartened, and with good reason. There was no backing out now unless she wanted to put the final nail in the coffin on Sophie's desire to marry.

"You're right," she told him. "You're a good man to allow me to drag you into this, Alejandro. I promise I'll make it up to you somehow."

"I'll hold you to that." He reached out and took her hand. Only this time it felt different. Not as dangerous, even though the butterflies in her stomach still flew in formation.

"Shall we go back to the party? I think we have some explaining to do."

He smiled. "Let the show begin."

Olivia should've known she wouldn't be able to fool her sisters. She shouldn't have even tried. But even though they'd gone along with the charade at the party, pretending to be just as surprised and convinced as everyone else by her love affair with Alejandro, Zoe and Rachel had shown up at her condo early the next morning with a box of doughnuts and plenty of questions.

She'd spilled the beans within the first five minutes.

"So we weren't convincing?" Olivia asked as she put the kettle on to boil water for coffee in the French press. "Please, at least tell me we weren't painfully obvious."

"You were absolutely convincing to the untrained eye," Rachel said as she took down coffee mugs from the cabinet above the stove. "You should know better than to try to pull one over on Zoe and me. Why didn't you tell us about the plan from the start?"

Olivia turned toward her sisters and braced the small of her back against the edge of the counter.

"I didn't have a plan per se. In fact, when I saw that Sophie hadn't snapped out of her funk by last night, I was in full panic mode. She missed the brunch and then the dinner where she was supposed to welcome her guests. It was starting to feel like something more than cold feet. I'm afraid if it goes on much longer, Mason won't be able to keep up her flu cover-up. Either that, or he's going to lose his patience. I mean, how would you all feel if your husbands had ditched the wedding events and told you they weren't sure they wanted to marry you less than a week before the wedding?"

Her sisters nodded in agreement.

"Thank goodness Mason is a very patient man," said Rachel. "So what are you planning to do? Are you counting on word of your affair with Alejandro magically getting back to Sophie? Or do you have a plan?"

Olivia bought herself some time by grinding the coffee beans she had measured out. It only took a few seconds, but by the time she'd finished, both of her sisters were staring at her expectantly, waiting for an answer.

"I definitely want to be proactive," Olivia said. "There's not enough time to leave matters up to chance. However, before I can do anything I need to figure out where she is. I haven't talked to her since Sunday. Have either of you heard from her?"

Olivia already knew the answer to that question. Because of course her sisters would've rushed to her the minute they had learned Sophie's whereabouts. No, this was a code red situation. And they needed to do something to avert a major catastrophe. Since the three of them were together and would soon be fortified by doughnuts, she was confident they'd come up with something.

Zoe cleared her throat as if she had something to say. That's when it dawned on Olivia that her sister had been uncharacteristically quiet as she and Rachel had been mulling over the situation.

"I know where Sophie is," Zoe said.

The tea kettle whistled as if punctuating Olivia's agitation.

"What? Where is she?" Olivia demanded as she took the kettle off the flame.

Zoe stood there silently, looking away from her sisters.

"You've been standing here all this time harboring this information?" Rachel said. "Are you going to make us pry it out of you, or are you going to tell us?"

Zoe shot daggers at Rachel. "She asked me not to tell."

"Honey, this is not an ordinary situation," Olivia said. "You're not betraying her trust by telling us. In fact, you just might be saving her marriage. Where is she?"

"I still can't believe she's been right here the whole time," Olivia said as she and her sisters climbed the stairs of their childhood home. "She was probably watching the party last night from her window. Alejandro and I were right down the hall from her."

Olivia stopped in her tracks causing Rachel to nearly bump into her. "Oh my gosh. I hope she didn't overhear Alejandro and me talking."

"I don't think so," Zoe whispered. "I spoke to her last

night and she didn't say anything. And you know she would've had plenty to say if she'd heard you."

"Good point," Olivia whispered back. "Let's—" She drew a finger over her throat in a gesture that meant *silence* and motioned for them to continue on to Sophie's room.

The three sisters traveled quietly down the long hall. Sophie's room was at the opposite end of the hall from Olivia's. She was grateful because if her sister had overheard the conversation it would have made matters even worse. Now, regardless of how dangerous the Alejandro plan felt, it was her last recourse. It had to work, because she certainly didn't have a plan B.

Nor did she have a plan for approaching her sister, she realized when they finally stood in front of Sophie's bedroom door. Zoe and Rachel looked at Olivia, as if they were waiting for her to do something. So she did what she did best and took charge. She gestured to Zoe, indicating that she should knock on the door and be the one to speak to Sophie first.

At first, Zoe shook her head, but through a series of pantomimes Olivia was able to impart that it was only logical for Zoe to be the one to knock because she was the only one who knew Sophie was here. With a resigned shrug Zoe acquiesced and gave the door a tentative rap.

"Sophie?" she said. "Are you in there? It's me, Zoe. I just wanted to check on you. See how you are."

When she didn't answer, Olivia tried the door. It was locked. Olivia motioned for Zoe to knock again. This time Zoe didn't argue.

"Come on, Soph. Open up. Please? You can't hide in here forever. Besides, it's getting kind of difficult to explain your absence to the guests. You're gonna have to make up your mind about what you want to do. You owe Mason that much."

Olivia gave Zoe the signal to tone it down a little bit. She appreciated what her sister was trying to do, but she was still holding out hope that the soft touch might work.

As if reading Olivia's mind, Zoe changed her tactic. "Besides, if you don't open the door I'm not going to tell you the gossip. And it's juicy. It involves Alejandro Mendoza. You're definitely going to want to hear this."

Sophie almost caught Olivia giving Zoe the thumbs-up. Because the tidbit about Alejandro seemed to be the magic words that made Sophie open the door for Zoe.

Of course, when she saw Rachel and Olivia standing there too, she tried to shut the door again, but the three of them were quicker than Sophie and managed to muscle their way in before she could lock them out.

Before Sophie could say anything, her sisters grabbed her in a four-way group hug as they cooed their concern and happiness about finally seeing her again.

"We were so worried about you," Rachel said.

"How are you doing?" Olivia asked.

"Have you changed your mind about the wedding?" Zoe asked. "Are you getting married?"

All Sophie could say was "I don't know. I don't know what I believe anymore."

Olivia noticed that Sophie didn't utter one word of protest about Zoe's sharing the secret of her whereabouts. That confirmed what Olivia had suspected—that Sophie had told Zoe because she knew Zoe wouldn't be able to keep the secret.

Zoe was the loose lips, Rachel was the vault and Olivia was the problem solver.

"You said there was gossip?" Sophie asked. "About Alejandro Mendoza?"

Olivia felt relief—her sister seemed to be playing right into their hands. Good thing, too, because Olivia didn't know how they would have steered her in that direction if she hadn't brought it up herself.

Olivia said a silent prayer that Zoe would pick up on her cue and proceed in a way that didn't look staged.

"Oh, that's not important," Olivia feigned. "We are here to talk to you, to see what we can do to make you feel better about everything."

Olivia held her breath.

"The best thing you could do for me right now is to talk about something other than the wedding. Because if you keep badgering me about it, you can't stay." Sophie walked over to the door and put her hand on the knob as if she were demonstrating how she would show them out.

"Then you're saying we can stay if we don't talk about the wedding?" Rachel asked.

Sophie eyed her sisters as if she were weighing the pros and cons.

"Olivia and Alejandro hooked up last night." Zoe spat the words so perfectly Olivia had to remind herself to look suitably offended. After all, if this had been a true hookup, she wouldn't have wanted anyone—even her sisters—gossiping about it.

The ploy seemed to be working, because Sophie's jaw dropped and her eyes were huge.

"Zoe," Olivia admonished, "you promised you wouldn't say anything."

Rachel rolled her eyes. "Well, you two made such a spectacle of yourselves last night that if Sophie didn't hear it from Zoe she would certainly hear about it from someone else."

Olivia stood there silently, channeling her best humiliated/indignant expression.

"This is nobody's business but mine and Alejandro's," Olivia said. "So just stop, okay?"

"Oh, I don't think so," said Sophie. Her eyes sparkled as she took the bait—hook, line and sinker. She grabbed Olivia's arm and tugged her toward the couch by the window. "You are not leaving until you tell me everything."

She looked at Zoe and Rachel. "This happened last night? At the welcome barbecue? And I missed it?"

Zoe and Rachel nodded, a little too enthusiastically.

"Yep. You missed it," Zoe said. "If you would've been there last night you would've had a front-row seat."

No. If she'd been there last night nothing would've happened. There would've been no need.

Olivia's mind replayed last night's kiss. The details were so vivid she could virtually feel Alejandro's lips on hers. Never in her life had she been at odds with herself like she was over this. Every womanly cell in her body couldn't wait for her to kiss him again, but every ounce of common sense in her brain reminded her to rein it in. Because if the plan worked like it seemed to be working, she was going to be kissing Alejandro a lot more. It was fine if she enjoyed it. In fact, it was probably for the best if she did since they'd be spending so much time together. However, it was in her own best interest to not get carried away.

"Olivia! Oh, my gosh," Sophie squealed. "He's gorgeous, and I knew he was interested in you because of the way he was looking at you Saturday night. Did I call it or what?" She looked at Zoe and Rachel. "I called it. Didn't I call it?"

Sophie clapped her hands gleefully, looking like she'd just opened the front door and found the prize patrol of a sweepstakes holding a big check made out to her.

"You called it, Soph," Rachel conceded.

Olivia crossed her arms and let her body fall back against the couch with a petulant *harrumph*.

Sophie angled herself toward Olivia. "Tell me everything. Start from the beginning and tell me every juicy detail. Come on, Liv. Spill it."

Olivia looked down and shook her head. "I'm glad you all think this is entertaining, but I don't want to talk about it."

"Wait, what?" Rachel asked. "Alejandro is gorgeous and we would all like to live vicariously through you for just a few minutes. I mean, it was just a hookup. What's the harm in sharing?"

Perfect.

Olivia took a deep breath and bit her bottom lip, doing her best to look sincerely offended.

"I'm not sure it was just a hookup," she said. "So you all just hop off, okay?"

"Are you saying you care about him?" Zoe asked.

Olivia gave a one-shoulder shrug. "Yeah, I think I do."

Sophie was watching, rapt. Olivia decided she needed to kick it up a level.

"I didn't think it was possible. Really, I didn't think it would ever happen to me. I thought I was immune."

She placed both of her hands over her heart. "But for the first time in my life, I think I'm in love. Truly, madly, deeply in love." One at a time, she looked each of her sisters in the eye, ending with Sophie. That's when she delivered the knockout punch. "I'm in love with Alejandro Mendoza and he feels the same way."

Sophie sat there looking stunned. When she didn't speak, Olivia feared that she'd been a little too melodramatic. Maybe the *truly, madly, deeply* bit was a little over-the-top. *Ugh*, it probably was. It was the title of her favorite Alan Rickman movie, and the name of that corny Savage Garden song, which had to be one of the sappiest love songs ever. Okay, so she'd secretly loved it ever since the time she and her sisters had gotten up and sang it at karaoke night at Señor Iguana's.

The fib had come to her in a rush, but that might have been the reason Sophie was just sitting there staring at her. Olivia said a silent prayer hoping she hadn't blown it.

Chapter 5

Alejandro was able to arrange a wine tasting for Wednesday afternoon at Hummingbird Ridge Vineyard. It was short notice, but he was psyched when Olivia was able to herd and organize a group of fourteen who were interested in going. It was his wedding gift to the brides and grooms.

Alejandro had left the outing to the discretion of the wedding party, and the final group ended up being comprised of family—Mendozas and Fortune Robinsons. It was great, in theory. The problem was Olivia's "we're in love" plan seemed to be working, as Sophie seemed to have miraculously recovered from her "flu" and had happily agreed to join them. That meant they had to put on a convincing performance for Sophie's benefit in front of key members of the family—Mason, Dana and Kieran; their fathers, Gerald Robinson and Orlando Mendoza; Orlando's fiancée, Josephine Fortune; and their siblings, Rachel and Matteo; Zoe and Joaquin; and Cisco and his wife Delaney. Rachel and Zoe were in on the ruse, but his brothers and Delaney weren't and they believed they were witnessing a romance unfolding right before their eyes.

As they had waited to board the small chartered bus that would take them to the winery, Dana's friend Monica had flirted with him. But then Olivia had walked up and draped her arms around his neck and greeted him with a kiss that made his eyeballs roll back into his head. After that, Monica had kept her distance.

Normally, he would have been enticed by the challenge of a beautiful woman's reserve—especially one who had shown interest in him. After all, it was the thrill of the chase, and it was one of his favorite games. But not only did Monica virtually disappear, his attention kept drifting back to Olivia, who was seated beside him on the bus.

He admired the way her long dark hair was swept back from her face, accentuating dark, soulful eyes, high cheekbones and full lips that begged him to kiss them again. His eyes followed the graceful slope of her neck to the place where her blouse ended in a vee at her breastbone and just a hint of cleavage winked at him. She looked sleek and polished in her snug-fitting beige pants and black tank.

She leaned in toward him. "Thanks for doing this." Her voice was quiet and husky and made him think of sex, even though he wasn't sure if she was expressing gratitude for the wine tasting trip or for going along with the ruse to draw her sister out of her prewedding funk.

"My pleasure." He watched her intently, realizing that in its own way this game of subterfuge was at once erotic and frustrating as hell. The two of them acted like they couldn't keep their hands off each other, like they were merely tolerating the others until they could finally sneak off to finish what they'd started.

Every single person here, with the exception of Rachel and Zoe, thought Olivia and he were sleeping together. The thought made his groin tighten even though the exact opposite was true. They were like the old back-lot Hollywood sets that looked real from the outside, but behind the scenes it was just prefabricated plywood braces and empty promises.

Even though he really could've used a cooldown, he put his hand on the back of her neck and caressed it. The gesture made her look up at him and when she did, he lowered his mouth to hers and planted a gentle kiss on her lips.

"Get a room, you two." Sophie laughed. Olivia had strategically chosen the seats in front of Sophie and Mason to give her sister a front-row seat for the show.

They ended the kiss and feigned embarrassment as Sophie leaned forward and braced her forearms on the seatback.

"So, my big sister isn't immune to love after all." Her voice floated between them on a note of wonder. "You know, Alejandro, I called this relationship even before the two of you realized you were perfect for each other."

"Yes, you did, Sophie," Olivia said to her sister. She placed her hand on his leg and traced slow circles and she continued to gaze at Alejandro, as if she was so deeply in love she couldn't bear to look away. "You nailed it. You did."

Alejandro smiled. "What do you mean you called it?"

"That night at the Driskill bar," Sophie explained, "I

said to Olivia that the two of you were perfect for each other. Not just because you're the last single Mendoza brother and she's the last single Fortune Robinson sister, but because you're perfect together. You're made for each other."

"We are perfect for each other," Alejandro echoed as he gazed at Olivia.

"Well, it's true," Sophie said. "You are the only person in the world that could make my sister believe in love. You're like King Arthur of Camelot, the only one who could pull Excalibur out of the stone."

He raised an eyebrow at Olivia. Had she really never been in love? What was it that would cause her to take such a hardline stance? What would make her close herself off? Granted, love was a risky endeavor. The heart was uncertain by nature. He'd learned that first-hand after he'd lost Anna.

"See, Olivia? I told you that there was someone for you. I told you that Alejandro was your man."

"Yes, you did, Sophie."

Something flickered in Olivia's gaze. She blinked and looked away. But it felt more like she was pulling away. Maybe she was performing the same reality check Alejandro himself was right now. Despite the hot kissing, tender touching and cozy embracing, it was all for show. Every bit of it. He needed to remind himself of that now and again. Hell, if he knew what was good for him, he would write a stern reminder on a figurative sign and nail it to the forefront of his mind. Because he could already see it would be very tempting to lose himself in this game.

Olivia scooted away from him and turned around in her seat to talk to her sister.

"I'm glad to see you're feeling better." Her voice was low. "You had us all worried for a while."

Alejandro didn't turn around. Instead, he sat facing forward and he caught his father, who was seated at the front of the bus, slanting a glance over his shoulder in Alejandro's direction. When the older man realized Alejandro had caught him looking, he pretended to be shifting so that he could more easily drop his arm around Josephine's shoulder. But Alejandro hadn't missed the curious look in his dad's eyes.

He pondered the vague conundrum of what he was going to say to his father and Josephine once they had a chance to corner him. Orlando was bound to be full of questions, and rightfully so. He was his father, after all. A father who wanted nothing more than for all of his children to be as happy as he was.

There was a long stretch of time after Alejandro's mother, Luz, died when he thought his father might never be happy again. Orlando had been so deeply in love with Luz that Alejandro and his siblings had feared that he might will himself into an early grave. That was so unlike the man who had always been so full of life.

When Luz died five years ago, Orlando had been bereft. Alejandro and his siblings had convinced him that he needed a change of scenery, that he needed to leave a lifetime of memories and the hustle and bustle of Miami for the more laidback pace of Horseback Hollow, Texas. That was when he met Josephine Fortune. Since then, Orlando had been like a new man.

Alejandro hated to lie to his dad. They'd always had a great relationship, but he'd promised Olivia he wouldn't tell anyone what they were up to. They couldn't risk anyone slipping up and tipping off Sophie. The more people who knew about the ruse, the greater the chance of someone spilling the beans.

Orlando was nothing if not understanding. As soon as the week was over and Sophie was happily off on her honeymoon, he would level with his dad. Orlando would understand.

Gerald Robinson, however, might be another matter.

Olivia's father sat in the front seat across the aisle from Orlando and Josephine. He'd arrived only moments before the bus left so Alejandro hadn't had an opportunity to introduce himself again. They'd met at his brothers' weddings, but it had only been in passing.

Alejandro ignored the dread that reminded him that Gerald Robinson would probably wonder about this sudden relationship. Any father with a daughter like Olivia would be protective.

He'd done a fair amount of research on Gerald Robinson the mogul, the genius businessman. The guy was formidable. He had a reputation for ruthlessly eliminating competition and systematically taking down his opponents.

Alejandro blinked away a sudden vision of Gerald enlisting his henchmen to teach him a lesson about messing with his daughter. But then he dismissed the thought because he wasn't messing with Olivia. He was helping her. Actually, he clarified to himself, he was messing around with Olivia to help Sophie.

This could get complicated in ways that he hadn't even thought of before he'd agreed to this farce.

Alejandro's hand instinctively found the tattoo on his forearm. He covered it with his palm, as if touching Anna's name might provide answers. The tattoo was his touchstone, anchoring him in the past and grounding him in the present all at once. It was a reminder that he'd been fortunate enough to know true love once. Not everyone was lucky like that. Olivia didn't even believe in love. He didn't know if it was because she'd been hurt so badly that it had cauterized her heart.

He glanced at her as she and her sister had their heads together, whispering and laughing, making happy sounds that had him convinced that their Saturday-night fight, the one that had nearly turned Sophie into a runaway bride, was not only a thing of the past—it was erased from the annals of their sister history.

The bus rounded the corner, bringing Hummingbird Ridge Vineyard into view with its inviting lodge and its acres of weathered grapevines standing like rows of stooped and gnarled old men waiting for the rapture.

The midday sun beat down, casting a golden light on the scene, making it one of the most beautiful sights Alejandro had ever seen.

The blood rushed in his ears as his pulse picked up at the thought of how hard he'd worked to bring his plans to life. Soon, this would all be his. His kingdom.

"Is that Hummingbird Ridge?" Olivia asked.

He nodded.

"It's beautiful," Olivia said. "It looks like a postcard. Isn't it sad that for as long as I've lived in Austin, I've never been to a Hill Country winery? So this is a real treat for so many reasons."

"Never?" Alejandro asked. "Why not?"

"That's a good question. I have no idea why not and I don't really have any good excuses. I guess I just haven't had time to venture out here. Or, actually, I've been so bogged down by the day-to-day grind that I haven't made time."

He wanted to ask her what she did for fun, if she even had fun. Or was she always all work and no play? He wanted to tell her that he could help her with that, if she'd let him. After all, he had made an art form out of having fun while working his way to success. But the bus was pulling into the winery's parking lot. He made a mental note—right across the large sign in the forefront of his mind that reminded him their escapades were all for show—to help Olivia learn how to have fun this week. Right now, he had a winery to show off and a captive audience that was eager to learn more.

As the driver parked, Alejandro told her, "I'm going to go inside to make sure everything is ready for us. Will you corral everyone outside until I get back?"

"You bet."

She already had her work face on, ready to take charge. It would be fun to see her spring into action organizing everyone.

"Thanks. Why don't you take them for a walk around the grounds? There's a sculpture garden around the back. I want to make sure everyone gets a chance to enjoy it. I'll come and get you as soon as they're ready for us."

Without even thinking about it, he leaned in and kissed her. It felt natural. Maybe a little too natural. But she kissed him back. When she pulled away, they both seemed to have the same question in their eyes: *Is this okay?* And the same answer: *It's fine.*

He stood and made his way to the front of the bus. Since it was a weekday the staff had agreed to close the tasting room for their private party. A sign was tacked to the large rough-hewn wooden door. It read: "Closed for private party from 1pm-3pm. Please come again." Alejandro reached out and grabbed the brass handle and pulled the door. It creaked open, exposing an airy reception area with high vaulted ceilings with dark beams. A marble-topped tasting bar crowded with wineglasses and corked bottles graced the wall directly across from the front door. In the center of the room, someone had set a wooden trestle table for the tasting. They'd laid it with breads and cheeses and other appetizers to pair with the various wines.

The rusty squeak of the door sounded behind Alejandro and he turned to see Gerald Robinson walk in. The man stopped just inside the threshold, scowled and took his time looking around, taking in everything as if he were judging the place and finding it wanting. Even after his gaze skewered Alejandro, Gerald didn't speak. He stood there silently, challenging him with his blank expression.

There he was—*the* Gerald Robinson. Creator of empires, eviscerator of men who got in his way… And of men who dated his daughter?

Obviously his brothers and Mason had battled the monster and lived to marry his daughters.

When Gerald agreed to join them today, Alejandro had known the mogul was bound to have a conversation with him about what Alejandro was doing with Olivia. What the hell was he supposed to say? Lying to Orlando was one thing—it wasn't really lying because he would confide the truth later—but lying to Gerald by saying he was in love with his daughter was another. It was best to be proactive and take charge of the conversation.

"Mr. Robinson, welcome." Alejandro walked over to Olivia's father and extended his hand. "I'm Alejandro Mendoza. We've met before at Rachel's and Zoe's weddings."

Gerald offered a perfunctory shake, but his grip was

firm and commanding. "I know who you are. Olivia tells me you're buying this place?"

"I am."

Again, Gerald's steely gaze pinned him to the spot. Alejandro steeled himself for the inevitable interrogation.

"Nice place," Gerald said. Unsmiling, he broke eye contact and gave the room another once-over. "You're from Miami. I take it you know something about wine."

They weren't questions. They were statements that proved the guy had already done some investigating. Hell, for all Alejandro knew the man might've hired a private detective to perform a full-scale inquiry.

It was fine if he had. Alejandro had nothing to hide. He made his living honestly.

"I know a lot about wine. Are you an oenophile?"

"I have no idea what you're talking about," Robinson said.

"An oenophile is a wine enthusiast," Alejandro explained.

Gerald scowled at him. "Why didn't you say that in the first place?"

It was a fair question. Gerald probably thought he was being pretentious, showing off. Maybe he was. But that wasn't something he'd admit out loud.

"I don't like wine," Gerald said. "But I read something just the other day about how over the past few decades, Hill Country wineries have been growing steadily and Texas wine production has become a viable player in the industry. Fascinating. The article said that winemakers are forgoing the Napa Valley because it's expensive and exclusive and basically out of their reach."

That was exactly why Alejandro had chosen to buy a place in Texas. When he'd discovered it was a viable option it had almost seemed meant to be, since most of his immediate family had relocated to the Lone Star State. In fact, if he'd believed in fate, he might have thought it'd had a hand in aligning the stars and moon to make this possible. It just seemed to make sense that this was where he would invest the money his mother, Luz, had left him when she passed away.

In typical Luz fashion, she'd made arrangements to take care of her children even after she'd left this earth. She'd taken out a small life insurance policy, leaving equal sums to each of her five kids. She'd left each of them a handwritten note telling them how much she loved them, that it had been a privilege to be their mother and that she hoped the money she was leaving each of them would help make their dreams come true.

Alejandro had invested the gift from his mother and, while it wasn't enough to allow him to buy Hummingbird Ridge free and clear, that investment, along with the money he'd saved, was the seed money he needed to interest his cousins, Rodrigo and Stefan, and a couple of investors who would be silent partners. Together they had the buying power to make the deal. They were almost there. The last hurdle was to clear due diligence and inspections and they'd be home free.

"That's exactly why I chose Texas," Alejandro said. "Most of my family has relocated to Texas. I've had my eye on wineries here. I've made several scouting trips, during which I became friendly with Jack and Margaret Daily—the couple that owns Hummingbird Ridge. They wanted to sell and I wanted to buy. It just seemed like a good fit."

Gerald grunted as he stood there with his arms crossed. Alejandro couldn't tell if he was boring him or if the sound indicated contemplative interest.

"Hummingbird Ridge has been in Margaret's family for several generations," Alejandro explained. "She inherited it and wanted to pass it on to their daughter, but the daughter's not interested. She's a surgeon and doesn't have the time or the inclination to take over the family business. I asked them if they wanted to adopt me, but they said they'd cut me a deal instead," he joked, but Gerald didn't laugh.

"If I would've known it was for sale, I would've bought it."

"Really?" This was unexpected coming from a guy who professed to not like wine. "You're interested in getting involved in the wine industry?"

Gerald shrugged. "To diversify."

"If you find a vineyard and you do decide to invest, make sure you've got a good crew. Even though this is becoming one of the top wine production states, it still has its challenges. It has distinct regions that are different enough to the point of being incompatible in terms of vine selection. Depending on the area, the microclimatic and geographic factors can vary considerably, but that's what I find so appealing about it."

Gerald didn't say anything. Alejandro could tell from the man's body language that it was time to stop talking. So he just stood there. The faint whir of the air conditioner was the only sound in the room.

"Well," Gerald finally said, "thanks for arranging this tasting. And if you hurt my daughter, you'll answer to me and there will be hell to pay."

The older man's forced smile reminded Alejandro of a great white shark as Gerald turned around and let himself out of the tasting room.

"Alejandro, welcome. We're excited that you could be here today."

Alejandro turned to see Margaret stepping out of the office, which was located down a hallway to the right of the wine bar.

"Hi, Margaret. Everything looks great. Thanks for going the extra mile to make today special for my guests."

"My pleasure. Will they be arriving soon?"

"They're already here." He motioned to the door. "They're enjoying the grounds until you're ready for them."

"We're ready when you are," Margaret said. "Shall we invite them in?"

As Alejandro and Margaret set off to find the party, she told him that Jack was sorry to miss him, but he had some business in Dallas he had to take care of.

Alejandro's phone rang, interrupting the conversation. His cousin Stefan's name flashed on the screen. "Excuse me, Margaret. I need to take this call."

"That's fine, honey. I'll find everyone and bring them inside."

"Stefan, my man," Alejandro said. "You must have been picking up the good vibe. I'm standing here in the Hummingbird Ridge tasting room. What's going on?"

Stefan didn't speak right away and for a moment Alejandro thought they'd lost the connection.

"Stef, are you there?"

"I am. I don't have good news. Masterson is pulling out of the Hummingbird Ridge deal."

Alejandro's gut contracted. "Bad joke, bro."

"I wish it was a joke. It's not. We're not going to have the money we need to buy the place. We're going to be short by a third."

Chapter 6

That evening, Alejandro stared straight ahead at the stretch of highway ahead of him as he drove Olivia to the barbecue, which was hosted by Mason's family. Losing the investor was nothing more than a setback.

Still, if he'd had a shred of a hint that the deal wouldn't go through, he wouldn't have brought everyone to the winery. He would've come up with some other way to celebrate the brides and grooms, but he certainly wouldn't have dragged everyone out in the middle of all the wedding festivities had he known that the vineyard might not be his. Or at least he wouldn't have announced that it was his new venture. But after the sting of the setback had subsided a bit, his mind turned to more constructive thoughts: getting replacement funds.

Before they'd boarded the bus to leave for Austin, he'd asked Gerald Robinson if he could meet with him on Monday morning after the wedding because he wanted to present an investment opportunity in Hummingbird Ridge. It was a long shot, but Robinson hadn't cut him off at the knees. Instead, he'd dug around in his wallet and come up with a business card.

"Call my assistant and tell her I told you to set up a meeting." He hadn't asked any questions or expressed any interest; he'd just walked away and gotten on the bus.

Immediately, Alejandro had excused himself and had gone back inside the winery and placed the call. Before the bus had left Hummingbird Ridge, he had an appointment with Robinson on the books at three o'clock Monday afternoon. He'd have to change his flight back to Miami from Monday to Tuesday, but it was a small price to pay for possibly saving the winery purchase.

The biggest problem was whether or not to tell Olivia he was meeting with her father.

He remembered what she'd said about the guys who had used her to get to Gerald. He didn't want her to get the wrong idea, that he was using her. Sure, they weren't dating, but after weighing it, he thought it was best not to involve her so that she wouldn't feel obligated.

He kept hearing her say, *I owe you. I'll make it up to you*, after he'd agreed to help her with her plan to make Sophie think Olivia believed in love.

He didn't want her to feel beholden. Plus, he really didn't want to get into the details of how the deal was hanging by a thread. Not when it came to a business deal of this magnitude. If Gerald said no, that would be the end of it. She'd never know. If he said yes, he would tell Olivia.

"Do you want to talk about whatever is on your mind?" Olivia asked from beside him in his car.

He slanted a glance at her, but returned his focus to the road.

He had worked damn hard to keep his poker face in place. He hadn't wanted to spoil the festivities. Obviously he hadn't been as good at hiding his frustration as he'd intended. "Talk about what?"

"What's had you tied up in knots since the start of the tasting."

"I got a phone call while we were at the vineyard. There's a slight snag with one of the investors. But it's not a problem. Everything will be fine."

Telling her that much made him feel better. Since she'd picked up on his mood, sharing that was more honest than if he'd tried to pretend that nothing was wrong.

He deflected the focus off himself with his next comment. "And speaking of fine, it seems like Sophie and Mason are doing well. It's nice to see that your plan worked. I guess we make a convincing match."

On Friday evening, the wedding rehearsal went off without a hitch and Sophie seemed to be herself again, in full bride-to-be mode. Now she was seated across the rehearsal dinner table from Olivia, laughing and flirting with Mason, stealing kisses and whispering private words in his ear.

Good. The plan had worked out exactly as Olivia had hoped it would. In less than twenty-four hours Sophie and Mason would be on their honeymoon and Olivia would officially be disqualified from receiving the title Prewedding Homewrecker of the Year.

Maybe Sophie had simply experienced a case of cold feet, but Olivia still owned the responsibility of pushing her sister into the desperate weeds of despair after she brought up their parents' dismal excuse of a marriage. Ever since the night of the Fuzzy Handcuffs, Olivia had limited herself to one alcoholic beverage during wedding festivities—at the winery she had only allowed herself a single sip of each wine they had sampled. It was at once her own self-enforced punishment for being so sloppy at the bachelorette weekend and insurance that it wouldn't happen again.

Being one of the few sober people at the parties was a strange experience. But it was necessary. She could enjoy herself without social lubrication, and it was the only way to ensure that her sister actually made it down the aisle, headed in the right direction for the start of the rest of her life.

The private dining room where the rehearsal dinner was taking place was awash in golden candlelight and gorgeous white flowers. The party planner had strung hundreds of tiny golden twinkle lights around the room. She had crafted them into hanging topiaries and stuffed them into glass cylinders that were grouped with dozens of candles and more flowers to create ethereal tablescapes. It was a dinner fit for a princess—two princesses, Sophie and Dana. Olivia almost allowed herself to breathe a silent sigh of relief—almost—but she'd hold off on that until Sophie and Mason had been pronounced man and wife.

Still, she had never seen her little sister look so happy, and she couldn't help but smile along with her. But then she realized that as soon as Sophie and Mason said *I do*, she and Alejandro would part ways.

She slanted a glance at him and remembered the kiss at the luau. How it had started as a means to an end and had turned into something electrifying. His hands on her body. The way her body had responded to his touch, and how neither of them had seemed to want to stop. But they had. And now that it appeared certain that Sophie would make it down the aisle tomorrow evening, Olivia needed to start mentally distancing herself from Alejandro. She was going to miss him and his kiss. Miami was a long way from Austin. Not that either of them wanted to try to keep this chemistry alive long distance. Because chemistry did not a relationship make.

Even so, too bad he didn't live in Austin. If he had, maybe they could see if this chemistry could evolve into something less ethereal. But he didn't live in Austin and that's why it was safe for her to daydream about what-ifs that would never happen.

Although if he did end up buying that vineyard, he would be in Austin now and again. She thought about the way he'd looked when he'd told her about the snag with the investor. It had been obvious that he hadn't wanted to talk about it. That's why she hadn't pressed him further. Since she didn't want to pry, she had no idea where his financing stood. Even though she shouldn't get involved, she had an idea about how she might be able to help him—just in case he needed it. After all, she owed him. If not for him, Sophie might not have gone through with the wedding. Olivia felt like the least she could do was help Alejandro find a replacement investor. Her gaze combed the crowd until it landed on her father.

Yes, she just might be able to secure Alejandro's vineyard purchase. She would talk to her dad after the brides and grooms had each said *I do* and the wedding was over.

In the meantime, she was going to make sure she played her role of Cupid-struck lover to the hilt, to make sure Sophie didn't have any reason to back out at the last moment.

Matteo, Mason and Joaquin were talking about the eighteen holes they'd played that morning. Alejandro had begged off on the round of golf because he'd needed to make some phone calls.

The guys talked about bogeys and birdies and the difficulty of the fifteenth hole, but Olivia wasn't a golfer and the conversation didn't hold her interest. Alejandro seemed to be in his own world, too. She wondered where that world might be and who he might be thinking about.

Olivia leaned over so that her arm rested flush against Alejandro's. She let her hand fall onto his thigh. Granted, his leg was hidden by the table and no one could see it, but it helped her get into character.

Following suit, Alejandro did the same thing, letting his hand wander over to her thigh. It happened so naturally. His thumb and forefinger toyed with the hem of her dress. The feel of his thumb on her bare leg sent shivers coiling outward from her belly.

In response, she traced tiny circles over his pant leg, on the inside of his thigh, going high, but not *too* high. This was for their own entertainment, of course, but it was just for play. He was teasing her and he was blurring the line between pretend romance and giving in to the attraction that they were both feeling. Last night's kiss had confirmed that. It had been filled with curiosity and longing and pent-up desire.

For a crazy moment she wondered what would happen if they just gave in to their feelings...

She thought it through, making a crazy attempt at justification. By making love with Alejandro, this act they had been putting on for Sophie's benefit wouldn't be a complete farce. It wouldn't be a total lie. Of course they wouldn't be in love as they claimed, but they would be involved. Even if she'd made love with Alejandro, they would still break up right on schedule and move on with their lives.

But in the end, common sense won because the thought of rendering herself so vulnerable to Alejandro, making love to him knowing that they would say goodbye, made her heart ache.

She laced her fingers through his and took his hand off her leg, putting it on the table, where everyone could see.

This was just another act in the play. A play that was for her sister's benefit.

"May I have your attention, please," said Gerald Robinson. The room quieted down at the sound of her father's commanding voice. "Sophie and Mason, Dana and Kieran, please come up here. Join me. I'd like to say a few words. Even though the Montgomerys are cohosting this evening with me, I hope they won't mind me proposing a toast to the four kids whose lives will change forever tomorrow night."

Olivia flinched, suddenly wishing she could muzzle her father, because he was a man who spoke his mind and she could never be sure exactly what was going through that head of his. She squeezed Alejandro's hand as she watched the foursome join him at the front of the room.

"You okay?" he said, looking at her with eyes so dark and soulful it made Olivia's breath hitch.

"I'm fine. Or at least I hope I will be—or everything will be—" She gave an almost imperceptible nod toward her father and leaned in closer to whisper to Alejandro. He smelled good—like citrus and something grassy and clean. It instantly calmed her nerves. "I hope he doesn't decide to unload his ideas about love and marriage. I did that and we saw where that got us."

Alejandro smiled that lazy, hypnotizing smile of his. For a split second Olivia wanted to lean in and kiss him.

"If he does," Alejandro whispered, "we will just have to put in some overtime."

His gaze dropped to her lips and lingered for a moment before he freed his hand from hers and put his arm around her shoulder, pulling her close in a display so convincing that Olivia wanted to believe it was real.

Good grief. What the hell is wrong with me?

She inhaled, trying to clear her mind, but all she managed to accomplish was filling her senses with the scent of him. She needed to get some air.

Her father was in the middle of giving his toast. He hadn't said anything offensive yet—then again, Olivia had only been listening with half an ear—but there was still time.

She sat forward in her seat. "Will you excuse me for a moment, please?"

As she stood, she caught Zoe's eye.

Out in the hall both Rachel and Zoe fell into step with her as she made her way toward the ladies' bathroom.

The restroom was decorated with dainty pink flowered wallpaper and gold fixtures. It was divided into two sections: a sitting area with a love seat and a vanity where guests could freshen up makeup or wait for friends to finish in the second area, which contained the toilets and lavatories. The two areas were separated by old-fashioned swinging doors.

"What's going on?" Zoe said, once they were inside the restroom.

Olivia considered making a sarcastic quip about being in here because nature called, but she was tired of pretending. That wasn't why she was here.

"For a moment, I was afraid our father was going to single-handedly undo all the hard work we've accomplished this week bringing Sophie and Mason back together. It's one thing for Sophie to get upset over my indiscretion—that's fixable, as evidenced by the events of this week. But if Dad is in one of his moods and he starts going to town and giving a dissertation on his views of the institution of marriage, I don't know if I'll be able to fix it."

"You can't worry about that," said Rachel. "She seems fine. I really doubt anything could sway her now. She loves Mason. I think if she did have another episode like she had last weekend, maybe it would be a good idea to question whether or not she was ready to get married."

"You're right," Olivia said. "It's just that we've come this far. I don't want anything to go wrong."

"I have something sticky on my fingers," Rachel said. "Come in here so I can wash my hands." She pushed through the double doors into the area with the sinks and stalls. Olivia and Zoe followed her.

"You are still blaming yourself and you need to stop," said Zoe. "You have done everything you can to ensure that Sophie makes it down the aisle. I mean, not many sisters would go to the lengths that you've gone to, pretending to be in love—although getting to cozy up to Alejandro Mendoza isn't really a hardship."

Rachel and Zoe laughed.

"I must admit you two have put on a pretty convincing performance this week," Zoe said. "There were times that even I believed you. I don't think anyone suspects that your relationship is anything but real. Certainly not Sophie. She'll be fine."

Rachel turned off the water and reached for a paper towel just as Sophie pushed through the double doors. Her smile was gone and so was her rosy glow. "So it was all an act? You and Alejandro have only been pretending to be in love with each other?"

Olivia's heart stopped. Rachel and Zoe stood frozen in place with huge eyes and gaping mouths.

"You lied to me." Sophie's voice was laced with hysteria and kept getting higher with each word. "Why would you do something like that, Olivia?"

Alejandro looked up at the feel of someone tapping him on the shoulder.

Rachel leaned down and whispered, "We have a situation. Can you help me, please?"

A feeling of dread spread over him as he glanced around the ballroom and realized that the other three Fortune Robinson sisters weren't in the room. He had no idea what was up. Had Sophie changed her mind again? She had looked perfectly happy a few moments ago when she had joined her father at the front of the room for the toast. Gerald Robinson had seemed uncharacteristically sentimental and Sophie had seemed to bubble over as she leaned in and kissed her father on the cheek. But Alejandro was quickly learning that the Fortune Robinson family was strangely complex. Just when he thought he had them figured out they left him guessing.

He followed Rachel to another room near the one where the rehearsal dinner was taking place and found Sophie reading Olivia the riot act.

"So this was all a horrible trick?" she asked.

"Sophie, I can explain if you'll just let me," Olivia said. She reached out to take hold of Sophie's hand, but Sophie pulled away.

"Don't. Don't touch me."

"Sophie, I did this for you. You were getting ready to make the biggest mistake of your life deciding not to marry Mason, and I felt like I'd caused it. I wanted to fix it. There's no reason for you to be mad—"

"No reason to be mad? You lied to me, Olivia. I suppose this has all been one big joke to you?"

"Calm down, Sophie," Zoe said. "You're acting like she stole your fiancé rather than try to help you make things right."

It seemed like Zoe's words didn't even register with Sophie.

"How many other people are in on this joke?" Sophie demanded. "How many? Tell me."

Olivia seemed to be stalling and stammering as Alejandro approached. She looked at him with desperation in her eyes, but she finally found her voice. "Only Zoe, Rachel and—"

"There you are, *querida*," Alejandro said. "I've been looking all over for you, my love. Is everything okay?"

"You can drop the act, Alejandro," Sophie said. "I

know all about your little game and I don't appreciate it one bit."

"Game?" Alejandro asked, lacing his right fingers through Olivia's and putting a protective arm around her shoulder. "I have no idea what you're talking about."

Sophie wasn't buying it. "This." She gestured at Olivia and Alejandro with a dismissive wave of her hand. "This lovey-dovey act. Olivia isn't in love with you. She doesn't even believe in love. She's made that perfectly clear too many times over the years. So just stop. Right now. Okay? This is insulting."

Olivia glanced up at him with a look that suggested she wished she could melt into the ground. He did his best to reassure her with his eyes. *Don't worry. I've got this.*

He dropped his arm from Olivia's shoulder and pulled his fingers from her grasp. "Wow. Did I read this all wrong? I'm so embarrassed. I think we need to talk, because obviously I've gotten the wrong message."

Sophie snorted. "Please don't tell me she used you. She concocted this elaborate scheme and didn't even clue you in? Olivia?"

"No," Alejandro said. "I know it started out as a way to convince you, Sophie, that love was real. Olivia thought that the best way to do that was to make you think she had fallen in love with me. The funny thing is, somewhere along the way in the midst of all this craziness, we really did fall in love. Or at least I did, and I thought she felt the same way."

He turned back to Olivia. "After everything we've shared. I… I just don't know how I could have been so wrong. I know you said you didn't want to tell your sisters about how things have changed between us because you didn't want to upstage the wedding. But all those kisses we shared felt so real. I'm in love with you, Olivia. Maybe we should leave and talk about this privately. I don't want to ruin your sister's night. However, I do need to know right now if this is just a game to you."

He was playing his part so convincingly that he almost believed himself. It wasn't hard. Olivia Fortune Robinson would be a very easy woman to love. But then something flashed in her eyes that made him get ahold of himself and he knew she understood what she needed to do.

"No, it's not a game. I love you, too," she replied.

Sophie exhaled impatiently. Her mouth was tight and her dark eyes glistened with tears. Alejandro half expected her to stomp her foot. But she didn't. She got right to the point.

"Just knock it off, you guys. This really is getting to be insulting. The more you lie the more furious it's making me."

Alejandro waited a beat, giving Olivia the opportunity to come clean. When she didn't, he knew it was up to him to pull out the big guns. So he did the only logical thing he could do: he fell down on one knee and took Olivia's hands in his.

Zoe, Rachel and Sophie gasped in unison.

"If you feel the same way I do," he said, his gaze fixed on Olivia, "if you love me as much as I love you, then, Olivia Fortune Robinson, will you be my wife?"

Chapter 7

Two hours before the wedding, Olivia watched as the stylist pinned a stunning cathedral-length veil to Sophie's head. The salon was abuzz with late-day clients. Dana, Monica, Rachel and Zoe had already come and gone. Madison, the owner of the salon where Olivia and her sisters had been coming for years, had already worked her magic on the rest of the bridal party. Sophie was the last of the lot since placing her long veil proved a little tricky. Unfortunately, it did nothing to quell her curiosity.

"When is Alejandro getting you a ring?" She turned to look at Olivia. Her expression promised she wasn't going to let this go.

"I need you to sit still and face forward, please," said Madison.

"Sophie, are you five years old?" Olivia asked. "Quit looking at me and do what Madison needs you to do.

Come on, the wedding is in two hours and we still need to get to the hotel so we can get dressed."

Olivia had appointed herself Sophie's handmaiden for the day. After everything that had happened, she was doing her best to make sure her sister made it down the aisle on time. In the meantime, she needed to distract Sophie from the details of last night's surprise engagement. *Surprise* being the key word. It was the last thing she had expected from Alejandro, but it had worked like a charm. Sophie's mood had turned on a dime. One minute she had been furious with her for the deception—and frankly, Olivia had been at a loss for what to do—and the next minute she had been crying tears of happiness for her sister whom she thought would never find love.

By the time she and Alejandro had left Sophie, she had seemed convinced. Today, not so much. She hadn't outwardly questioned the sudden proposal, but she was full of questions.

"Well, if you would just answer my question, I wouldn't have to keep moving my head to look at you," Sophie said. "If you would just tell me, I could close my eyes and relax. You don't want to be the cause of the bride's anxiety, do you?"

Olivia walked over and stood in front of Sophie, and leaned her hip on the vanity in front of the chair. "I don't know when he's going to get me a ring, Sophie. His proposal was as much of a surprise for me as it was for you. I—"

"Wait," said Madison, stopping midpin. "You're engaged? When she was talking about a ring, I didn't realize she meant an engagement ring. I didn't know you were even dating anyone, much less engaged. Oh, my gosh! Olivia! That's fabulous news. Congratulations! Have you set a date?"

Olivia cringed inwardly, but she dug deep, determined to keep up the happy, newly engaged charade. Really, all she wanted to do was change the subject. Last night, Sophie had been so upset. Even though Alejandro had shocked her with a fake proposal, in hindsight it really was just about the only thing that would've worked.

Alejandro had indeed saved the night, but it was a temporary fix.

Olivia couldn't help but feel that they had dug themselves in deeper and wonder how she was going to mend things with her sister when she and Alejandro called off the engagement. They had a couple of weeks before they would have to deal with that. It wouldn't be an issue until after everyone got home from their honeymoon. By that time Alejandro would be back in Miami and Olivia would be left with the task of announcing the broken engagement. But that seemed worlds away.

"Madison, today is Sophie and Dana's wedding day," she told the hairdresser. "I don't want to steal their thunder by putting the spotlight on me. So let's focus on them and I will give you all the details the next time I see you. Is that a deal?"

"Of course," Madison said, returning her focus to Sophie's veil.

"Hey," said Sophie. "Dana's gone to the hotel. I'm the only bride here and I say I want to talk about the engagement. Did you really not have any inkling? I mean, I'm so happy for you, but you guys met a week ago." She turned her head slightly to look at Madison. "Well, actually, they didn't just meet. They've seen each other at

Zoe's and Rachel's weddings. Alejandro is the brother of their husbands. My sisters have a thing for Mendoza men, I guess. But I digress." She turned back to Olivia. "*Inkling.* Did you really not have an inkling this was going to happen?

"Come on, Soph," Olivia said. "I mean it. I don't want today to be about me. Let's keep the proposal on the down-low for the time being. Okay?"

Sophie shrugged. "I'm almost more excited about this news than I am to walk down the aisle."

"I'm going to pretend you didn't just say that," Olivia said.

Sophie rolled her eyes and turned her head away from her sister. Madison sighed and put both hands on either side of Sophie's face and gently moved the bride back into position.

"If you keep moving your head, I'm going to stick a bobby pin up your nose."

Sophie squinted at Madison. "How could you stick a bobby pin up my nose if I'm looking in the opposite direction?"

Madison cocked a brow. "Obviously you don't understand. If you don't sit still, I'm going to stick a bobby pin up your nose on purpose. To get your attention. I really don't want to do that to you on your wedding day. So, please?"

Sophie looked momentarily stunned, but sat up straight and faced the front, folding her hands primly in her lap. "Okay. I'm sorry."

Olivia chuckled to herself. Madison was one of the few people who could get away with saying something like that without making Sophie mad.

"You know, it might be a good thing that he hasn't

gotten the ring yet," said Sophie. "That means you can pick out exactly what you want."

She held up her left hand. The two-carat diamond glistened in the overhead lights. "Mason proposed to me with the ring of my dreams. He knows me. He gets me. I am so lucky."

Sophie paused for a long moment and Olivia thought that they had turned a corner, until her sister said, "But don't worry, you and Alejandro will have the rest of your lives to get to know each other. I mean, on one level, I think you two know each other better than some couples who have been together for decades. That's what love at first sight is—or in your case, second or third sight." She smirked at her own joke, then went on, undeterred. "I think we need to announce your engagement tonight."

Olivia held up her hands. "No. Stop. Look, we have talked about nothing else but Alejandro and me since we've been here. That's precisely why I'm asking you to not say anything about our engagement tonight. No, scratch that. I'm asking you to not even *think* about my engagement tonight. I want you to focus on your own wedding. Soph, this is *your* night. I promise we can make the big announcement after you all return from your honeymoons. And not a minute sooner, okay?"

God help me.

Sophie shrugged. She looked like an angel in her lace veil. Her dark hair was pulled back away from her face, accentuating her exquisite cheekbones. The makeup artist had done a beautiful job creating a smoky eye that brought out the almond shape of Sophie's without looking too heavy. It was sweet and sultry… It was just right.

"When we get home from Tahiti," Sophie said,

"Mason and I are going to throw the biggest, splashiest, most spectacular engagement party for you and Alejandro. We're going to invite everybody in Austin and Miami. Because it's a pretty spectacular happening when my sister, who had sworn for as far back as I can remember that she didn't believe in love, finally meets the man who makes a believer out of her. How does that sound?"

Sophie looked Olivia square in the eyes and held her gaze. Olivia did her best not to squirm.

Liar, liar. Pants on fire.

"That sounds—" Olivia's voice broke. She cleared her throat. "That sounds fabulous. But you might want to discuss the rather large guest list with Mason before you commit."

Still holding her sister's gaze, a slow Mona Lisa–like smile bloomed on Sophie's face.

"Mason will be happy to host the engagement party of the century for you and Alejandro. After all you've done for us."

Olivia couldn't breathe.

Oh, no. Oh, boy. Here we go.

She hoped she didn't look as pale as she felt.

"But you know," Sophie said, "it really was just a temporary case of cold feet. I would've married Mason no matter what. Because I love him and I can't imagine my life without him."

To Olivia's great relief, the double wedding went off without a hiccup. Sophie and Mason, Kieran and Dana were joined together as husband and wife in the grand ballroom of the Driskill Hotel, in front of nearly five hundred of their closest friends and family members.

The ballroom was festooned in white flowers— peonies, roses, lilies of the valley, freesias and hydrangeas arranged in tall gold-toned vases. The place looked like a florist's shop had exploded and it was glorious. The guests sat in gilded chairs situated in two sections on either side of an aisle. But tonight there weren't brides' and grooms' sides. The bridal couples had made it clear that everyone was gathered for the sake of love.

The place proved a perfect backdrop for her sister and sister-in-law.

Sophie looked stunning in her satin-and-lace ball gown, with its long train and veil trailing behind her. She looked like royalty.

Dana looked artistic and beautiful in the vintage silk shantung wedding gown that belonged to the grandmother of her maid of honor, Monica. She had graciously lent it to Dana for the special day and it served as both her something old and something borrowed. If Dana had designed a wedding gown for herself, it couldn't have been any more perfect than that one.

Honestly, Dana and Sophie both looked so radiant they could have worn bathrobes and slippers and still looked gorgeous. They were both so full of love as they promised to love, honor and respect their grooms for the rest of their lives.

As Olivia listened to the minister's touching opening words, her gaze picked Alejandro out of the guests. When he caught her looking at him, Olivia couldn't look away. Emotions she'd never experienced before zinged through her—happiness for the two couples pledging their love before God and everyone, wistfulness at the beauty of that love, and maybe even a touch of envy.

She may not believe in love, but never in her entire life had she wished she did more than that moment.

Little Rosabelle, Dana and Kieran's adopted daughter, was the one who drew her out of her reverie. Bedecked in her pink princess dress, complete with floral crown, four-year-old Rosie was the flower girl. She did a fabulous job strewing rose petals down the aisle. Her new nanny, Elaine, stood at the side of the dais, smiling encouragingly at the little girl, poised at the ready to gently correct Rosie's course should she veer off track. But the child played her part perfectly, smiling bashfully at the guests seated on her either side. Given that she was so young and it was getting close to her bedtime, Rosie couldn't have done a better job.

At the beginning of the ceremony she stood with the bridal party. It was no surprise when she grew a little restless. Standing next to Olivia, she began to entertain herself by playing with the skirt of Olivia's dress. She grabbed a handful of skirt and pulled it around herself like a cape. It enlisted titters and *awwws* from the audience. The sound made Rosie hide her face and then peek out from the fabric. When she saw everyone looking at her, she stepped around behind Olivia and hid. Olivia placed a reassuring hand on the little girl's blond curls. Actually, she didn't blame her one bit for wanting to hide. She was getting a little weary of these wedding games herself. There were many times this week when she had wanted to hide her face from the world. But her sister was happy and within a matter of minutes she would be married. It was all worth it.

Alejandro was smiling at her again. He looked so handsome in his dark suit and white shirt. It was a different look from the cool Miami casual that he had projected most of the week. The more dressed-up look suited him. He was such a handsome man. All of his brothers were married. Why wasn't he?

Olivia recalled the conversation she and her sisters had last week at the bachelorette party before everything blew up. If she were inclined to be a romantic she might have believed that the reason Alejandro had never married was because he had been waiting for her.

But that was just crazy.

"By the power vested in me," said the officiant, "I now pronounce you husband and wife. Err—husbands and wives?" The man shrugged and looked out at the guests. "Ladies and gentlemen, it is my pleasure to present to you Mr. and Mrs. Mason Montgomery and Mr. and Mrs. Kieran Fortune Robinson."

The guests erupted into boisterous applause as the recessional music sounded, signaling the end of the ceremony. Olivia handed Sophie her bouquet, scooped up Rosie, balancing her on her hip as she waited her turn to walk back down the aisle.

The bridal party exited the room where the ceremony had taken place and waited for the wedding planners to usher everyone out and into the room where they could enjoy cocktails and hors d'oeuvres. Then the bridal party and immediate family returned to the ceremony room for pictures.

They were using the same photographer as they'd used for Rachel's and Zoe's weddings, because she had done a beautiful job. But Olivia didn't remember the photos taking this long.

Joaquin and Matteo Mendoza were in the photographs because they were married to her sisters and therefore full-fledged immediate family. As with Alejandro, they had not been in the bridal party, so at first impulse it seemed strange that they would be in the pictures and Alejandro wouldn't. But it made sense.

I think maybe Alejandro would be a perfect match for Olivia.

She tried to blink away the memory of her sister's words. It was just crazy girl talk.

Isn't it a coincidence that he's the last single Mendoza and you're the last single Fortune Robinson?

Obviously it was time for a reality check. There were good reasons that the two of them were still single. Good sense topped the list.

It had been a long week of wedding festivities and pretending. She was tired and her defenses were down. That always happened when she let herself get worn out. That was the only reason she was thinking these irrational thoughts as she watched her sisters interact with their husbands.

As the photographer arranged them into a grouping for a shot of the entire family Sophie stepped out of place and surveyed the group.

"Where is Alejandro?" she asked. "It's my party and I'll do what I want to," she said with a sassy smile. "And I want Alejandro in the family picture. It's important."

"It's not just your party," Olivia reminded her sister.

"Dana?" Sophie asked. "Do you mind if Alejandro is in the family picture?"

Dana shook her head. "Of course not. It's fine."

"Mason? Kieran?" Sophie said. "Any objections?"

As they indicated their approval, Sophie shot her sister a triumphant look.

Sophie wasn't letting this go. Olivia realized if she put up too much of a fight, things could get ugly.

Granted, Sophie and Mason were married. Technically, her job was done. However, if she took this opportunity to announce that there was no engagement or that they had called off the engagement, pretending it was too sudden or logistically difficult, it would cast a dark cloud over the festivities.

This was one of those times when it was best to lose the battle so she could win the war. In that spirit, the best thing she could do was to just go along with it.

"In that case, if nobody objects I will go find Alejandro," Olivia said. "I'll be back as soon as I can."

It wasn't hard to locate him. He was standing with his father and Josephine, sipping a cocktail that looked like scotch and soda. He was holding a flute of champagne in the other hand. As she approached she was about to tease him about being a double-fisted drinker, but he smiled the warmest smile at her and held out the champagne.

"This is for you," he said. "You look like you could use it."

"I look that bad, huh?"

His smile faded. "No, not at all. It was just a figure of speech. You look beautiful."

Olivia felt her face warm at the sincere compliment. She never blushed. It was unfortunate that her body was choosing this moment to start. Then again, her body seemed to have a mind of its own when it came to Alejandro.

Just accept the compliment, she told herself. It was only a compliment. "Thank you. Hello, Orlando. Josephine, you look lovely. I'm so glad you both could be here for the wedding. It means a lot to our family."

They exchanged pleasantries about the ceremony

and about how adorable Rosabelle was in her flower girl debut.

"You're so good with children," Josephine said. "Do you have any of your own?"

A hiccup of a laugh bubbled up in Olivia's throat. "Oh, heavens no. I'm not married. Of course, you know that since— I mean, I've never been married."

Her gaze fluttered to Alejandro, and she felt her face heat up again.

"I'm sorry to barge in but, Alejandro, your presence is requested in the photo room."

Photo room? Ugh. Get ahold of yourself.

"I mean, the bridal party would like for you to be in some of the pictures, if you don't mind."

She smiled and tried to look normal, but she felt like one of those grimacing emoticons.

"I don't mind at all," Alejandro said, just as calm and cool as if she had asked him to bring the car around so they could escape this circus.

Now, there was an idea. Maybe they should get in his rental car and just keep driving until they were far away from here. Maybe they could go to Miami. She could stay until both couples were back from their honeymoons, when she could announce that she and Alejandro were no longer engaged. Then it wouldn't be a bombshell. In fact, Sophie might be so wrapped up in her own marital bliss that she wouldn't want the gray clouds of a broken engagement to shadow her own happiness.

"Where should we go?" Alejandro asked, waiting on her to lead him.

"Miami," Olivia mused aloud. "Let's go to Miami. Right now."

Alejandro shook his head and laughed. "That's one of the things I like the best about her," he said to his father and Josephine. "She has the best sense of humor. She always keeps me laughing and guessing."

The three of them laughed again and Olivia joined in so that they would believe that she really was just making a joke that hinted at her being a weary maid of honor.

If they only knew.

Actually, no. She didn't want them to know the truth. She didn't want anyone else to know about the ticking time bomb that she had created. She simply wanted to pacify her sister until the married couples got into their respective limousines and drove off into the night toward the first days of the rest of their lives.

She took his arm to lead him toward the photo room. After they had said their goodbyes to Josephine and Orlando and were out of earshot, Alejandro asked, "Why do they want me in the photos?"

Olivia slanted him a look that suggested he should know why. "Because, darling, you are my fiancé. Remember?"

"Right." He ran a palm over his eyes and raked his fingers through his hair, a tic that Olivia was beginning to associate with him being stressed. "Did Sophie tell everyone?"

Olivia shook her head. "No, but she is definitely testing me. I can't tell if she's on to us or if she's just excited because she thinks I've finally come over to the dark side."

"The dark side? Is that what you think of marriage?"

Maybe she was being overly sensitive, but there seemed to be a bit of rebuke in his tone.

"Don't you?" she answered. "I mean, you're not married and how old are you?"

"I'm thirty-four. And no, I don't necessarily think of marriage as the dark side."

"Then why aren't you married?" She instantly regretted asking the question that had been lurking in the back of her mind since she realized he was the last single Mendoza. "Or do weddings make you sentimental?"

He shot her a look. "I was actually engaged once."

The revelation hit Olivia like a sucker punch. "Really? What happened? I mean, if you don't mind me asking. I really thought you and I were similar in our thoughts about marriage."

One side of his mouth quirked up. "That's what happens when you assume."

She made a show of flinching. She remembered the old saying—*when you assume you make an ass out of u and me.* She arched a brow as she asked, "Are you calling me an ass, Alejandro?"

"Don't be ridiculous." The way he looked at her had her blushing, and inwardly going to pieces. It should be illegal for a man to look at a woman like he looked at her, making her feel things she shouldn't be feeling in this elaborate charade that they had orchestrated. Especially when he was set to leave in a couple of days.

"Again, when you assume, you run the risk of jumping to wrong conclusions," he said as he reached for the door to the ballroom where the ceremony had taken place. "Here we are, my most cherished fiancée." His dark eyes danced with mischief. "Let's give the bride the show she's expecting."

They were already inside the ballroom when Olivia realized how neatly Alejandro had evaded her question.

He'd been engaged. Who was the woman he had loved enough to want to spend the rest of his life with—or at least want that for a brief period of time? What had happened to break up the engagement?

Now wasn't the time, but she fully intended to find out.

Alejandro's participation in the photos hadn't taken long. Sophie had only wanted him in one shot: the family photo. He had stood on the end and quietly joked with Olivia that they could cut him out of the picture if they wanted to. He probably should've found a way to gracefully bow out of the photo session. She could've told them she couldn't find him. But it was done now. He was officially part of the family photo.

He got the distinct feeling that Sophie might've been calling their bluff by including him in the family shot. If she was, then she knew she was taking a chance. Maybe she'd had the photographer snap a few shots without him after he'd left.

This wasn't the first time he'd wondered if he'd pushed the envelope too far when he had proposed to Olivia in front of Sophie and her sisters. But seeing Olivia in distress had made him desperate to fix the situation. He'd just wanted to see her smile again. Of course, he wanted Sophie to be okay, too, but for a crazed moment, when he'd seen Olivia in such turmoil, he'd known he had to make things right. His knee-jerk reaction had been a proposal.

There was no getting around it now. The fake-proposal die was cast.

Before he returned to Miami, he would help Olivia clean up any family repercussions the "breakup" might cause. It was important they left family relations as good as possible. Olivia had already said she would be the heavy and take responsibility for the breakup. She'd claim they'd gotten swept away by the romance of the double wedding, but with distance and a fresh perspective, she realized she wasn't ready for a life-time commitment.

Alejandro was prepared for the breakup. What he hadn't thought through was that he would have to delay his meeting to present the investment proposal to Gerald Robinson until after they called off the engagement. He didn't want it to appear that he was using Olivia for his own personal gain.

He'd debated whether or not to tell Olivia about his plan to ask her father to invest in Hummingbird Ridge. He'd ultimately come to the conclusion that it was best not to involve her. It was a long shot that he would buy in anyway.

If Robinson said no, Alejandro was perfectly prepared to leave it at that—no hard feelings. He didn't want Olivia to feel as if she needed to plead his case because she owed him.

Most people wouldn't feel the need to get involved on someone's behalf, but Olivia was different. Once she invested in someone, she was all in. Making sure her sister made it down the aisle was a case in point. She'd said more than once that she would make it up to him for helping her. A sixth sense told him that if she knew about the investor dropping out, she'd make it her mission to make that right. He couldn't take that chance. He'd fight his own fight.

If Gerald wasn't interested, he'd return to Miami and continue the frantic search for replacement funding. He could only hope that the Dailys wouldn't find another buyer before that. They had been so kind to refund his deposit, though they had every right to keep the money as stated in the contract. But Jack Daily had said he couldn't take the money in good conscience. That was one of the things that Alejandro loved about that winery in particular. It came from good stock, and he wasn't simply talking about the vines. He was talking about the family who had invested generations of blood, sweat and tears to make it what it was today.

They were good people and if he was given the chance, he wanted to carry on that legacy.

However, the way they'd left things was that if a viable buyer materialized before Alejandro could come up with the money, they would have to take the offer.

The Dailys were ready for the next phase in their life. They deserved the chance to write this next chapter. He hoped he would be able to write his own next chapter at Hummingbird Ridge. It would put him a hell of a lot closer to Austin than Miami. It would be easier to see Olivia if she was into seeing him. Maybe then he'd be able to figure out what had made her so down on marriage and romance.

The band leader called the crowd to order, putting an end to Alejandro's reverie. The man's deep baritone voice introduced the bridal party. As Olivia walked in, Alejandro watched her scan the crowd and find him.

He'd never met anyone who could flirt with her eyes the way Olivia did. She had great eyes. He felt mesmerized as she stood with the other bridesmaids and groomsmen until the brides and grooms had entered the room, acknowledged their guests and took to the parquet floor for their first dance.

She looked confident and happy—not a bit worried—as she closed the distance between them. If she wasn't worried, he wouldn't worry. At that moment, he decided he was going to forget all the challenges he was facing with the vineyard and the charade and just enjoy himself tonight. It was one of the easiest decisions he'd made in ages.

Olivia couldn't remember when she'd had so much fun at a wedding. It wasn't usually her preferred way to spend a Saturday night. But Alejandro knew how to show a girl a good time. The ballroom was awash in gold and white and there were so many flowers and tiny golden twinkling lights it seemed like their very own secret garden right in the middle of the busy city.

Sophie and Dana opted not to torture the bridal party by confining everyone to a head table. Instead, the two newly married couples dined together and the rest of the bridal party was dispersed among the guests. It was no surprise that they had seated Olivia and Alejandro together. If they hadn't, Olivia had been prepared to do some place card swapping—all for the sake of keeping up their charade, of course.

After dinner—a salad of warm goat cheese with gold and red baby beets; a surf and turf of filet mignon and sea bass served with truffle mushroom risotto—the dance floor heated up.

Alejandro was a good dancer. Olivia had no idea why she thought he might be reserved, but he wasn't at all. They danced to every song and by the time the band slowed things down with a ballad, it seemed perfectly natural when Alejandro, her fake fiancé, pulled her into his arms and held her close.

In the past, Olivia had always had a problem with slow dancing because most of the men she'd danced with had accused her of trying to lead. They would tell her to relax, to feel and respond to the subtle messages they sent with their bodies. Obviously either they were much too subtle—subtext: not man enough—with their bodily messages or she simply wasn't picking up their vibe.

Tonight, as she and Alejandro swayed to the music, was the first time she understood what it meant to let the man lead. Or maybe it was the first time she'd wanted to let someone else lead.

For the duration of the song, Olivia let herself imagine what it would be like if this pretend relationship was real. What would it be like to really be engaged to Alejandro Mendoza? She let herself go there, envisioning everything from what dress she would wear at their wedding—a mermaid-style gown that had caught her eye when she'd gone with Sophie for her final fitting—to what would happen on their honeymoon.

Ooooh, the honeymoon.

The thought made her breath catch. She closed her eyes as tiny points of warmth radiated out from her belly, making her lean into Alejandro and snuggle into his shoulder as they danced.

By the time the song ended, Olivia felt a little off-kilter. The two of them stepped apart, allowing a respectable amount of space between them. Sophie's voice broke the spell.

"I hope you all are having fun," she said. She was holding the lead singer's microphone with one hand. She had a champagne flute in the other. "Before the night gets away from me, I wanted to take this opportunity to give a shout-out to my sister, Olivia."

Olivia's heart leaped.

Oh, no. Please tell me she's not going to do what I think she's going to do.

Olivia grabbed Alejandro's arm to steady herself. He covered her hand with his left hand. She didn't dare look at him because she was trying to catch Sophie's eye to silently beg her not to do what it was becoming more and more apparent that she was about to do. But Sophie skillfully looked everywhere but at Olivia.

"My sister Olivia is my rock," Sophie said. "She's always thinking of and doing things for others. So often, she sacrifices her own needs for those she loves, and she doesn't get the credit she deserves. Olivia and Alejandro, I'm sorry for doubting you two. They know what I mean by that, so I won't bore you with the details. But I will say this—and my sister asked me not to say anything about this because she didn't want to steal my and Dana's thunder—because I just can't resist. Olivia and Alejandro have some great news."

She lifted her champagne flute and smiled broadly. "Everyone, please raise your glasses to the most recent Fortune Robinson bride-to-be and Mendoza groom-to-be. Olivia and Alejandro are engaged to be married."

Chapter 8

After the wedding, as soon as the brides and grooms were off in a send-off shower of sweet-smelling lavender buds, Alejandro drove Olivia home to her condo in the Barton Hills neighborhood of Austin.

All she wanted was to get out of her bridesmaid dress and the pinching heels, take her hair down and get away from the flood of congratulations that had washed in after Sophie's little announcement.

They were both exhausted and contemplative, so they were mostly quiet in the car. They didn't talk about a plan, but Olivia knew they needed to before Alejandro left her place tonight.

As she changed into her heather gray yoga pants and a soft white T-shirt, she came up with a plan and was ready to present a strong case when she walked back into the living room. Alejandro was on the same page because he took the words right out of her mouth when he asked, "What are we going to do now?"

"First, I'm going to open a bottle of wine," she said. "That's what I'm going to do right now."

"Sounds good to me. Do you think that we're okay sticking to the original plan?"

She stopped on her way into the kitchen and looked back at him. "You mean breaking up tomorrow?"

He shrugged.

"I was hoping we could stay in character at least until after Sophie and Mason were home from their honeymoon and settled into married life. Does that work for you?"

"When will they be back?"

"They're only going away for a week. Mason has some business he needs to take care of. Then I think they're planning a longer trip in the fall."

He seemed to mull things over for a moment. "Yeah, I think I can make that work. I have some Hummingbird Ridge business, but nothing I can't tend to while I'm here."

"Great! A week should be long enough for the wedding sparkle to wear off and for us to realize we were swept away by the romance. Then we can 'take a break.'" She bracketed the words with air quotes. "I'm happy to be the heavy. I'll tell everyone I felt like things were just moving too fast. I'll confess that I got caught up in the romance of the wedding and while I think the world of you, I need time to think things over. My family won't be surprised, believe me. In fact, I'll bet they're already placing wagers on how long it will take me to call off the engagement."

Alejandro frowned at her. "I thought maybe your

cynicism about love was all an act, but you've almost convinced me that you're really not a believer."

He was quiet for a moment, as if he was giving her the chance to tell him he was wrong, that it really was an act. When she didn't say anything, he asked, "What happened to sour you on love?"

Biting her lip, she looked away, toward the kitchen. Why did he care? She could read all sorts of things into that, but she wasn't going to.

"How about that glass of wine?" she asked, trying to buy herself a little more time. "After the day I've had, I'm going to need a glass of wine or two if we're going to have this conversation."

"Sure, thanks. That sounds good."

"Is red okay? I have white, but it's not cold."

"Red is perfect. May I help?"

She opened the cabinet and took down the wine-glasses, hoping by avoiding the question he would get the hint that she didn't want to talk about it. "I'm good. I've got this."

The phrase was a pep talk for herself. Even though she didn't really want to talk about it, maybe she owed him a little insight about her parents' dynamics. After all, two Mendozas were part of the family and they were bound to pick up on the tension, if her sisters hadn't already filled them in. Alejandro had been so good to help her, and he did care enough to ask. He didn't strike her as the type who would dig just to be nosy. But why was he asking? What did that mean? She supposed it was possible for a man to care about a woman in a purely platonic way, although she had never had any success-ful relationships of that nature with men. And truth be told, if circumstances were different—if they weren't practically family—maybe she would want more than something platonic with Alejandro. But if it got messy… No, she'd better leave well enough alone.

"When are Dana and Kieran back?"

"They are going to be gone longer. They're heading to Paris for ten days," she said. "Did you meet Elaine Wagner tonight—the new nanny they'd hired to care for Rosabelle? She was the kid-wrangler tonight. She has a son who's just about Rosie's age. She's going to look after Rosie and her dog Sammy. You know that Dana and Kieran adopted Rosie after her father died, right?" She didn't wait for Alejandro's response before she continued.

"Having Elaine come on board has given Kieran and Dana enough peace of mind to know that they can get away for a while. After all they've been through— and with this whirlwind wedding—they deserve some time away."

She looked across the open-concept kitchen and saw Alejandro watching her intently. Since talking about Dana and Kieran had seemed to divert the conversation from her folks, she decided to continue.

"When they get back they're going to live at Dana's house. They want to get a new place together, but with the wedding put on the fast track and the honeymoon trip to Paris they haven't had a spare minute to begin the search. But Dana's house has a nice big yard for Rosabelle and Sammy to play in. Really, there's no need to rush the process. Everything will happen in good time."

She paused to pull the lever of the corkscrew and yank the cork out of the bottle. She knew she was rambling, but it seemed to have worked.

She set aside the cork from the wine, a Cabernet

Sauvignon from the Columbia Valley, which *Wine Spectator* had scored a ninety-six. She wasn't a wine connoisseur, but she knew what she liked and she hoped this would be suitable for Alejandro. She poured the wine, secured both glasses between the fingers of her left hand, grabbed the bottle with her right and joined Alejandro in the living room. He was sitting on the couch, with one arm stretched out along the back. He looked so at home, like he belonged there.

As she set the wine bottle down on the coffee table, she realized she was nervous. Even so, she took a seat next to him on the couch rather than choosing the gray toile-print wingback chair. It reminded her of that first night in the Driskill bar when she'd moved from the chair to sit next to him. She hadn't been so drunk that she didn't remember it had felt so natural to sit next to him and just lean in and start kissing him. Of course, they'd kissed many times since. She wondered what he would do if she leaned in and kissed him right now.

She was tempted, but she didn't do it. Instead, she handed him a wineglass.

As had become their custom, they purposefully locked gazes before clinking their glasses. She thought about making another joke about good sex, but she just couldn't summon words that wouldn't sound rehashed or recycled, like ground they had already covered. Was that because she knew they were coming up on the final act of this performance?

With Sophie married and away on her honeymoon, did they really need to stay together? Wouldn't it be easier to end it now? Sophie was a big girl, and if Olivia was perfectly honest with herself she knew that Sophie had gone through with her marriage of her own volition. Olivia and Alejandro dating or not dating, being engaged or not, would not make one bit of difference in her sister's relationship.

If she knew what was best for both Alejandro and herself, she should tell him right now that it would be better for him to leave as planned. Funny though, she really wasn't ready for this to end. She'd gotten used to him being around. Even if it was a farce, she had gotten used to being part of a couple with him.

Alejandro and Olivia.

Olivia and Alejandro.

She liked the sound of that.

She traced the rim of her wineglass with her finger. Even after only a week it sounded natural to link their names. Would they remain friends and keep in touch after he went back to Miami? Would he make a point of ringing her up when he came to Texas on vineyard business? She hoped so. In fact, she wanted that very much.

She looked at him, mustering the will to tell him he was free to go if he needed to, but instead, what came out was "If we're going to make this engagement look convincing, don't you think you should check out of the Driskill and move in here with me?"

He looked surprised, as if he hadn't considered the possibility, and she braced herself for him to be the voice of reason, to not only decline but say everything she had been thinking only moments ago. That it was time to break up. Time to come clean. Time to move on.

"Are you sure?" he asked.

"Since short-term rentals are hard to come by and hotels are uncomfortable and expensive, you can move into one of the spare bedrooms in my condo," she said.

"Short-term rental?" His brows knit together. "I thought we were only talking about a week."

"Yes, well, I was just thinking that you might not want to pay for a hotel. Unless you want to, of course."

She cringed inwardly. This wasn't going the way she'd hoped. Maybe she should just make it easy on both of them and cut him loose.

"No. I see what you're saying and I appreciate it," he said. "I just don't want to impose. It's not easy having someone in your space, even for a week."

True. But it was definitely easier to host a guest when you wanted the person there. And she didn't mind Alejandro being in her space.

"It'll be fine. And it'll appear more convincing if we're living together. It's the least I can do after all you've done to help me."

"It wasn't such a hardship," he said. For a moment, something shifted between them. She swore he was going to lean in and kiss her. But then she glanced down at her wineglass and when she looked back up the spell was broken.

"I will have to cook dinner for you while I'm here," he said. "It'll give me the chance to show off my culinary chops. I'm happy to say I know my way around the kitchen."

"Did you learn to cook so you could get the girls?"

He laughed. "Of course. Works every time."

She loved the way his eyes came to life when they bantered. Kissing him felt almost as natural as verbally sparring with him.

"How about this?" he said. "I'll earn my keep by cooking for you."

"Works for me. I've been told I have many talents, but domestic pursuits are not among them." She chuckled.

"Hey, my birthday is next week," she said. "Why don't you cook dinner for me then? Otherwise, my parents might insist on celebrating with us."

"Do you think so? I got the distinct feeling that your parents were avoiding me tonight after Sophie's announcement. I'd mentally prepared myself for what I would say to them, but it was probably for the best that they focused on your sister's and brother's wedding. If your dad is one of those old-fashioned types that gets offended if a guy doesn't ask for his daughter's hand, I didn't want to face the wrath of Gerald Robinson. That would've definitely been a party foul."

"You don't have anything to worry about. My father isn't really the traditional type when it comes to love and marriage. In fact, if you asked his permission to marry me, he would probably think you were up to something. Or at the very least sucking up."

"Have they said anything to you?" he asked.

"My mother cornered me earlier tonight. She said she was happy for us and she wants to get to know you better. She and my father want to take us out for dinner. Which means *she* wants to go out to dinner and my father probably knows nothing about it. She was trying to get us to come over tomorrow night, but I told her that we were both busy. I'll keep putting her off as long as I can. Especially for my birthday."

He picked up the bottle and refilled her wineglass. "What day is your birthday?"

"It's next Saturday."

"Maybe you should celebrate with them. When I

was growing up, birthdays were always a big deal in our house. My mother would have a cake for us and we got to pick whatever we wanted for dinner."

Olivia shifted, and pulled one foot up and balanced it on her knee. She began to massage her foot. When she noticed him watching her hands, she said, "Sorry, my feet hurt after standing in those heels all night."

"Here," he said, "put your feet in my lap. I give a mean foot massage."

She looked a little taken aback. For a moment he thought she was going to refuse, but she swung her legs up onto the couch and stretched out so that her feet were in his lap.

He used his thumb to draw small, firm circles on the ball of her foot.

She tilted her head back and moaned. It made him think of the night in the Driskill bar when she kissed him. He had a nearly overwhelming urge to lean over and see if her lips tasted as sweet as they had that night. But it probably wouldn't be a good move since he was going to be moving in with her and they needed to keep things cool just a little longer.

"That feels so good," she said. "Are you close to your parents? It sounds as if they made a big deal over making you feel special on your birthday."

"I'm close to my dad. My mom passed away about five years ago."

"I'm sorry."

He shrugged. "Thanks. My mom was a wonderful woman. We all took her loss pretty hard. But it's good to see my dad happy again with Josephine. There was a time when it seemed like he would never be the same again. I know you and your sisters are close but are you close to your folks? You seem like you're avoiding the question."

"Maybe I am." She sat up and pulled her knees into her chest, hugging them and still managing to hold her wineglass. "My sisters and I are solid, but my parents? They sort of live in their own worlds. Separate worlds. I guess I might as well tell you because you're bound to hear about it anyway. This reporter, Ariana Lamonte, has been doing a big exposé on my family. My dad mostly. Last year, evidence surfaced that he is actually part of the Fortune family."

Alejandro nodded. "The Fortunes are a big Texas family. Seems like everybody's related to them in one way or another—or at least most people have a close degree of separation. My brother Cisco is married to Delaney Fortune."

Olivia shrugged. "This is still new for me. I'm still trying to digest it, because the implications are pretty damning. Not only does it mean that my father has been lying to us about his identity for as long as my brothers and sisters and I have been alive, but we are also coping with the fact that my father seems to have other children who keep popping up. Illegitimate ones."

She closed her eyes and rested her forehead on her knees. A moment later, she looked up at him.

"I probably shouldn't be telling you all this, but for some crazy reason I feel like I can trust you."

He reached out and put a hand on her arm. "You can trust me, Olivia. It sounds like you've been through a lot of change this year."

She nodded. "Not just this year. The truth has been a long time coming. I've always known that my parents didn't have a great relationship. I just didn't know why. But now that all of my father's illegitimate children keep crawling out of the woodwork, it's just hard for me to be around my parents. Their relationship is such a farce. I have no idea why they stay together because it's all a lie. So you can see going to dinner with them for my birthday would be the ultimate torture. Will you please be my knight in shining armor and save me from that?"

He brushed back a strand of hair that had fallen into her face. He had heard rumblings about Gerald Robinson's Fortune connection, but nobody seemed to know the true story. He hadn't heard about illegitimate children. No wonder Olivia was freaked out about love and relationships.

"I wouldn't want to do anything else," he said. "You know, love is a tricky thing. My parents showed me the best example of true love and commitment. It was real and perfect. Not only did I see it in my parents' relationship when my mother was alive, I've experienced that deep kind of true love myself. Yet I'm even screwed up when it comes to love. That's because when you fall in love, you're so vulnerable. You open yourself up and you expose yourself to the worst pain—"

The words got lost in his throat. Olivia put her hand on his. He looked at her sitting next to him on the couch in her yoga pants and fitted T-shirt and somehow the possibility of falling in love didn't seem so out of reach anymore.

"Sounds like you're speaking from experience," she said. "How did Anna break your heart?"

It had been years since he'd talked about this, but he heard himself speaking before he could stop himself.

"Anna Molino was my high school sweetheart. We

would be married right now if fate hadn't been cruel. Anna died in a car accident when we were just twenty years old."

"Oh, Alejandro, I'm sorry."

Maybe it was all the pent-up emotion that he had been harboring for years; maybe it was because he was actually starting to feel something for this beautiful woman. Whatever the reason, he reached out and ran his thumb along her jawline, moved his hand around so it cupped the back of her neck and lowered his mouth to hers.

When their lips met, he lost all sense of time and space. All he knew was things hadn't felt this right in ages.

"Do you want to stay here tonight?" Olivia whispered. "We can go to the Driskill and get your things tomorrow." Her expression was so earnest, he almost said yes, but if he stayed he wasn't sure what might happen. He needed some space to think about what he was getting into by moving in with her—even if it was only for a week. He needed to figure out if he could handle it.

"In the guest room," she amended as if she was reading his thoughts. "Because we probably shouldn't be kissing like that unless we mean it."

"You're right," he said. "I'm sorry. I shouldn't have done that."

"Don't be sorry," she said. "I'm not. But we probably should save the action for our adoring public."

He stood.

"On that note, I should get back to the hotel tonight."

Chapter 9

Alejandro checked out of the hotel and was at Olivia's condo by eleven o'clock on Sunday morning. After the kiss last night, she wasn't sure what to expect today. Olivia had even prepared herself for the possibility of Alejandro deciding to stay at the hotel rather than with her.

They were both a little shy this morning as she showed him to the spare bedroom down the hall.

"Here's the closet where you can hang your clothes. I put some extra hangers in there for you. There's a dresser if you need some drawers. I'm sorry this room doesn't have an en suite, but the bathroom is right across the hall. Here, let me show you."

She knew she was talking too much, rambling away like a Realtor showing a house rather than someone welcoming a houseguest. But he wasn't just a houseguest. The thought that she and Alejandro would be sleeping under the same roof made the muscles in her stomach knot a little too tight.

He smiled at her. "This is perfect. Thank you for letting me stay here."

"It's for a good cause. I'll leave you alone while you get settled in. Please let me know if you need anything else to be comfortable. I put fresh towels in the bathroom and—"

"I can unpack later," he said. "What I'd really like to do right now is go get something to eat. Are you hungry?"

She hadn't really thought about it until he'd asked, because she'd been so anxious about whether or not he would end up bailing on her. She put a hand on her stomach and realized that she was famished.

"I am hungry," she said. "Did you have someplace in mind? I would offer to whip us up something but I don't have any food in the house. And that's probably a good thing because I'm not much of a cook."

He laughed. "I was serious last night when I said I was happy to serve as the chef while I'm staying here with you. I might even teach you some of my secrets."

She would love to learn Alejandro Mendoza's secrets, and not just those that pertained to the kitchen. And just like that, all of the potential awkwardness she feared would be spawned from last night's kiss melted away like ice cream on a hot Austin day.

"I'll hold you to that," she said. "Maybe you can give me a cooking lesson tomorrow? But in the meantime why don't we go to the South Congress Café? They have carrot cake French toast that is to die for."

Olivia's condo was just a short walk to the restaurant. It was a beautiful, sunny day, cool enough to make it pleasurable to be outdoors, but warm enough that the walk had Olivia working up a thirst even in the light sundress and sandals she wore.

Alejandro looked crisp and cool in his khaki shorts and ivory linen shirt.

When they arrived at the restaurant they found there was a short wait for a table. This was one of her favorite places to eat and Olivia was happy to see it doing such brisk business.

Even though she'd been there more times than she could count, the place looked both familiar and brand-new as she tried to see the exposed-brick walls and blond-wood-beamed ceilings through Alejandro's eyes.

Once they were seated, Alejandro asked her, "Do you have to do anything constructive today? If not, do you want to order Bloody Marys? One of those would really hit the spot right now."

"I scheduled myself to do absolutely nothing today but recover from the wedding," Olivia said. "A Bloody Mary sounds good, but I think champagne is what I need."

They ordered the drinks along with water and coffee, but asked the server to come back for their food order.

It was nice to be out like this with Alejandro. The pressure of the wedding was off her shoulders, and there was nobody around that they needed to impress. The entire day was theirs. It dawned on Olivia that this was the first time they had been together without any expectations weighing them down.

"I'm guessing that your day is clear since you're drinking?"

He gave a one-shoulder shrug. "For the most part. I have some calls to make later this afternoon. I need to get in touch with my cousin Stefan. He and his brother Rodrigo are my business partners. Since I was basically out of pocket yesterday, I need to go over some things with them."

"Do they live in Miami?" she asked.

"They do."

"Will they be relocating to Austin once you take over Hummingbird Ridge?" That was a clever way of asking whether he'd found a new investor without appearing too nosy.

He shook his head. "Right now, I'm the one who will be in Texas. I know the Dailys so it stands to reason that I would be the one stationed here. Basically Stef and Rod are silent partners. Although I imagine they will want to take a much more hands-on approach once the wine starts flowing."

Well, that sounded encouraging.

"Who wouldn't?" Olivia said. "In fact, if you're ever in need of a taster, I'd be happy to volunteer. It's a tough job, but I am willing to step up and sacrifice myself."

He laughed. "That's magnanimous of you. Not many would sacrifice themselves like that."

Their server reappeared and they ordered—the French toast for Olivia, and the goat cheese and bacon omelet for Alejandro.

"How long have you lived in Austin?" he asked once the server had refilled their water glasses and left to turn in their order.

"All my life. I was born and raised here. I've done a fair share of traveling—you know, study abroad semesters and a postgraduation backpacking trip through Europe. But I keep coming back to Austin. It's home.

My life is here. It's where my heart lives. Are you sad to leave Miami?"

"I don't know that I will completely leave. It's hard to say where I'll be after everything is settled with the winery."

Oh.

Disappointment tugged at her insides. She hadn't realized it, but she had been hoping he would say he was eager to call Austin home. It was a crazy thought, though. He was so Miami sophisticated, so big-city, he probably wouldn't be happy here long-term. For all its quirks and artistic originality, Austin had a different vibe from Miami.

"So Miami is home?"

He shrugged. "For now. But less so than it has been. My uncles and cousins still live there, but my father and my immediate family are all in Texas now. As I told you, we're a pretty tight-knit bunch."

"That's nice. Maybe you should think about joining them and making the move. Austin has a lot to offer thanks to the university, and the town has a pretty progressive music scene. Have you ever been to the South by Southwest festival? It's a fabulous film and music festival."

"I know what it is. Or maybe I should say I've heard of it, but I've never been. I'll have to catch it sometime."

"It's always in March. So you just missed it by a couple of months. But there's always next year."

He raised his glass to her. "Here's to next year."

They spent the next ten minutes or so asking personal questions, in a verbal dance of getting to know each other: colleges, careers and craziest things they'd ever done. When their food finally arrived, they ate in the companionable silence that came from good chemistry, each digesting the fresh information they had gleaned—until a familiar voice pulled Olivia out of her reverie.

"Olivia? I thought that was you."

She turned to see Pamela Davis, an accountant at Robinson Tech.

"Hi, Pam. Happy Sunday."

Pamela looked expectantly at Alejandro, obviously waiting for Olivia to introduce her. She was opening her mouth to do just that when the older woman beat her to the punch.

"And this must be your fiancé." Alejandro was a good sport as the woman introduced herself and fawned all over him.

"I was so excited for you when Sophie announced the big news. I had no idea that you were even seeing somebody." Pamela reached out and grabbed Olivia's left hand. "Where's the ring?"

Olivia shot Alejandro a glance. She should have anticipated this. She should simply go to the mall and buy a suitably impressive, but budget-friendly, cubic zirconia because this would surely not be the last time this happened. But then again, if they were going to call off the engagement by this time next week, a ring might complicate matters.

"I wanted to take her to pick out the ring of her dreams," Alejandro said. "We've been so busy with Sophie's wedding that we haven't had a chance to do that yet." He turned to Olivia. "*Querida*, would you like to do that as soon as we finish here?"

"That sounds lovely." For Pamela's benefit, they made googly eyes at each other.

The older woman put her hand over her heart. "Be still, my heart. There's nothing like young love. It makes an old woman like me feel like a kid again. Alejandro, it was so nice to meet you. You take good care of our girl. She's a keeper. And I'm sure you are too if she chose you. I'm going to leave you lovebirds so that you can finish your breakfast and go get that ring. I'll come by your office first thing tomorrow and get a good look at it."

As soon as Pamela cleared the doors of the restaurant, Olivia turned back to Alejandro. "What kind of a fiancé are you to not give me a ring?"

He laughed.

"*Querida*, you heard what I told the lady. We are going right now to pick out the ring of your dreams."

When the dishes were cleared and the server presented the check, Olivia tried to reach for it, but Alejandro was faster. "This is on me."

"Don't be ridiculous," she said. "Please let me split it with you. You need to save your money for that ring."

"Yeah, I'll do that, but this is my treat." He smiled at her. It was a knowing look that made her feel like he could see right through to her soul.

"You can't stand not being in control, can you?" he said.

What was she supposed to say to that? Of course, the answer was yes, but she wouldn't acknowledge it, nor would she admit how she was feeling—as if she and Alejandro had just had their first date.

As they made their way back to her condo, arms bumping and hands brushing occasionally as one or the other slightly leaned into the other's space, they passed a block of storefronts. Olivia paused to linger at the windows. She wasn't in any hurry to get home. Out here they were a man and a woman spending time together, getting to know each other. Once they got back to the condo, he would make his phone calls and she would prepare to return to work tomorrow after being off this week for the wedding. And they would be swept back into their separate lives—separate lives lived under the same roof for the next week. At least she had him to herself right now.

One of the storefronts was an art gallery. They slowed down so she could look at the display cases housing original, handmade jewelry. Earrings and necklaces of hammered silver and burnished metals shared space with ornately rendered rings boasting gemstones of all colors. Olivia caught a glimmer of an exquisite fire opal ring set in an ornately carved rose gold band.

"That's gorgeous," she said, pointing to the ring. "I've always wanted something like that. I'll have to come back and try it on. I'm guessing that you're not a shopper. Am I right?"

"I'm guessing you've got me pegged. But if you want to try it on, you might as well since we're here."

She shook her head. "I don't want to subject you to that torture, because once I start in a shop like that I can't promise how long I'll linger."

She flashed him a flirtatious smile as she started walking away from the shop. "But since we're getting married, maybe that could be my engagement ring."

"Ariana Lamonte of *Weird Life Magazine* is here to see you," Judy Vinson, Olivia's administrative assistant, said over the phone. "I know she doesn't have an appointment, but she asked me to see if you could give her a few moments of your time. She said she's been trying to get in touch with you for more than a month."

"Ugh," Olivia groaned into the phone.

No! Not Ariana Lamonte. The woman was the last person Olivia wanted to see today. It was her first day back and all day she'd felt as if she had been stuck in first gear when she needed to be in fourth to make serious progress toward catching up. Work did not stop even when the boss's daughter got married.

Olivia had already fended off Pamela Davis who, as promised, had appeared in her doorway first thing that morning expecting to see the ring. Olivia was surprised the woman hadn't brought her jeweler's loupe. She stopped her sarcastic thoughts. She was just being defensive because she felt bad for having to tell yet another white lie—this one about the ring being sized.

Lies begat lies. She should be used to that by now. But it didn't mean she had to like it.

Now she had to contend with Ariana Lamonte. The woman was relentless. She had been dogging Olivia for over a month now, trying to pin her down for a meeting. Until now, Olivia had been able to avoid her. Ariana was writing a series of articles about the Fortune family, more specifically about her father's children. She'd been interviewing both the legitimate and illegitimate children of Gerald Fortune Robinson. It was juicy news that Austin's resident genius had sown his seeds far and wide.

"Olivia?" Judy said. "Are you there?"

Olivia sighed loudly. "I'm here, Judy. Look, I can't deal with Ariana Lamonte today. I am drowning in work. Can you get rid of her, please?"

"I'm sorry. Ordinarily, I would have already done

that," Judy said, her voice low, "because I know how you feel about her. But I think you might want to talk to her today. She says she has some news that you need to know."

Oh, for God's sake.

Olivia leaned her head back on her chair. If she sent the reporter away, she would only come back. She might as well deal with her once and for all and make the problem go away today.

"Okay, Judy, tell her I'll be with her in a few minutes. I'm going to take a walk with her outside the building. She makes me nervous being in here. Please make sure she stays put. Don't let her wander around. She has a knack for finding the exact place she shouldn't be."

"I hear you," Judy said. "No worries. I have it all under control."

"Thanks, Judy."

Olivia took a moment to smooth her long dark hair— she was wearing it down today. Thank goodness she had taken the extra time to flatiron it smooth. She retouched her powder and reapplied her crimson lipstick. Finally, she stood and smoothed the wrinkles out of her black pencil skirt and white silk button-down blouse.

If the truth be told, she had put in the extra effort for Alejandro's benefit. Why else would she have subjected her feet to the black stilettos she'd chosen if not to show him her professional side. When she'd walked into the kitchen this morning he'd given her a cup of coffee and a look that said he approved, one hundred percent.

Actually, as painful as the heels could be, they made her feel pulled together and in command. They made her feel badass. So, with that in mind, there couldn't be a better day for Ariana to ambush her.

As Olivia walked down the hall toward the reception area, she chuckled to herself because she really was feeling pretty badass today. That meant the notorious Ms. Lamonte, who thought she could stage this surprise attack, would soon be discovering that the joke was on her.

When Olivia walked into the reception area, she saw a woman who looked to be in her mid to late twenties. She had a curvy figure, long brown hair and dark eyes. Her outfit was boho-artistic. Probably chosen to present an image of creative free spirit meets investigative reporter. She had pretty skin and her makeup accentuated her features but wasn't heavy-handed. She wasn't at all what Olivia had expected. Then again, Olivia didn't know what she had expected when it came to Ariana Lamonte.

But here they were, face-to-face.

Olivia stuck out her hand, immediately taking charge of the situation. "Ms. Lamonte, I am Olivia Fortune Robinson. How can I help you?"

The reporter stood. She was probably close to Olivia's height, but the high-heeled boots she wore made her seem much taller.

"Thanks so much for seeing me. I don't make a habit of showing up unannounced, but I've called several times to set an appointment to no avail. So here I am. I had a feeling this would work."

Ariana tilted her chin up a notch and smiled.

"Yes. I can only give you five minutes because I'm very busy. I'm in the process of digging myself out after being out of the office all week last week."

Ariana's eyes flashed. "Yes, I know. For your brother's and sister's weddings. I hear the ceremony and reception were absolutely beautiful. And I understand congratulations are in order for you, too. You're engaged! Even though it does seem rather sudden, all of Austin is abuzz with the excitement of the happy news."

It had been less than forty-eight hours since Sophie had opened her big mouth at the wedding and spilled the news. How could "all of Austin" already be abuzz?

"Is that so? You must have some very good inside sources because we haven't announced that news yet. Who told you?"

Ariana widened her eyes and smiled an innocent smile. "Oh, Olivia, surely you know a good reporter never reveals her sources. But I can say this—everyone is very complimentary about your fiancé. I hope I will have the honor of meeting him sometime soon?"

Yeah, not on your life.

"Yes, well, what can I do for you today?"

Ariana hitched her leather handbag up onto her shoulder. "As you know, I have been writing a series called 'Becoming a Fortune.' I was hoping you would allow me to interview you for the next installment."

"Why don't we take a walk, Ariana." Olivia didn't wait for the reporter to weigh in. She simply started walking. "We can talk while we walk."

Olivia cast a glance over her shoulder and saw Ariana stepping double time in those high-heeled boots to catch up. When she did, she fished in her shoulder bag and pulled out a small notebook and pencil.

"What can you tell me about your fiancé?"

Olivia frowned. "He's a very private person, Ariana. I'd rather not talk about him in his absence." They exited the front door of the office building and started walking down the path. "What other questions do you have? If that's it, I really do need to get back to work. I hope you understand."

"Of course. Well, I wanted to ask if you know anything about your father's life before he moved to Austin. I have uncovered some evidence that he may have been married before. Can you tell me anything about that?"

Olivia felt the edges of her peripheral vision go fuzzy for a split second. What? Oh, the fun never ended. Was her mother now going to have to deal with a harem of Gerald Robinson's ex-wives in addition to the flock of illegitimate children? If so, maybe the wives—or *wife*, singular, as Ariana had said—would legitimize some of her father's newfound offspring.

"Ariana, I have no idea what you're talking about. All I know is that my father has been married to my mother for many years. If he had been married to someone else before her I can hardly see how that matters or is any of your business, frankly." She turned on her heels. "I need to get back to work now. For the record, I'd rather not be interviewed. Please don't contact me anymore."

Chapter 10

Alejandro knew there were many different facets to Olivia, but he'd never seen her quite as overwrought as she was when she got home from work on Monday evening.

"I don't know who Ariana Lamonte thinks she is, but she basically ambushed me at work."

Alejandro poured her a glass of Saint-émilion Grand Cru from the bottle he had opened an hour earlier so that it could breathe for a while.

"Thank you." She took a sip and continued. "Wouldn't you put two and two together and figure out that if somebody didn't return your calls it was a hint that they didn't want to talk to you?"

"I know you mentioned her the other night, but who is this woman?"

"She's a features writer for *Weird Life Magazine*. It's an Austin-based magazine. She's been doing a series of articles called 'Becoming a Fortune.' She is completely obsessed with the Fortunes and all my father's illegitimate offspring."

"Why did she want to interview you?"

"She's been profiling my siblings and basically anyone who has a connection to the Fortunes. I can't believe how many people have cooperated and spoken to her. I don't understand why. It really weirds me out to think that she's putting my father's indiscretions out there for all the world to see."

Olivia sipped her wine. "This is good."

"I thought you might like it. It's one of my favorites. But did you talk to her?"

Alejandro motioned toward the living room. Olivia followed him into the room and they sat on the couch with their wine.

"I tried. Really, I did. But when she started asking about our engagement, that was the beginning of the end. She knows about us, Alejandro, and Sophie spilled the beans less than forty-eight hours ago. She's that obsessed with us."

"How do you think she found out?"

Olivia shrugged, then sipped her wine. "There were a lot of people at the wedding. It could've been anyone really. For all we know, she might be paying someone close to us for information."

"What did you tell her?"

"I shut her down. Changed the subject. And she tried to follow up with the most ridiculous assertion that not only had my dad fathering children with women other than my mother, which we do know is true, but she says she has uncovered evidence that my father was married before he was married to my mother. That was the last straw. I asked her to leave."

"How did she take it?"

"In all fairness, she was actually civil about it. She told me if I didn't want to be interviewed, I didn't have to do it. That's how we left it."

"I'm glad she was decent enough to realize she couldn't force you into something you didn't want to do. Do you think she'll leave you alone?"

"I do. Or at least, I'm hopeful. I think she knows better than to show up at my office again."

"I hope so."

Olivia shook her head and stared off into space for a moment. "Every day it's something new. Some new revelation or surprise about my parents that jumps out and hits me between the eyes. That's why it's easiest to not believe in anything that has to do with love and relationships," she said. "Because just when you think you have a handle on it, that you know what's what, a new piece of evidence surfaces that proves that everything you thought was real and good was all a big lie." She turned to him. "Do you know what it's like to live a charade?"

His right brow shot up. "I'm in the middle of living one right now," he said. "I don't mean to make light of your family situation."

She reached out and touched his hand. "I know you don't. The funny thing is, our relationship feels more real and substantive than anything that my parents have lived for decades."

Her expression softened. And she looked like she had surprised herself by saying it.

"That might've sounded awkward or inappropriate," she said. "I don't mean to put any pressure on you. It's just that you and I are more open and honest with each other than my parents have ever been."

She shook her head and waved her hand as if she were clearing her words from the air.

He wanted to reach out and hold those hands, but he stopped himself. "We are open with each other, Olivia. If I lived in Austin, I think I might want to see if things could work out between us—"

"I was hoping you were still considering moving to Austin. Or at least that Hummingbird Ridge would keep you here for a while, while you look for a new investor."

He silently muttered an explicative. He couldn't tell her that he'd planned to talk to her father about investing, but today he had called Gerald Robinson's assistant and canceled the meeting that was supposed to take place at three o'clock because he didn't want to solicit an investment while he was masquerading as his daughter's fiancé. He didn't want her to feel pressured into intervening or going to bat for him, and he didn't want to seem like one of the many guys who'd used her just to get to her father. But he was going to have to tell her *something* now. "I didn't want to mention this until after the wedding, but that slight snag with the winery purchase is turning out to be more challenging than I first thought."

"What's happened?"

He shook his head, trying to decide how much to tell her. "It's complicated, but it's nothing we can't work out. It's not over yet. I just need some time to reconfigure the timeline. But on a much better note, I have a surprise for you. How about something to brighten your day?"

She narrowed her eyes. "Sounds good to me. What did you have in mind?"

"I got you something. Actually, it's a birthday present, but I'm no good at holding on to gifts. Especially for the better part of a week. It's burning a hole in my pocket. May I give it to you now?"

A smile spread over Olivia's face and some of the stress from the day seemed to melt away. He got up and walked to the kitchen island and came back with a small square red velvet box. Balancing it on his right hand, he offered it to her.

"What is this?" she asked.

"Open it and see."

She held the box for a moment, glancing up at him with a skeptical look on her face. Finally, she opened it.

It was the fire opal ring she had fallen in love with at the shop in downtown Austin yesterday. The sight of it took her breath away.

"Alejandro, what is this?"

He slanted her a glance. "The ring you liked? It is the right one, isn't it?"

"Of course it's the right one." She slid it onto her finger and admired it for a moment before she got up and threw her arms around him. "Why did you do this?"

"It's for your birthday. I guess I should've sung 'Happy Birthday' to you, but I'm sure you would've asked me to stop."

"You shouldn't have done this. It's too much. I know how much it cost."

He shrugged. "Nothing is too good for my fake fiancée. Now when they ask you to see the ring you can show them."

"If I was engaged, this is exactly the ring I would choose."

Olivia framed Alejandro's face with her hands and before she could overthink it, she kissed him.

It was supposed to be a quick thank-you kiss. A peck

on the lips to show him her appreciation, but somewhere between *quick* and *kiss*, it turned into something more.

Kissing him had become so natural these days. But this was different. It began leisurely, slowly, starting with a brush of lips and a hint of tongue. But at the contact, reason flew out the window.

When she slid her arms around his neck and opened her mouth, inviting him in, he turned her so that he could deepen the kiss. Deeply, fervently. Desperately.

Olivia fisted her hands in his shirt and pulled him closer.

Her entire body sang. Every sense was heightened as his touch awakened the sensual side of her that had been sleeping for far too long.

She heard the ragged edge of his breathing just beneath the blood rushing in her ears. She felt the heat of his hands on her back. He smelled like heaven: a heady mix of soap and cologne with subtle grassy notes mixed with something leathery and masculine. Yet despite the intoxicating way he smelled, it was the way he tasted—of red wine and something that was uniquely him—that nearly made her drunk with pleasure. The two combined were a heady, seductive mix that teased her senses and made her feel hot and sexy and just a little bit reckless.

Here in his arms, she didn't feel like she had to have control. She wanted to melt into him, let him take charge for a while.

As he tasted and teased, the last bit of reason she possessed took flight. It felt too good to touch him, kiss him. It had been far too long since a man's touch had made her blood churn and her body long to be fully taken.

Was this really about to happen? Was she about to

make love to Alejandro? Finally. After pretending to be lovers, they were about to stop lying to themselves. After nights spent dreaming about him, about this, it was about to happen. She wanted it to happen.

Judging by the way he shifted and groaned, he wanted it just as much as she did. His kisses made her body hum, her heart sing. It had been so long since she'd been with anyone and even longer since she had let herself trust anyone the way she trusted Alejandro. She took in a deep breath and squeezed her eyes shut, fighting the wave of feelings swelling inside her, threatening to break.

He untucked her blouse from her pencil skirt and slipped one hand beneath the fabric, the warmth of his hand teasing her bare skin, his fingertips gently caressing her before he grasped the hem of her blouse and pulled it up over her head. She wriggled out of it, helping him by straightening her arms and ducking her head so they wouldn't have to worry about undoing buttons. Next she shed her bra and unzipped her skirt. He pushed her skirt down, taking her panties with it.

Clothing was a barrier and she wanted nothing between them. The realization that they were about to be naked sent a shiver of longing coursing through her.

Sure, they had kissed and touched each other and made everyone around them believe that they were lovers, but this was a new level of intimacy. Skin on skin. This time it was just for them.

But that wasn't going to happen if he remained fully clothed. She tugged his shirt over his head, and let it fall to the floor. Sliding her hands over his bare back, she relished the feel of his muscles beneath her fingertips before going for the button on his pants.

"Alejandro Mendoza, we should've done this a long time ago," she said, moving her hands down his back and cupping his backside.

"Might've been overkill if it had been a way to prove to Sophie you really do believe in love."

"Seeing is believing."

"I'll say," he conceded.

A half smile curved Olivia's lips. "I had no idea what I was missing." Especially now that she had him completely naked.

He leaned back, his eyes intent on her. "Damn." His voice was hoarse in his throat.

"I'm guessing it's a good thing that I've reduced you to one-syllable words?" she said.

He didn't answer; he simply leaned in and pressed a kiss to the sensitive spot behind her ear, his breath hot and delicious on her neck. Anticipation knotted in her stomach as he walked her backward down the hall toward her bedroom.

Once there, he moved his hand down her hip to her thigh. She parted her legs, and he nestled himself against her.

He kissed her again, moving his hands along the curves of her body. Reaching between her legs, his fingertips traced her sensitive skin, dangerously close to her center, where she was aching for his touch.

Olivia feared she might spontaneously combust or possibly melt into a puddle of her own need right at his feet. And when he finally moved his hand, sliding his finger over her center, she heard a low sound rumbling and realized it was coming from her.

After that, she lost all ability to think lucidly. The only thing she was aware of was the way Alejandro was teasing the entrance to her body with his fingertip before sliding it deep inside her. Her head lolled back. He increased the rhythm and everything went hot and bright like a sparkler on the Fourth of July. She was electric, sizzling like a live wire or a rocket ship launched into space. And when she finally landed, Alejandro was right there with her, kissing her lips. She could feel the hardness of him pressing against her. He was ready for her.

And she was ready for him. She wanted him so badly she felt she would burst into flames.

He eased her down onto the bed. Everything that was dark about his eyes grew even darker.

"Do you have a condom?" he said.

"Me? No, I don't have any." There had been no need. Until now. Oh, for God's sake, why hadn't they thought about this before now? Why? Because they had sworn this wasn't going to happen. A hiccup of laughter nearly escaped her lips. Just making that promise should have been her first clue that she needed to have some on hand. She supposed she should've been relieved that he hadn't come prepared because that would've meant he'd been planning this seduction. But, good grief, if they had come this far and had to stop for lack of protection, she just might actually die.

"I may have one in my shaving kit. If I do, I don't know how old it is, though."

"Not much action lately, huh?"

He groaned and kissed her. "I'm not quite sure how you want me to answer that. Still, it's worth a look. I'll be right back."

She watched him walk across the room naked and fine. Funny, she thought, you can tell yourself you're immune, you can tell yourself you don't want something or you shouldn't have something, when all the while the *don'ts* and *shouldn'ts* are a colossal lie. Seeing him like this, she knew she had been lying to herself since the night she saw him in the Driskill Hotel bar.

She wanted him. And on some very basic level, she'd known they were going to end up like this—whether she'd wanted to admit it to herself or not.

Olivia turned over onto her side and drew in a deep, measured breath, trying to calm her shallow breathing and slow her thudding heart.

This is happening. This is really happening.

And she couldn't believe how right it felt. It was probably going to make things harder when he went back to Miami; she was well aware of that. But she had known it would be difficult from that first moment, after that first kiss, when they'd started down this thrilling, rocky road. But the thing was, even after that first kiss, things had never been awkward. Even the public displays of intimacy they'd put on for Sophie's benefit hadn't been awkward. In fact, the lack of awkwardness had blurred the line between fantasy and reality that should've been so distinct. She could only hope this wasn't a mistake, that after all was said and done, making love to Alejandro wouldn't be the straw that brought everything crashing down.

He returned a moment later, holding a small square packet.

"Victory is ours," he said. "And it is still well within its shelf life. I am happy we can give it a decent burial."

Olivia propped herself up on her elbow and laughed at the double meaning. "I never dreamed a rubber could make me so happy."

"You obviously need to expand your horizons, *querida*."

She loved how he called her that. The endearment warmed her from the inside out. As if she could be any hotter right now.

"What I meant was, it would've been a real mood killer if you would've had to have gotten dressed and gone to the drugstore."

He ripped open the foil packet.

"No worries. This time. We might want to keep that in mind for the future, though."

The future.

The thought caused Olivia's heartbeat to kick up again. Would there be a next time? She hoped so. But why was she thinking about next time before *this time* had even happened. And it was about to happen.

It had been a long time since she'd been intimate with a man, but he was worth the wait.

She watched, mesmerized, as Alejandro positioned the condom over himself and rolled it down his hard length. Arousal ripped through her, knocking the breath right out of her lungs. But that was nothing compared to when Alejandro slid into bed next to her and, with one swift motion, had her lying flat on her back.

Alejandro kissed her senseless. It was as if his next breath depended on it. Need had her fisting her fingers in the hair at the nape of his neck until he grabbed ahold of her wrists and lifted her arms over her head. He deepened the kiss and positioned himself between her thighs, his hard manhood bumping against the private entrance to her body. And suddenly she needed him inside her.

His gaze locked on hers, he thrust gently to fill her. She raised her hips to take him all the way in. His breath escaped in a rush, and he held absolutely still for a moment, as if he were afraid to break the fragile moment of their joining. Looking into his eyes, Olivia reveled in the sensation, in the wonder of this man inside her.

"You feel even better than I imagined," he whispered, his voice sounding hoarse and raspy.

His eyes were the darkest shade of brown she'd ever seen. As he moved inside her, she couldn't take her eyes off him. He pulled back slightly just before thrusting deeper, closing those dark eyes, getting lost in the rhythm of their love.

The driving need that led to her release grew with every pump and thrust. She held on to him, watching him, his expression, his eyes squeezed shut, his jaw clenched tight.

This was Alejandro. Gorgeous, sexy Alejandro. And he was lost in her.

She looked away, unable to deal with the intensity as he pushed into her one last time and she caught a glimpse of his tattoo. That tattoo. Another woman's name branded on his arm. She turned her face away so she wouldn't have to see it, wouldn't have to think about him in love with someone else.

She refocused on the passion, on how right they felt together, on the feel of him moving inside her, and the next moment pleasure exploded within her, and she felt as if the clouds had parted on a gray day and she was looking directly into the sun.

His eyes closed and his neck tendons strained as the orgasm shook his body. She slid her hands along the rock-hard muscles of his arms to end up with her fingers curled into his hair. He swayed above her for a moment before she pulled him down on top of her. He bowed his head and rested his forehead on hers, kissing her again as if drawing a sustaining life's breath from the final moments of their coupling.

He rolled off her onto his back and she curled herself into his body, amazed by the heat radiating from his skin.

He covered his eyes with his palms. Then, keeping his elbows crooked, he slid his hands beneath his head. She wasn't sure if this was the right thing to do. Her instincts were telling her to hold on to him, snuggle into him, because that's what lovers did after making love. But he wasn't making any effort to hold her. As right and intuitive as the lovemaking had been, this part felt awkward.

The last thing she wanted was for her vulnerability to morph into neediness. Because that was so not who she was. She had never been a clinging vine. And she didn't want to start now.

But, dammit, she felt clingy.

She didn't want to have feelings for him. He made her want things that didn't make sense. Things that she didn't even believe in. He was part of the extended family. She had even hoped after their short-term engagement that they could be friends.

Family and friendship. Those things were far too valuable to mess up. Why was she just considering that now?

She supposed that somewhere deep in her psyche she thought making love to him would exorcise whatever demon had possessed her when she met him. While it had been mind-blowing, it hadn't satisfied that craving. No, she still wanted more. She needed more. She wondered if rather than satisfying the beast, she had simply awakened it.

She lay there lost in thought, heart thundering as she tried to sort out her emotions.

"You okay?" he asked.

She nodded, but he didn't say more. They just lay next to each other, until she couldn't stand the silence anymore. She turned over onto her side, facing him. She stared at him through the golden early-evening light, filtering in through the bedroom's plantation shutters.

Olivia studied his profile as he lay there with his arm raised over his head, his tattoo in full view. She reached out and touched it. She hadn't pushed him to talk about it the other night because it'd felt too personal, as if she were crossing the line. But here they were in the most emotionally vulnerable space. It felt like nothing should be off-limits.

"Tell me about Anna."

He was silent for a long time, and for a moment she thought he wasn't going to answer her.

But she wanted to know. She needed to know. So she decided to prod him.

"You loved her." The words escaped before she could stop herself and she felt awkward after saying them, because obviously he had loved Anna and he didn't love her.

"I did. I still do. I have to be honest with you, I always will."

Olivia felt small, and irrationally jealous of the dead woman.

"We met in our freshman year of high school in English class. Anna was new to the school. She'd just moved to Miami from Venezuela. We were reading *Romeo and Juliet* aloud in class. She read Juliette's part and I read Romeo's. It was love at first sight. I was so taken by her grace and beauty, I wanted to marry her when we turned eighteen. I'd even saved my money and bought her an engagement ring. But Anna's father asked us to wait to get married until after we'd graduated from college. We weren't happy about it, but we honored his wishes. It was important to Anna. But we still got engaged. We ended up going to different universities—she was at Florida State in Tallahassee and I was at the University of Florida in Gainesville. We alternated weekend visits, taking turns making the drive to see each other. Sophomore year, she was killed instantly when a semitruck driver fell asleep at the wheel and hit her car.

"I have always felt responsible for her death. If only I had insisted she leave Sunday afternoon when it was still light outside rather than staying one more night with me and leaving before sunrise the next morning to make it back for an early class."

She heard the pain in his voice, but it was her pain she felt when he said the next words.

"I guess I've always believed each person was only granted one true love in a lifetime. I always believed Anna was mine."

He lowered his arm, held it in front of him, tracing the intricate lines etched into his skin.

"I got her name tattooed on my arm so that I would always remember that once life wasn't hard and happiness wasn't impossible."

She wanted to ask, *What do you think now? Do you think you could be happy with me?* But she couldn't force the words out of her throat.

Chapter 11

The following Saturday was Olivia's birthday. Alejandro had planned a perfect birthday celebration for her—a feast featuring filet mignon and butter-poached lobster, and of course it would be accompanied by continuously flowing champagne since it seemed to be Olivia's favorite. And flowers. Lots of flowers. The condo looked like he had robbed a florist. Even though he had given Olivia her birthday present, the fire opal ring, earlier that week, he'd sent her out to the spa to be pampered so that she could relax and he could prepare for their romantic evening in.

During the day, while she was at work, Alejandro had been spending time at Hummingbird Ridge, proceeding as if the deal was still on track despite the fact that they'd suspended the closing indefinitely—or at least until he could secure another source of funding.

It was difficult knowing he had a potentially untapped investor in Gerald. But he had to bide his time.

He could not give the impression that he had proposed to Olivia to get the inside track on securing the deal. His conscience simply wouldn't let him do that. He had to wait until after Olivia broke up with him. If she was the one to walk away, Gerald would know that he hadn't broken Olivia's heart, and Olivia would know that he hadn't been like every other guy who had seen an opportunity and used her to further his ambitions. His new plan was to talk to Gerald first and see whether he was interested. If Gerald decided to invest in Hummingbird Ridge, Alejandro would talk to Olivia and explain why he had done things the way he had done them. She would be off the hook and wouldn't feel beholden to him for helping her with the Sophie debacle.

Technically they wouldn't be together, wouldn't be dating or engaged or be lovers— Okay, so they were lovers. That was the one part of the equation that was real. Maybe he should've exercised some restraint and waited until all the pretense was over, all the business deals were closed, and then they could've entered into a relationship of their own volition, but it was pretty clear he had no restraint when it came to Olivia.

Once everything was settled and Hummingbird Ridge was his, Alejandro would move to Austin and he had every intention of starting over and dating Olivia the right way, treating her the way she deserved to be treated.

He had just taken a pound of butter out of the refrigerator to make a compound butter for the fresh French bread he had purchased when he heard someone entering the condo.

"Hello?" he said.

"Hey, it's me." Olivia was home about an hour earlier than he was expecting her and judging by her expression something wasn't right.

"What's wrong?" He walked over and kissed her.

"I hope dinner can keep."

"Why?"

"Sophie and Mason decided to come back from their honeymoon a day early because of bad weather," she said. "There's this tradition in our family, that we have a big dinner to welcome the newlyweds home their first night back from their honeymoon. That means we are cordially invited to my parents' at six o'clock this evening. Attendance will be taken."

Alejandro raked his hand through his hair. "How can they expect us? Can't you tell them we already have plans? It's your birthday."

"Coming home from your honeymoon trumps a birthday, I'm afraid," she replied. "Besides, when my mother called, she said we would be celebrating my birthday tonight along with Sophie and Mason's return. So she gets her way after all. Should've known. She always does."

Alejandro frowned. "But how can they pull together a dinner party on such short notice?"

"The plans have been in place since before the wedding. The menu was planned, the flowers, the decorations, the tablescapes, the guest list. Even though it was planned for tomorrow night. Oh, I guess I forgot to tell you about that, didn't I? Sorry. If it makes you feel any better, there will be another dinner when Dana and Mason get back next week. Just be glad you won't have to attend that one."

What she didn't say was: *You won't have to attend because by that point we will be broken up.*

The unspoken words hung between them.

He thought he saw regret and sadness in her eyes, but maybe he was just projecting his own feelings onto her. The plan was to break up after Sophie and Mason returned. He needed that to happen so he could execute the next phase of his plan. However, Olivia told him about the dinner tradition. Probably because she had no idea that he was trying to avoid her father. The two of them had bonded over a joke of avoiding her parents for a completely different reason than the one that had him steering clear of Gerald. It appeared that he would have no choice but to go tonight. Unless—

"We haven't really talked about the logistics of our breakup," he said. "Maybe it would facilitate matters if I didn't go tonight."

He knew it was a bad idea before Olivia started shaking her head. That's when he realized how weary she looked.

"I know it's a lot to ask, and I've already asked way too much of you." She looked too vulnerable and tired. "Can you just hang in there one more night? If I go without you, the attention will be focused on where you are and why we aren't together. Not only will it detract from Sophie and Mason's homecoming, but..."

She stared at her hands for a moment. When she looked up at him again, that's when he noticed that she had tears glistening in her eyes.

"It's my birthday, Alejandro. It's bad enough that I won't get to celebrate the way I want to, but I really don't want to break up on my birthday."

* * *

They were supposed to start the evening in the living room with drinks and hors d'oeuvres and a toast to the newlyweds and Olivia.

She had asked her mother if they could just focus on Sophie and Mason tonight. After all, her birthday happened once a year; her little sister only returned from her honeymoon once in her lifetime. But when Charlotte Robinson had a plan, no one changed her mind. That stubborn streak was probably what had kept her married to Gerald all these years. She lived in one of the largest homes in Austin; she had money and a lofty position in Texas high society. Those things mattered to Charlotte. Olivia supposed that was why she stayed with her husband despite the humiliation of everyone knowing that he had not only cheated on her repeatedly, but had flesh and blood souvenirs from those dalliances. Souvenirs who shared his DNA.

Compared to that, a birthday party was inconsequential. Still, Charlotte wasn't about to change the plans and forget tonight was Olivia's birthday. It didn't matter what Olivia wanted as long as Charlotte could put on airs and pretend like everything was fine.

Olivia led Alejandro down the polished wooden hallway to the first door on the left—the living room—and they joined a handful of family members who were already there. Sophie and Mason had arrived and were sipping champagne and happily mingling with the others.

Olivia wished she and Alejandro could stay in the background, that they could be flies on the wall and observe the festivities from a safe distance, because talk was bound to meander to the engagement. Olivia's thumb found the back of the fire opal ring Alejandro had given her for her birthday. The makeshift engagement ring burned her finger. As much as she loved it she wanted to take it off and stuff it in her purse. She loved that ring, but with everyone oohing and ahhing over the gorgeous stone, she wondered if she would be able to look at it the same way after Alejandro returned to Miami and she resumed her life. Funny, she used to feel she had a full life, a fulfilling life—no one to answer to, no one to consider, no one to make her realize she really did lead a small and lonely existence that consisted of getting up in the morning alone, working sixteen-hour days, coming home and falling into bed alone, only to get up in the morning and do it all over again. She was twenty-eight years old and this was all she had to show for herself. She balled her hand into a fist so she couldn't see the ring.

A server stopped in front of her and Alejandro with a tray of champagne. He grabbed two flutes and handed her one. The two of them locked gazes before they toasted each other. She wondered if he was thinking the same thing that she was thinking—that yes, the sex had been great. Mind-blowing, in fact.

In that instant, he slipped his arm around her, falling so naturally into the part he had been playing so well, and she knew she didn't want it to end. She didn't want to tell everyone the engagement was off, that they had broken up. She encircled his waist with a possessive arm. Because somewhere along the line Alejandro Mendoza had proven to her that there were decent men left in the world. Men who were trustworthy. Men who didn't use you for your father's wealth and your family's social standing. In fact, this man had selflessly helped her and wanted absolutely nothing in return.

And now he was about to walk out of her life.

They were too good together for her to let him go without knowing exactly what he meant to her, what she felt for him. She had to have faith that he was starting to feel the same way. Because how in the world could two people be so good together and not want to last?

It would be her birthday present to herself. Tonight, after they got home, she would tell him exactly how she felt.

She smiled at him and he leaned down and kissed her. It was just a quick, whisper-soft kiss, but it filled her heart and nourished her entire being.

"Olivia!" Sophie said, coming up to them and huddling in close so that no one else could hear. "Look at you two. If this is still an act for my benefit, I do beg you to stop. I mean, I appreciate all the trouble you went to, but look at you two." She turned to Mason. "Honey, besides us, have you ever seen two people who are more perfect for each other?" She turned back and whispered to Alejandro, "Please tell me the two of you have figured that out."

Sophie and her exuberance. You had to hand it to her. Only, Olivia wished that all this enthusiasm was coming after she'd had a chance to talk to Alejandro, because she wasn't quite sure what to say. Of course, the plan was to keep up the ruse through tonight. Alejandro had been so gracious about not spoiling her birthday by staging the breakup tonight. So all she had to do was tell Sophie of course they were in love, just like they always had been, and always would be.

Until the breakup.

All she had to do was open her mouth and say it—except for the part about the breakup. That would come soon enough. Unless it didn't. But pretending tonight made Olivia fear that it might jinx everything.

They were here, together. The less said the better.

Before she could say anything, Sophie took Olivia's left hand and lifted it up. She gasped at the fire opal. "This is new. This is beautiful. Is this the engagement ring? Because if it is, I am starting to believe that this game you've been playing might in fact be real. Please tell me it's real and you two really are in love."

Before she could answer, her parents joined them. They were making the rounds greeting their guests, pretending to be the perfect host and hostess. Olivia wanted to roll her eyes and say to her sister, *If you want an act, talk to the two of them. They are insufferable.*

"Hello, Alejandro, I'm Charlotte, Olivia's mother. I'm sorry we haven't had the opportunity to formally meet before now." Charlotte extended her hand as if she expected Alejandro to kiss it. He did, and somehow he made it look so incredibly natural and genuine.

"It's nice to meet you, Mrs. Robinson. Thank you for allowing me to join in the celebration tonight."

"You're family, Alejandro. Of course you would be included this evening. I'm sure very soon we will be planning a similar party for you and Olivia."

Gerald had been talking to Mason while Charlotte had been addressing Alejandro. As if perfectly choreographed, they switched. Olivia's stomach knotted as Gerald zeroed in on Alejandro.

But she was confused when her father said, "He does exist. I was beginning to think that you were a figment of my imagination since Olivia doesn't make a habit of bringing many men home. Or, after you canceled our meeting, I thought maybe the Hummingbird Ridge deal had completely fallen through and you had left town."

"Meeting?" Olivia said. "What were you two meeting about?"

"Alejandro here has a business proposal for me. I did some investigating and I learned that a large portion of his financing for Hummingbird Ridge fell through. I'm guessing he wants me to plug the gap. I was interested." He turned to Alejandro. "But I must admit I'm a little skeptical since you haven't shown very good follow-through."

Olivia's blood ran cold. She looked at Alejandro. "Are you going to ask my father to invest in your business?"

Alejandro looked panicked, but when he nodded the edges of Olivia's vision turned red.

"I'm getting ready to leave on a business trip day after tomorrow," Gerald said to him. "If you're serious about this you need to get in before I go. Otherwise I think the window of opportunity is closed. The only reason I'm giving you a second chance is because of Olivia. If she loves you, that has to speak to your character. And if you marry her you'll need to be able to support her in the manner in which she is accustomed."

So Alejandro Mendoza was no better than any of the others. Oh, wait, yes he was. He was much smoother. He had actually convinced her that she could trust him.

"Excuse me," she said, fighting back hot, angry tears. "I need to leave. I'm not feeling well."

Alejandro excused himself and went after Olivia. Sophie came after her, too, but Alejandro said, "If you don't mind, I'd like to talk to her privately."

"Is she okay?" Sophie asked. "I don't understand what just happened."

Alejandro didn't try to explain. "Liv, please wait, please," he said, and went after her. Sophie must've stayed back, because he was alone as he stepped out the front door and made his way to the driveway where he caught up with her. "Will you please let me explain? Because I can explain."

"I'm sure you can," she said. "The only problem is I don't want to hear it. However, I do need you to take me home. Or if you'd rather, I can call for an Uber. But you will need to come and get your things tonight so you might as well drive me. Unless you'd like to go in and see how much money you can get out of my father."

That hurt. But he knew from her point of view she thought he deserved it.

"Get in the car and I'll explain."

Miraculously, she complied. Once they were inside he said, "It's true, I did ask your father for a meeting to discuss investing in Hummingbird Ridge. But I asked him before you and I got serious. That day at the winery when we were there for the tasting, I got a call from my cousin telling me that one of the key investors had pulled out of the deal. Minutes earlier, I'd been talking to Gerald and he had been saying that he was intrigued by the Texas wine industry and had been looking into investing. After I got the call—actually, before we left Hummingbird Ridge—I asked him if I could meet with him to discuss possible investment opportunities. I scheduled an appointment for Monday. This past Monday. At three o'clock. But after things took a turn and everyone thought we were engaged, I canceled the meeting with him. I canceled because I didn't want to go into that meeting under false pretenses."

"But you're still going to meet with him. You made love to me knowing full well you have a plan. Otherwise you would've told me about it. Why didn't you tell me, Alejandro?"

She sat there with her arms crossed, walls up, glaring at him, a mixture of hurt and rage contorting her tearstained face.

"I didn't tell you because I didn't want you to feel like you had to intervene, or feel like I was using you. Because I wasn't, Olivia. I didn't want you to know anything about it until it was a done deal. I didn't want you to think my business deal with your father had any bearing on us or that I expected anything from you."

She shook her head. "But don't you see it has everything to do with us? You kept it a secret. You went behind my back and didn't tell me—"

Her voice broke. He reached out to touch her and she shook him off.

"Liv, please."

"Alejandro, we were going to break up after Sophie and Mason got back anyway. This is as good a time as any to end it. Please take me home and we can both get on with our lives."

Chapter 12

"Olivia, open up. I know you're in there."

Sophie's voice sounded between the bouts of intermittent knocking.

"Olivia, if you don't open the door I'm going to call the police to do a safety check," she continued. No, wait, that sounded like Rachel.

"Don't test us, because we mean it." And there was Zoe.

All three of her sisters were standing outside her condo door. Experience reminded her that they were absolutely serious about calling the police. They would do it. This wasn't a mere battle of wills. It was three Fortune Robinson sisters against one. There was no winning that battle.

Olivia dragged her yoga pant-clad self off the couch, raked a hand through her tangled hair and opened the door.

"Why aren't you three at work?"

They glanced at each other. "Because it's Sunday?" Zoe offered.

Was it only Sunday? Yikes. Time really did stand still when you had a broken heart. Since Alejandro had left, she had been dozing on and off, in and out of a fitful, tearful, nightmare-laden sleep. She'd confined herself to the couch, because she couldn't make herself sleep in the bed that she and Alejandro had shared the previous week, the bed in which they had made love. The bed in which she had given herself to him body and soul.

She was such an idiot.

How had she allowed herself to fall for him? To be so taken in, so gullible, so ready to believe that he was different from any of the other jerks who had used her.

She looked at her sisters, all three of them happily married to good, decent men. Sure, they'd had their own challenges when it came to finding true love, but never like she'd had.

What was wrong with her?

A saying came to mind. *If every guy in the whole world uses you, maybe it's not every guy in the whole world who has a problem.*

It went something like that, some permutation of that. But it didn't matter if she'd mentally quoted it exactly. She got the gist.

Apparently not every guy in the whole world was a scumbag since her sisters were all happily married. So that meant something was wrong with her that she kept attracting the users.

Zoe held up the doughnut box and smiled. "We brought you something. They're birthday doughnuts, since you didn't get cake yesterday."

"I'll make coffee," Rachel offered.

"I'll help Olivia wash her face," Sophie said.

Like a child, Olivia allowed her sister to shepherd her into the bathroom. Olivia caught a glimpse of herself in the mirror and winced. She looked like hell. She hadn't bothered to take off her makeup after Alejandro left. Her tears had washed away most of it, but there were still vague brown and black streaks where her mascara had meandered down her cheeks, mixing with her foundation and bronzer.

Sophie opened the bathroom linen closet and took out a washcloth. She wet it and gently blotted Olivia's face.

"Rough night?" she asked.

Olivia shrugged, not quite sure what to say. Because really what could she say? Sophie would probably think this was what she deserved. Maybe her sisters were right. Maybe her bad attitude was what drew the negative to her. Maybe because she expected all men to be the same, the ones she met were exactly that.

But she had let herself believe that Alejandro was different.

Dear God, what a mistake that had turned out to be.

"Where's your ring?" Sophie asked.

Olivia tamped down the irritation that sprang to life at Sophie's question.

Have you not been paying attention? The words strained and pawed at the tip of her tongue, but somehow, in the haze of her grief, she knew better than to unleash them.

"I gave it back to Alejandro. I don't need it anymore."

Actually, what she had done was return it to the little red box it'd come in and slide it into his briefcase when he had been in the guest room packing. She knew he would've never accepted it if she had handed it to him. But she couldn't keep it when all it would do was serve as a reminder of how he had broken her heart.

"You know, in Texas some courts have said that the woman is allowed to keep the ring if the guy breaks off the engagement."

Olivia frowned and blinked up at Sophie. "And why do you know this?"

"Who knows? I heard it somewhere and my brain has a knack for hanging on to useless information. I probably retained it for the same reason I can still sing every single word of *Sesame Street*'s 'Rubber Duckie' song. Want me to sing it for you? Would that make you happy?"

Olivia held up her hand. "That's okay. Really."

But the joke made Olivia smile. Her sisters. What would she do without them? Especially sweet Sophie, who should be spending this Sunday with her new husband, not helping her spinster sister nurse her broken heart. The warmth she felt at the gesture began to sting her eyes and soon the tears had started again.

God, she hated feeling out of control like this.

Sophie grabbed her into a hug. "Oh, Liv, I'm so sorry you're hurting. You really do love him, don't you?"

Adding to the out-of-control feeling, she realized she was nodding her head when she should've been shaking it and convincing herself that she didn't love him.

"I know your relationship started off as a ruse to get me back in the wedding, but from the minute I saw the two of you together I was holding out for you. I knew this was real even if you all didn't know it."

She wanted to tell Sophie to stop. It was over. She'd

loved and lost and now her heart was broken and she didn't want to talk about it anymore. Rehashing everything was only making it worse. Salt in the wound. Insult to injury.

"Olivia, if you love him, why are you sitting here? Why are you letting him get away? I don't even understand what happened last night."

The two of them sat down on the edge of the jetted tub. Olivia found her voice and gave Sophie the lowdown.

Sophie listened without saying a word until Olivia had talked herself out. When she was quiet, Sophie said, "Okay, let me get this straight. You're upset with him about a winery deal that he already had going before he met you. The one that would keep him here in Austin. And you're upset because he intended to ask our father to buy in to save the deal, but he put off asking him because he didn't want to approach dad under false pretenses and he didn't want to involve you because he didn't want you to feel obligated to help him after you had roped him into this wedding farce he gained absolutely nothing from. Hmm... Let's think about that for a minute."

Sophie let the words hang in the air.

"I don't know, Liv. I'm not quite seeing the same picture of a liar and a scoundrel and a cheat that you seem to think he is. Am I missing something?"

"Yeah, I'm not seeing it, either," Rachel said. Olivia looked up to see Rachel and Zoe standing in the bathroom doorway. "I think you're in love and you're scared. I think you're projecting your fears onto him so that the relationship will end and you'll be exactly where you thought you would be."

Olivia sucked in a quick breath.

"Well, congratulations," said Zoe. "You did it. You wanted him to leave. And he did. Happy now?"

"Zoe, *shush*," said Rachel.

"No, she's right," said Olivia. "She's absolutely one-hundred-percent right. I've been so busy wallowing in my misery over being left, over thinking any man who is interested in me is a scoundrel who wants something. But that's not Alejandro. I may have lost the best thing that's ever happened to me, because I'm an idiot."

"No, you're not an idiot," said Sophie. "You are a smart, wonderful, generous person with a huge heart. You will go to the ends of the earth for those you love. You proved that in what you did for me. Now be kind to yourself and go after him. Go get your man."

"I will," Olivia said. "I mean, I would, but I don't know where he is."

"He didn't tell you where he was going?" Rachel asked.

"He had to sleep somewhere last night. Obviously he didn't go to his brothers, because you would know if he had. He didn't stay with Cisco and Delaney. Maybe he went back to the Driskill?"

"Let me get my cell phone and I'll look up the number and we can call and see if he's registered there," said Zoe. "Rachel, you call Cisco and ask if he's there."

"Or we could just call his cell phone," Sophie said.

Of course. Why hadn't she thought of that? It was the only logical thing to do, but her brain had been so addled she hadn't even considered the obvious.

Olivia got her phone and called Alejandro's number. When it started ringing, they heard a strange ringing sound coming from the spare bedroom. The four of them went to investigate and finally found Alejandro's cell phone underneath the foot of the bed. It must've fallen out of his pocket as he was packing.

Olivia sighed. "Well, now I have a valid reason to see him again."

"Olivia, your feelings for him are a valid reason to see him again," said Zoe. "You need to think positively. As positively about the outcome of things for yourself as you do for those you love. Because you are worth it. You deserve the same kind of love that you bestow upon other people."

After her sisters left, Olivia sat in the silent living room for a long time thinking. Rachel had called her husband, Matteo, and had gotten the phone numbers of Rodrigo and Stefan, Alejandro's cousins and business partners.

Now Olivia placed a call to Stefan.

"Hi, Stefan, this is Olivia Fortune Robinson. I'm a friend of Alejandro's. He was staying with me in Austin while he was here for the wedding."

"Hey, Olivia, I know who you are. Alejandro had a lot of nice things to say about you."

Her heart clenched. He had nice things to say about her, but she'd thought the worst of him. Well, he probably wasn't thinking nice things about her now. With just cause.

"He left Austin yesterday and I'm not sure where he went, but he left his cell phone here and I'd like to get in touch with him to let him know I have it. Is he back in Miami, by any chance?"

"No, he's still in Texas. He went to see his dad in Horseback Hollow. If you want, you can probably get in touch with him through Orlando."

Stefan gave Olivia the telephone number.

"Stefan, can you tell me a little bit about Hummingbird Ridge? As an investment…and what you're looking for in an investor. I know that one of your investors pulled out. Can you give me a ballpark dollar amount? I may know someone who is looking for an investment opportunity."

It was a whim, and she knew a whim could be dangerous because, as a general rule, spontaneity had always gotten her in trouble. But then again so had planning everything out to the last painstaking detail. So she took a deep breath and threw caution to the wind.

He filled her in on the details.

"Thanks so much, Stefan. I'll get back with you. Or Alejandro when I see him."

"Hey, no problem. It's nice to talk to the woman who has stolen my cousin's heart."

Alejandro had confided his feelings in Stefan?

The thought renewed her hope.

She called Alejandro's phone. She knew he wouldn't pick up, but that was beside the point. She wanted to hear his voice. That's all she meant to do—call, listen to his voice on his voice mail greeting and hang up. Instead, she ended up leaving him a message, even though she knew he wouldn't get it until she gave him back his phone.

"Alejandro, it's Olivia. I'm sorry. What I hate most about this fight is that I might've ruined something that could've been so good. I hope that we can talk about this. Will you give me that chance? Because if I don't get the chance to tell you I love you, I know I'll regret it for the rest of my life. I love you."

He might not want to hear from her. He might want

her to mail the phone to him since he would probably be back in Miami soon. But she had to tell him how she felt.

Since Rachel lived in Horseback Hollow, and Stefan said Alejandro was there... If he was still going to be there tomorrow when her sister went home, maybe Rachel could take the phone to him. Or maybe Olivia could go with her and deliver it herself.

One way or another he had to hear her message.

Alejandro should've trusted his instincts. If he hadn't gone to the party, Gerald wouldn't have had the opportunity to dump on them like that in front of Olivia. But who was he kidding? If he hadn't gone to the party, Olivia would've gone by herself and her father probably would've sent a message home through her about what a flake he was for canceling the meetings and avoiding him.

In hindsight, he should have been upfront with Olivia. He could've told her he didn't want her to get involved in his offer to her father. If only he could go back and do it over again. But he couldn't. He had to deal with the way things were. He needed to focus on finding another investor for Hummingbird Ridge.

On his way out of Austin to Horseback Hollow he had stopped by the winery. Jack and Margaret Daily had agreed to give Alejandro first right of refusal if another buyer came along. That motivated him to quit moping and get the job done.

In the meantime, it was good to be sitting at the Hollows Cantina in Horseback Hollow having a beer with his father before returning to Miami.

"I'm sorry the engagement is off," Orlando said.

Alejandro waited for his father to add that everything had happened too fast and they'd probably gotten caught up in the moment, but he didn't. They sat in companionable silence not needing to talk, just happy to be in each other's company.

Alejandro had already decided that he wouldn't tell his father that everything started off as a farce, a ruse to get Sophie down the aisle, and somehow it had turned into something real. That, for the first time since Anna, he had been able to feel again.

"You love her," Orlando said as if reading his mind.

"Yep."

"Then what are you doing here when you should be there telling her that?"

By the time Olivia talked to Orlando, Alejandro had already left Horseback Hollow.

Her heart sank. Orlando hadn't been very forthcoming with information about Alejandro's whereabouts. She couldn't blame him; after all, he was protecting his son. However, he had promised to relay the message to Alejandro that she had called and she had his phone.

It should've been enough, leaving messages with both Stefan and Orlando, but Olivia spent a restless Sunday night tossing and turning and coming up with a crazy plan. By six o'clock Monday morning she was at Austin–Bergstrom International Airport, boarding a flight to Miami.

Rachel was the only person she told of her plan. Olivia knew it was a crazy thing to do, but she had never been the type to sit around and wait for things to happen. In fact, when it came to love she had proactively prevented anything from happening. Not this time. When she went to bed tonight, she would know that she had done everything possible to save the best thing that had ever happened to her.

When she landed in Miami armed with Alejandro's address, she got a cab to his house. The only problem was Alejandro wasn't there. He wasn't at his office, either. That's where she met Stefan and Rodrigo in person. They told her he was still in Texas.

"But Orlando said he left," she told them.

His cousins seemed truly baffled. Or maybe they were just good actors covering for him—after all, his acting ability might run in the family. Maybe he didn't want to see her and his family was running interference.

She tried to leave his cell phone with them, but they refused. "I know he has a meeting at Hummingbird Ridge at the end of the week," Stefan said. "I think you would be better off taking the phone back with you. He can pick it up from you when he's there. If he needs a cell in the meantime, he can get one of those disposable phones."

"If he does, would you please let me know the number?"

She sounded desperate, even to her own ears. Well, she was desperate.

Maybe Alejandro was right. Maybe true love only came around once in a lifetime. He'd had his with Anna. Olivia had found hers—as short-lived as it had been—with him.

Olivia and her bruised heart returned to Miami International Airport. Disappointment was her only companion. Instead of leaving with the fulfillment—or at least the closure—she was certain she'd find when she saw Alejandro and he realized the great lengths that she would go to for him, she left feeling uncertain and small.

By the time she landed in Austin, it was nearly seven thirty in the evening. She was tired and she should be hungry, but she wasn't. All she wanted to do was go home and put on her jammies and pull the covers over her head.

She was intently digging in her purse for her car keys as she exited the airport and she wasn't really watching what she was doing.

"Excuse me, miss. Do you need a ride?"

In the split second before she could fully register who was speaking, the deep, masculine voice still sounded hauntingly familiar. She flinched and looked up, her heart nearly jumping out of her chest as her eyes focused on Alejandro. He was standing there holding a sign that said Fortune Robinson.

Instinct took over. She dropped her purse and ran into his waiting arms. He greeted her with the deepest, most possessive kiss and for a moment the entire world faded away. If she'd fallen asleep on the flight home, if she was dreaming this, she never wanted to wake up.

When they finally came up for air, he cupped her face with his hands. "I got your message."

"Which one? I left messages with both your dad and Stefan, who is very nice, by the way. I met him in Miami."

Alejandro smiled. "I heard. I can't believe you went all the way to Miami. And I wasn't talking about either of those messages. I got the one that you left on my cell phone."

"How could you hear that message? I have your phone."

That reminded her that her purse and its contents were on the ground. When she stooped down to pick it up and gather her belongings, Alejandro bent down and helped her.

"Here it is, right here." She handed him his phone.

"I have a computer program that allows me to check my messages remotely. When I heard your voice and what you had to say, I knew I had to come to you right away. Olivia, I love you. How could we just walk away from each other?"

All she could do was shrug and shake her head.

"Let's never do that again. I almost grabbed a flight to see if I could meet you in Miami. But with the way we've been narrowly missing each other, I figured it would be best to be right here when you got home. Rachel gave me your flight information."

She hugged him again. "Alejandro, I'm so sorry for everything. I hope you can forgive me for pushing you away."

"Let me think about that for a moment." He turned over the sign and held it up. The other side read, "Olivia, will you marry me...for real?"

Her heart felt as if it would burst out of her chest. "You know how much I love champagne?"

"Yes," he said, his eyes locked with hers.

"You know I love it more than anything. But I love you more. I would give up champagne forever to have you."

"There's no need for you to give it up. Especially now."

"Why is that? Is it because you heard that there's another investor interested in joining you in the Hummingbird Ridge venture?"

His eyes flashed and she waited for him to ask if it was her father, but he didn't. So she offered the information. "It's me. I want to invest in you and Hummingbird Ridge and make it possible for you to be in Austin permanently."

"I would be here with or without Hummingbird Ridge. We will definitely talk about that later. But I want you to know I want to be with you, wherever you are. Obviously it isn't a good time to give up champagne. Because we'll need it to toast both of our partnerships—business and personal," he said. "But first, this time, I need to do this right, *querida*."

He pulled a familiar small red box out of his pocket and opened it. It was the fire opal ring she had put back in his briefcase.

He fell to one knee. "Olivia Fortune Robinson, will you do me the great honor of being my wife?"

"Yes! This time, I am not letting you get away."

As he slid the fire opal ring on her finger, a crowd of people broke into a rousing round of cheers and applause. It was her family—her sisters and brothers and their spouses. And his family—Orlando and Josephine and his sister and brothers. They were all there to see him propose.

He pulled her into his warm embrace, into that spot in his arms where she fit so perfectly. For the first time in her life, Olivia Fortune Robinson knew with her whole heart that love was real.

* * * * *

"The Joshua trees and saguaros sure are pretty," Jack
said reflectively. "This sort of looks like the land west
of the Three Rivers Ranch house. Where you showed
me the North Star, remember?"

Remember? Those moments had been burned into
Vanessa's memory. Even if she never saw him again
for the rest of her life, she'd always have those special
moments to relive in her mind.

The thought unexpectedly caused her throat to
tighten, and she wished the waitress would get back
with their drinks. She didn't want Jack to think she was
getting emotional. Especially because she could feel
their time together winding to a close.

"I do. And I just happen to know a place not too far
west of here where there's another special view of the
evening star."

His eyelids lowered ever so slightly as he looked across the table at her. "After we eat, you should show me."

Did he expect her to look at him in the moonlight and not feel the urge to kiss him? Or maybe she'd get lucky, Vanessa thought, and the moon would be in a new phase and the light would be too weak to illuminate his face.

Damn it, Vanessa. Who are you fooling? You could find Jack's lips in the darkest of nights.

Thankfully, a waitress suddenly approached their table, and the distraction pushed the mocking voice from her head…but not the idea of being in Jack's arms again. She was beginning to fear she'd never rid herself of that longing.

Don't miss
The Other Hollister Man *by Stella Bagwell,*
available August 2022 wherever
Harlequin books and ebooks are sold.

Harlequin.com

Love Harlequin romance?

DISCOVER.

Be the first to find out about promotions,
news and exclusive content!

f Facebook.com/HarlequinBooks

𝕏 Twitter.com/HarlequinBooks

⊙ Instagram.com/HarlequinBooks

ⓟ Pinterest.com/HarlequinBooks

You Tube YouTube.com/HarlequinBooks

ReaderService.com

EXPLORE.

Sign up for the Harlequin e-newsletter and
download a free book from any series at
TryHarlequin.com

CONNECT.

Join our Harlequin community to
share your thoughts and connect
with other romance readers!
Facebook.com/groups/HarlequinConnection

HARLEQUIN

Heartfelt or thrilling, passionate or uplifting—Harlequin is more than just happily-ever-after.

With twelve different series to choose from and new books available every month, you are sure to find stories that will move you, uplift you, inspire and delight you.